Debbie Johnson is base
lives with her family. Aft
people's stories through her
to make up some of her own
Prize in 2010, before goin
her debut novel.

To find out more, go to:
www.facebook.com/debbiejohnsonauthor

Praise for *Dark Vision*

'A sizzling debut about goddesses, vampires and
rock 'n' roll. You'll love Debbie Johnson's sassy page-turner'
Jane Costello

DARK
VISION

DEBBIE JOHNSON

DEL REY

1 3 5 7 9 10 8 6 4 2

Published in 2014 by Del Rey, an imprint of Ebury Publishing
A Random House Group Company

The Random House Group Limited Reg. No. 954009

Addresses for companies within the Random House Group can be found at:
www.randomhouse.co.uk

A CIP catalogue record for this book is
available from the British Library

The Random House Group Limited supports The Forest Stewardship
Council® (FSC®), the leading international forest-certification organisation.
Our books carrying the FSC label are printed on FSC® -certified paper.
FSC is the only forest-certification scheme supported by the leading
environmental organisations, including Greenpeace.
Our paper procurement policy can be found at:
www.randomhouse.co.uk/environment

MIX
Paper from
responsible sources
FSC® C016897

Printed and bound by Clays Ltd, St Ives PLC

ISBN 9780091953591

To buy books by your favourite authors and register for offers visit:
www.randomhouse.co.uk

For my dad, who loved reading, and my mum,
who always believed I could write.
Wish you were both here.

Before

Lily McCain stood a few feet away from the crowd. She was dressed the same as everyone else – school blazer, knee-high white socks, purple tie – but something about her was different. Had always been different since she was six years old and her parents were killed in a car crash. Even the other kids knew she was odd, and instinctively avoided her.

She was thirteen now, and she'd already experienced a world of pain. The kind of pain that made boyfriends and make-up and the new Britney Spears or Robbie Williams single seem dull and irrelevant. The kind of pain that made it hard for her to enjoy gossip, or friendship, or school trips. Or anything at all.

'This song is, like, a million years old,' said Gemma Gardiner, a plump blonde with orange skin from her daily sunbed sessions. 'So old I bet my dad has it.'

The song in question was 'Ferry 'Cross the Mersey' by Gerry and the Pacemakers, and the opening bars were blaring fuzzily from speakers stationed around the boat. The *Royal Daffodil*, en route from the Pier Head to Seacombe in the Wirral. The day was grey, with drizzle slanting horizontally from a thunderous sky on to the bored school-children below.

vii

It was only a river, but it was a big river. So big, thought Lily as she stared down into the churning waters below, that you could almost believe you were aboard some ocean liner, destined for a fresh start in the New World. Which, she decided, spotting a flock of seagulls pecking at a flotilla of old lager cans gathered around the base of the ferry, had to be better than this one.

'What's up, weirdo?' asked Gemma, coming up behind her and giving her a poke in the ribs. 'Thinking of ending it all? Just don't expect any of us to jump in after you.'

'Get lost, Gemma,' Lily said, looking warily at the small group of girls that had followed their Queen Bee over.

'No, I won't,' Gemma snapped back. 'I always thought you looked a bit like a ginger witch . . . maybe we should see if you float! What do your reckon, girls? Should we duck her?'

The crowd behind her tittered uncertainly. Gemma was known for taking things too far. Last week she'd held Penny Fox's head down the toilet for so long she'd blacked out.

Lily was terrified, but she stared Gemma down, locking gazes, noticing the way her eyelashes clumped together under a mascara overload. She'd obviously avoided Miss McDonough's traditional morning baby-wipe attack to get rid of outlawed make-up.

Gemma, knowing she couldn't back down in front of her disciples, reached out to grab Lily's bony wrist, and twisted it, hard.

Lily jerked in pain, squeezed her eyes shut, and felt that weird thing happen. The weird thing that had started when she was six years old, when Mum and Dad went out to work one morning and never came back. The weird thing where she just . . . knew stuff. Stuff she shouldn't know, and stuff she really didn't want to know. Stuff that made her feel like throwing up. Gemma had touched her – and that was a very big no-no in Lily Land.

'You need to stop using those sunbeds,' she said

moments later, staring at Gemma's near-fluorescent face. 'They're going to make you sick. They're going to give you something called melanoma. And they're going to make you look really old and wrinkly and ugly.'

Gemma dropped her hand like she'd been burned with acid.

'You're fucking mental, you know that?'

Lily nodded. Yes, she knew that.

Gemma strutted away, glancing back over her shoulder and giving her the evil eye as she retreated in a cloud of disapproval and the scent of her mum's Obsession perfume.

Lily shook off the image, as she'd learned to do, and went back to the side of the boat, leaning over and looking down. The off-white froth of the water slapped against the sides of the ferry as they ploughed on to their destination. Gerry continued to crackle on about life and Liverpool.

It was then that she noticed the man over on the far shore. He was distant, but she could see him clearly, like her eyes were superpowered, or she was looking through one of those telescopes dotted along the prom. He was dressed in dirty grey robes; a crucifix swung from his neck as he pulled some kind of small boat back on to land. He was . . . a monk. Like out of the films, but scruffier. A monk with a fishing boat.

He looked up, met Lily's eyes, and dropped his wooden oars to the sand. He seemed as shocked as she was, and made a swift sign of the cross over his torso. She could see his mouth forming words as he shouted to the other monks behind him, running towards them and pointing back over his shoulder.

They were the only people there, on the shore. And there were no buildings, either; no dock wall or buoys . . . no ferry terminal, no factories, no terraced streets. No flotillas of lager cans. None of the stuff that should be there. None of the stuff that had been there moments ago. Just the water's edge, trees in the distance. And the monks – about five of them now – running round their boat, all staring and pointing at Lily, a small, skinny figure at the side of the *Royal Daffodil*.

As quickly as she saw it all, it disappeared. She blinked her eyes, stared harder: they were gone. The monks were gone. And the buildings were back where they were supposed to be, solid and grimy and grey behind the sheets of rain.

Gerry had skipped a few verses. He was on to the chorus, telling anyone willing to listen how much he loved this land.

Lily felt a rush of heat to her cheeks – felt what she could only describe as a blurring sensation in her brain – then fell to the floor, wet red hair straggling over her face.

'Miss!' yelled Gemma. 'Miss! Lily's thrown a whitey!'

Chapter One

My name is Lily McCain, and I'm a music writer for a newspaper. You might conclude from that information that my life is a roller coaster of sex, drugs and rock and roll.

Well, one out of three ain't bad, as the old song doesn't say. And tonight, it was rock and roll. Again.

I drained the final few dregs of my beer, but kept hold of the bottle. I didn't want anybody offering to buy me a new one. I'd had enough already, and my feet were feeling pleasantly fuzzy in my boots, toes tapping to the heavy bass beat of the band on stage. The Dormice.

They were, I'd been told, the Next Big Thing. They were going to be Bigger Than The Beatles. In my head, I always give these things capital letters: they are catchphrases I hear again and again. Along with There's Never Been Anybody Like Us Before, and We Can't Be Pigeonholed. As an arts reporter for the *Liverpool Gazette*, they are words that have been repeated to me a million times.

Also capitalised in my mind are the other phrases, the ones that go with them: Actually You're A Bit Crap, You Sound Just Like The Beatles, and Please God Send Me Some Earplugs. Then there's my personal favourite: You'll Be Driving A Taxi In A Few Years' Time.

Lily McCain, girl reporter. So young – ish – and yet

1

so cynical. Still, at least this lot could play. The punk ethos is all well and good, but after the hundredth time listening to sounds that resembled cats being tortured with toasting forks, it's a drag.

I've heard some wonderful music over the years. Soul-searing acoustics, heart-pumping rock, and even some Scouse cowboy-folk. In some cases, it was a privilege to be there at the beginning. But I've heard even more terrible music. If I had to do a pie chart on it, there'd be a huge chunk of mediocre, a sliver of great, and a fat wedge of awful.

The awful is made up of music that has sledgehammered my brain and violently assaulted my ears. In fact, I have the ears of a ninety-year-old, even if the rest of my body hasn't yet reached thirty. But those ears were here tonight to do a job: to review the band in question for my weekly pop page in the paper. I'd try not to be too harsh: they were all seventeen – young, dumb and full of strum.

Music is a nasty business, and the Liverpool scene has its fair share of sharks swimming in melodic waters, but these guys were too young to know that yet. So I'd give them their write-up; give them a few hyperbolic words to send off to potential managers and record companies. Make their mums and dads proud. Mums and dads that were there that night, in the Coconut Shy, taking snapshots and beaming at their talented offspring.

I stood alone near the bar, far from the madding crowd. I don't like being too near to people. Don't like them touching me without my permission. Don't like the uninvited brush of their skin on mine.

All of which makes my choice of profession quite an odd one, as I spend vast amounts of time in nightclubs, theatres and crowded gigs. But there is safety in a crowd: a certain anonymity that appeals to me. Some people know who I am, and will try to latch on, but it's easy to keep my distance. I can make fake friends to chat to over a beer, share an occasional cigarette with outside in the rain, but whom I never have to see in the real world. It's that type of environment. There is a high turnover of potential fake friends: young kids in bands who split over musical differences (The White Stripes would *so* kick Nirvana's ass), students who grew up and moved on, the 'businessmen' who soon shifted their cash to more reliable investments.

You can be best friends one day, and they've moved to Prague the next. Which is fine by me. I'm weird that way. In fact, I'm weird most ways.

The band finished off their final song, the cute singer with the floppy hair doing a spectacular scissor kick off the stage. He won't be trying that move in ten years' time. Assuming he hasn't popped his clogs from a drug overdose by then. Again, cynical, but I've seen it a few too many times. Even a hint of success brings a hoard of yes-men, all desperate to service your every depraved need. And showbiz types, I've learned, are needier than most.

I can feel it oozing from them: their craving for applause, for money, for sex, for approval. For oblivion, in some cases, from the seething mass that lives inside their brains. I can feel it, and on a few occasions, I've seen it too: a casual hug at the end of the night as the roadies pack up their gear and wheel the amps into the back of the van. That's all it takes, sometimes – that unrequested embrace. Then the blur appears, along with the vision – of them and their future. All very well when it involves a job at Costco or getting their girlfriends knocked up. Not so good when it involves needles and spoons and sordid corners of squalid rooms. Bad juju, and nothing I want to know about, thank you very much.

Hence me keeping my distance. And wearing long sleeves all the time, even on hot summer nights when the sweat threatens to drown me. The flashes don't happen often, and there needs to be flesh-on-flesh contact to kick-start the spinning brain. I've picked up a few coping techniques over the years, and wrapping myself up like a mummy is one of them. Still, as long as I dress in black – the unofficial uniform of the music world – nobody seems to think it's odd. This is also an environment that tolerates – in fact, encourages – the unorthodox: another thing that appeals to me.

As the tech guys came on stage to fiddle with the backline, I felt someone stand next to me. Felt it strongly, with such a tug that I had to fight not to turn round and stare at them. I'm usually hyper-aware of other people around me, logging them purely as obstacles to be avoided. But this was different. This felt . . . magnetic.

I gripped the beer bottle in my right hand and, in readiness, fished my mobile phone out of my pocket with my left. Like a good Girl Scout, I am always prepared to avoid human contact, although I am fairly sure that wasn't in the Girl Scout handbook.

I glanced around for Kevin, the barman who usually kept an eye out for me, but he was nowhere to be seen.

'You'll like the next band,' the man said in a whisper. A whisper I shouldn't have heard so clearly, not with the near-nuclear noise levels in the club as the DJ kicked in, playing 'Uprising' by Muse very loud indeed. Loud enough that everyone else had to shout into each other's ears through cupped hands.

Not this guy, though. Not Mr Whisper. His voice – tinged with the soft lilt of Ireland – came in loud and clear, like it was hot-wired directly into my head.

'Will I?' I asked, quietly, hoping he wouldn't hear and would go away. Again, I fought not to turn around. I don't know why. I just had the strangest feeling that I shouldn't. Like I said, I'm weird.

'Oh yes. They're kind of Velvet Underground meets Mazzy Star,' he said, naming two of my favourite bands. Again, I heard him, clear as day. And he'd heard me too, which was even odder.

I gave in. Couldn't resist any more. Maybe he had hearing aids or something. I turned round to get a look at Mr Whisper, the man with the supersonic aural abilities.

He was tall, a few inches over six feet. Which meant that even at my five nine, I had to gaze upwards. Thick dark hair, just touching his shoulders. Shoulders that were broad and nicely filling out a skinny-fit black T-shirt that left little to the imagination. I suppose if I were built like Captain America, I'd dress like that too. A wide mouth, high cheekbones, and eyes that were . . . odd. Under the near-fluorescent tube lighting of the bar, they were an unusual shade of deep blue. Almost purple, in fact. Must be some kind of freaky contact lenses.

'They're not. Contact lenses,' he said, smiling. Before I could wonder how the hell that happened and whether I'd accidentally said it out loud, he offered me his hand.

'I'm Gabriel,' he said. 'Gabriel Cormac.'

I ignored his hand, held up both of mine to show they were occupied with beer and phone, did my usual apologetic grin as I lied and said it was nice to meet him. In fact, it wasn't nice to meet him. It was scary and strange and it felt all wrong. And I was sure as hell glad I'd taken the time to prep my handshake-avoidance routine.

'Nice tactic,' he replied, nodding down at my hands. 'Almost like you've done that before. Have you considered gloves?'

I stared at him, trying to decide what he meant. Did he know? Or did he just have a glove fetish? I couldn't tell, and was left wondering whether I should leave to get a taxi home or hit him with the beer bottle. He was alarmingly gorgeous, and seemed to know far too much about me. Probably a hallucination, I decided. Let's face it, it wouldn't be the first time. Because when I'm not busy getting psychic future-flashes of random people's lives, I sometimes see dead people. Or imaginary people. Or future people. I never quite know, and it never lasts long enough for me to figure it out – mainly due to the whole going-unconscious-and-falling-over thing that tends to happen just after.

OK. Deep breaths. Cool, calm and collected. That, at least,

was the plan. I edged away from Gabriel a few inches. That tug I'd felt earlier was getting stronger: I actually wanted to touch him. And that is something that has never happened to me before in living memory. I have some vague images of my mother before she died: of hugs and cuddles and the holding of hands. But they are so painful, so raw and agonising, that I learned long ago to shut them down straight away.

Since then, since I was six, I've avoided physical contact with anyone. Even my nan, who took me in and raised me after my parents were killed. She's a hard woman anyway, not given to physical displays of affection. Or any other kind, in fact. The one time she did touch me – a brief hand on the shoulder at the funeral – I saw her death. I saw her in a hospital bed, with tubes in her nose, and her heart beating on a machine. And I saw a woman I now recognise as the grown-up me, sitting next to her. Fun times.

Even back then, when I was little, I didn't tell anyone. I knew they'd think I was nuts. Distraught after losing my parents. Unbalanced. All of which may well have been true, but it's happened so many times since that I now accept it as a part of my screwed-up life. The lesson? Don't touch people. Ever.

And yes, brothers and sisters, that whole not-touching thing has been fantastic for my sex life. My non-existent sex life. I may be the only twenty-six-year-old virgin left in Liverpool. Or possibly the world.

Now, out of the blue, along comes this man – this Gabriel Cormac – with his wry comments and his violet eyes and his white skin over perfectly sculpted biceps. Making me want to reach out and touch him. A lot. I clenched my hands into fists, and shoved them into my pockets.

'Sorry, I can't hear you properly,' I lied, deciding avoidance was the best policy. Hey, it's worked for years, why change now?

'Yes you can, Lily,' he replied, looking incredibly amused. And incredibly smug.

'How do you know my name?'

'I know a lot about you, Lily McCain. And you could know a lot about me as well, if you'd been polite enough to shake my hand . . .'

Yeah, I thought. Like how you die; the day you first cough up blood; how depressed you feel the night you decide to take that whole bottle of diazepam . . . all of which I've encountered before. Quite the head-fuck. And somehow, I had the feeling that the man with the eyes would have a very interesting future ahead of him. One I wanted no part of. He already seemed to know far more about me than I was comfortable with.

'Anyway,' he said, his gaze drifting over my shoulder and towards the stage. 'The band's on. Tell me what you think.'

Glad of the distraction, I turned away from his piercing look, and watched as the stage lighting – set to 'moody' – kicked in. The band was already in place, dark silhouettes against the purple haze. A spotlight homed in on the girl singer, and a collective 'wow' hummed through the audience. She cradled the mic like a lover, held it close to lusciously full lips painted a vivid blood red. Hair you could only describe as sable flowed in thick waves over her shoulders, trailing over creamy white skin to a dramatically plunging neckline. Boobs you'd kill for, or at least spend a good few grand paying Dr Feelgood to create for you.

She waited until the crowd stilled, which miraculously it did. Her voice purred into the mic, a whisper of liquid honey backed by a steady thrum of bass. A low murmur ran through the room as the pace picked up, a seduction of sound so sensual that I started to feel a responding thrum in my hips. I looked around the Coconut Shy. Everyone was watching her, even the bouncers at the back and the professionally bored girl who ran the coat check-in.

I looked back at the band, and let out a quiet yelp. They'd changed. They were . . . skeletons. The singer was nothing but bone, microphone grasped by yellowing metacarpals, the sable hair gone and replaced by the curved dome of a bare skull, glowing in the spotlight.

The enchanted swaying of the crowd continued, mesmerised. No recoiling in horror. No gasps of shock. I was clearly the only one witnessing this transformation. Lucky old me.

I knew what would happen next, and leaned back against the bar in preparation, feeling the beer bottle slip from my fingers and smash unheard on the floor. The buzzing started, then the heat, then the slow-motion slip from sanity. It feels like fainting, on steroids.

I woke up God knows how long afterwards, with my face resting against something warm and hard. Warm and hard, and pounding with a throbbing heartbeat. Strong arms around me; gentle breath on my face. It was Gabriel, and my head was nestled against his chest.

My instincts didn't know which way to react: panic, because I was in a man's arms, or regret because I knew I had to get out of them. And soon.

'It's all right, Lily,' he said, that whisper straight into my brain again. His arms tightened slightly, pulling my body closer against his.

'No, no it's not . . . you don't understand,' I stammered, wriggling to try and break free, and succeeding only in increasing the contact between us. He smiled, his eyes hypnotic, and reached out to my face. He stroked my cheek, ran his fingers slowly along my jaw, held me still.

'I do understand. And it's all right. Just relax.'

I felt his skin burning into mine, and a whoosh of sensation I'd never experienced before. Like my nerves had been jolted with electricity.

I saw it then: the vision. Me. Him. Naked. Tangled in sheets, with a whole lot of kissing going on. My body on fire with need, his fingers stroking places that had never been touched before.

As quickly as it came, it went. I screwed up my eyes, tried to shake it from my mind. Reality. Back to it, pronto, girl. Get loose, get up, get away.

I clambered to my feet, holding on to the bar to keep myself upright, feeling about as steady as Bambi on speed. Realised, luckily, that nobody had noticed, and if they had they'd assumed I was just drunk. The band was still on, still human. Still holding the whole room in thrall.

Gabriel stood up with a lot more grace than I had, which I don't suppose would have been hard. He looked at me quizzically, his head tilted to one side, the violet eyes shining from his undeniably beautiful face.

'What did you see?' he asked. 'Was it interesting? Fun?'

I was so not going to answer that question, and instead, once I'd regained the power of speech, parried with one of my own. A big one.

'Who are you?'

'A friend, Lily. But more to the point – who are you? Did you know that Lily McCain isn't even your real name? And what do you know about your parents?'

I slammed my fists into his chest as hard as I could, and shoved. I suspect it was only the element of surprise that made him budge, as I'm not blessed with superhuman strength. Just superhuman weirdness. I ran for the door, and out into the chill October night.

I stood in the street, heart racing, the driving rain slapping my face like dozens of icy hands.

I scanned the road for a black cab, felt the soaking splash of tyres hitting a puddle as a car screeched in response to my upraised hand.

I climbed in and slammed the door behind me, hard.

He was right, I thought, as the engine revved and the boxy black cab started to cut its way through the neon night. What *do* I know about my parents?

Chapter Two

I headed for safety: the *Liverpool Gazette* office. Not home – where all I'd find would be a cold bed, junk mail, and the tangle of my own thoughts – but work. The place where I'd been gainfully employed for the last five years, and the place where I knew I'd find the closest thing I had to a friend.

The office is vast and open plan, mainly empty at night, like a call centre without the staff. And without the cleaners: a thick layer of dust always seems to coat everything, even the wide green leaves of the neglected potted palms that are scattered around the hangar-like room.

Even in the day, the lighting is industrial, due to the fact that there are no windows. The perfect working environment for the creative mind. Not.

I swiped my security card, nodded at the sole guard, who was busy reading a Jackie Collins novel at the front desk, and ran into the newsroom.

Clusters of desks were set up in small pods according to their function: news desk, reporters, feature writers, subeditors, designers. Upholstered swivel chairs that had seen better days were dotted around at various angles, as though invisible bodies had abandoned them mid-swing.

I heard Carmel on the phone, saw her leaning forward with her face in her hands, dark hair falling on to the desk as she sighed in exasperation.

'Yes, Mr McCauley, I do understand. The alien invaders are coming, attracted by the wheelie bins. Because they're purple. I get it. What I'd suggest is this – why don't you go outside, and spray paint your wheelie bin a different colour?'

She paused, taking the opportunity to bang her head gently on the desk, then said, 'Yes. I think orange would look lovely. Goodbye, Mr McCauley. Sleep well, and don't forget to take those tablets the doctor gave you.'

She hung up and met my eyes as I sat down opposite her.

'Aliens?' I said, raising my eyebrows. 'Again?'

The night shift at the *Gazette* is notorious for the freaks and weirdos that crawl out of the woodwork, feeling the need to communicate their fears and paranoia. You need to be part news hound and part psychiatric nurse to cope with it. It's probably why I've always felt so comfortable there. I don't have to come in to the office during the day, and by 2 a.m. my life seems comparatively normal next to the stories that pour in to Carmel's 'news' hotline.

'Yep,' she said, 'again. Mr McCauley calls me most nights, bless him. He's become almost a friend. In fact, I'm starting to believe him . . . Maybe I should be looking for a different job.'

She stared at me, taking in my skin, which I knew was even paler than usual, my wet hair and generally freaked-out countenance.

'You all right?' she said. 'I only ask because your pupils are so dilated they look like dinner plates. Have you been dropping pills and shagging boy bands?'

I snorted with laughter: she knew it was the last thing I'd have been up to, even though she'd said a million times I should. Carmel O'Grady thought my life would be a whole lot better if I just got what she termed 'a good seeing to'. We've agreed to differ on that.

'No, I'm not so good,' I replied, feeling some of the wired energy drain from my body as I started to feel safe. Well, safer, anyway. Carmel had been adopted into a family of six boys when she was a baby, and could kick the shit out of any man, woman or beast who looked at her the wrong way. And as we are friends, I knew I'd fall within the circle of protection should any passing strangers – say, hot guys called Gabriel – have followed me to the building.

'Tell me all,' she said, leaning back in her chair. The phone rang, shrill and insistent in the silent office. I looked a question at her.

'Ignore it. It'll be that man in Freshfield telling me the demon squirrels are in his garden.'

'What if they are? What if you're missing the scoop of the decade?'

'Stop avoiding the issue. What's wrong?'

I wondered how I was going to explain everything without sounding like a total lunatic. Carmel is used to me and my eccentricities, but I have an underlying suspicion she thinks I should be accompanying Mr McCauley on his trips to pick up his clozapine.

'I met this man . . .'

'That's a good start,' she interrupted. I gave her a look, and she made a silly zipping gesture across her lips.

Deep breaths. Out with it – some of it, at least.

'I met this man, in the club. And he was . . . well, he was gorgeous, but that's not really relevant. I just thought it would keep your interest level up. I've never met him before, but he knew my name. And then he said it isn't my real name. And then he asked what I know about my parents, who are kind of dead. And then I knocked him over and ran away. And then I got a cab and came here. And Frank outside is reading *The Stud*, which is odd, 'cause I thought he'd be more of an Andy McNab man.'

I stopped and sagged back against the chair. I'd run out of energy. It sounded even weirder out loud. Even though I'd left out the good bits, like the skeleton singers and the sweaty sex.

'Can I speak now?' she asked.

I nodded, feeling slightly nauseous at the thought of even having this conversation.

'OK,' she said, frowning in concentration. She does that a lot, and the two creases at the top of her forehead are the only things that mar an otherwise exceptionally pretty face. Despite her solidly Scouse-Irish name, Carmel O'Grady was born to an Egyptian mother, and her heritage shows in her deep-honey skin, high cheekbones and wide, whisky-coloured eyes.

'So, first off, Lily – if that is in fact your real name – why do you seem to be taking this bloke seriously? Surely he's just a random nutter trying to get your attention? Probably wants you to listen to his band's demo, or something . . .'

She had a point. Bands and their PRs go to extraordinary lengths to get in the paper. I've been offered bribes in every shape and form, from chocolate drumsticks to 60-year-old bottles of Scotch. I've remained, of course, too noble to accept. By which I mean that Carmel always takes them instead. And the way she ate those chocolate drumsticks would have made a docker blush.

'I don't know. It felt . . . real. And I don't know much about my parents. They died when I was six, in London. They went out to work one day and didn't come back. I was told it was a car crash, and then before I knew anything, I was whisked up here to live with my nan, who I never even knew existed until then.'

She nodded. She knows all this already. I'm not much of a sharer when it comes to my past – there isn't much to share – but Carmel has heard versions of most of it, dragged out of me during late-night chats. I was really just saying it out loud to straighten my own head, and she was letting me.

'And having met your nan,' said Carmel, doing a fake shudder, 'I can only presume she was the last resort. I don't think I'd even want to leave my dog in her care. But what about the name thing? Presumably you have all the usual stuff – birth certificate, passport?'

I paused. Made myself think about the little brown envelope of paperwork I have back at the flat. She was right. I do have all that stuff – and until now, I've had no reason to question it. It was only my encounter with the head-fuck Superman clone that had nudged something loose.

'I do, yes. But there is something . . . something at the back of my brain that wants to get out. I don't remember much about that time, or the time before it. And who'd want to? It was all horrible. But after the funeral, I remember being in a small room with my nan, and some men in black . . . I assumed they were with the undertakers. I'd never seen them before. Nan was scared of them, I could tell. The whole thing was odd anyway, with hindsight – I mean, it was at night. Who holds a funeral at night?'

'Goths?' said Carmel, one eyebrow up.

I ignored her, which is often for the best. 'And they were handing her a package,' I continued, 'and telling her something about it all being for my own good . . . and the next day I moved here. Everything changed. Everything. And I think . . . I think that might have included my name.'

'And you're only just remembering this now?' said Carmel, incredulously.

'Yes!' I snapped, feeling as angry with myself as her. It was all there, but hazy, like a scene from a film I'd watched as a child. 'And I know that's weird! If I could just drag it out of my memory . . .'

It was so frustrating. Here I was, the human oracle, able to see any number of futures I had no interest in – but completely incapable of seeing into my own past.

'Hmm,' she said, 'maybe we should call Mr McCauley. See if he has a spare alien mind probe lying around. Look, this is probably nothing, but I can see you're upset. Why don't you tell me what you do know – when they were killed, where, their names – and I'll log on and see what I can find out for you? It's not like I've got a newspaper to produce, or anything. And while I do that, you go and get us some coffee from the machine. I'm still not convinced your drink wasn't spiked.'

I nodded gratefully, and recited the little information I had. Carmel had access to online libraries for all the newspapers in the UK, and was a whizz at pulling out facts and stats. It was how she revised for her weekly pub quizzes and filled in the down time between calls from the Prank Parade. She jotted it all down, and I stood up, fishing for change in my pocket. I paused, looked at her.

'Am I being mad?' I asked.

'Yeah. Probably. But I'm not one to quibble over an identity crisis, am I?'

Carmel has spent years and a small fortune trying to trace her birth mother, to no avail. She's in an off-spell at the moment, but I know it's only a matter of time before she starts again.

'Now, shoo!' she said, gesturing me away with her hands. 'I have magic to work! Get me a cappuccino . . .'

I left her, and ambled towards the break room. The canteen closes at night – there aren't enough staff to justify opening it – but one wall is banked with vending machines offering soggy BLTs and Mars bars that usually get stuck in the mechanical arms on their way down. The lights were flickering on and off, and I blinked to adjust to the fit-inducing rhythm.

My phone buzzed, and I reflexively pulled it out to check. A text. *I can help*, it said. *Meet me at Lime Street Costa tomorrow morning at 10*. From an unknown number, but somehow I instinctively realised it was from him. Gabriel. The list of things he knew about me obviously extended to include my phone details. He was one scary dude.

I ignored it, and with shaky hands approached the drinks machine. It took three attempts and robbed me of £1.50, but I finally managed to extricate two steaming cups of brown gunk. I pulled my sleeves down and wrapped the ends around my hands to prevent scalding as I gripped the thin plastic cups, and walked back to the newsroom.

Carmel was sitting staring at her computer, that frown doing overtime as she scanned the screen. I put the drinks down and waited for her to speak. Wondered if I should reply to the text; if I should meet him in the morning; if I should just buy a ticket to Rio and reinvent myself as a cocktail waitress.

'This is odd,' she said, tapping at the screen with a pencil.

'There's a surprise,' I replied, sipping bitter black coffee so hot my lips recoiled in protest.

'No, it's really odd. I can't find anything about your parents . . . or at least about the McCains. What I have found, though, for exactly the same time and the same place, is a car crash in St John's Wood. A Volvo estate, same as you said, in collision with a white Transit van. The driver of the van was never found.'

'Yes, that's what I told you – that's how it happened. I do remember that part.'

'But this is the odd bit. The Volvo wasn't driven by your parents. It was driven by a man called Francis Delaney. He died in the crash, along with his wife, Sarah, who was in the front seat. And there was a third fatality . . . a child. A six-year-old girl. Their daughter, Maura Delaney.'

I dropped the coffee, saw the searing-hot liquid soak through my clothes to my skin, but felt nothing.

Maura Delaney.

I knew that name.

I knew it because it was mine.

Chapter Three

I parked my car outside the house, in front of an anonymous door painted an anonymous cream, on an anonymous street in the Anfield area of Liverpool. It wasn't far out of town, and the rows of terraces were overshadowed by the might of Liverpool Football Club, quiet in the week and awash with traffic on match days. A whole industry has built up around it: kids offering to 'watch' cars for a quid, the implied promise being that if you didn't pay up, your car might accidentally lose a window while you're gone.

Today was a Sunday, and all was quiet. Kids played on bikes; litter blew around in mini tornadoes, and a few women were out scrubbing their steps. They really do still do that here.

Number 19. The house I grew up in. The house that had, technically, been my home from the age of six upwards, but had always just felt like a collection of walls and windows and roof tiles.

I knocked just to let her know I was there, then used my key to let myself in. I knew she'd be up. She barely sleeps – never has – too much nervous energy fizzing round her clogged veins.

'Nan!' I shouted, making my way through the hall and

into the kitchen. She was exactly where I knew she'd be: sitting at the table, listening to Radio Merseyside, a Silk Cut hanging from the corner of her mouth.

She's not that old, my nan. Coleen McCain. She's only sixty-five, in fact, but she looks a lot older. Has one of those faces you see a lot of in Liverpool: faces that have weathered one too many storms, smoked one too many fags, witnessed one too many tragedies. Her hair is straggly and streaked with grey, and her face is always clear of both make-up and expression. Her eyes are an icy blue and about as welcoming as the Arctic. Not your archetypal loving granny figure, by a long stretch.

'All right, girl?' she asked, surprise flickering across her creased face. 'Want a cuppa?'

Without waiting for a reply, she stood and flicked on the kettle, sucking on her ciggie the whole time.

'Bit early for a visit, isn't it? What's up with you?'

I sat down at the table and scratched the plastic gingham cover with a fingernail, watching as she dunked a tea bag haphazardly in a mug. It was early. Barely past eight, a time of day I rarely see. But I hadn't slept, my mind tortured by visions of burning Volvos, and men in black, and a little girl trapped in the back of a hunk of twisted metal.

'I want you to tell me who I am, Nan,' I said, taking the tea from her and using the mug to warm my hands. It was cold in the house. It always has been. Nan is obsessed with the price of fuel, and, wrapped in seven layers of clothing, always hoarded heat like precious jewels, only ever agreeing to switch on the radiators when we were both shivering and our lips turned blue.

She stubbed out the cigarette in an already overloaded ashtray, and stared me down. I looked away first. Too much conditioning to challenge her.

'Don't be bloody stupid, Lily. You know who you are. You having one of them mid-life crises a few decades early, or what?'

'No,' I replied, fighting to stay calm. 'Just a my-life crisis. I want to know who I am. And I want to know who Maura Delaney is. Don't pretend you don't know.'

She ignored me, reached for her Silk Cut with trembling hands, lit it up and sucked for dear life. I could feel the lie coming a mile off. It didn't take psychic powers to see she was stalling, preparing a good one. Her eyes narrowed behind the haze of smoke.

She opened her mouth to speak, and I felt anger seething through me. I'd had enough. The night from hell, no sleep, and adrenaline for breakfast. Not a good combination.

This woman had raised me, sure enough. She'd taken me into her home. Fed me, clothed me, made sure I went to school. But she'd never offered me affection, or encouragement, or anything that vaguely resembled the love a young child needs. Whoever she was, whoever I was, I was sick of the lies. Of the fact that I'd suffered through a miserable childhood that was based on fiction.

I reached out and grabbed her wrist, holding it tightly as she struggled. Opened my mind, willed it to happen, urged it on, wanting to feel that familiar buzz, the mental tingle that told me I was about to see something I shouldn't. I waited. And waited.

Nothing. Just an old lady trying to prise my death-grip from her papery skin and birdlike bones.

I howled in frustration and dropped her hand to the table. I felt like crying. My whole life I've avoided human contact, avoided the touch of others, for fear of what I'll see about them. Scared of my freaky-ass visions. And now, when I wanted them, when I needed them – nothing. They'd gone AWOL. Bloody typical.

My nan rubbed at her wrist, and I felt a pang of guilt, knowing there'd be finger-shaped bruises there later in the day. I might be screwed up, but that didn't make me feel good about committing assault and battery on a pensioner.

'There's nothing I can tell you,' she said. 'Nothing you

need to know. So shut up and drink your bloody tea. This is your life; this is who you are. Sorry if the surroundings aren't grand enough for you, milady, but you're Lily McCain. From Anfield. Live with it.'

I shut up. I drank my tea. I tried to talk to her, about my life, about hers, all the time feeling the impenetrable barrier she'd always kept up still firmly in place. Coleen was the definition of the term 'tough old bird'. I didn't know why I'd even tried.

Eventually, mug empty and heart saddened, I agreed to leave. She said she wanted me to. Said she had to get to Mass, had things to do. She always had things to do. And none of them were ever going to involve honesty, I knew.

She was lying, had been lying for so long that maybe she'd lost sight of the truth. I paused in the doorway as I left, saying goodbye.

'Take care of yourself,' I said, recalling that image of her in the hospital bed. The tubes. The machines. Me having to make the decision to switch them off. She might be a bitch, but she was the only family I had.

'I always do,' she replied, a rare truth from cigarette-puckered lips. 'Make sure you do the same, kiddo. No bugger else will, that's for sure.'

The Costa was full, as usual. The station was cold, as usual. And I was confused, as usual.

I sat at a table for two, feeling the familiar melancholy I always get at train stations. I've never understood it, but think it's something to do with the swirl of emotions that congregates there. People saying goodbye. People being reunited. People lost, or worried, or just waiting for a train that never comes.

What can I say? I'm a sensitive flower.

I gripped my mug, wondering how long my body could last sustained by nothing but hot beverages, and looked around me, also wondering if Gabriel would even show up. If it wasn't all some sick practical joke, that is. The three calls I'd already missed from Carmel told me otherwise, but I lived in hope.

He arrived exactly as the hands of Lime Street's grand station clock clicked on to ten. He might be a raving insaniac, but at least he was punctual.

And he was, still – I couldn't help but notice – dropdead gorgeous, his muscular torso encased in a snug-fitting black sweater, his dark hair falling in thick waves to touch his shoulders. In daylight, his skin was even paler, his eyes darker – still with that hint of violet, but less supernatural outside the confines of the nightclub. He smiled, sat down and placed what could only be described as a man bag on the floor next to him. It probably contained a laptop; maybe some back copies of *Psychic Weirdo Weekly*.

'I'm glad you came,' he said, eyeing my cup as though he was about to swipe it.

'Get your own,' I replied. 'I don't know you well enough to be sharing saliva.'

'Don't you? My mistake. Maybe you didn't see what I thought you did, then . . .'

His gaze travelled slowly across my face, resting on my lips, which I was now nervously biting. I felt a slow blush crawling up from my neck as I remembered the vision. All that skin. The curves and planes of his musculature. The throbbing need that engulfed my body as he explored it.

The blush raced up to my cheeks, and I knew they were now as red as my hair.

'That's pretty,' he said, his voice a sultry Irish whisper. 'Does it go all the way down?'

I shuffled the collar of my coat a little tighter around me, even though I was feeling suddenly very hot. His knees brushed against mine under the table, and I could tell from his laugh as I jumped back that he'd done it on purpose.

'Why did that band look . . . dead?' I asked, surprised that that was my first question. There was so much to ask, but for some reason, that was what snuck out. The image had been bothering me ever since I saw it, lying there dormant behind all my own personal identity issues. I mean, I've seen some odd shit in my time, but skeletons playing bass? That's is pretty much at the top of the list.

'They looked dead because they are,' he replied, still staring disconcertingly at my mouth. 'They're vampires. You'd be amazed how many successful rock bands are.'

'Hmm,' I muttered, because I couldn't think of anything else to say. I should have been totally freaked out. Should have been running for the nearest exit. Should have been surreptitiously dialling 999 on my mobile under the table. Yet somehow . . . it rang true. I knew what I'd seen, and while I'd never got to grips with my visions, I'd also never known them to totally lie. That'd be like fibbing to myself, wouldn't it?

Even that incident with the monks on the school trip had turned out to be scarily rooted in reality, when I looked into it years later. There *were* monks there, centuries ago, and they did ferry people across the Mersey. And that band last night…they *were* dead. Surprisingly good musicians for the tragically deceased, but dead all the same. As for other bands, he was right – the very best, the very biggest, they had a certain charisma, a certain appeal, that went beyond their music and their Goth-chic clothes. So. Vampire rock. Brilliant.

'You don't seem surprised,' said Gabriel, who was now playing footsie with me, forcing me to shuffle my boots around like a demented tap dancer to avoid his touch.

'Stop it!' I snapped, stamping down on his feet with all the weight of my size-eight Doc Martens. He grimaced, issuing a small ouch. It felt surprisingly good to see him in pain.

'Is that what *you* are, then, a vampire?' I asked, struggling to believe I was having this conversation at all. Never mind in full public view, in front of Costa Coffee, with the hissing announcements about the delayed 10.20 to Newton le Willows echoing in the background. Also struggling to believe that as I asked it, I found myself checking out Gabriel's luscious lips, imaging what it would feel like to have them pressed against my neck . . .

'No. Don't be stupid. I'm here, aren't I? Haven't you ever watched *Buffy*, for goodness' sake? I'm not disappearing in a puff of smoke, ergo, I'm not a vampire. I'm something entirely different. I'm something like you.'

'You mean you're a socially retarded music critic with parent issues?'

'No. And you're not retarded, Lily, you're just . . . waiting to blossom. As for the parent issues, isn't that what you really want to know? About them? Your parents?'

Ah. He'd done it. Cut to the chase. Gone to the heart of the matter. The matter I was subconsciously trying to avoid. Because while I knew that being Lily McCain, orphaned granddaughter to a cold-hearted fake nan, isn't ideal, it's what I know. It's who I've been for most of my life, and it's all I have. Having this conversation could change everything I've assumed to be true. And does anybody really like change that much? Speaking as a person who's been wearing the same brand of eyeliner for the last twelve years, I can could safely say I don't.

'My parents,' I repeated, looking into his eyes for . . . what, reassurance? He was the one who'd started all this. He was the one who'd exploded my dull but perfectly satisfactory life into chaos.

'It would have happened anyway, Lily, with or without me. It's time. People are coming for you, and you need to be ready.'

'What the hell are you talking about, Gabriel? And stay out of my bloody mind, will you?'

He smiled, and my heart thudded extra hard at the curve of his lips, the flash of white teeth. Inappropriate reaction, I told myself. Think fear, think anger, think escape . . . think anything but sex.

'I'm not in your mind all the time, if that's what you're worried about. I just get little flashes every now and then. I have no control over it, so your secrets are safe . . . most of them, anyway. And other things I can figure out for myself. Like the fact that your heart's beating faster than normal. That your pupils are dilated. That you're feeling warmer than you should. That you're imaging what it would feel like if I leaned over and kissed you right now . . .'

I screeched my chair back, feeling my face flame.

'Actually, that last one was a guess,' he added slyly, clearly amused by my reaction. 'And while this flirting is fun, we need to get serious. I'll call you Lily if you want, but that's not your name. Things are about to change for you, for all of us. That's why I'm here.'

'But why are you really here? Apart from, you know, to totally freak me out?'

'I'm here to keep you safe,' he said. 'From the people who want to kill you.'

Chapter Four

As I let those cheery words sink in, all hell let loose around us. Armed police thundered into the station lobby, wearing body armour and brandishing plastic shields. Everyone stopped what they were doing and stared.

'Get out!' shouted someone from the entrance to the coffee shop. 'I mean, leave calmly, by the emergency exits!'

Predictably enough, the words 'leave calmly' resulted in a mass exodus of running feet, a chaos of bodies tripping over suitcases on wheels, and several high-pitched female screams. A man pushed to the front of the crowd, wearing a suit and brandishing a walkie-talkie. Gabriel stared at him intently, and I realised he was using that supersonic hearing of his to eavesdrop.

'Bomb scare,' he said, standing up and throwing his bag over his shoulder. 'Come on – we have to leave – now!'

He grabbed my arm, dragging me to my feet and along behind him so fast I felt like I was skating. But instead of heading towards the exit as I expected, along with the rest of the thoroughly spooked tide of humanity, he raced towards the ticket barriers. Stumbling, I followed, and we both burst through the turnstile and on to the platform.

'Faster!' he yelled, as we galloped along the platform,

right to the edge, to the spot where trainspotters usually stand with their notebooks. 'Down!'

He jumped deftly on to the tracks, beckoning for me to follow him.

I hesitated, not knowing what to do. Behind me, there was chaos. And potentially a bomb. In front of me, miles of train track, and a man who could read my mind. Over my shoulder I saw two figures in black approaching us. Not running, not panicking, just searching. They homed in on me, seemed to share some kind of communication, then speeded up. Nobody else was here, on the platform – the carnage outside had everyone's full attention. It was just them and us, with the 'them' getting closer and closer every second.

I made my decision – which went something along the lines of 'better the lunatic you know' – and jumped. Gabriel caught me under the arms and held me steady, but I still felt the impact of the ridged steel tracks ricochet up my ankles.

'There's no bomb,' he said quickly, 'it's just a distraction. It's you they want. Now run!'

I ran. As fast as my boots would carry me, I ran. Down into the deep, dark tunnel that would ultimately lead to the next station; the tunnel hewn from rock and earth; the tunnel that Gabriel was disappearing off into way too quickly for me to keep up.

I lost sight of him, and felt panic rising up in my throat. I could hear the dull, regular thud of footsteps behind me: whoever they were, they were following. Fast and hard. Gabriel was right – there was no bomb. Or if there was, it was Lily-shaped.

Chest heaving with the effort, eyes half-blind in the subterranean lighting, I fled, all my instincts telling me I had to get away from the men behind me.

As I stumbled over a break in the tracks, strong hands gripped me, pulled me off to one side. Gabriel. He jerked me against him, and I slammed into his body. We were in an alcove, a tiny metal door in front of us. Maybe it was a workman's hatch. Maybe it was a storage unit. Maybe it was a way into the magical realm of Narnia – I didn't care, I was just glad when Gabriel threw his bodyweight against it and heaved it open.

He grabbed my hand again, and for once I didn't stop to worry about the implications of his flesh touching mine. I held on and ran beside him, inside another tunnel now, this one narrow and black, drops of God knows what dripping down on to our heads.

After what felt like hours but had probably been minutes, he stopped and indicated for me to do the same. I panted, my lungs screeching from the exertion, sucking in gulps of fetid air. Gabriel, infuriatingly, hadn't even broken a sweat.

'Stay still, stay quiet,' he said in a voice that I wouldn't dare argue with. He might have the looks of a Calvin Klein model and carry a man bag, but right now, his word was law. As the thought crossed my mind, a truth clicked into place: his word *was* the law. Because he was the king. Sounded crazy, but hey, I was used to that – and somehow, I just knew.

Before I had time to process that particular snippet of weirdness, he made a waving gesture with his hands, and started to mutter under his breath. It was gloomy in the tunnel, and I was starting to sense the furious scamper of rats around my feet. Gabriel's eyes were glowing in the darkness, bright and violet. His body seemed to swell, to enlarge, his chest expanding and his arms elongating, until he filled all the space between the ancient arches of brickwork. I hunkered back, not wanting to get squashed, and watched as he threw his fingers forward as though aiming a javelin.

There was a thundering crash, and the air filled with crumbled particles of masonry, covering my face and making me sneeze.

'Rockfall, further down,' he said. 'They won't be able to

get through. We're safe – for now. Come on, we need to get out of here.'

He stooped over his bag, clicked it open, and pulled out a torch. A bloody torch – of all the mundane, boringly human things. He flicked it on, and a bright beam of light shone into my flinching eyes.

'You look a real mess,' he said, laughing and pulling a chunk of plaster from my hair.

'Yeah, well . . .' I replied, fresh out of witty repartee. Near-death experiences will do that to a girl, I suppose. 'What now?'

'Now, we walk out of here. We leave, calmy, through the emergency exits.'

And that's just what we did, picking our way slowly and carefully along the abandoned tunnel until Gabriel spotted another door, similar to the one we'd entered. It was rusted shut, and next to it was a rolled-up copy of the *Gazette*. From 1979. I guessed these tunnels hadn't been used in quite some time.

With a quick curse, Gabriel managed to pull the padlock loose and manhandle the door open, this time using sheer brawn instead of any flicky-finger stuff. We emerged, blinking, into the light. I looked around, and realised I knew where we were.

Edge Hill. The old one – the original nineteenth-century station that was now disused. We'd walked a few miles underground, and were now near the edge of the former platform. Very *Harry Potter*.

Gabriel jumped up nimbly from the track on to ground level, as easily as stepping up a steep kerb. He reached down for me and, after a moment's hesitation, I took hold of his hands. There was no other way I was going to get up there myself, unless someone conveniently brought me a dwarf to stand on.

He hauled me up, and I fell, probably with a great deal of comedic value, on to the concrete.

I wasn't bothered about that, though. I was too busy coping with the buzzing head and the mega brain tingle as his fingers twined into mine. Great timing, I thought, as I sank on to the floor, and into the vision.

It was of me. Again. Which was an alarming trend, but not as alarming as the fact that I was screaming in agony. My stomach was wracked with cramping pains, and when I looked down, it was huge. The size of a hump-backed whale. I was pregnant and, it seemed, about to give birth. He was there, Gabriel, at my side – not holding my hand or offering breathing advice like dads on telly, but wielding a vast golden sword. A sword that was . . . on fire.

I regained consciousness as quickly as I lost it, and found myself yet again lying in Gabriel's arms. This was getting to be a habit, and bearing in mind the subject matter of that last flash, not one I wanted to encourage.

'You OK?' he asked, half an eye on me, half scanning our surroundings, presumably for mysterious and threatening assassin types.

'Yeah,' I said, looking at him cautiously. 'But before we go any further, I should make one thing clear: I will not, under any circumstances, be having your baby!'

Chapter Five

'I need to go home,' I said.

'You can't go home,' he replied.

'You can't stop me,' I said. OK, so that last statement was patently untrue, but I've got my pride. And I really, really needed a shower.

'You can shower at my place,' he countered, doing that infuriating mind-reading trick again.

'I don't think so, lover boy – not after that last vision. That was like living birth control, as far as I'm concerned. No more touching. Of any kind.'

'Are you sure?' he asked, pulling his dust-covered sweater over his head and shaking it. Underneath he was wearing a grey jersey T-shirt that clung like water to every ridge of muscle, every perfectly outlined abdominal. Which really wasn't playing fair.

I averted my eyes, like a proper lady should, and tried to ignore his smirking expression. We could both do with a shower, truth be told. And, in my case, possibly a new identity and a safe house.

We were in a small playground near the old station. Gabriel thought our pursuers would be patrolling the mainline routes looking for us, so we'd retreated to the park to regroup. For him, that involved being very bossy, and for me, it involved trying exceptionally hard not to lose my now-fragile control.

'They're looking for you. They want to kill you. What part of that don't you understand?'

'All of it,' I replied, sneaking a look to check he was decently clad again. 'I don't even know who "they" are.'

'Do you trust me?' he asked, grabbing hold of my chin and twisting my face upwards so I was looking into his eyes. I slapped his hand away viciously.

'No! I don't even know you. Why should I trust you, when all you've done so far is evade my questions, raid my brain and drag me through collapsing tunnels?'

'You missed out the bit about saving your life.'

'I only have your word for that, Gabriel. If that's even your name. So you do what you like, but I'm going home. I'm going home, I'm having a shower, and I'm going to work. That's just the way it is.'

He stood tall, in fact even taller than he usually was. I couldn't tell how it was happening, but his body seemed to be getting bigger. His face was set and determined, and the violet in his eyes had dimmed and deepened and was now almost black.

'I won't allow it. It is my duty to protect you, and I will die trying if I have to.'

O-kay. There was clearly going to be a personality clash here, and frankly I didn't know how to handle it. I live an independent life. I've learned to cope with a whole lot of weirdness and isolation, and have formed my own existence despite that. But growing up with Coleen also ingrained in me a deep respect for – by which I mean fear of – authority. I never choose direct conflict, and have instead evolved a set of behavioural rules that usually allow me to live how I want to without the need to butt heads. Rules such as working night shifts, and living alone. Now the Incredible Hulk seemed set on derailing it all.

Time for a change of tactic.

I sat down on the roundabout, kicked at the damp clumps of grass with my boots. He'd obviously decided he was my protector. And I'd obviously decided to go along with it – at least for the time being. Now it was a matter of managing that situation without the use of sledgehammers or nail files to the eyes.

'Look, Gabriel,' I said. 'You need to understand how I see all of this. You say you're here to protect me. Fine. There's clearly a whole other world out there I don't get. And yes, I believe you when you say those men were after me. But if we're going to work together, if I'm going to *let* you protect me, I need to do certain things. And going home is one of them. I'll compromise on the shower, but I do need to call in to my flat, grab a few things. Things that are important to me.'

'Things that are more important than your life?' he said softly, giving the roundabout a gentle push so it started to spin. The wind was cold and fresh on my face as I whirled, and by the time I returned to face him, I was ready to answer: 'Yes. That important.'

His expression softened, and he finally nodded his agreement. I tried very hard not to look smug as we walked towards the main road and hailed a cab.

My flat is tucked away in a side street in a part of Liverpool known as Lark Lane. Anyone who's been there will describe it as 'bohemian', which means you get vast Victorian villas full of actors, writers, students and smack-heads, all living side by side in uneasy harmony. At the bottom of the road is a vast green space, Sefton Park, with a boating lake and an aviary and loads of Peter Pan-style statues. It's a nice place to visit, on those days when you're not running for your life.

As we approached the house, I felt Gabriel place a hand protectively in the small of my back, and I can't say that I felt any urge to pull away from it. I hadn't got a good look at my pursuers back at the station, and that wasn't filling me with regret. I knew – I sensed – that they intended me harm. And Gabriel? He intended me something else entirely. I just didn't know what.

I fished the key out of my pocket, but there was no need. My front door, down the side of the building, was already open, banging in the breeze. Gabriel pulled me behind him, and I let him. There is a time for bravery, and this wasn't it.

As we tiptoed into the hallway, I heard screams and crashes coming from the living room. A shrill female yell, a barrage of thuds. The sound of something formerly made of pottery smashing into pieces.

'Stay here!' he ordered, shoving me up against the wall. He took a deep breath, and this time I wasn't mistaken – he started to swell, to enlarge, gaining a couple of inches in height and even more muscle. He reared back and kicked the living-room door so hard it swung off its hinges.

Inside were two men. Both dressed in black. One was collapsed in the corner, blood coming from his nose. The other was lying unconscious on the floor, his head wearing a plant pot and half a bonsai tree. Above him, arms raised and preparing to deliver another whack with the remaining plant pot, was Carmel.

Gabriel dashed in, heading towards them, and I saw Carmel about to change course and go for him instead. He flicked his fingers and the pot disintegrated into smithereens, the pieces clattering harmlessly to the wooden floor.

'It's OK!' I shouted, following him in and standing between them. I didn't know who I was more worried about: Gabriel might be some kind of magical warrior dude, but Carmel still had bloodlust in her eyes. That usually ends badly.

'Carmel, it's me! Gabriel, this is my friend!'

Carmel ignored Gabriel and lurched towards me, swallowing me up in a hug. That showed exactly how upset she was – she knows better than most how little I like to be touched.

Gabriel looked away from our happy reunion and crouched down, touching the neck of Plant Pot Man with his fingers, then doing the same for Nose Bleed.

'They're out, but still alive,' he said, with an element of regret.

'Shame,' said Carmel, kicking the one nearest to her in the ribs. 'I was aiming for annihilation. Now – is someone going to tell me what's going on? I was worried about you, Lily. You didn't return my calls, and I thought you were freaking out about the whole Maura Delaney thing.'

I saw Gabriel's eyes brighten at the unexpected mention of the name.

'Yeah, I know,' I said to him. 'I'm not quite as dumb as I look. What happened, Carmel?'

'I came round to check on you, used that key you keep so well hidden under the recycling box out back. Within a minute of me arriving, those two bastards came in, shouting something about death to the Mother of the Mortals, and full-on *Lord of the Rings* mayhem ensued. I tried to tell them I wasn't the Mother of the Mortals, whoever the fuck that is, but, well . . . they weren't very nice. And you know how upset I get when people aren't nice.'

'How did you do this?' asked Gabriel. 'When you entered the building you triggered a surveillance spell, and they attacked. They will have been waiting nearby. These men are warriors. How did you defeat them? What kind of martial art do you use?'

Carmel stared at him, as though seeing him for the first time.

'The martial art of having six big brothers. I don't take shit from anyone.'

She turned to me and gave me a small grin.

'You were right, he is.'

'Is what?' asked Gabriel, as he started to drag the men feet-first into the centre of the room.

'Nothing!' I snapped, still enough of an immature girl to

want to hide that I'd described him as gorgeous the night before. 'Now, if you two can give me a few minutes, I'll grab what I need – are we OK for that, Gabriel?'

'Yes,' he replied. 'But make it very few minutes, or there will be more of them. They're like cockroaches: however many you stamp out, more appear.'

Nice image, I thought, making my way into the bedroom. I grabbed a backpack and started to shove in a few essentials – underwear, clothes, phone charger, iPod – before pulling out my top drawer and getting what I'd really come for. The photograph. The only one I had of my parents before they died, apparently with me along for the ride. So many questions, and so little time – this whole fleeing-from-death scenario was getting seriously tiresome.

The door opened, and Carmel peeked her head in. Her thick black hair was wild, her whisky eyes still bright from battle. She was wasted on that news desk, when there were wars to be waged.

'Come on! Mr High and Mighty says we need to leave – now!'

I nodded, slipped on the backpack, and we ran back out into the street. As we reached the pavement, a silver Lexus pulled up across the road. The windows were tinted a nice shade of drug-dealer black so I couldn't see who was inside, but from Gabriel's reaction I could hazard a guess.

'Run!' he shouted, taking hold of my hand and dragging me yet again down the street. Carmel sprinted ahead, even faster, and I could feel the adrenaline flowing from her as she headed for the park.

We dodged traffic as we crossed the road, ran through the wrought-iron gates and on to green fields that were dotted with kids playing football and mums pushing prams. Gabriel was doing a weird thing as we ran, kind of sniffing the air like a bloodhound, his head swivelling around like a satellite as he checked the layout of the park.

I'd heard the dull clunk of expensive car doors slamming,

and the sound of feet thudding behind us as we ran, so I didn't need to look back to know we were being chased. Again.

'This way!' Gabriel shouted, after an especially big sniff, pointing towards the gleaming glass of the park's Palm House.

The Palm House was built in the nineteenth century, a magnificent dome made of a cast-iron frame and hundreds of panes of glass. It houses exotic plants and statues, like an especially big, especially beautiful, greenhouse full of art and flowers.

It was also, I realised as we ran inside, currently being used as a wedding venue. Luckily, your average Scouse wedding party is a raucous crowd, and nobody seemed to even notice as three wild-eyed strangers covered in dust, brick and soil appeared.

Gabriel scanned the room, ignoring the fancy frocks and the band playing the opening chords of 'Brown Eyed Girl', and headed for a statue. Typical nineteenth-century, mock-Classical woman leaning over an infant, as though about to kiss its forehead. 'Mother and Child', said the plaque in front of it.

'Hold my hands!' said Gabriel, gesturing to both Carmel and me. She looked at me, eyebrows raised, and I nodded. I didn't know who he was, and I didn't trust him, but he'd gotten me this far. And I'd never been a big fan of Van Morrison.

We grabbed hold of his hands, and the world went black.

Chapter Six

We were standing in a large room, in what appeared to be the top floor of one of the huge towers that had sprung up on the Liverpool waterfront in recent years. The floor-to-ceiling windows offered stunning views of the river, and put us almost at beady-eye level with the Liver Birds.

We were also, I realised, still holding hands. I snatched mine away, which Gabriel took as his cue to laugh. Irritating pig.

Carmel laughed too, but hers was tinged with hysteria as she glanced around. I can't say that I blamed her; I was feeling less than grounded myself. A natural enough reaction to our whole Beam Me Up, Scotty experience, I suppose.

The room was vast, decorated in modern block colours, furnished with black leather couches and dark wood. On one wall was a huge flat-screen TV, surrounded by fancy-looking speakers and a kitted-out games console. A bar area was home to a beer fridge and a full set of optics, with gleaming glasses in neat rows. Everything your off-duty mystical warrior would need for a spot of R&R.

'Sorry about the mess,' said Gabriel, picking up a lone magazine from the glass-topped coffee table. 'I wasn't expecting guests.'

Carmel stared at him, stared at me, then did what comes naturally to her: walked to the bar and poured herself a very stiff vodka.

She gulped it down, poured another one straight away, then handed me a bottle of Peroni. The journalists' creed: if in doubt, get drunk.

I pulled off my backpack and coat, dropped them to the floor, and slumped on the sofa. God, it was comfortable, and God, I was exhausted. If this was one of my hallucinations, it was a real humdinger.

Carmel joined me, and I felt instantly better for the warmth of her body next to mine. Close enough to comfort, not too close to crowd. I may have got the shitty end of the stick when it came to my childhood, but, I was starting to realise, I'd won the friend jackpot.

'Gabriel,' I said, after a few minutes of silence. 'I hate to break it to you, but the charm of your international man of mystery act has officially worn off. We need answers. And we need them now.'

He nodded, and pulled up a leather footstool, perched himself in front of us. His face was still speckled with dust, the dark waves of his hair matted with cobwebs and clumps of masonry.

'All right, Lily. No more games. What do you want to know?'

'We'll start with how we got here. One minute we're wedding crashers. The next we're here in your shag pad. How?'

'Shag pad?' he replied, the corner of his mouth quirking up in amusement. Carmel made what I can only describe as a growl, and he dropped the attitude. He had more common sense than I thought.

'Would you settle for "it was magic"?' he asked.

'No,' Carmel and I replied in unison.

'Thought not. But it is . . . at least, that's the best word I can find in your language.'

In our language? I thought.

'Do your best to translate,' I said, saving that particular query for later.

'OK. This city, this place, is special. And not just in the touristy, birthplace of The Beatles kind of way. It's special because of the energy here. The water, the land, the way they come together. Everywhere has an element of it, but sometimes, there's . . . more. For the whole of its existence, it's been a place that's drawn people, their hopes, their dreams. Their needs. An emotional melting pot, you could call it.'

'And that's what gives it this . . . special energy?'

'No, it's the special energy that draws people in. They don't understand why, but they come, and they stay. It's not just here you find it; it's all over the world. Parts of Dublin, too. New York. Vancouver. Cleethorpes.'

Carmel snorted on her vodka, and Gabriel smiled.

'I was kidding about that last one. Look, you've heard that phrase they use, the Pool of Life? Well it's accurate. That's what this place is. And at certain key locations, the magic is thicker, the energy stronger. It wasn't an accident the Palm House got built where it did. Think of it like . . . a power socket, waiting for someone to come along with a plug.'

'And you're the plug?'

'On this occasion, yes. I used the power I found there, to get us here. I could explain the physics of it, if you like . . .'

'No thanks,' I said. 'Not while I'm on my first beer. Look, I can't argue with the fact that it happened, and maybe I'll never understand the hows and whys of it. So for now we'll move on – why me? Why am I involved in this? There's nothing special about me—'

'She has self-esteem issues,' interrupted Carmel, a vodka-induced heat creeping over her cheeks. 'I've been working on it for years. I blame her nan.'

A shadow flitted momentarily across Gabriel's face,

and his eyes darkened to a deeper shade of purple. A far stronger reaction than her flippant comment merited. There was more than met the eye there, I thought, and I wanted to find out about it, sometime soon.

'You *are* special, Lily,' said Gabriel, leaning forward so his face was inches from mine. 'Very special. I don't know how much of this you can take in in one sitting, but you at least need to know who you are.'

'That would probably be a good start,' I replied, feeling nervousness coil in my stomach like a pit of restless snakes. This was it. This was what I wanted to know. This was the moment we'd been building up to since we'd met . . . and now that moment was here, every instinct I possessed was telling me to run. From this room, from this building, from this beautiful man. From a past and a future I knew I didn't want.

'Don't worry,' he murmured, reaching out to place his hand on my knee. I saw Carmel notice, and knew she expected my usual reaction. But I let him be. I needed that contact, for once in my life.

'You're not Lily McCain,' he said. 'You know that. Coleen isn't any relation to you at all, as I think you'd started to suspect as well. You're not even Maura Delaney. You're more than that. You're Mabe, the Mother of the Mortals. The giver of life and bounty. A seer, a matriarch, the root of the whole human world.'

I opened my mouth to speak. Closed it again. Because really, what was the appropriate response to that little speech? I wanted to scream, and shout, and call him a madman. I wanted to leave all this behind, go to the office and write a review of the Dormice. I wanted to accuse him of being a liar, slap him around the face and make a grand exit, stage left.

But I couldn't. Because as soon as he said it, I knew, somewhere deep down and hidden, that it was true. However insane it sounded, however crazy and far-fetched and

Twilight Zone it seemed, it was true. I was Mabe. Mother of the bleeding Mortals. Whether I wanted to be or not.

'There were three of you,' he said, gauging my reaction until he thought it was safe to continue. 'The power of three made you strong. But . . . now they're gone. They were hunted, taken, until only you remained. You were hidden, kept safe, kept ignorant. Until now. Now they're here, and the threat is too great to allow you that ignorance any longer.'

'Who's here? Who are "they"?' said Carmel, her innate nosiness getting the better of her. My friend, the news hound.

'The Fintna Faidh.'

'The what-na what?'

'Fintna Faidh,' he repeated, pronouncing it 'Fie'. He shook his head and sighed. 'This is really complicated... Look, there are three realms. Let's call them Heaven, Earth and the Otherworld. It's more complex than that; I'm dumbing it down. There always have been three, although humans are mainly concerned with the one in the middle, apart from occasional looks towards the other two. For us, now, the two we need to be concerned with are Earth and the Otherworld. Throughout time, the three have coexisted. There've been skirmishes; there've been collaborations – usually resulting in genocides or world religions – but the three coexist, separate but together. Mostly peacefully. Mortals are regarded by the Gods and by the Otherworld as troublesome and under-evolved, but we let them be. Apart from the odd fairy-tale incursion, we leave them alone. I don't expect you two to understand straight away, but that's the system, and it's always worked.'

I felt a big 'but' coming on, and was one hundred per cent sure I wasn't going to like it. I'd also noticed the way he'd used the word 'we', neatly excluding himself from the troublesome and under-evolved category.

'But now . . . the Fintna Faidh want to end that. End the

duality of human and other. To extend the power of the Gods and the Otherworld, to dispense with mortals completely . . . and to do that, they need to stop us. You. Mabe. The Seer, the Mother of the Mortals.'

'Stop me from doing what?'

'From fulfilling your role in the cycle. Giving your blessing and bounty to the human world. From combining the strengths of deities with the needs of the mortals.'

'And how, exactly, am I supposed to do that?' I asked, fearing I already had the answer, locked away in a drawer in my brain marked 'never to be opened'.

'You already know how,' he said, dark eyes looking unwaveringly into mine. 'You've seen it already. You're the Mother of the Mortals. I am the High King, Cormac mac-Conaire. Your mate.'

Chapter Seven

'Wow,' said Carmel, emptying her glass. 'This is just like being at work. I need another drink.'

She stood and walked slightly unsteadily to the bar, glass dangling from her fingers.

'So, that's quite a name you have there,' she said, over the sound of free-glugging vodka. 'What's with the Gabriel?'

His eyes never left mine, but he grinned at the question.

'I just liked it,' he said.

'Oh. Cool. And when you say you're Lily's – Mabe's – whoever's – mate, do you mean in the meet-you-down-the-pub way, or the naked-rutting-beasts way?'

'The latter,' he responded, 'but you don't need to put it so crudely.'

Her only response was a snort.

'Are you all right, Lily?' he asked, reaching out to touch my hand. I recoiled, told him not to touch me, and pulled the sleeves of my top tight around my fingers. Skin on skin was bad, High King or not.

'Yeah,' said Carmel, topping her drink off with an inch of tonic. 'You see, Gabriel, that's going to be a problem. That whole not-touching thing she has going on. Unless you've invented some fancy new way of doing it?'

I'd heard enough. Carmel was invoking the spirit of Bill

Hicks to help her cope with the shock, and Gabriel was looking at me like I was nitroglycerine sloshing round in a fishbowl. Mother of the Mortals or not, I needed a break. I live on my own for a reason.

'I have to be alone for a minute,' I said, standing up and grabbing my backpack. 'Where can I go?'

Gabriel stood as well, went to touch my arm to guide me, then stopped when he noticed my expression.

'Down the hall,' he said, following me as I walked towards the door. 'Third on the right. Everything you need is in there.'

I nodded, felt his eyes on me as I entered the corridor, tried to ignore the fact that his gaze provoked a throbbing heat between my shoulder blades. I lost count of the doors, but needed to get away, so I grasped the first handle I saw.

'No! Not in—'

I turned, pushed.

'There,' he finished lamely, rushing to catch up with me.

Inside, the room was dim, windows tightly curtained and the lights off. In the middle, an enormous bed. And on the enormous bed, the band I'd seen last night. All of them. In the centre was the woman, the voluptuous singer with the black hair. She was naked, and surrounded by the rest of the group, all nude and coiled around each other like sleeping kittens. Sleeping kittens with really big teeth.

I backed out, closed the door behind me as quietly as I could. I didn't know if they were dead, drunk or drugged, but I thought it was probably best to let sleeping vampires lie.

'Next one,' said Gabriel quietly, pointing further down the corridor. 'Are you sure you don't want to talk some more? I could come with you, try to explain better . . .'

'No,' I replied, hardening myself to the flicker of hurt I saw in his eyes. 'That was enough for now. Are we safe here?'

'Of course. We're protected. Spells are in place, and my

people are nearby. My sword is ready, and we'll lay down our lives to keep you from harm.'

A simple 'yes' would have done, but there didn't seem to be space left for 'simple' in my life any more. I nodded my thanks, and left him, hands hanging loosely at his sides, looking less like the High King and more like a teenager who'd just been dumped.

My room was lighter, brighter, and altogether better for being completely devoid of the living dead. My own bathroom, already supplied with towels and toiletries; a wardrobe containing clothes that were my size, if not to my taste. A few books – Celtic myths and legends, ha bloody ha – and food, in a small fridge. Hunger kicked in as soon as I saw it, and I pulled open the glass door and scooped out a ham salad sandwich and a bottle of water.

I sat down on the bed, ate, drank, tried not to think. Then I emptied out my bag, pouring the irrelevant clothes over the vivid red silk of the sheets, and found it.

The photograph. The one tangible connection I had with the people I thought of as my parents.

I didn't even look like them, I thought, as I stroked the curled edges of the paper. My mother was blonde, round, soft. I remembered that softness: the warmth of her body when I curled up against it; the whisper of her voice as she kissed my hair. The way I'd felt so safe, so small, so happy. My father was fair as well, with sparkling blue eyes. I didn't recall him as clearly, just knew he used to come home from work and spin me round in the air, call me his Fairy Princess. Me. Their little changeling: all gawky limbs, big green eyes and long, flaming red hair. I don't know why it had never occurred to me before, the fact that I looked so different.

I don't suppose it was something I'd wanted to dwell on. Growing up with Coleen had been hard – cold both physically and emotionally. Remembering the days before that, when all had been well in the world of the Fairy Princess, was too raw and painful to cope with.

I touched the image of my mother's face, allowing the tears welling up in my eyes to finally fall. She'd been my only happy memory. And now, it turned out, that one was probably fake as well.

I crawled under the silk sheets and curled up beneath them, placing the picture on the pillow next to me.

I wondered if they'd known – my parents, the Delaneys. Francis and Sarah. If they were part of the great conspiracy, or if they'd believed I was actually their own flesh and blood.

And, I wondered as I drifted off into a fitful sleep, I wondered who the girl was. The one who'd died with them in the Volvo that day. There'd been a body, and it definitely hadn't been mine. So who was this girl? The girl the world thought was me . . .

I was having a wonderful dream. A dream where silky fingers were stroking my face and shoulders, smoothing strands of hair away from my face. I sighed and rolled on to my back. The touch continued, drifting down along the side of my neck, round to the front of my throat, light and sensual and arousing in all kinds of ways. God, it felt good. Better than good. It felt sinful, and delicious, and . . . real.

I jerked awake, jumped up, scrambled to the other side of the bed. There was a man in there with me, and it wasn't Gabriel.

'Good evening, Lily,' he said, smiling at my reaction. His eyes – a deep, chocolate brown – were sparkling with laughter. Dark-blond hair, tucked behind his ears. Olive skin, the kind that pegged him as Mediterranean. A body to kill for, draped along the edge of the bed. Where we'd obviously been having, well, some kind of cuddling session.

'Who are you?' I snapped, snatching the covers and pulling them in front of me, even though I was fully clothed. Something about his look, his predatory glance, made me feel vulnerable. And confused. And just a wee bit hot.

'I'm Luca,' he said. 'You have nothing to fear from me, Lily.'

He smiled as he said it, but the glimpse of sharp, shining teeth did nothing to make me feel reassured.

'Why were you touching me?' I asked. That wasn't really what I wanted to know – that went more along the lines of, 'Why didn't it plunge me into a nightmare world of visions?' – but it would do for starters.

'Because I wanted to,' he said simply, stretching out on the bed like a panther, black T-shirt riding up from jeans and flashing a glimpse of smooth, taut stomach. 'Because you looked so pretty, like Sleeping Beauty, your skin so white and smooth. I didn't mean any harm. Anyway, you seemed to like it. You were purring, like a little cat.'

I blushed, suspecting he was right.

'Please don't do it again,' I said. 'I don't like people touching me.'

'Then we have nothing to worry about. I'm not "people". I,' he said, letting out a fake Gothic horror-movie laugh, 'am Vampyr!'

He bared his fangs, and I all but fell off the bed in a tangle of clothes, sheets and panic. He carried on laughing, and my fear was replaced by an urge to hit him with something very, very hard. If this was an example of vampire humour, I wouldn't be queuing up for the Undead Comedy Club any time soon.

On the other hand, I thought, remembering the way my skin had tingled under his touch, there could be other . . . advantages.

'So, you're dead,' I said.

'Technically,' he replied. 'But I still have the full complement of male urges, if you get what I mean?'

He winked, leaving me in no doubt at all as to what he meant. And interestingly, I wondered if his non-living status meant I could give in to a few urges of my own.

Did normal rules not apply with vampires? Did touching the undead somehow chase away my propensity for mind-numbing visions? Did the fact that he had no human future mean I could get a pass on the brain-freeze? I supposed it made sense ... It's not like I've ever had a future-flash when stroking a dog, or anything. Non-human might mean non-invasive, which was damned fine news. I've lived with the burden for so long, the thought of losing it, even temporarily, made me giddy.

I looked him up and down, and my newly emerging inner slut gave him the thumbs up. Being dead looked good on him.

I crawled back over the bed, enjoying the flash of surprise on his face as I kneeled next to him. This had been a day for revelations. Painful revelations that were still tormenting my mind. Would it hurt to try for a few that might feel good instead? To find out something new about myself that would result in something other than a full-blown anxiety attack? Maybe I deserved a treat. Just for a minute or two.

I reached out, tentatively touched his arm. Oh. Cold, hard. Nice. I paused: no visions. Ran my hand down to his fingers, linked mine into his. Still no hint of what his future might hold: no tears, no heartbreak, no agonising pain. Nothing apart from the very delicious sensation of my flesh on his. He'd gone very still, and a small warning sign flashed in my brain: he was *absolutely* still, like a predator tricking his prey ...

I ignored it, and touched his chest, feeling only one thudding heartbeat where there should have been more. Yep, definitely dead. He looked on in curiosity as I moved further down his body, slipping my hand beneath his T-shirt and up on to his torso. Yikes. That felt really, really good – lots of ridges, smooth skin over hard muscle. Still no visions, not even that tiny spider's web of sensation that warns me one is on its way. Different sensations instead, as

I traced the contours of his abs, then further up. Nipples, erect; a trail of silky hair. Wow. So this is what a man feels like. I suddenly understood why everyone is so obsessed with sex.

'Might be an idea to stop that now, Sleeping Beauty,' Luca said, his voice edgy and frightening, all playfulness gone. 'I may be dead, but I'm not *that* dead. Get away from me for a moment, or I might hurt you.'

I snatched away my hand and flew to the other side of the bed, scrambling off it. I settled myself down in a chair under the window, and hoped that was far enough. Great. I find a man I can touch without fear of seeing the future, and replace it with one that wants to drink my blood. Could life get any more complicated?

Right at that moment, the door to the bedroom burst open, and Gabriel stomped in, puffed up so tall with High Kingly magic he had to stoop to fit under the frame. He was, literally, almost seven feet tall, and built to match. I really needed to add that to the barrage balloon full of questions that were piling up.

His fists were clenched, and he glared at Luca, who was grinning up at him smugly. He was apparently unimpressed by the Popeye routine.

'Are you all right, Lily?' said Gabriel. 'I felt . . . something odd.'

Ah. Yes. That would be me experiencing full-on sexual arousal for the first time ever. There wasn't really a polite way to phrase that, so I just nodded, let the blush have its wicked way with me, and stayed quiet.

'She started it,' said Luca, unfolding himself from the bed and shoving his way past a now-deflating Gabriel. 'Quite the little minx, this Mother of the Mortals.'

He waved, leaving the room, and I found myself unable to meet Gabriel's eyes. I knew they'd be flaming violet. And quite possibly a tiny bit angry.

'I'm fine,' I said at last, once I realised he wasn't going

to start the small talk. 'Luca came to say hello, and, well . . . did you know that's the first time I've ever touched a man's chest?' I blurted out. Dignified, as usual.

'And that's the way you chose to start?' he asked. 'With a vampire drummer?'

The drummer. Of course. They were always the ones to watch, quietly dangerous in the back. Explained the fabulous arms as well. I quickly shut down that train of thought, uncertain when Gabriel's pesky telepathy would kick in.

'I'm sorry,' I said. 'Didn't mean to upset you. It was just . . . I needed it, I suppose. After everything that's happened. To be able, finally, to touch someone. It's been . . . for ever. I got carried away.'

I knew I had no need to apologise. Despite his belief that I was his mate, I still hadn't consented to that and was, as far as I was concerned, a free agent. But he looked so hurt, so worried, that I wasn't enough of a heartless bitch to remind him of that. That was probably something I needed to work on.

He nodded, and I could feel the effort it took for him to drop the subject.

'I understand. Just be careful,' he said. 'With Luca. With all of them. They're allies, but they're animals. Their control can slip.'

Right. Another gem to add to the list: don't poke the vampires.

'Where's Carmel?' I asked, deciding to change the subject.

'She's gone home to call work – said she was "throwing a sickie", whatever that means – and she'll meet us later. She said she needed to feed the cat, but to be honest, I think she was drunk. I need to restock the vodka if she's coming round again.'

'And is she? Coming round again? You're not going to do some, I don't know, Jedi mind-control trick and erase it all from her memory?'

He sat down opposite me, eyes running over my face, lingering on my neck as though checking for potential vampire mayhem.

'I could, if that's what you want. I have the magic to do that. But apart from the alcoholism, she seemed to take it all in her stride. For a mortal. And she is tough, also for a mortal. It would help my mind rest easier if I knew she was with you, when I can't be.'

I pondered the issue, not overly thrilled at the prospect of a new life where I seemed to be in need of a bodyguard twenty-four/seven. But I needed Carmel as well – not only for babysitting duties, but because she was mine. In this world of weirdness, she was my friend. I didn't doubt Gabriel's dedication to his duty, but to him, I was Mabe. Mother of the Mortals and potential consort. To Carmel, I was Lily McCain, retarded pop girl and late-night news desk buddy. And whatever else I got dragged into, she'd always see me as that.

'Will she be safe?' I asked, trying hard not to be selfish.

'I can't guarantee it one hundred per cent,' he replied. 'But we'll do our best to guard her. It's something we do well. I have no intention of letting anything happen to you, Lily, or to Carmel.'

'And Coleen? Nan?' She might be a grade-A battleaxe, but I was in no rush to sit by that hospital bed.

'Don't worry about her. She's being watched.'

'Right,' I said, tucking my knees up to my chin. Ugh. My jeans were smelly. I still hadn't had that shower. 'Well, let's ask Carmel. I'm fairly sure what the answer will be, but we'll let her make an educated decision. What time is it anyway? I assume after dark, unless Luca's the kind of vampire who takes sunshine risks?'

'Luca takes no risks at all when it comes to his own well-being,' said Gabriel, 'so don't worry on his account.'

There was an edge to his voice, a slightly bitter anger I'd not heard before.

'Are you . . . jealous?' I asked, unable to keep the grin off my face. 'Are you, High King Cormac macConaire, feeling a touch of the green-eyed monster?'

He stood up. His usual height, which was quite tall enough. Looked at me with slight haughtiness, the kind of expression I supposed a High King would have been practising for years.

'Of course I am,' he replied. 'I am consumed with it. I feel the need to run a stake through Luca's heart, disembowel him and spread his entrails in the midday sun. He touched you in a way you won't let me touch you. You touched him in return. I felt it all, every one of your breathless sighs, every one of your heartbeats. And I hate him for it. Does that answer your question, *a ghra*?'

Uh. Yeah. I suppose it did. Even if I didn't know what that last bit meant.

Chapter Eight

Same time, same place, different world.

We were back at the Coconut Shy, and I was nursing another beer. This time, Gabriel was by my side, as my High King totty, and just a few hours earlier I'd been feeling up the band's hunky dead drummer boy. And, last but not least, the fate of the whole world now rested upon my shoulders.

What a difference a day makes.

The band – The Cloaks of Darkness – were on stage, doing an ironic cover of The Smashing Pumpkins' 'Bullet with Butterfly Wings'. As Isabella, the singer, drawled that opening line about the world being a vampire, my heart constricted: even knowing what she was, I'd have happily walked over and opened a jugular for her.

I tore my eyes away, and instead looked at Gabriel.

'Why are we here?' I asked, accepting now that he'd hear me, despite the din.

'You need to meet some of my people,' he replied. 'So you know who is on your side, and who to avoid.'

'And your people – you – where do you fit in? You look mortal, and you say you're a king, which *sounds* mortal. But then there's the whole body-swelling-up thing, and the fact that you talked about humans as "them". Sorry if it's a drag but I need to know a few things.'

He nodded, still scanning the room for his killer leprechauns. Or whatever.

'The High Kings were mortal once. They ruled in Tara, and the Otherworld was the realm of the Tuatha de Danaan – kings, gods, the dead, that kind of thing. And at the start of each High King's reign, the sacred stone – the Lia Fail – would shout his name, and the new king would be ceremonially mated with Mabe, which would ensure well-being across the mortal lands.'

'Mabe? That would be me, then?' I asked, pretty sure I'd not done any ceremonial mating in recent times.

'No, not then. Then it would be the priestess that represented Mabe in the mortal world. But over the millennia, the lines have become blurred. The lines of the High Kings . . . mingled, shall we say, with those of the Tuatha de Danaan. The blood mixed, and the race developed. I am the High King of the mortal realm, but I am also a descendant of gods.'

I took a sneaky look at him – the violet eyes and the master-race body – and decided I could believe that. He certainly looked like one, and he was definitely bossy enough to be both.

'So where do you live, and, you know, hang out? When you're being human?'

'Dublin, mainly, sometimes New York. But I move around. I'm what you might call an older man, and too many questions would be asked if I stayed in one place for too long. My body clock doesn't work in quite the same way as a mortal's. I can pass as human, but I'm not. I can visit the Otherworld and pass as Tuatha, but I'm not. I'm both.'

'So . . . what am I? I feel mortal. I get hangovers. My nails need cutting. I don't see a goddess when I look in the mirror.'

He laughed and, before I could stop him, stroked my face, with the speed of light.

'That's in the eye of the beholder, Lily. But to answer your question, you are the spirit of Mabe, born into human flesh. Your sisters were, also. And I've been waiting a very long time for you.'

Right. To do the whole mating thing. Yay.

'Why me? Why this whole spirit-into-flesh affair? Why not the priestess, like it's always been?'

'Because that cycle has ended and a new one has begun. It was always prophesied that this would happen. I was raised to believe it, to wait for you, to secure the fate of humanity. It is a moment of great weakness in time, and one the Fintna Faidh are looking to exploit. That's why I need to keep you safe, Lily. That and a few other reasons.'

My mind was a whirl of questions, and there was a whole new sister issue I was having to clamp down on for the time being, but any further conversation was halted by the arrival of a short, stocky, dark-haired man. Not quite a leprechaun, but stick him in a green suit and he could give it a go.

'Finn,' said Gabriel, clasping him on thick shoulders with both hands. Finn grinned at me in a manner that can only be described as impish, and gave me a quick bow.

'My Lady,' he said, 'it is an honour to be at your service. My sword arm is yours to command.'

'That's . . . very nice of you,' I replied, unsure of the whole goddess/leprechaun etiquette. Behind me, Kevin the barman approached, his floppy blond hair falling over one eye as usual.

'And this is Caemgen,' said Gabriel, 'although you might know him as Kev.'

I stared at Kevin, who was grinning while he cleaned a glass with a dirty tea towel. Kevin, apparently pronounced Kwe-veen. The barman who'd always kept an eye out for me.

'Kevin!' I said, feeling even more out of control. For a goddess, I didn't have much of a sense of power. 'Are you . . . one of them?'

'Aye, milady,' he said. 'Caemgen ni Niall. Also yours to command. And to supply you with fresh bottles of Peroni whenever your heart desires.'

'Who else?' I asked Gabriel. 'Which of your other secret squirrels have been watching me all this time?'

'A few. Remember Miss McDonough?'

'My old head teacher?'

'Yes. She was with us. And Roisin, your friend at university?'

'The one who mysteriously moved to Peru as soon as we graduated?'

'That's the one. You're too important to risk, Lily. Coleen . . . wasn't enough.'

Damned right she wasn't. She wasn't enough for anyone, never mind a six-year-old girl who'd just lost her parents. I swallowed down the bitterness. I had no idea why I'd ended up with her, but I'd always carry the scars. Someone had made a very bad choice somewhere along the line, and when I found out who, there'd be a hefty wet-kipper slapping session.

'These men are to be trusted,' said Gabriel. 'With your life. They would give up their souls for you, Lily.'

I wasn't sure I wanted anyone giving up their souls for me, whether they were willing to or not. I was starting to yearn for the days when the most responsibility I had was whether to give a band three stars or four.

I could feel all of their gazes upon me, as though they were waiting for something, some command, some request, some sign that I was anything but an ordinary screwed-up Liverpool girl in a battered pair of Doc Martens.

'I need to pee,' I said, which may have been slightly less than they were hoping for. Gabriel nodded – as though giving me permission – and I headed towards the ladies, slamming my way through the metal-clad doors and leaning against the graffitied wall.

I didn't actually need to pee. I needed to breathe. Away

from all the testosterone and mumbo jumbo. Away from the noise and the crowd and my new-found soul-sacrificing friends. I considered climbing out of the window and making a run for it, but it was too small, and the ledge was covered in a suspicious-looking brown gunk. Ah, the glamorous life of a goddess.

My hyperventilating was interrupted as the door slammed back again, and a woman walked in. A woman who actually looked like a goddess: tall and slender, with a swanlike neck and lustrous ebony hair.

She smiled at me, and walked over to the mirror, fluffing her already perfect do into a big, black cloud. She pulled out a lipstick, and started to draw a blood-red circle over her lips.

I had the feeling she wasn't a regular at the Coconut Shy. And I had an even stronger feeling that she was one of *them*. Privacy was clearly a thing of the past. I should have locked myself in a stall, but it probably wouldn't have done any good.

'So,' she said, pouting and checking the lippie, 'he's given you the spiel, has he? Cormac Mor?'

'If you mean Gabriel, then . . . yes, I suppose he has. Are you with him? Are you one of his people?'

'Hardly!' she said, laughing. 'I'm one of the bad guys. Or at least I suspect that's how he painted it. He always was a little narrow-minded. Pretty enough, I'll grant you that, but haughty with it, don't you think?'

I shrank back against the wall, feeling a wave of strength flow from the modelesque creature in front of me. I felt its shadow wrap around me, like tendrils of invisible smoke, clogging my nostrils.

'Well, sweetie, he hasn't told you the truth, the whole truth, and nothing but the truth, so help me, Goddess. I am Eithne, of the Tuatha de Danaan. And I'm here to tell you that we don't wish to annihilate the mortals – we wish to improve them. Make them better. Bring them . . . up to standard. To reclaim what was once ours, and to share all that we have learned. Has he told you what the Otherworld is like? The Land of the Young? No illness, no pain, no age-ing. Doesn't that sound better than' – she gestured around the admittedly less than glamorous surroundings of the Coconut Shy lavatory – 'this?'

It did sound better, but the picture of well-being she was painting was offset by the fact that I felt like I was choking to death. Nausea was rising from the pit of my stomach, and every breath I took in was tinged with a rich, sickly perfume. Like apples fallen off the tree and left for too long.

She looked at me, at the way I was struggling to exhale, at my clenched fists and whitening skin, and her eyes narrowed.

'Interesting,' she said, reaching out to stroke my hair. 'You can . . . feel it. You can feel my power. I didn't expect that. Still, I'm telling the truth. This mortal world is – how might you put it? Fucked up? They've covered their sacred groves with shopping malls, their shrines with housing estates. They've blocked the magic of their rivers with pol-lution and waste. They had their chance at bounty. Why should we – why should you, Mabe? – give them another? I mean, it's not as though they're worth the effort, is it? Look at that woman he put you with, the dried-out bone that raised you.'

She held up a finger, touching it against my lips, and I felt my mind prised open. I saw the vision clear as day: me, as a child. Six years old. Serious face, and hair in plaits. In a small, dark room, surrounded by strangers. The woman I'd been told was my nan looking at me like I was poison. The two men in black, the men she was scared of. One of them handing her the brown-paper package . . . Gabriel? His face flashed into view: the cut of his cheekbones, his fine white skin, those unmistakable eyes. He looked exactly the same then as he did now. It was definitely Gabriel. He was the one who'd given me away. Who'd left me to my fate with her, with Coleen, a woman who'd never loved anything in her life. The woman who'd raised me in silence and fear.

Eithne pressed harder on my lips, and I choked in a breath that I knew could be my last.

'Ah . . . you didn't know, did you? Well, now you do. And you have a choice,' she said, looking at me like I was an insect being divested of its wings. 'It's up to you. You don't have to let him in your mind. You don't have to feel his touch. You don't have to play the part he has all laid out for you – the sacrificial spirit, ready to birth a nation. You can choose us. You can choose freedom.'

I couldn't reply. I couldn't speak. I couldn't even breathe. She could end it right now; win this war I wanted nothing to do with. Snuff me out like I'd never existed. I dragged my thoughts together, tried to come up with some way to fight back, but she was too strong. That last breath choked in my throat, and my eyes started to blur from lack of oxygen. She had a beautiful face, but it was cruel, and not the one you'd choose as your last sight.

The door slammed back yet again, so hard it took a chunk of plaster from the wall. Eithne, distracted, dropped her touch, and I sucked air into my sore lungs, sliding down on to the floor, huddling there with the discarded tissue paper and hardened globs of chewing gum.

It was Isabella. The singer. A fury of hair and hands, she grabbed Eithne around the neck and threw her hard across the room. Eithne slammed into the sinks in a way that would have broken a human back, and I heard the hiss of water as disconnected pipes spewed out.

Isabella roared, and sank her fangs into Eithne's shoulder, blood seeping. More blood oozed out as she tore into flesh. Eithne rallied, gripped Isabella's hair to yank the vampire's face from her body, then grabbed her arm and pulled with such ferocity that I heard the shoulder dislocate. Shoving her away, she ran for the door, leaving a trail of Eau de Rot behind her.

Isabella stood up straight. Rammed herself repeatedly against the wall until the joint was knocked back into place with a sickening pop. Wiped her mouth clear of blood with the back of her hand, and turned to me.

'Bloody Tuatha,' she said, making a gagging sound. 'They always taste of battery acid.'

Chapter Nine

I've been to a few after-show parties in my time, including one with Liam Gallagher, but nothing that could compare with the weirdness in Gabriel's apartment later that night.

The vampires were glowing with energy, alive with the adrenaline of their gig and the willing post-performance snacks they'd 'romanced' just enough to leave their conquests with dreamy memories and mysterious love bites. Luca was prowling round the room, topless and wearing a pair of leather trousers, and Isabella was languid and luscious, draped over the sofa like a Renaissance painting come to life.

Morgan the bass player was on a high, playing *Call of Duty* on the Xbox with Marcus, the guitarist. I'd be surprised if there was anything left of the handsets by morning. They too had dispensed with the need for shirts, which made for entertaining viewing.

Finn, Kevin and Gabriel were huddled in a corner, drinking whisky and drawing up battle plans, and Carmel had finally joined us.

'There was this man outside my house,' she said, dumping a bag of her stuff in the corner and sliding down next to me on the couch. 'And when I say "man", I mean god. Blond, well fit, like Daniel Craig on steroids. He nodded as

I went out, got in his car, and followed me here. Did I just get really lucky, or is it something to do with the World of Warcraft over there?'

'Probably,' I said. 'He'll be your guard, and he'll have some stupidly unpronounceable name, and if you ever speak to him, he'll witter on about duty and laying down his life to protect yours.'

'Hmm . . . could be worse, I suppose. So, how are you holding up? And what's with the semi-naked stud parade? Are they Gabriel's men?'

'Oh. No,' I replied. 'They're my new vampire friends. And you see that one over there, with the shiny hair and the eyes? I was in bed with him earlier.'

'No way!' she said, voice bubbling with laughter and disbelief. 'Was there kissing?'

I love Carmel, I realised. Really love her. I'd just broken the news that she was in a room full of the living dead, and the first question out of her mouth was about my sex life. I understood why *I* could deal with all of this – with my visions, I've been on the fringes of the supernatural my whole life – but her easy acceptance of it amazed me. That's what three years on the night desk will get you, I suppose.

'No. But quite a lot of bare skin. It was . . . nice.'

'I bet it was,' she said, surveying Luca like he was a box of chocolates. 'So how did that happen? Why did you drop the whole "no touching, dahling" routine? And while we're sharing, what's with that anyway? Why don't you like to be touched? Is there something . . . off, from when you were a kid?'

Her tone had lowered, and the sparkle had gone from her eyes. She obviously expected some sordid tale of abuse to be heading her way.

'Nothing like that,' I said quickly. 'It's complicated . . .'

'I think,' she said, gesturing around the room, 'that if I can handle this, I can handle anything.'

Fair point.

'Sometimes, when I touch people – skin on skin – I see things. I see visions . . . of their future. And a lot of times that's fine – it's mundane, it's normal, or even really happy. But other times, it's . . . not so happy. It's how they die, or how they get ill. Which is—'

'Bloody depressing!' she butted in. 'I can see that. So – if I held your hand now, you could see what my future holds?'

'Not necessarily,' I replied, feeling uncomfortable at the thought. I couldn't bear to see a future that held anything bad for Carmel. 'It doesn't seem to happen with the vampires at all. And with humans I don't have any control over it, or know when it will happen. Which is one of the many things that suck about it. Why? You don't want me to, do you?'

'No way!' she answered solidly. 'I can't think of anything worse. The present is plenty interesting enough, thank you. And it does explain a lot – all these years I thought you were just being weird. I didn't mind, it was all part of the package, but I know you freaked a lot of other people out. Like the canteen staff, when you insisted they put your coffee down on the counter so you didn't have to touch their hands. They thought you were a real stuck-up cow.'

Good to know. Lily McCain, social pariah.

She paused, cast her eye over Morgan and Marcus, squatting bare-chested on the floor in front of us.

'So, you can touch vampires . . . again, could be worse, if this lot is anything to go by. And I noticed that you gave the old High King a bit of the cold shoulder earlier. What's up? Have you two had a falling out? The path of true mating not running smoothly?'

She'd noticed, of course. Being a girl. She was right – I had been off with him. Following the revelations in the Coconut Shy bathrooms, I was finding it hard to fall back into the routine of banter and sarcasm that Gabriel and I had established. After my encounter with Eithne, he'd been so worried I thought he'd explode, insisting that he stuck by my side the whole night. I guess he thought he'd failed in his protection duty – which he had. They'd all been shocked that she'd come in person – the Fintna Faidh usually stuck to their men-in-black foot soldiers on Earth, apparently – and Finn thought it was to do with something called Samhain.

Samhain, it transpires, is an ancient festival when the walls between the Otherworld and ours come down. In the modern era we've claimed it as our own with Halloween, taken its mystery and magic and made it safe by dressing it up with Frankenstein masks and candy baskets. And in the approach to Samhain, the walls waver, allowing more contact between the two planes. The fact that Eithne had been able to come and go undetected was plain good luck for me. Hurrah.

Gabriel had explained all this on the way back from the nightclub, in a cool voice that suggested he'd also noticed my stand-offishness. He'd got the message and kept his distance since, which was fine by me. Because the news that Eithne delivered, however hideously, had changed the way I felt about him.

Knowing that he was keeping secrets, that he was the man who had calmly handed me over to Coleen and my miserable fate, had changed everything. It's not like I was one hundred per cent sold on him before, but I had believed him when he said he was on my side. And I had, truth be told, not been totally repulsed at the thought of being his mate.

But now . . . now I was even more confused. My life had been plunged into this netherworld of madness without so much as a by-your-leave, and throughout, Gabriel had given me the distinct impression that there was nothing I could do about it, apart from cling to him and hope. That my role had been decided in advance. Then along came Eithne, slinking and stinking her way from the Otherworld, to tell me I had a choice. That I could decide my own destiny. Change my own future.

I can't say that the thought of allying myself with her

appealed in any way – she had almost killed me, after all – but I now felt a deep-rooted dissatisfaction with what was happening around me. I could feel the change inside me, feel the need for control swimming through me, like an infection in my cells. The time for dumbly doing what I was told was coming to an end.

So, it appeared, was the war meeting. Gabriel walked towards us, Finn and Kevin behind him. All three looked worried, serious, but also excited. Like they'd come to a decision.

'I need to return to the Otherworld,' said Gabriel. 'I need to meet with our allies there and find out what is going on.'

'Fine,' I replied icily. 'Off you pop, then.'

'To do that, I need to go somewhere. And you will come with me. I will not risk leaving you alone with . . . these,' he said, looking round at the frolicsome vampires with an air of distaste.

'So where are we going?' asked Carmel, who'd obviously decided to throw in her pounds with her pennies.

'To the nearest *sidhe*,' he said, pronouncing it 'shee'. 'You know them as fairy mounds. The few obvious ones remaining have become tourist attractions, which has rendered them defunct. But there is an active *sidhe* nearby – at Bidston Hill.'

'The Observatory?' I asked, knowing the place as a local weather station on the Wirral.

'Yes. We will leave right now,' he said, dispensing with any of the niceties, such as asking my permission.

The vampires stirred, and I could feel electricity buzzing in the room. Isabella was smiling and unfolding her limbs from the sofa. Luca let out a whoop, and the others dropped their gaming handsets to the polished wooden floors. They were obviously happy to be on the move again, apparently having the attention span of three-year-olds.

'Lily can come with me,' said Luca, grinning. 'I think she'd like that.'

'Lily will not,' said Gabriel, glaring at him in a way that suggested his disembowelling plan was coming back to mind. 'I am her protector, and I will not leave her side.'

A debate ensued, and Carmel and I followed it as best as we could, our heads turning from side to side like we were at Wimbledon.

'Enough!' I shouted, standing up. I was sick of being argued over; of my own will being ignored. Silence fell over the room, and I felt a strange power surge inside me, rising in my veins like a drug.

Goddess-time.

'Cormac macConaire, I shall not accompany you. I will go with Luca. This is what I wish, and this is what I command.'

Gabriel's eyes flared, and I saw a slight contraction in the muscles of his T-shirt-clad arms. I held my breath, expecting him to swell and shout and generally act all kingly about it. Instead, he lowered his head slightly, the merest fraction of a bow, and replied: 'Then it shall be so, My Lady.'

Chapter Ten

Moments later I was starting to regret that decision. Vampires drive like maniacs and shouldn't be allowed anywhere near the wheel of a Mercedes. They certainly shouldn't be allowed into the Mersey Tunnels, the monumental underground routes that run beneath the river.

The concepts of 'Do Not Change Lanes' and '40 mph Speed Limit' were clearly lost on Luca as he propelled us forward, bathed in harsh fluorescent lighting. The concrete of the walls whirred past, and I could hear Carmel cursing as she was thrown around in the back seat.

'Slow down!' I said, gripping the dashboard. 'You might already be dead, but we're not!'

'My apologies,' he replied, easing off the gas until we reached a leisurely fifty. 'We're just in a hurry. To get to the Otherworld, and see our lord.'

'And who might that be?' I asked, as my heartbeat settled back into a regular pace. 'And why are you all involved in this anyway? You're not mortal.'

'We all were once, Lily,' he said. 'I was a musician. I lived in Siena. I had a wife, children, work I loved.'

He looked sad beneath his Mediterranean tan, and I had a million questions to ask.

'I'll tell you all about it when we have more time,' he

said, cutting me off before I had the chance. 'But for now, know this – we are allied with Cormac Mor because Donn, the Lord of the Dead, commands it. He has no desire to see the end of the mortal realm.'

'Bad for business?' I asked.

'Yes, and because he has an . . . affection for mortals. For their failures and triumphs. Their spirit. The way they battle on through their lives, completely devoid of meaning. It gives him pleasure, watching their trials and tribulations, knowing all the time that whatever they do, they will end up with him.'

'Sounds like a lovely bloke,' piped up Carmel, obviously earwigging in the back.

'Not really,' said Luca. 'But he is our lord. And we ourselves have our own reason for wanting to keep mortals around.'

'What's that?' she asked.

'Food,' he said, flashing a wicked grin full of white teeth. 'You would be especially tasty, Lily.'

Nice. At least if I didn't cut it as the Goddess, I had a bright future ahead of me as a vampire buffet.

After throwing a handful of coins into the toll basket, we followed the convoy of cars to the hill. As soon as we'd parked and got out, Gabriel descended, huge and scary, his white skin shining in the darkness, the violet of his eyes luminous.

He moved to touch me, retreated at the last minute and settled instead for giving me an eyeball inspection for damage.

'I'm fine,' I said, twisting my neck round to show him. 'Look, Dad, no teeth marks. Almost had a heart attack with his driving, though. Now what?'

'Now we climb the hill. Or I can carry you?' he suggested, with a hint of a dare in his voice.

I ignored him, not ready to resume business as usual just yet, and started up the pathway, Carmel at my side. It was pitch black, as was to be expected at 4 a.m. The distant lights from the motorway below rose in a faint orange glow, blurred with the occasional passing car headlights. Normal people, going about their normal lives. I bit down a twinge of bitterness. That was never going to be my life again.

Carmel stumbled as we climbed, and a dark figure rushed up to her side. Tall, blond and 'well fit', as she had described him. He had a torch in one hand and offered the other to her. She took it after approximately a nanosecond of deliberation.

'Connor macEoghan,' he said, the Irish name lilting lyrically from his lips. 'At your service.'

'Lovely to meet you,' she replied in a tone that suggested some kind of internal combustion was occurring. I smiled to myself and ploughed onwards. Carmel has always had an eye for the boys, and it was good to see that some things at least hadn't changed.

I could feel Gabriel hovering nearby, presumably ready in case I stubbed a toe or got attacked by a passing owl, but I blanked him out. I was, I was starting to learn, pretty good at sulking. Must be a goddess thing.

We reached the top of the hill, and Finn led us round to the back of the Observatory complex, through a clump of shadowed bushes, and into a small clearing. The space was lit only by our torches and the moon, which drenched Gabriel's face in silver, making him look even more magical than usual.

He walked towards me, placed a hand on the back of my hair, pulled me so close our hips were touching. His expression was so solemn that I let him. I felt a sizzle of his power run through my body, so strong I was glad I was wearing Docs. Those rubber soles were the only things keeping me earthed as I sank into the violet of his eyes. For a second I felt we were alone, in the wild wind on top of the hill. Alone in the whole world.

'I don't know what I have done that has upset you so

much, *a ghra*,' he said. 'But I am sorry. I won't be gone for long. Stay with Finn and Kevin. They will protect you while I am away. Be safe, and know that my heart is with yours.'

It was such a pretty speech, and said with such conviction, that I almost lost myself. Almost gave in to those instincts to lean closer, touch my lips to his, tangle my fingers in the midnight of his hair. Almost, but not quite.

'Now,' he commanded, 'stay where you are and do not – I repeat, *do not* – wander off on your own. This place is dangerous.'

He turned and walked away, leaving me breathless at how fast he could change from tender suitor to bullying bastard. I knew which one I liked best.

I deliberately turned away, not wanting to see him go up in a puff of smoke or whatever he did to re-enter the Otherworld. I heard footsteps and knew the vampires were following him. Connor remained at Carmel's side – a man who had his job and was sticking to it – and Finn and Kevin looked towards Gabriel's retreating back with yearning in their eyes. This Otherworld must be a heck of a place.

Taking advantage of their momentary distraction, I deliberately disobeyed Gabriel and immediately wandered off on my own. Take that, High King, I thought, as I ambled along the path that curved around the hill.

I was angry and hurt and mind-numbingly cold. I was fed up of being surrounded by people, none of whom had any respect for my personal space, and I wished I was alone, in my flat, with a good book and my iPod.

Mainly, though, I was sick of being treated like a child who'd been put in the naughty corner. I was a grown woman – nay, goddess, if he was to be believed – and if I wanted to wander off on my own, I'd damned well do it.

Wrapping my arms around myself against the chill in the air, I stumbled towards a small hollow in the side of the hill. It was tiny, just big enough for little children to play hide-and-seek in, but I quite fancied sitting in it, on my own, away from the drama and the magic and the stupid names.

As I approached, a pinprick of light appeared, followed by several more. The sound of pattering footsteps. A face no bigger than the palm of my hand – a perfect heart-shaped peach of a face. Shimmering blonde hair, a dazzling silver haze hovering around child-sized shoulders. Ah, so pretty.

The creature let out a shrill shriek, and leaped towards me. It wrapped its arms and legs around my torso like a fierce monkey and pulled at my hair as I tried to bat it off. We whirled around together – me much bigger; it much stronger and a lot more determined – until I fell, flat on my back in wet grass. It hunkered down on top of me, pointy knees digging into my sides.

'Drink!' it screeched, trying to force a goblet to my mouth.

'No!' I shouted, trying to wrench unfeasibly strong fingers away from my face.

It grabbed hold of my nose, pinched so hard that I felt tears spring to my eyes. Unable to breathe, I was forced to open my mouth to gasp for air. As my lips parted, it tipped the rim of the goblet up and over, and warm liquid flowed between them.

Chapter Eleven

When I opened my eyes, I was still lying flat on my back. But the grass was dry – warm, even – and the hissing hell-child that had attacked me had disappeared. It was also daylight, and most definitely not the kind you got in Liverpool in October. I felt aglow with it, and all of the cold and tension and tiny aches and pains that racked my mortal body had been washed away.

I sat up and looked around. I was lying in a valley between two gentle hills, a rich emerald green that dazzled my eyes. Around me were technicolour flowers and trees dripping with ripe fruit, humming with honeybees. Horses were grazing, flicking the whites of their manes, and damselflies hovered over a brook that gurgled and bubbled its way over rocks.

I definitely wasn't in Kansas any more. Or even, I suspected, the world as I knew it.

Two people were making their way down one of the hills towards me. They were dressed in white, and holding hands. I knew this should be my cue to run, but I couldn't. My body wouldn't move, and my brain didn't even want it to. I . . . knew these people. And they meant me no harm.

The couple approached, and one of them sat beside me

on the warm grass. I looked up into a face I recognised, but hadn't seen for years. A face that had become almost fictional in my mind.

The face of my mother.

She reached out to stroke my cheek, and I knew it would be fine. That her warm touch would not result in visions – not here, in this place. Because this was the Otherworld, and, like Luca, she was . . . dead.

I saw tears streaming down her face, and felt my eyes moisten in response as I threw myself into her arms. She held me tight, kissing my hair, murmuring to me in a language I couldn't understand. It sounded the same as the words Gabriel sometimes used, the heavy cadence of Old Gaelic.

'I can't understand you!' I said, pulling away from her embrace.

'Yes, you can,' she replied, nodding at me reassuringly. 'Just try. Relax and listen. This is your language as well, Lily.'

As she said it, I realised she was right. I could understand her. And I could speak to her – to the woman who had given me the only years of love and comfort I could remember.

She looked just the same, hair long and blonde around her shoulders, her body smooth and plump. She looked beautiful, and happy, and like every good thing in the world. Everything I'd lost. Everything that had been taken away from me when I was thrust into the world of Coleen and the withered rock she kept where her heart should be.

'How's it going, Fairy Princess?' said my father, squatting down beside us. He reached out and held my hand, and I wanted him to pick me up, and spin me around like he used to.

'Am I dead?' I asked. 'Am I dead and in heaven?'

'No, Lily,' said my mother, smiling like she used to when I'd done something especially silly, like ask if zebras were horses with stripes painted on them.

'You're not dead. You're here with us. In Tir na nOg. The Otherworld. You already know that.'

I looked around at the green hills and the flowers, feeling the soothing flow of sunlight on my head, and wondered how Gabriel could ever tear himself away from this place. And I understood why Kevin and Finn had looked so desolate to be left behind.

'Can I stay?' I asked, clinging on to the hope that I could. Even though, deep down, I knew that wasn't to be. That whatever fate had landed me in the role of Mabe, Mother of the Mortals, wasn't going to let me off that easily. Even the thought of leaving brought on a fresh batch of tears, which she wiped gently away.

'No,' she said. 'You know you can't. You have work to do, Lily. Important work. We just wanted to see you again. To answer some of your questions. To tell you how much we love you.'

'I love you too. When I found out about all this, I wasn't even sure if . . . if I was your child!' I blurted out.

'Of course you are,' she replied. 'Our child, and more than that. You know who you are. Cormac Mor wasn't lying to you, Lily. About your role in the world, about what needs to be done if the mortal realm is to be saved. The time is getting nearer, and it will all be up to you. To make your choice. To keep everyone there safe.'

'But why?' I said, knowing I sounded like a whining child. Two minutes in my parents' company and I'd already regressed. 'Why do I need to save it? That woman, Eithne – she said I didn't have to. That she and her kind just want to make things better for humans, make them happier . . . Could they make them like this? Make Earth like this?'

'That's one way of looking at it, sugar,' said my father. 'But not the only way. The Fintna Faidh have their views. They believe the mortals are unnecessary now, an inconvenience. That the Otherworld should have dominion. That would mean the end – the end of people. The end of their loves, their hopes. The end of the balance between worlds. The end of everything. Is that what you really want?'

'I don't know,' I said, thinking of Coleen. Of my childhood. Of the other bullies who'd made it a misery. Of the death and cruelty I saw every time I opened a paper or switched on the TV. Was it all really worth saving? Was I really the right person to choose? Shouldn't it be someone more . . . happy? Someone with more to lose?

'But think of the other things, Lily,' said my mother, without me having uttered a word. 'I know you don't have too many good memories to hold on to, but think of us, and the way we were. The love we shared. That's the way the mortal world can be – the way it is for most of them. And for every act of hatred, there is one of love. More than one. Think of Carmel and how she's never understood you but has always accepted you; the way that even now she's willing to put her life at risk for you. Humans do that. They are willing to sacrifice themselves in a way that the Fintna Faidh aren't. Isn't that worth saving?'

'Yes. No. Maybe,' I said, decisively. 'When do I have to decide?'

'Soon. The night of the Feast of Samhain. That's when you need to make your choice. Do you trust him yet? Do you trust Cormac Mor? Gabriel?' she asked. 'Do you trust him enough to be his mate?'

I felt a momentary tug of amusement. This was too strange. My long-dead mother was asking me if I planned to have sex with a man I barely knew. It was a bit too late for the birds and the bees talk, but the question was a good one. Did I trust him?

'I don't know,' I replied. 'I need more time . . .'

'You don't have time, Lily. Whatever decision you make, it will be made soon. I know this has all been a terrible shock for you. If things had been different, we would have prepared you for it. But your sisters were taken, and we had to keep you safe. Even then, the Faidh knew what power you would have. They're here, by the way. Your sisters. Here with us. And Lucy, the girl who was in the car with us. Well, she wasn't a girl really; she just had the shape of one because that's what we needed to keep you safe. She was a friend, and she gave her mortal life to save yours.'

'Can I meet them?' I asked, looking around hopefully. I only saw one other figure, standing tall and still at the crest of the hill, casting a long shadow under the golden blaze of sunshine. Whoever it was didn't seem to want to join us.

'Not this time, no,' said my mother, following my line of vision to the solitary figure on the hill, in plain sight but somehow hiding. She frowned slightly, and I strained my eyes trying to make out who it was. 'In fact, it's probably time for you to go,' she said firmly. 'You can't stay here for long. I know it only feels like minutes to us, but you've been gone from the human world for hours, perhaps days already. He'll be worried about you.'

Too right he would, I thought, not needing to ask who she was talking about. He'd have his High Kingly knickers in a right royal twist when he found out what I'd done, if he got back before me. I'd get a proper telling-off this time, maybe even get sent to bed without my supper.

I put that thought to the back of my mind. I'd deal with him later.

Sisters, I thought. And Lucy. The girl who died in my place. My parents. All of them here, in this magical place I had to leave. To return to what? An angry, arrogant king in a cold city? A nan who'd choose a pack of Silk Cut over me? To the canteen ladies who thought I was a stuck-up cow? To long, empty years, free of human touch or comfort? It didn't sound that tempting.

My father stood up, held out his hands and pulled me to my feet. Despite my adult height, he whirled me around so hard my feet left the ground, and I landed against him, dizzy and laughing and crying all at the same time.

'Time to go, Fairy Princess,' he said. 'And you'll make the right choice. I know you will.'

'OK. I'll go. But I'll miss you so much it hurts,' I said. 'I always have.'

'We know that, Lily. Take care – and remember who to trust.'

Chapter Twelve

I woke up in a bath. A nice bath, with hot soapy water up to my neck, and fragrant candles burning all around me. Cinnamon. Mmm.

Maybe, I thought, sinking a bit lower into the foam, it had all been a dream. Like Bobby in the shower in *Dallas*. Maybe I was at home, in my flat. In a new bath that I must have forgotten getting installed.

'Sorry, but no,' said Gabriel, smirking at me from a chair by my side. 'Still here.'

I yelped, splashed around a bit, then realised that all the movement was in fact revealing more of my body, which had been perfectly well covered by bubbles anyway.

'How did I get here? How did I get . . . naked?' I asked, feeling a rush of priggish modesty that I found almost embarrassing. I've never been undressed by a man before, and it would have been nice to be conscious the first time it happened.

'Isabella,' he replied. 'What kind of a man do you think I am?'

'The kind who's probably pretty angry with me right now,' I replied, deciding to jump straight into the fight. I'd come to no harm in the Otherworld, other than endur-ing a big dose of mind-boggle, but he didn't know that.

Hadn't known that, while I'd been gone. And whatever his motives, I knew he took the whole save-the-pop-writer-save-the-world routine very seriously.

'I was angry,' he said. 'Furious. Livid, in fact. I got back a day ago, and you were still gone. Finn was almost ready to fall on his own sword he was so distraught at losing you. Carmel's been in a frenzy. And I . . . broke a few things.'

'A *day* ago?' I asked. Wow. They'd been right when they said mortal time moved faster. 'And you all stayed on that hill waiting for me to come back?'

'Yes,' he said. 'In shifts. I was in and out – there, the Otherworld, back at the apartment – in case you were somehow here. And when you reappeared, you were unconscious. At first we feared you were dead, so I broke a few more things. But then you smiled. Still out cold, but smiling. Like I've never seen you smile before, despite my best efforts. You looked so happy. So I knew – I knew where you'd been and who you'd been with. Your parents.'

I sighed, sank further down into the bubbles. Tears sprang from my eyes and I didn't have the will to stop them. Gabriel sucked in a sharp breath, and I knew he'd be fighting not to reach out and comfort me.

'Don't,' I said simply. 'Not now. I'm a mess. I was only with them for a few minutes . . . it was too short. Tell me about them, Gabriel.'

'They were brave, Lily. They died to save you. There have always been mortals who know our secrets, share our goals. And after your sisters were taken, they decided to sacrifice themselves to try to keep you safe. They are people of great honour, and great love. Everything they did was for you, even down to faking your death. I can tell you more, when you're ready to hear it . . . maybe when you have clothes on . . . and I'm sorry. I'm sorry you had to leave them so soon.'

I wondered if he meant when I'd had to leave them this time, or the one before – the time when I'd left them for the not-so-loving arms of Coleen. The time when he'd made the decision to abandon me to her, and her twisted version of parenting. And I wondered if he'd tell me the truth about that, if I asked him directly. Whether he'd tell me about Lucy, the girl who died, and her role in all of this. She'd only been six – in body at least. How had that happened?

'*I can tell you,*' said a voice in my head, deep and soft, like words wrapped in velvet. I snapped my chin up and stared at Gabriel.

'Was that you?' I asked, not at all happy with the idea of him speaking directly into my brain.

'Was what me?' he asked, frowning. 'What did you hear?'

'Ah . . . nothing,' I replied, deciding to keep it to myself. I'd probably imagined it anyway. I'd been to the Otherworld. Maybe I was suffering from some kind of cosmic concussion. Maybe I could now add hearing-voices-in-head to the visions and hallucinations. Party on, dudes.

'Did anything else happen while you were there?' he asked, leaning forward and searching my face. 'Did anybody bother you? Did you meet anyone else?'

'No,' I replied quickly, meeting his probing eyes and praying that my secret didn't show. 'Just them. That was quite enough.'

Technically speaking, I hadn't met the man who stayed on top of the hill, so I kept that one quiet for the time being. I wasn't actually lying, simply being economical with the truth. Not that I was going to suffer any moral hangover about it even if I did lie. Gabriel's overbearing concern for my safety was starting to chafe, and I needed to learn to think for myself, and look after myself.

I wouldn't be much good at saving the world if I had to run to the big boy for help every time I grazed my knee. Especially when I wasn't at all sure I trusted the big boy in question. Eithne had shown me there was an alternative version of this reality, and as soon as I got some quality alone time, I'd be asking the voice in my head to tell me more. As the madman said to the doctor.

'OK,' I said, changing the subject. 'What do you think we should do next? My parents told me the time for me to make my choice is coming soon.'

'Choice?' he said, suddenly sounding angry. Clearly not a word that hit his happy spot. 'What choice? There is no choice, Lily. At least not one that results in anything but death for the world you grew up in. You are Mabe, whether you want to be or not, and I am your mate, no matter how hideous you find the thought.'

Oops. Angry time was back.

I bit back my own anger, knowing it wouldn't achieve anything. Beside, I didn't find the thought of being his mate hideous. In certain lights I found it pretty appealing, in fact. Spending quality naked time with Gabriel was the kind of thing normal girls would lie awake at night dreaming about. But I wasn't a normal girl, and I was starting to find his one-sided view of my future about as attractive as genital warts.

It wasn't just Eithne who'd told me I had a choice to make: my mother and father had too. And their opinion meant a lot more to me than hers, or the High King's. Goddesses always had a choice, and railroading me and blanketing me in half-truths was only going to make me more determined.

'So you say,' I replied, 'but please don't completely discount the fact that I have my own mind, Gabriel. That I have other people to listen to. That I'm not just some well-behaved child sitting around waiting to be told what to do. Insisting I have no choice in the matter doesn't make it true.

'Now, I'm sick of reacting to all this, sick of running. Sick of not knowing what's going on in my own life. Sick of you bossing me around. And if I stay in this bath much longer, I'll turn into a prune. I'm getting out. And then I'll either listen to your plan, or come up with my own.'

He snorted so hard I thought he might choke, stood up and handed me a towel. He turned round to avert his eyes, playing the gentleman.

'I'm not stupid,' I said, standing up straight and holding the towel in front of my breasts, 'I know you can see me in the bloody mirror.'

I saw myself reflected. Tall, shining with moisture, my hair draped in a deep-red swathe over my shoulders. Long legs, slender body, boobs that would pass the pencil test. This was me. Naked. And you know what? I looked pretty damned good.

I dropped the towel, deliberately, feeling an uncharacteristic urge to flaunt myself. Power ran through me when I saw his reaction: a clenching of lips, a sway of hips, a distinctly mate-like twitching in his groin. It was the same power all women feel when they realise the control their bodies have over men. The power of the goddess all of us can be. I was just starting to get to grips with mine, and decided I liked it. At the very least, I knew what to do to distract him now.

'Plan?' I asked, brazenly stepping out of the bath, noticing that he'd now clamped his eyes shut. Wuss.

'Dublin,' he said, voice strained. 'We go to my house in Dublin.'

'And how do we get there?' I asked, using the towel to rub my hair dry. 'Magic portal? The wings of Pegasus?'

'No, he said. 'Ryanair.'

We travelled at night, for the sake of the vampires, and arrived at Gabriel's Dublin home just before one in the morning. Carmel had been knocking back the miniatures on the flight, and was still upset at my disappearing act.

'He smashed everything in his apartment. The flat-screen, the Xbox. All the glasses in the bar. And I texted you, like, a dozen times,' she said. 'I was worried sick.'

'I'm sorry about that,' I answered, 'but I couldn't get

much of a signal in Fairy Land. I'll have a word with Vodafone next time, see if I can upgrade my tariff.'

'No need to get all sarky on me,' she snapped, as the car pulled up into Merrion Square. I gave her a very human shove out of the door, grabbed my backpack before following her out, and we stood looking around us.

Gabriel's home was a magnificent Georgian town house, tucked between others like it in a red-brick terrace. The buildings were clustered around a park that would probably be very pretty in daylight. The pavements were empty, with a few sleek and expensive-looking cars parked alongside them.

'Crikey,' said Carmel. 'This is pretty fucking awesome. You remember that time we came here with work?'

I nodded. I did indeed. Against my better judgement she'd persuaded me to join her for a journalists' shindig in Dublin, which involved less of seeing the fair city than getting hammered in most of the fair city's excellent pubs.

'That night in McDaid's, when I snogged the fiddle player?' she continued, obviously reliving a happy memory. Mine? Not so happy, and mainly involving the wandering hands of our Guinness-drunk picture editor. Wandering hands are an inconvenience to most women. To me, they are a potential catastrophe. Ah, fun times.

Gabriel unlocked the door to the house, and we walked into a long hallway. Protected, as usual. Gabriel led, with Finn and Kevin at his side. Then Carmel and I took our places behind them, carrying our bags, followed by Connor and the vampires. In fact, once I started to ponder it, I realised I hadn't been left alone for a single minute since all this started, apart from my brief excursion into the Otherworld. It did make me feel safe, but also slightly claustrophobic. I'm used to being on my own, and once all this was over – one way or another – I'd be locking myself in a darkened room for a very long time.

Carmel and I were told to wait in the corridor, as the

front door closed behind us. Ahead, Gabriel and his men were carrying out some kind of security check, and outside, we could hear Luca and Morgan doing the same. After a few minutes they all returned to the hallway, and as none of them were covered in blood or carrying severed limbs, I assumed they'd met with no resistance.

'No hostiles,' said Luca, slinking back inside the house. Gabriel nodded, frowning, still scanning around him, slightly taller than he should be.

'All clear here as well,' he said. 'Which feels wrong. I expected trouble. Time's running out, and they must be getting desperate – so where are they? Where's the ambush?'

His tone made me feel jumpy, and I gazed up the stairs, half expecting one of those 'Death to the Mother of the Mortals' types to come hurtling down at me. But actually, I hadn't seen one for days. Not since we'd been chased through Sefton Park, in fact. He was right – it did feel wrong. They'd been at Lime Street, chasing us through the tunnels until Gabriel made them go splat. They'd been at my flat, waiting. So where were they now? Strangely, I felt worse for not being surrounded by brainwashed assassins baying for my blood.

'*They are in retreat,*' said that voice in my head. The same one as before; the one made of velvet. '*I commanded it. There will be no attack upon you, Goddess.*'

I tried not to show any reaction, especially as Gabriel was looking right at me. Now would so not be a good time for a mind-link moment. The voice in my head belonged to me – it was private, a Goddess-to-mystery-shopper kind of thing. Gabriel knew way too much about me already, and I had the feeling that another man in my brain would send him over the edge. He'd expand to the size of the Statue of Liberty and lock me in a trunk for the rest of my life, all in the name of keeping me safe.

'*Why?*' I said, or, rather, thought, all the time trying to keep my expression bland.

'Because there has been enough death,' the voice said. *'Now is the time for life. I would rather talk to you than kill you, Lily.'*

Fair enough. I liked the sound of that. Especially as talking to me was something Gabriel only did as a last resort. He was more of the 'sit down, shut up, do as I say' kind of guy. He could justify his strong, silent behaviour as much as he liked, but at the end of the day he was just stupidly bossy. Perhaps he couldn't help it, having been raised as a High King and all. But I – thanks to him – was raised by a not very pleasant mortal. One who also expected me to sit down, shut up and do as I was told. I've had a lifetime of being ordered around, which isn't very dignified. Not for anyone, and certainly not for the Goddess, if that's what I really was.

'You are the Goddess. Never doubt it,' said the voice. *'You have the power of choice. Yours to use.'*

I nodded to myself – to the voice. It was instinctive, to respond in some way, but obviously looked pretty weird to anyone watching me. Which Gabriel, of course, always was. It was his life's mission.

'Are you all right?' he asked, taking hold of my shoulders so hard I could feel his fingers digging deep into the flesh beneath my coat.

'Yes. And get your hands off me – right now!' I said, my voice louder and harsher than I'd meant it to be. His fingers dropped away, and the tension level in the hallway ratcheted up a few notches. I heard Luca snigger behind me, muttering something about trouble in paradise.

'You can shut up as well!' I snapped, whirling round and poking him in the chest. Which admittedly hurt my finger a lot more than his chest.

'Why are we here, Gabriel?' I asked. 'What's the master plan, oh great King? Or don't you even have one? This lot seem to follow you round like lapdogs, but I wouldn't mind knowing what's next in your grand vision, if it's not too much trouble?'

There was a strained silence, and Finn couldn't have looked more shocked if I'd slapped him. Kevin was shaking his head at my blatant disrespect, and even Carmel was biting her lip nervously. It could be possible that I'd overstepped the line a tiny bit. Gone a smidgeon too far.

Hey. Even goddesses make mistakes.

I refused to back down, despite Gabriel's everexpanding presence before me. His head was brushing the ceiling and his shoulders were so broad they almost touched the walls on either side. Everyone but him was blanked from my vision, and I felt like Alice in Wonderland, as though I was getting smaller instead of him getting bigger.

It was a mind-twisting sight, and ever so slightly terrifying.

'You'd better calm down,' I said. 'Or you'll demolish the building.'

Chapter Thirteen

The next afternoon, I woke up in a decadently large four-poster bed, wrapped in a silk-covered duvet. Small men with pointy hammers were living inside my brain, apparently mining for coal. My mouth was dry, and I was desperate for the loo. I half fell out of bed, and staggered to the en suite bathroom. My feet were sore from too much dancing, and there was a large mystery bruise on my right hip. I'd seen those before. They usually sprang from excessive alcohol consumption, and my ensuing loss of all spatial awareness. I'd clearly been doing some hard-object surfing the night before.

I groaned, sluiced water from the cold tap over my face, and into my mouth. I looked into the mirror, and immediately regretted it. Dark circles. Pale skin. Hair in backwards-through-bush mode. The type of face that should be plastered on the side of alcopop bottles to turn teens teetotal.

I dragged on some clothes from my backpack, and stumbled to the room next door. Carmel was splayed across the bed, covers draped haphazardly over her, looking even worse than I did. I could see she was naked apart from her shoes, and her eyes were caked shut with last night's mascara.

'Help me,' she muttered. 'I think I've gone blind.'

'No. You just need a baby wipe,' I said. Ever the professional, she'd taken two bottles of water and a can of Diet Coke to her room with her. They stood on the bedside table, next to a blister pack of paracetamol.

As I grabbed one of the bottles and sloshed down a couple of painkillers, she emerged fully from the sheets.

'Is your hair always like that in the morning, or did you stick your finger in a plughole last night?' I asked.

'I don't know. I might have done. How are you?'

'I woke up with the world's worst hangover.'

'You're lucky that's all you woke up with,' she said, crawling upright and making three attempts to get the top off the remaining water bottle. Those sports caps can flummox the best of us.

'What do you mean?'

'I mean Luca. Jesus, he was persistent. I don't know how you managed to keep saying no . . . mainly no, at least.'

I grimaced, feeling a trickle of remembrance about last night seep through the cracks in my brain. Oh yes. Luca. Bare-chested, as usual. Golden skin, lots of it. Muscles, even more. Me not quite keeping my hands to myself. The disapproving glances of Finn and Connor, who'd been left on babysitting duty. A lot of crazy jiving to Doors songs. Luca lifting me up and dancing me across the room to 'People Are Strange', my legs wrapped around his hips. Luca's very obviously turned-on boy bits grinding into me, making me feel all squishy and wriggly . . . and . . . oh *God*. How bloody embarrassing! I'd behaved like the school slut at the Christmas disco, and in front of everyone, too. At least Gabriel had gone to bed by then.

'Fuck!' I said, falling on to the bed next to Carmel. She stroked my hair and made sympathetic noises. 'I feel like such an arse. I can't believe I did all that . . . stuff. I'm never drinking again.'

'Of course you are,' she said. 'And it wasn't that bad.

Just a bit of touchy-feely. I don't care what they say, you're only human, and he is hotter than hot. It's not like you've been sleeping around all these years, is it? You deserve a bit of fun.'

'Not that much fun. And not here, in Gabriel's house. That's . . . icky. He'll go nuts.'

'How will he know? He was the party pooper who left early.'

'Believe me,' I groaned. 'He'll know. And he won't be happy. I didn't do anything else, did I?'

'Nah,' she replied. 'Not for lack of trying on Luca's part. I couldn't tell if he wanted to eat you or screw you or both. But you remained steadfast and true, and tottered off back to your room about four. I don't think the Serious Squad would have let anything major happen, anyway. Finn and Connor were in full-on serve-and-protect commando mode all night. Couldn't get either of them to dance at all. Even to "Groove is in the Heart". I'm rethinking my crush after that.'

There was a polite knock on the door, then a pause. Carmel shouted, 'Go away! I'm not here!' and slid back under the covers until her head disappeared from view. The door opened, and Gabriel's face appeared around it.

'Are you decent?' he asked.

'Depends on your definition . . .' she muttered from beneath the sheets, sticking out one hand in a wave. 'Morning, Gabriel.'

'Good morning, Carmel. I take it you enjoyed yourself last night? Is there any chance there's a single drop of alcohol left in the house at all?'

'No,' she replied. 'I puked it all up this morning.'
Gross.

Gabriel pulled a 'yuck' face at me, and I waited for it to change to the 'you have failed me again, evil slut' face.

'Fancy coming with me for some breakfast? Or a late lunch, as it's half past two?' he asked, lifting one eyebrow.

'If you don't mind being seen with me in public,' I said, gesturing at my shameful state.

'I've been seen with worse,' he replied, with a slow, easy smile that made something deep in my tummy do a flip-flop. Easy-going Gabriel was back, when I least expected it.

I popped back to my room to grab my coat and bag, then we walked out into sub-zero sunshine. The air was crisp and cold and still, and you could see frost shimmering on the iron railings in the square. We walked along Grafton Street to Bewley's, where a sign told me we'd find the best coffee in Ireland. You can't argue with that kind of claim, and I was ready to drink gallons of the stuff.

As we entered, a small, dapper man wearing round, wire-rimmed glasses nodded at me. His hair was slicked back like it was the 1940s, and he wore a suit that looked like he'd been demobbed in it. I nodded back, automatically, and felt Gabriel's hand tighten on my back. He stared the man down in such a ferocious way that I felt embarrassed for us all, and stormed off ahead to get a seat. So much for easy-going Gabriel.

'What was that all about?' I asked, as he joined me a few minutes later. 'It's not like he was about to kidnap me and sell me into slavery. Especially not looking like this.'

'People aren't always what they seem, Lily,' he said, placating me with a mug of Ireland's finest.

'*He's right,*' said the voice in my head. '*They're not. Like him, for example. Gabriel. Can you trust him?*'

I looked blankly ahead, desperate not to betray the whole secret-inner-conversation routine. The voice – maybe it was my subconscious, although the voice was male – had asked yet another good question: *Could* I trust Gabriel? I'd tied my fate to his with less research than I'd normally give to buying a new smoothie maker. Admittedly, I hadn't had much choice at the time: events had moved a lot faster than my mental processes. When it had been a fifty-fifty between him and the death squad in black, I'd opted for him. But now, here, I could pause, breathe, allow my thoughts to catch up with themselves, and ponder that question: Could I trust him?

There were things about Gabriel that I liked. Admired. Lusted after. But there was a lot I didn't know, and some definite black marks against him. Like being bossy, domineering, economical with the truth, and treating me like an especially slow-minded toddler. Plus, oh yeah, giving me away to a nasty old coot when I was six, and abandoning me to a desperately lonely life for the rest of my childhood.

As the last thought skittered across my mind like a poisonous spider, he dropped his spoon to the table with a clatter. His eyes blazed so bright I saw several heads turning to stare at him. He looked less than human right then, and there was an ominous stretch to the sleeves of his sweater. I had no idea how much control he had over his body changes, but was pretty sure Bewley's wasn't the place to test it out.

'Are you in my head?' I asked cautiously.

'Yes. Just for a moment there, I was. Is there something you've been wanting to ask me, Lily?'

I could feel the surreptitious glances around us, hear low-level whispers as people wondered what was wrong with him. I drew in a long breath, spoke quietly. 'There is. And we should discuss it. But you need to take a chill pill, Gabriel, or someone's going to film the amazing inflatable you on their phone, and stick it on YouTube. Can you do that? Calm down a bit?'

He nodded, picked up a knife, and twisted it round and round his fingers until it looked like a stainless steel spring. Displacement activity, I presumed; redirecting his angst and taking it out on a poor innocent dining utensil.

It seemed to work, and his eyes dimmed to navy blue, his shoulders relaxing out of warrior pose. The trick now was how to have the conversation without it all going nuts again.

'It's all right,' he said. 'It was just the shock of it. I'm usually more in control – you know that. I even managed to stay in my room last night while you were riding Luca like a bucking bronco.'

Low blow. I screwed up my eyes, let the blush flame over my face. Told myself I had nothing to be embarrassed about. But it didn't quite wash. The new me was taking quite a bit of getting used to.

'I think you'll find that's called dancing, Gabriel. Maybe you'd understand, if you weren't, you know, a thousand years old.'

'I'm younger than Luca,' he said maliciously. 'And after that performance, he's lucky to be sleeping through another sunrise. Anyway. That's irrelevant. You were thinking about Coleen, weren't you? About how you came to be with her?'

'I already *know* how I came to be with her, Gabriel,' I said, leaning forward across the table. 'You gave me to her. I remember it. You, dressed in black after the funeral. Passing me on like excess luggage.'

'It had to be done, Lily,' he replied, his fingers inches from mine on the tablecloth. I knew he was itching to touch me, but I was glad he didn't. I might have stabbed him with the remaining knife. 'Your parents were dead. And as far as the world knew, as far as the Tuatha knew, you were dead as well. For a while they thought they'd won, which bought us the time we needed to hide you. With Coleen.'

'But why *her*, Gabriel? You must have known what kind of person she was. You must have known that wasn't the right environment for a child.'

'I didn't see you as a child,' he said. 'I saw you as the Goddess, or at least a potential Goddess. I saw you as—'

'Something you needed to keep safe. Yes, I know. But I was six, for Christ's sake. And I'd never even met the woman before. Do you know what she did when we got back to her house that night? After the funeral? She sent me straight to bed so she could watch her TV programmes. Didn't talk to me, or touch me. Just told me that from now on I'd answer to Lily, 'if I knew what was good for me', and that it was bedtime. There was no heating and I was freezing cold. It was pitch black, and she wouldn't even let me put a light on. Said that was for babies, and I'd better get used to the dark. I lay there, with the sounds of *Coronation Street* coming up the stairs, shivering, scared half to death and wondering why my mummy had left me with this horrible old woman who didn't even know my name.

'When I woke up the next day, I cried so hard. I'd dreamed about my parents, and I was convinced they'd come and rescue me. Then Coleen ordered me out of bed so she could tell me her house rules: Don't speak unless spoken to; no television without her in the room; three meals a day and not a scrap more; no friends allowed back there; and absolutely no arguments unless I wanted to feel the back of her hand. And the back of her hand had a pretty hefty sovereign ring on it. Then, for the rest of the day, she ignored me while she did crossword puzzles and smoked. We had variations on that theme until I was eighteen and I went off to college. I didn't have a single birthday present for all the years I lived with her. That might not mean much to you Otherworldy types, but for a human girl? It was shitty. So I ask you again, Gabriel – why her?'

He closed his eyes, silent for a moment. God knew what was going on in his brain. Hopefully guilt, and regret, and remorse.

'Because,' he said, 'it needed to be someone who would make you forget. We needed to erase your old life. You had to give it up, become someone else. You were young, we knew you'd adapt. That you'd become someone new. Coleen was a tool, a way of changing your future. Protecting you by creating distance from your past.'

'Yeah, well. That worked. But she didn't just distance me from my past; she distanced me from everything. And you're right – I did give up. I gave up hope that my parents would come for me. That anyone would come for me, ever again. I learned how to be alone, and how to like it. Being alone is the only thing I've ever known. And then you turn up, years later, and expect me to calmly accept my new life? Expect me to forget all that learned behaviour, and become your mate? Have your baby, even? Really, how did you expect that one to go?'

'What else could I do?' he said, slamming his fists on the table so hard the salt and pepper danced. 'Ask to be your friend on Facebook? I miscalculated. I should have come sooner, given you time to accept it. I should have allowed you to be prepared. I'm sorry, for that and for your life with Coleen. Truly sorry. But what's done is done, and we don't have much time. I can't court you, can't woo you the way I should, the way human women expect. The Feast of Samhain is almost here, and that is when you need to accept me. Their strength is growing. When I was in the Otherworld, I felt it. The Tuatha used to rule the mortal realm – and some of them want it back. You, me, we are the only ones who can stop it. So please, accept my apologies, accept my regrets – but stop resisting me. You've seen our future. Seen our fate. Why fight it?'

'Because,' I said, 'I don't believe you. I don't believe that is my only option. I don't believe you're telling me every-thing I should know. I don't believe you even see me as a real person, Gabriel. You dismissed my feelings when I was a child, and you're still doing it now. What I do believe is that I can choose for myself – and I might not choose you.'

Chapter Fourteen

Our mutual contempt was cold enough to freeze lava by the time we arrived back at the house. He was an arrogant, heartless prick who expected mindless obedience. I was a selfish, immature prima donna with no sense of responsibility. We both played these roles to the hilt, walking through the streets of Dublin, screaming, shouting, and on one occasion, slapping. That would be me, and the slap was a compromise. What I'd really wanted to do was push him over the edge of O'Connell Bridge and into the River Liffey.

We'd wandered around the city until it was dusk, raging at each other, pausing only to buy bags of chips that we ate with chilled fingers. In a strange way I enjoyed it. The fighting, not the chips. It was the first time I'd ever really argued with anyone, and I was getting pretty good at it. Even when I thought he was right, I didn't budge an inch, and I found the fact that I could provoke so much fury satisfying in the extreme. If it had been a film, we'd have ended up with passionate make-up sex against the wall in the hallway. As I still half hated Gabriel, and had my strange debilitating skin allergy, it actually ended with a lot of slammed doors, and me wondering if Luca was awake yet. I needed someone to pummel.

As soon as I walked into the living room I knew something had changed. Connor, Finn and Kevin were standing up, with fixed expressions on their faces. The vampires, very much awake, were scattered around, looking unusually well behaved; and Carmel was curled up in an easy chair, legs tucked beneath her, arms wrapped around her own body as though she was cold.

'Thank fuck you're back,' she whispered as we entered. 'You've got visitors.'

I could tell from the aroma curling into my nostrils that one of them was Eithne, my old friend from the Coconut Shy toilets. I knew the normal reaction would be fear, but my blood was still up from sparring with Gabriel, and I glared at her viciously. If she fancied round two, I was up for it.

She giggled, a sound that seemed completely alien to her, and smiled. 'Nice to see you too, Goddess,' she said. Her nose wrinkled slightly. 'Mmm . . . chips?' she asked.

Standing next to her in front of the marble fireplace was a man, tall and lean, with long black hair tied back in a loose ponytail. His skin was caramel brown, his eyes dark and slanted upwards, and he was clad head to toe in black leather. Kind of a medieval Asian assassin look. I'd never seen him before, but I could tell he was important from the body language of the vampires, who were all casting sneaky glances in his direction.

'High King,' he said, nodding at Gabriel, then turned to survey my frostbitten cheeks and damp hair. 'Goddess,' he said in greeting.

'Lily will do fine,' I replied, unbuttoning my coat and wondering when someone was going to tell me what was going on.

'My name is Donn,' he said simply, and a few things fell into place. Like the fact that Isabella was looking at him like a scared puppy, and even Luca was sitting quietly, fully clothed, with his hands neatly folded in his lap.

'I am the Lord of the Dead, and ally to Cormac Mor,' he added formally.

I shrugged off my coat, slung it over the back of a chair with my bag. Not so long ago I'd have run screaming from the room, but now? Lord of the Dead? All in a day's work.

'What's with this Cormac Mor business?' I asked. 'You're the third person I've heard call him that.'

'It means "great",' said Eithne sneeringly. 'Which he thinks he is.'

I cast a look in his direction. He was bigger than usual, and edging towards me, placing his outsized body between Eithne's and mine.

'Yeah, he does, doesn't he?' I said. 'Now, not to be rude, but why are *you* here? Last time we met I got the impression you didn't much like me.'

'Sorry about that. I got a bit carried away – nothing personal.'

'You tried to kill me. That's about as personal as it gets.'

Gabriel advanced towards her, and in response, Connor, Finn and Kevin tensed. I noticed that all three had swords in belts at their sides, and their hands were inching towards the pommels. There'd been a lot of talk about sword arms in the past few days, and now it looked like I was about to see them in action first-hand.

'This is not the time for conflict,' said Donn, his voice as deep and exotic as his eyes. 'Much as I'd like to rip out Eithne's still-beating heart and eat it, we are here to talk. Eithne is here to represent the views of the Fintna Faidh, and I speak for the rest of the Tuatha de Danaan.'

'Where is Fintan?' asked Gabriel, giving a slight shake of the head to his warriors. Their hands moved; postures marginally relaxed. 'Why does he not come himself?'

'He's ... busy,' answered Eithne. 'People to see, things to do. But he has sent me on his behalf, to discuss the future of the alleged Goddess, and the balance of power that holds sway over her.'

'Alleged'. Huh. What a cow. I looked at Carmel, and she made a little catlike 'meow' noise. Seemed that bitchiness was a female hobby in the Otherworld as well as in ours.

'The Goddess is in my care,' said Gabriel. 'And will remain so. Any balance you seek was made void when Fintan sent his minions to kill her. Her sisters were taken in their eighth and ninth years respectively, and she has been attacked several times. I will not release her into danger.'

He made a valid point, but I still bristled at his use of the word 'release'. I was not Gabriel's property, child, mate or prisoner. I didn't know quite what I was yet, but I did know I could make decisions for myself.

'We haven't been attacked for days now, Your Greatness,' I pointed out. 'And I don't feel threatened by anything other than you.'

It was true. I didn't feel threatened. Scared and freaked out, yes, but not threatened – because, well, the voice in my head had told me I could relax. That the men in black would not be pursuing me again. My mental visitor had said he wanted to talk to me, not kill me, and I believed him. I wasn't sure how well citing 'voice in head' would go down as proof, so I didn't elaborate.

'Who is Fintan?' I asked instead, as Gabriel struggled not to splutter out loud at what he would undoubtedly see as another example of my 'foolhardy and contrary' nature. That had been just one of the many complimentary gems he'd thrown at me earlier.

'He is my lord, leader of the Fintna Faidh and the greatest of the Tuatha de Danaan,' announced Eithne proudly, sticking her boobs out like a pageant queen in front of the judges.

Donn rolled his almond eyes, and snorted. 'Self-styled,' he murmured.

'He is your enemy,' said Gabriel, violet sparks flaring from his eyes. 'And whatever she says, he wants you dead.

The only way to prevent you from saving humanity is by killing you.'

'Not strictly true,' said Eithne. 'Admittedly that is a path that was followed in the past, but it is not the only way, Cormac Mor, and you know it. You are conveniently forgetting that the Goddess has a choice. And that she may choose us.'

Not bloody likely, I thought, as her sour-cider smell assaulted me. I wouldn't choose her, anyway. But seeing the effect her words had on Gabriel was enough to keep me quiet. He was rigid with anger, planted in front of me like a colossus, his shoulders wide enough for two, his chest physically blocking me from the others.

'She speaks the truth, High King,' said Donn, 'although I wish to hear it as little as you. The wench should not have a choice; she should be forced to accept her role, in the way she would have been in your father's time. But whether we like it or not, Fintan's case has been accepted by the rest of the Tuatha. In the old ways, the Goddess would have been prepared, trained to control her power and embrace her fate. And yet she remains here, raw and unschooled. You know that if it were up to me, that would not matter – she is but a vassal, and should be treated as the property she is. Sadly, that is not my decision to make, and the Faidh are insisting she is given free will.'

I wasn't sure that Donn and I were going to end up as friends. His attitude made Gabriel look like an enlightened modern man. If this was an ally, something was very wrong. All my instincts fought against Eithne, and yet she was the one saying the words I wanted to hear.

'The old ways became irrelevant once her sisters were killed, Donn,' replied Gabriel, his voice haughty and cold, even to his supposed ally. 'They were taken, and they were slaughtered. The same will not happen to Lily. I will die to protect her.'

'That's very touching,' replied Eithne. 'And typically

heroic of you, Cormac, but have you ever thought to ask Lily what it is that she wants?'

I knew I was being played for a fool, that she was exploiting the obvious rift between us, but even as I battled my distress at the image of what had happened to the sisters I'd never met, her words slammed right into its target. I didn't want to give Eithne the satisfaction of agreeing with her, so I fought down the urge to scream, 'No, he bloody hasn't!' at the top of my voice. I was starting to wonder if 'Tuatha' wasn't Gaelic for 'manipulative bastards', and didn't really want anything to do with any of them.

I coughed, drawing attention away from the mounting tension between Eithne and Gabriel, and back to me.

'Sorry to distract you from your glaring competition, but you're talking as though there are options, and you two have come all the way here to discuss them,' I said, pointing at Donn and Eithne. 'So would someone care to tell me what they are? I'm busy too, you know.'

'Really?' said Eithne, voice dripping with disbelief. 'What could you possibly have to do right now that's more important than this?'

Sadly, I couldn't think of a damned thing, and decided that poking her in the eye was probably the best response. If I could reach past King Swello.

'She has to file her pop page. It's deadline day,' said Carmel, piping up in a small, slightly scared voice. I turned to look at her, hiding under a pile of cushions, hair still rocking electric-shock chic, streaks of old mascara under her eyes. I grinned. She'd never looked more fabulous.

'Thank you,' I mouthed silently. She was right: I had my real life as well. Deadlines and editions and copy to file. I'd almost forgotten it, and I shouldn't. It mattered, at least to me. And the Dormice. I was not, and never would be, anybody's 'property'.

'Yes. That. And I've never missed a deadline in my life. So hurry up, and get on with it. What – what are the options?'

I saw Gabriel take a deep breath, about to protest. There is only one option, blah-de-blah-de-blah.

'Shut up,' I said, meeting his eyes. 'Shut up now, or I'll never be able to forgive you. For any of it.'

For a moment, I thought he'd argue. Or explode. Pink fingers of anger were crawling across his skin, and his fists were clenched into balls the size of claw hammers. He was now a good two feet taller than everyone else in the room, and the floor tremored whenever he moved. Even Donn looked on in interest, glancing up at the quaking chandeliers.

I stood tall too, held my head as high as I could, fixed Gabriel's gaze with mine. Tried not to blush, or gulp, or faint at his feet. Channelled as much regal as I could.

'As you wish, Goddess,' he said after a few beats. His tone was neutral, which, I knew, was the best I was going to get. Around us the warriors and vampires exchanged significant glances, and Donn looked thoroughly disgusted at his acquiescence. I blinked, and looked away from Gabriel. I could feel the raw power of his disappointment, his soul-deep sense of defeat and rejection. Eithne smiled, and I had a moment of doubt: surely anything that pleased her was wrong?

'Your "option",' he said, his voice sarcastic and cold, 'is to leave here. To leave my protection. To leave *me*. Is that what you want, Lily?'

'To leave you and go where?' I asked, knocked off balance at the thought. Leaving him. Escaping. That's what I wanted, wasn't it? And if it was, why did I suddenly feel so empty at the very thought?

'You will go to Fionnula the Fair,' said Donn, ignoring the significance of the moment Gabriel and I were sharing. Gods, I supposed, learned to be insensitive after a couple of eons or so. 'She will be your teacher. She will answer your questions, show you the way to gain control over your . . . emotions. She will equip you to make your *choice*. The decision that must be made.'

My questions. My choice. My decision. All the words I'd been wanting to hear. And yet, looking at Gabriel, now merely the size of a larger-than-average mortal man, I felt a slither of fear. Of pain. He turned his eyes deliberately away from mine, and even that tiny separation stung.

It looked like I was on my own.

Chapter Fifteen

I don't know what I expected Fionnula the Fair to look like, but an ageing blonde bombshell complete with Marilyn curves definitely wasn't it.

She was fair, I'll give her that, but I suspected her golden sheen had more to do with Loreal than luck. Her eyes were a piercing shade of blue, and she had a way of blinking very slowly as she spoke, making everything she said seem outrageously important.

Fionnula lived in a whitewashed stone cottage in a tiny fishing village between Dublin and Skerries. The coastline was wild and wet, the dark grey waves of the Irish Sea crashing up and over harbour walls and promenades, like probing fingers trying to grab the car and drag us into the abyss. I looked silently out of the window as we drove, taking in the shops and cafes and stands offering boat tours, the tourist facades fading as we headed further north.

Gabriel had the radio on to drown out any attempt I made at small talk, and Morrissey was drawling out 'Everyday Is Like Sunday' as we crawled our way through coastal towns that looked closed down. I was sure they were pretty in summer; now life seemed cold and hard, with heavy October sleet drenching the streets and people scurrying round with umbrellas bent backwards by the wind.

The cottage was miles away from anything other than a postbox, up a potholed drive and in the middle of dense forest. We arrived in darkness, greeted by the hoots of unseen owls and the plaintive lowing of cattle in the fields beyond.

I felt about as happy as the cows as I unpacked my backpack and followed Gabriel to the front door. He'd been playing it strong and silent for the whole journey, giving his full concentration to changing gears and braking round the winding cliffside roads that had led us here.

Carmel had been in the back, trying to keep up a one-sided conversation, but Gabriel's face remained as set as the slabs of stone that had been used to build the cottage walls.

The door had opened without him knocking, and she'd emerged. Fionnula the Fair. Wearing a pair of mulberry-coloured skinny jeans and a low-cut top with 'Eat Me' printed across the front in tiny cherries. My first thought was 'ugh'. My second was that I knew her, somehow. That her face was familiar, half recognised.

'So this will be the Goddess, now, will it?' she said, walking out to greet us. The rain was heavy, but it seemed to bounce off her do, a lacquered bonnet of platinum blonde.

'This is Lily,' said Gabriel, lifting my bag easily out of my hands, and walking inside. Strong, silent and severely lacking in social skills.

'Don't you be worrying about him, now,' said Fionnula, smiling as he strutted away. 'He'll just be in one of those huffs that kings are always so good at. He'll get over it, so he will. Now come in, get yourself nice and dry.'

I was expecting something rustic, maybe a blazing log fire and pictures of hay wains on the walls. Possibly a spinning wheel, complete with magical golden thread. At the very least, a mysterious black cat padding around the place.

Instead, the interior of the cottage was like something out of *House Beautiful*: all glowing white walls and polished chrome; central heating and warmth; a dining kitchen with gleaming black granite surfaces.

'Excuse the mess,' she said, gesturing around her picture-perfect home. Gabriel had said exactly the same about his spic-and-span apartment. These people clearly took their cleanliness very seriously.

'Wow,' said Carmel, dumping her own bag and sinking down into a tan leather sofa, 'this is excellent. It's so warm in here.'

Fionnula turned her attention away from me, and gave Carmel an appraising stare. She blinked, very slowly, her eyes a flash of blue under the fashionably dim ceiling lights.

'And who would you be?' she asked, lipsticked mouth curved.

'I would be Carmel,' my friend replied. 'I'm Lily's . . . champion. Don't ask me where that word came from; it just popped out. And I think . . . it should probably have a capital "c", just for effect.'

'Are you, now?' asked Fionnula. 'You don't look the Champion type to me.'

'I know,' she replied. 'Weird, isn't it? But that's the word that came into my head, so I suppose it must be right.'

Fionnula blinked, again very slowly, and put out a hand to stop Gabriel as he made to leave the room.

'A moment, if you don't mind, Cormac Mor?' she said, the way she used his title implying complete disrespect for it.

He stopped and nodded, apparently used to the sarcasm.

'Surely you have people better suited to being the girl's Champion than . . . that? What about Finn, or even one of Donn's bloodsuckers? If you think she needs protection here, at least be serious about it.'

I noticed Carmel's eyes narrow, but she stayed silent – on the outside, at least. Inside, I knew she'd be storing up the insults, filing them away in her 'people who aren't very nice' box. I wouldn't be at all surprised if Fionnula the Fair found her freezer switched off at the wall on the day we left, or her Touche Éclat mysteriously relocated into a cowpat.

Gabriel cast his eyes over Carmel, a slim, dark-haired girl wearing Karen Millen jeans, and shook his head.

'I know she doesn't look much, but she is right. She is Lily's Champion, in ways we don't understand. It is a sacred role, and one she was carrying out in her own way long before we arrived. And don't underestimate her because of that puny mortal form. I have seen her fight: she defeated two of the Faidh using nothing but her bare hands and a plant pot. Lily has chosen to leave my protection and come here, and if she chooses Carmel as her Champion, then so be it. I'm sure you'll look after them both well, Fionnula. Not many would risk breaching your land, would they?'

'That's the truth, Cormac Mor, so it is,' she said, 'and it'd pay you to remember that. I know this is not what you wish, but it has been decided. Lily will stay with me until she is ready, and you are not to return here until you are invited. Do you understand me, now?'

'I understand you very well, Fionnula. And I will not break the agreement. Lily will be free of me for as long as she wishes.'

He nodded his farewells to Carmel, and finally turned to face me. I hadn't left him much choice, as I was standing in the doorway, deliberately blocking his path. His eyes darkened, and his lips looked like they'd never smile again. I felt a leap of his sadness, a shock of sorrow and regret arcing between us.

'I know you think this is wrong,' I said, placing a hand on his chest, wishing it could be more. 'But you're always talking about me trusting you. Always telling me that's what I need to do. Always assuming that's easy for me, after everything that's happened. Everything I've found out. But maybe now is the time for you to show some trust in me, Gabriel. I need to do this. I need to find out more about who I am, and the part I play in all of this. And when

I've done that, I'll come back to you. I promise. We'll at least have a chance to make things right between us.'

He covered my hand with his, and my flesh was instantly engulfed in warmth and comfort. His fingers were entwined in mine, and for once I let them be.

'I hope so, *a ghra*,' he said. 'Because this isn't some silly game. This isn't about a man and woman. This isn't about me, or you, or Coleen. It's about the whole of humanity. I'm still not sure you realise how high the stakes are, and what you are risking by leaving me.'

'Maybe you're right,' I murmured. 'But it's the only way I can do this. So what about you? Can you trust me, Gabriel?'

'I'll try,' he said, kissing me gently on the forehead and moving me bodily out of his way. He turned as he opened the door, and added, 'If you need me, for anything, just call me. Fionnula will show you how.'

He left. I heard the car door slam, the sound of wheels screeching on gravel, and felt something wet on my face.

That would be me. Crying like a big fat baby.

Chapter Sixteen

'Come on, now,' said Fionnula, fussing around me. 'You don't want to be crying over him. You must know what his hearing is like; he'll be sitting in the car feeling all smug about it. You've made your choice, now don't go and give him the satisfaction of regretting it. Anyway, I know what you need.'

She bustled over to the kitchen area, and emerged with a bottle of Chardonnay and three long-stemmed glasses.

'Wine,' she said. 'The answer to all women's woes.'

At that, Carmel's interest level peaked and she roused herself enough to leave the sofa.

'Maybe you're not such a hag after all . . .' she murmured in a stage whisper. Fionnula ignored her as she poured, but I knew, as I had with Carmel earlier, that some kind of mental score sheet had definitely been opened. That battle had commenced.

But right at that moment, I didn't care. About either of them. Gabriel was gone. I'd been left here, with my night-news-editor Champion, and a teacher I'd only just met. And in a few days' time, at the Feast of Samhain, I'd have to make a decision that would change the world as I knew it.

A glass of wine was suddenly sounding like a very good idea.

*

The next morning, I found Fionnula already up and about in the kitchen. She'd lost the skinny-jeans-hot-mama ensemble in favour of a sequinned tank top and a black lycra miniskirt that barely covered her backside. It was the kind of look that embarrassing aunties go for at weddings, but I wasn't stupid enough to say anything along those lines. I wasn't too sure about Carmel, though, who staggered into the room stretching her arms and shaking her crazy black hair.

She sat down at the kitchen counter, swinging her legs from the stool, watching as Fionnula popped the toaster and flicked on the kettle.

'Top o' the morning to you,' she said, in her best *Father Ted* mock-Irish voice. I cringed, and concentrated on buttering the toast Fionnula passed to me. Forget the end of the world – I was in the middle of Armageddon already.

Fionnula sat down opposite Carmel, pointing a butter-slathered knife in her direction. She blinked very slowly, which had the usual effect of making me listen even harder than normal.

'It'd be best if you lost a bit of that attitude, *Champion*,' she said, her voice gentle and soft, a mocking emphasis on the last word.

'Why?' said Carmel, crunching a slice of toast she'd lifted from my plate. 'Will you turn me into a toad if I don't?'

I barely saw Fionnula's fingers move, but I heard the lyrical flow of Gaelic beneath her breath, felt a stirring of magic in the room. A few strands of my hair lifted into the air, as though they were responding to the static of a balloon.

Immediately, Carmel started to choke, spluttering and coughing as the food became lodged in her throat. She clasped her hands to her neck, gurgling as she tried to gulp in air. I jumped up and whacked her on the back, hard, and a half-chewed piece of toast came flying out of her mouth, landing in a soggy clump on the counter top. Very ladylike.

She dragged in oxygen, glared at Fionnula suspiciously, her whisky-coloured eyes narrowed to slits.

'Was that you?' she asked, once she could talk again. 'Did you do that?'

'Might have done,' replied Fionnula nonchalantly. 'But you'll never know, will you? Just watch that mouth of yours. I'm not a patient woman, and while you're in my home, you'll show me some respect.'

The two of them indulged in a spot more glaring, and then Fionnula stood up and walked over to the kettle, which had now boiled.

'Now, can I tempt ye with a nice cup of tea?' she asked, in a crazed parody of every fictional Irish woman I'd ever seen.

'Yes,' croaked Carmel, still holding her throat. 'Please.'

We finished our breakfast in a decidedly uncompanionable silence, until Carmel's quiet allergy kicked in. She sees it as one of her life goals to let no moment of peace go uninterrupted.

'So, what, are you like Lily's Mr Miyagi?' she asked warily, breaking the silence and earning a blank stare from Fionnula. 'You know? Wax on, wax off?'

It was obviously a pop culture reference too far for my new teacher. I don't know what Fionnula the Fair got up to in the mid-Eighties, but sitting in the cinema watching *The Karate Kid* clearly wasn't it. Carmel is a couple of years older than me, and I am a retro chick who doesn't like much company apart from hers – we've spent hours sitting in darkened rooms eating popcorn and watching Eighties classics. Perhaps we could open a magical branch of our private Movie Club to bring ageing witches up to date?

'She means,' I said, 'are you going to teach me stuff? Be, I don't know, my spiritual mentor, or whatever? That was the impression I got from Donn, but I didn't really understand what he was talking about.'

'Oh, I know, that drives me mad as well,' said Fionnula. 'He's all dark and mysterious, isn't he? He only does it to hide the fact that he spouts crap, half the time . . .'

I couldn't keep the surprise from my face, and Carmel cracked up into laughter. I wasn't sure where Fionnula's place in the pantheon of Otherworldy types was, but she didn't seem scared of any of them. Or even vaguely impressed. Which was good, I decided – I wouldn't want to be getting my Goddess life lessons from a wuss, after all.

'But in answer to your questions, yes. I will be "teaching you stuff". That's my role, always has been. You'd be amazed how many times some wannabe god needs etiquette lessons, or a High-King-in-waiting deserves a slap round the ear.'

She grinned at me, and I suspected I knew who that High King was. The thought was tremendously entertaining, and even overshadowed the pang of grief I felt when I heard his name echo around my mind.

'Everyone's young once,' she said. 'And everyone needs to learn. You will learn too, Lily – albeit a little later than usual. That'll make it harder, of course. Children's brains are more open, more accepting. You'll fight it all the way: you've had too many years in a rational human world. Mind like a steel trap, closed off to potential and truth; cement where your imagination should be.'

I stiffened a little, feeling bizarrely offended. Nobody had ever accused me of having a cement brain before, and I wasn't sure I liked it. And as for imagination, I've never really needed it – my real life has been wacky enough.

'She's done all right so far, witchy bitch,' said Carmel, standing to her less than impressive five foot four. 'She's had more weirdness thrown at her in the last few days than most people get in a lifetime, and coped with it all. So maybe you should show a bit of respect as well.'

Fionnula blinked like a sleepy iguana, and I held my breath. Here it comes, I thought: fireballs, thunder, Carmel turned into a piglet and stuck in a roasting pot for supper.

Instead, Fionnula laughed, the sound like glass bluebells tinkling in the breeze.

'Well said, Champion. Now go and make yourself scarce, so I can get on with being this Mr Miyagi you speak of. There are books in your bedroom, woods to walk in, and I have a pretty good Wi-Fi connection too.'

Carmel looked at me for a decision, and I nodded.

'Go,' I said. 'While you can still walk upright and don't have a curly tail.'

Grabbing an extra slice of toast, she sauntered out of the room. Heading, I guessed, for the Wi-Fi. Walks in the woods aren't really her thing.

'Now,' said Fionnula, gesturing for me to join her on the sofa. 'Down to business. First of all, do you remember me?'

I sat, sinking into soft leather upholstery, and tried to recall where I knew her face from. Drawing a blank, I shook my head.

'I was at the funeral. Your parents' funeral,' she said. 'Which was very naughty of me, really. But I hoped you'd end up here one day, and wanted to see you for myself. The bossy boots in charge wasn't too happy with me, but I didn't care. I could tell, Lily, straight away, that you were special. With your funny little ginger plaits, scaring people off with your eyes. You probably think Coleen and your visions were responsible for making you different, but that's not true. You would always have been different. There would always have been a distance between you and the normal world you inhabit.'

'Maybe,' I replied. 'But I'm pretty certain Coleen and the visions didn't help. Why weren't you supposed to be there, anyway?'

'Because I'm neutral,' she replied. 'My job is to teach, not to influence. And I only do that on request. It's the only reason they allow me the life I have, independent and away from them and their politics. You wouldn't believe how much they argue. It gets tiresome after the first century or so.'

I could only imagine. I'd found it tiresome after the first day.

'OK,' I said, 'you're Switzerland, then? You don't prefer one over the other?'

'"Prefer" isn't the right word, Lily. Some High Kings are easier to like than others, and I will always have my affections. But my role is to teach you – about your history, about your powers, about the decision you will face on the night of Samhain. I'm sure you must have questions about it all; I imagine Cormac was too busy being Mor to explain it properly to you, and you haven't even met Fintan, have you?'

Fintan. The leader of the Fintna Faidh. My nemesis, or my liberator, depending on how you viewed it. I hadn't met him as such, but I was starting to have the suspicion that I'd at least seen him – the shadowed man on the hill in Tir na nOg. The man who'd been leaping in and out of my head like a pop-up ad ever since.

'No, I haven't met him,' I replied, which strictly speaking was true. Fionnula lifted one über-plucked eyebrow at me, and I knew she had her suspicions. She was a teacher, for God's sake – they always had their bullshit antenna switched on.

'We all have our secrets, Lily,' she said, letting it drop. 'Just make sure you don't keep them for too long. Now – before we start – any questions?'

About a million, I thought, as a jumble of queries scrambled for prominence in my brain.

'Samhain,' I said, deciding on one. 'What happens? When Gabriel says I have to become his mate, to bless the human world with bounty, et cetera, what does he mean? Will I have to – you know – do it then?'

I blushed as I spoke, and realised my fingers were making vaguely obscene gestures to illustrate the point.

'Ah. Focusing on the practicalities. I like that in a woman. What you mean is, will you need to have sex with him?'

'Yes!' I muttered, fearing my complexion would never recover. I'd live the rest of my days with the face of a lobster. God, this was excruciating.

'There's no need for embarrassment, Lily. Sex is a natural part of life. There's not man or beast I haven't witnessed rutting at some point in the past.'

She paused, as if allowing me to savour that particular image would make me feel more comfortable.

'But to answer the question, no, you don't need to seal the deal, as it were, that night, as long as you accept him in principle. There'll be a ceremony at Tara, in County Meath, and you'll be asked if you are willing to take him as your mate. If you do, that will be taken as your consent. If you don't . . .'

'What? What if I don't? Donn said something about being forced to accept my role, like in his father's time. What does that mean?'

Her face darkened, and her lips curled downwards in a vicious sneer.

'The attitude of the Tuatha de Danaan is not always what you might call enlightened, Lily. Donn would have Gabriel take you, any way he needs, to achieve his goal. In the way that ruthless men have taken women since time began. Do I need to draw you pictures?'

'No . . .' I murmured, feeling a strange mix of fear and anger flow through me. 'I understand. But that's not going to happen. I won't let that happen. And Gabriel . . . he wouldn't.'

'Perhaps you're right, my dear. Gabriel was always a sweet child. But he is the High King, and he is ruthless. They all are. He has already made choices on your behalf that a mortal man would not be proud of. How far he will go in his defence of this realm, I do not know.'

I thought of Coleen, of the way he'd bundled me off to her and left me in her cold hands as soon as my parents were dead in the ground. I couldn't deny it. He was ruthless. But I still couldn't believe that he would go that far. I refused to believe it.

'No,' I said again, more firmly. 'That will not happen.'

'All right, child. Leave that thought alone for now. Tuck it away and forget about it a while. You have a lot to learn, and mere days in which to learn it. You are the exception to all our rules. You've grown up in the wild human world, and I for one have no idea what you are capable of. Take my hands, and I will show you some of what you need to know.'

I hesitated, my fingers instinctively curling away from her. Fionnula didn't look worried, but I was. After a lifetime of avoiding my Grim Reaper visions, opening myself up to them wasn't going to be a walk in the park.

'Don't be scared,' she said, holding out her hands. 'You won't see my future. I won't allow it. This can all be controlled, and I will teach you how. For now, take my hands, and I will show you my past. It will be all right, Lily.'

Fingers trembling like I had the shakes, I let her take my hands into hers, and steeled myself to see her racked with pain, or pumping blood from an arterial vein.

Instead, I saw her . . . younger. Astonishingly beautiful, her bold blue eyes shining out across luscious hills and valleys. Dressed in long grey layers, hair in braids along the sides of her face. A darker shade of blonde, so this was clearly the pre-Loreal era. There was a man. Dark hair, handsome, muscular arms peeking out from a leather vest.

'Is this the Otherworld?' I asked, eyes closed.

'No,' she said. 'It's here. Ireland. A very long time ago.'

The man walked towards her, and she ran into his arms. He picked her up by the waist, twirled her around, her bluebell laughter making him smile. He leaned down to kiss her, a kiss full of fire and passion. Even looking at it made me sigh.

There was a shimmer, a hazy background flicker, like moving from one dreamscape to another. The man again. Older now. Hair grey, body slow-moving, joints gnarled with arthritis. Fionnula, still young and beautiful, crying as she stroked his forehead. He was dying, and there was nothing she could do to save him. It was breaking her heart.

I snatched my hands away as I felt her pain cross over into me, become my pain. The fierce swell of it had threatened to break my heart as well.

'You said it would be all right!' I shouted, rubbing my fingers like they'd been scalded. 'That most definitely wasn't all right!'

'Yes, it was, child,' she replied, blinking tears from her eyes. 'That was humanity. That was love, and the pain that flows from it. The way I felt, when Brannigan kissed me? The way I felt as he lay dying? That is what Cormac fights for.'

'Then it's not worth the effort!' I said. 'It's too . . . raw. If that's humanity, I don't want it. Maybe they're right, the Faidh . . . maybe they're right to want to end it all!'

'Maybe they are, Lily. And only you can decide that. You've been to the Otherworld, haven't you?'

'Yes,' I replied, feeling a yearning to return, to be safe with my parents, to meet my sisters and Lucy, who'd died instead of me. To be away from all this confusion and hurt and second-hand agony.

'Then look now, again, and see it more clearly. See Fintan's world, and what he would wish for yours.'

She grabbed my hands and held them tight, refusing to let go despite my struggles. She was much stronger than she looked, and other than allowing my arms to be torn from their sockets, I had no choice but to go along with her.

To go with her to the Otherworld. To a quiet grove, a canopy of trees overhead filtering the sunlight on to a dappled carpet of leaves. People lay around, laughing and joking among themselves, feasting on the fresh fruit that fell around them. They were calm, and happy, and at peace. It felt like heaven.

Then one of them, a woman, pushed herself up to her feet, walked off on her own. She twined golden hair around her fingers, and looked off, beyond the twisting trunks of the trees, into the distance. A single tear flowed from her eye, trailing down her cheek. I could feel her emotions as though they were my own: she was in misery. She was trapped. She was a slave to a life she hadn't chosen. The fruit was bitter in her mouth; the sun was chill on her head, and the laughter of the others was shrill in her ears. She was alone, and had been for too long. She wanted to go . . . home. To a place that no longer existed.

Fionnula dropped my hands, and I quickly sat on them to make sure she couldn't grab me again. She was looking at me keenly, awaiting my reaction.

'You are *not* Switzerland!' I said. 'How can you claim to be neutral and then show me things like that?'

'That's the way it is. The way it will be. I don't suggest one or the other to you, Lily – I show you what they both are. This human world you know? It screams and battles and rages against itself, but there is always choice. And love. If you choose the Faidh, then it will all pass. All of the screaming and the battling and the raging will be gone. But so too will the choice, and the love. Humanity will pass into a thing of legend, and most will forget it ever existed, and be happy. Most, but not all. Those who remember, who yearn, will suffer for all of eternity, like the woman you saw then. I'm here to teach you, and these are the realities we face. This is the decision you must make when the Feast of Samhain arrives.'

'I don't want to!' I yelled, feeling a whopper of a tantrum coming on. 'I'm sick of all this! Why should I have to make the bloody decision? Why me? Why can't you do it, or someone else?'

'Because you are Mabe, Mother of the Mortals. Or Murderer of the Mortals. Whichever you choose. And there's no bloody use crying about it.'

Chapter Seventeen

The rest of the day was less spectacular. Fionnula seemed to sense that I'd rather saw my own hands off with a nail file than let her touch me again, and fell instead into school-marm mode.

First, there were the history lessons. I learned about the beginning, and the Overlord, the deity who held sway over all his creation – the being I'd grown up knowing as God.

I learned about the Tuatha de Danaan of old, and how they'd ruled all the worlds together. There were stories, of other gods and goddesses, and human heroes, of battles and victories and labyrinthine politics. Of jostling for position, and marriages of convenience, and the mighty women warriors who held sway over both war and fertility.

Then the invaders came, a mighty race that defeated them in battle, and the Tuatha were forced to retreat. To fade, *Lord of the Rings*-style, into the West. The human lands became the realm of the High Kings, and the Tuatha instead reigned in the Otherworld.

Most were happy with that, she explained. With their life of feasting and hunting and sex and song. And on the whole, they left the mortals alone. Some because they lost interest; others, like Donn, because he needed them;

and yet more because they were convinced that their day would come again.

They watched what the mortals did with their land – the shopping malls and pollution so despised by Eithne – and for a time they waited, sure that, eventually, humanity would do their job for them and wipe itself out.

In the meantime, the clock kept on ticking. The High Kings were wed to their land via the welcoming arms of Mabe's priestess, and the world continued to turn, and to change. But over the centuries the cracks started to show. Famines. Droughts. Tsunamis and earthquakes and floods. The apocalyptic stuff my generation has grown up with, and gives no thought to other than buying a charity single or donating a tenner to the Red Cross.

For the High Kings and for the Fintna Faidh, though, all of these things were signs. Signs that the power of the priestess was fading and that Mabe needed to return – to renew her blessing on the land; to restore balance and to bring fresh hope.

Mabe. That would, of course, be me.

I couldn't help thinking that they could have chosen better, but apparently it was nothing to do with choice. The Goddess goes where she likes, and she liked the look of me. And my sisters. But they didn't last long – the Faidh saw to that. They killed them, and they tried to kill me, in the hope of speeding up the fall of the human race. If they could do that, then they could reclaim this world for themselves. Take humanity and give it a Cybermen-style reboot.

I still wasn't convinced that was such a tragedy. Humans *have* made a mess of their world, and much as I like shopping malls, didn't the Faidh have a point? Do we deserve all we have? Fionnula and Gabriel could witter on as much as they liked about the splendour of mankind, but I've seen a lot of bad things. A lot of death, of pain, of the sickening ache in a woman's heart when she opened those test results from the hospital. And my upbringing hadn't helped.

Gabriel might have thought he was making the right decision when he gave me to Coleen, but he hadn't. Not unless his intention was to create an emotionally jaded goddess with a world view that rivalled Nietzsche's. He hadn't just protected me from the wicked; he'd protected me from the noble as well.

Even on a good day, I've never been truly happy. I've carved out my life, lived it quietly, with a minimum of fuss and messy human contact. Tried to keep myself safe, and never intentionally hurt anyone. Had a job that doesn't really matter, and friends whose surnames I don't know. Pretended to have fun and enjoy it all. Pretended to be as normal as I can. None of which makes me the poster girl for carefree humanity.

I tried to remind myself of the high points – of Carmel; my parents; the shiver of pleasure I'd felt when I touched Luca's body; the way my heart did a tiny tap dance when Gabriel looked at me the right way – but it wasn't enough. I still didn't feel the joy that had coursed through Fionnula's veins when she saw Brannigan running towards her. I've seen it in other people's lives, and I know it exists, but I've never felt it myself. I'm not sure I ever will – I'm too closed off, too private. Too damaged.

So, evil plan to kill off the whole of the mortal plane? I'm probably not the best person to ask. I've been faking my way through the mess of humanity for as long as I can remember, willingly taking my place on the sidelines, watching the party without ever really joining in.

I mentioned none of this to Fionnula, and she didn't ask. I was here to be taught, not to be shaped, and she was taking that bit seriously, without any touchy-feely regard for my finer emotions.

I took what she offered, and I learned. I learned the names of High Kings and gods, and I learned how to defend myself against fairies, and I learned about the origin of the vampire race. I learned that there were other creatures out there in the worlds, some of which we don't even have names for, and I learned that Gabriel had been born in Tara 270 years earlier, which really did make him a much older man.

I learned that, like Gabriel, Fionnula herself was of mixed bloodline, neither human nor Tuatha, and that she was even older than him.

I learned about Fintan and his followers, and I learned about Cernunnos, the God of Nature, and about Lugh, the God of Light. I learned that other nations, other continents, had their equivalents.

In fact, there was a whole lot of learning going on.

By the end of the day, I was all learned out, exhausted with the information competing for space in my brain. Fionnula, like all good teachers, knew when her students needed a break, and moved on to the importance of good posture, how to apply liquid eyeliner without smudging it, and the best way to mix a Mojito. The secret is gently bruising the mint leaves, apparently.

Celtic gods and cocktails. Just your average day in the la-la land that had become my life.

While I was occupied with my learnathon, Carmel had been keeping herself busy surfing YouTube, picking up self-defence tips from the ju-jitsu masters and would-be ninjas of the cyber world. I'd seen her out in the garden practising her moves, skilfully kicking over piles of logs and jabbing imaginary foe in the eye with two fingers.

She'd also emailed Big Bill, our boss at work, and told him she was suffering from severe 'women's problems'. It's what we always do when we need time off: Big Bill is a middle-aged bachelor who becomes so flustered at the mere mention of anything menstrual that no further questions are asked. I'd written my pop page for the week before leaving Dublin, and wouldn't be missed for a few more days. That, at least, is one of the advantages of living a shadow life.

It was only after dinner – a slow-cooked stew that had been filling the cottage with its spicy aroma all day – that I asked a question I'd been itching to ask since my self-styled mate made his dramatic departure the night before.

'So, how do I call Gabriel?' I said, once the last of the plates had been stacked in the dishwasher.

'There are these amazing modern inventions,' said Carmel from across the room. 'Called tel-e-phones.'

I ignored her. Ass-kicking the Invisible Man all day had left her even more sarcastic than usual.

'That's not what you mean, is it?' said Fionnula.

'Obviously not. I've been aware of the existence of phones for some time now.' I laughed. 'But last night, he said I could call him, and you'd show me how. Assuming I'm capable of hitting speed dial all by myself, what did he mean?'

'He meant with your mind. You've felt him, I presume, in there? Poking around?'

'Uh . . . no. Not really. I know he can do it, and I know it's really irritating, but he says he can't predict when it's going to happen. The first I tend to know about it is when he pulls a thought right out of my head before the paint's dry.'

'He's telling the truth. He has little control over it. And your skills in that department are sadly lacking.'

She shook her head, apparently very disappointed in her star pupil. Her expression made me feel like I should be sitting in the corner wearing a dunce's hat.

'Well,' I replied, 'that's because I had what you might call a deprived childhood. So why don't we try it now? What can I do, and how do I do it?'

Fionnula glugged down half a glass of wine in one go, poured herself a top-up, and nodded. Drunk in charge of a goddess. She could probably get three points on her witch licence for that.

'There is a link between the two of you, forged over

centuries,' she said. 'The connection between the High
King and Mabe is a strong one, which is why he can sometimes appear to read your mind. But the control of that lies
with you, Lily. You can stop him doing it, or you can choose
to let him in, and you can – if you need to – do the same to
him.'

'What? I can read Gabriel's mind?'

Carmel was sniggering in the background, and I didn't
need telepathy to know her mind was firmly in the gutter.
As usual.

'I'm not sure I'd do that, if I were you,' she said. 'Not
with all this talk of mating. You couldn't stand the shock
of it. You blush when you watch a raunchy episode of
Hollyoaks.'

'Bugger off and kick some trees,' I said. There was way
too much wine flowing in the room for my liking. 'Fionnula,
seriously, how do I do it?'

'Which part?'

'All of it, but start with the calling. I want to see if it
works, if I can do it. I'll work on the rest later.'

The voice in my head – Fintan, I presumed – had told me
that I could stop Gabriel from messing with my mind. He
might be Darth Vader as far as the Tuatha were concerned,
but I'd not caught him out in a lie yet. And, I realised, he'd
been very quiet since we arrived at the cottage. Not a peep
from him, even during Fionnula's less-than-balanced pre-
sentation of life in his Otherworld Utopia. In fact, since we'd
been there, my phone hadn't rung, no texts had landed, and
my head had been empty of both voices and intrusions.

The first two were probably down to poor mobile signal, but the rest? Probably down to that fear of 'breaching
Fionnula's land' that Gabriel had mentioned. She could be
pretty darned scary when she tried. Which, I thought, looking at her pouting and wobbling on her bar stool, was not
right now.

'All right, as you wish,' she said. 'But don't blame me if

you fail – this kind of thing normally takes months of training. I can't be held responsible when I'm working with
substandard materials.'

Ouch. More wine, Vicar?

'First of all, it would help if we knew where he is, and if
you could visualise the scene. Draw a picture in your mind
to ease the connection.'

'OK. I can do that part, at least.'

I walked over to her landline, dialled his number. Waited
until a few buzzes and clicks gave way to a solid dial tone.

After a few seconds, he answered, with one snapped
word, 'Gabriel.'

'It's me,' I said. 'Lily.'

'Yes, I know who you are. Is everything all right?'

'Yeah, fine. She's not turned me purple, or anything. Yet.
But, well, we're trying something new, and I need to know
where you are.'

'I'm in the basement of the house,' he replied. I strained
to hear, and caught the sound of music pumping in the
background: Nirvana's 'Nevermind'. Loud.

'What's the basement? What does it look like?'

'It's the weapons room, and the gym. Swords mounted
on the walls, some crossbows. Shields. Daggers for close
combat. Rowing machines and treadmills. Punchbags. I'm
on the flat bench doing weights.'

'Oh,' I said, insanely surprised at the idea. 'You work
out? I thought it was all . . . you know, magic.'

'I wish,' he replied, laughter in his voice. 'And yeah,
some of it is. The rest I have to sweat for. Anyway, I like it.
Helps me get rid of my . . . frustrations.'

I paused, glad we weren't on a videophone so he couldn't
see my face flame at the innuendo.

'I know you're blushing,' he said smugly. 'And I didn't
even need to read your mind to find that out.'

Wonderful. Looked like I could also add 'predictable' to
my ever-growing list of glaring flaws.

'Right. Great. Umm . . . what are you wearing?' I asked.

'Oh, it's going to be one of *those* phone calls, is it? Shouldn't you give me your bank details first?'

'No! Stop flirting and be serious! I'm trying to imagine the scene, to visualise it. So . . . so what are you bloody wearing?'

'Shorts. Sweaty ones.'

'Nothing else?'

'Not a thing, sweetheart. And they're pretty short shorts too. That visualisation getting any clearer?'

It was. So clear that my pulse rate had shot up a few notches, my mouth had gone dry, and I was squirming in my jeans. No matter how many bad things I learned about this man, how much I argued with him, my body seemed set on fancying him rotten. It was all very unfair.

I hung up without answering and turned round to see Carmel biting her lips to stop herself from laughing, and Fionnula pouring yet another glass. I tucked my hair behind my ears and tried to rise above it all. I am the Goddess, for fuck's sake, not a hormonal teenager with a crush.

'And?' I said as haughtily as I could, making 'wind it on' gestures with my hands.

'And, well, the next bit is hard to explain,' said Fionnula, slightly slurring her words so there were a few too many s's knocking around in that sentence.

'You need to sit still, and concentrate. Might help to close your eyes. Ignore me, and Carmel. Shut this place out as much as you can. Try to clear your mind of all the nonsense that's floating round in there. Imagine Gabriel, where he's described, the way he's described himself. Get that picture so clear in your mind that it's as real as we are – as real as this room is.'

I did as I was told, and found it alarmingly easy to picture him. He was in my mind most of the time anyway, like a mental squatter. I made another small 'move it on' gesture with my finger, and ignored her 'humph' of annoyance.

'Then you push your thoughts out to him,' she said. 'Let them flow, like a wave, towards him. It needs to be natural, not forced. When the wave hits, he'll know. You'll be there with him, in his mind, and be able to communicate with him. Talk out loud if it's easier, but for feck's sake, keep it clean, will you?'

Slightly insulted at the thought that I'd engage in public telepathy-sex, I sank down on to the sofa in a bit of a huff. I tried to do as she said, but clearing your mind is so much harder than it sounds. The minute you try to concentrate on nothing, a thousand thoughts scamper through your head like tiny rodents: did the copy editor get that Dormice review safely? Did I pay my credit-card bill on time? Will I be able to put that bonsai back together? How short *are* those shorts?

I shook my head, imposed a blank white wall where my thoughts were running riot, and used it like a mental scoop to push them away. None of them mattered, not right now. I crushed them all to one corner and squashed them flat like bugs, leaving myself with nothing but the clean white space: a bright, empty room. Now all I needed to do was keep it empty.

I breathed deeply, remembering the lessons of those three yoga classes Carmel had dragged me to a year ago, and tried to relax, letting the white emptiness expand and fill my mind like a cloud. After a minute or so, everything started to slow down, physically and mentally. I was conscious of the steady, languid pace of my heart beating, of my blood thrumming a gentle pulse at my wrists. My face felt pleasantly warm, and there was a slight buzz humming in my ears. Not an unpleasant one – a kind of benign, throbbing tinnitus.

I took the white space and replaced it with Gabriel: with the weapons he'd described; with the treadmills and the shields; with him sitting on a bench, drenched in sweat, barbells at his feet. I held the image, let it grow and develop. And eventually it clicked into place, like a camera when you press the button and it all zooms into focus: all motion stopped, all the blurring of everyday thought was removed, and a new reality took shape in my mind.

I could feel the basement walls around me, could listen to Kurt Cobain's anxious words screeching from the speakers, could inhale the musty smell of a room where battle-ready men work out. Carmel and Fionnula and the cottage all disappeared as my mind fled to the cellar of a red-brick Georgian town house in Dublin.

Time to push, I thought. It felt right. Not forced, Fionnula had said, but natural – like a wave. I nudged my thoughts along, the humming sound building to a slow roar, the kind you hear when you have a seashell pressed up against your ear. I sent my thoughts away from me, and towards him.

I opened my eyes. And I was there. In the basement in Merrion Square.

And those shorts really were short.

Chapter Eighteen

Gabriel jumped up, so shocked he almost fell over the weight on the floor in front of him. Two hundred kilos. Yikes.

'Are you here?' he asked. 'Or just in my head?'

'I . . . don't know,' I replied, looking around. The room wasn't exactly as I'd pictured it – he'd failed to mention the Athena poster of the blonde girl with her arse-cheeks hanging out of her tennis dress – but it was pretty damned close.

Gabriel came towards me, eyes sparking a bruised shade of purple. His body was glistening with sweat, and there was more of him on display than I'd ever seen of any man in real life. His slightly-too-long hair curled darkly to the bulked muscle of his shoulder, and I could see the heat radiating from his torso. My hand lifted up to touch his chest, deciding it wanted to know if it felt as good as it looked.

Nothing. I felt a thud of disappointment hammer through me, quickly replaced with relief. Probably not a good idea to get all hot and heavy during my first out-of-body experience.

He looked down at my hand and realised that neither of us could feel the touch.

'You're here . . . but not here,' he said, frowning in confusion.

'Yep. That seems to sum it up. I'm actually sitting on Fionnula's couch right now. Carmel's probably laughing her backside off, and Fionnula's . . . well, a bit pissed, actually. She thought I might not be able to do this. To connect with your mind. And now I'm confused, because I got the impression it would just be talking. Like on the phone. Not being here, like this, actually in the room . . .'

I realised I was rambling, just as eloquent in spirit form as I am in the flesh.

'And anyway, do you think you might be able to put some clothes on now?'

Gabriel thought about it, his expression serious, and then he grabbed a black T-shirt from the back of the bench and pulled it over his head. I felt marginally calmer when some of that shiny muscle disappeared from view. There was still a lot of leg on show, but I could avoid that by not looking down.

'This has never happened to me before,' he said, 'and I've been around for a long time. It's . . . interesting.'

'Maybe for you. I'm totally freaked out. And also – I think – a bit disappointed,' I said, only realising it was true once the words were out of my lips. I'd told Fionnula I only wanted to make contact, to 'call' him – but the devious part of my brain had obviously been a tad more ambitious than that.

I walked round the room, trying to distract myself by getting a better eyeful of the weapons he'd mentioned.

It felt a bit like being in an especially hideous museum exhibition. There were massive swords with razor-edged blades, the kind that could cleave a man in two and still shine, and which had undoubtedly been used for exactly that. One of them was mounted over the fireplace, taking pride of place. The blade was double-edged, the hilt decorated with elaborate designs of animals chasing each other in endless circles. On the pommel was a raised engraving of a woman, her features hidden by a sheet of hair, arms held out at her sides. Belly swollen with child. Even an idiot like me could tell it was a fertility symbol, carved in such intricate detail that it looked more like a drawing than something created from metal. The entire sword appeared to be made of gold.

'The Blade of Lugh,' he said, standing beside me. 'You've seen it before, I think? It was my father's. Passed down to our family by the Gods. He died wielding it, and so will I.'

Nice. I stared at the sword. I did remember it. And last time I saw it, he'd been brandishing it in front of me as I screamed my way into motherhood, flames blazing from its shaft. Not one of my happiest moments.

'What did you mean when you said you were disappointed?' he asked. 'This is unprecedented. Your spirit has left your body and travelled here to be with me. What else were you hoping for?'

I screwed up my nose as I pondered the question, resisting the urge to reach out and touch the shining Blade of Lugh. It looked so sharp I reckoned it could even cut my spirit-fingers.

'I don't know, Gabriel . . . I think I was hoping I could just, you know, sneak into your mind. The way you do into mine. Fionnula says it's possible, once I have enough control. Which apparently isn't quite yet.'

He was silent, his eyes dark as he stared at the gold blade hanging before us, absorbing the bitter tinge that had coloured those last few words.

'I see,' he said finally, and I couldn't tell from his tone whether or not he was angry at my planned incursion into the inner recesses of his brain. I wouldn't have blamed him if he was – I can't say I've ever enjoyed it when he does it to me. It seemed a bit unfair to expect him to be happy about me returning the favour.

We both stayed quiet for a few moments, 'Lithium' crashing away in the background.

'Well,' he said eventually, raising an eyebrow at me, 'why don't we try that now? You're here, sort of. My mind is open to you, Lily. Whether you need my permission or not, I grant it.'

I stayed quiet, not sure how to react. Not sure if it was the right thing to do, or whether I was even capable of it if I tried.

He tapped the side of his head with his fingers and gave me a stomach-melting smile.

'Go on. Try. Knock yourself out.'

What the hell, I thought. I had nothing to lose, and he was clearly willing. What was the worst that could happen? I nipped that train of thought in the bud right away. It's never a good idea to ask that question when you live the kind of life I do.

Instead, I revisited the clean white vision I'd found earlier, urging my friend the fluffy white cloud back into my headspace. I focused on Gabriel, and nothing but him, shutting out the music and the heat and the distractions of all the shiny objects around me. I would have touched him, maybe held his hands, but my body had gone all *Ghostbusters* on me, so I settled for just looking at him. A lot. Drinking in that perfect face and those hypnotic eyes, opened wide and sparkling with . . . anxiety? Excitement? I couldn't tell. He'd braced himself, feet planted firmly apart, as though expecting some kind of attack.

There were several failed attempts, when it felt a bit like my mind was being used as a battering ram against a metal door. I'd push, and be repelled. I'd shove, and it wouldn't budge. But, eventually, the door opened. I reached out with my mind, and it swung back to let me in. No words were spoken, no touch exchanged; there was no brass band or choir of angels. I just took a quiet mental step forward, and landed slap bang in the middle of his consciousness.

It was overwhelming, to start with. Like a film reel playing at the speed of light, projecting snatched images and half-formed conversations: battles and brawls, feast days, celebrations, a small child running free through fields of corn. A mother and a father, cousins and friends, a changing world filled with wonders. A wild, windy hill and a screaming stone. Horses and carriages and trains and cars and planes. And Gabriel, weeping, hunched over the battered, bloodied bodies of two little girls. The sisters I'd never known.

I saw him recoil as he felt me in there, fumbling around with all the finesse of an ice pick, and I took a slow, deep breath. Focused on the here and now. On the Gabriel I knew. Tuned into what mattered, like I was fiddling with a radio dial, searching for the best reception.

Passion. He felt passion. For this world, for its people. For his job. He was driven by responsibility and duty, and really hadn't been lying when he said he'd die to protect me. I saw it there, shining like a diamond embedded in rock: complete and utter devotion to the Goddess. It ran through him, deep and divine, and had made him everything he was. Given him his purpose in life. And there I was, tucked away in his brain, as a tiny child, scared and frightened as Coleen led me away to my new life. I felt his regret, his worry, his anger at what he'd been forced to do.

I saw him on the back row at my school nativity play, watching as I played third angel on the right, head wrapped round with silver tinsel. And later, at my university graduation ceremony, applauding on a day I thought I'd been alone. He was proud of me, of what I'd achieved with a minimum of encouragement. A silent spectator, looking at me from afar, never making contact but always there, always distant.

Nearer to the here and now: me again, leaning against the bar in the Coconut Shy, trying to avoid his gaze on the night we first properly met. I saw it from his eyes as

I collapsed into his arms after my vision, the way he felt when he cradled me against his chest, lifting me from the beer-stained nightclub floor. The warmth and the protectiveness that surged through him, shaking his self-control.

Then I was with him days later, while I'd been lost in the Otherworld. Smashing his flat-screen and camping out at the side of Bidston Hill, desperate for me to return. I felt his fear and anger and desperation when he couldn't find me. And when he did find me, when I finally woke up and he saw my eyes blink open for the first time, I felt what he felt: love. Love so strong, so unyielding, that it scared me. Terrified me like nothing I'd ever encountered.

I snatched my thoughts away, felt them race from his mind like smoke billowing out of tunnels, away from the pure emotion that was too much for my poor, undeveloped psyche to handle. I was so shaken that if my body had been there with me, I'd have needed a lie-down. I retreated to the other side of the room, needing some distance between us, scared of accidentally falling into his head again, of getting sucked into a mental black hole.

'Are you all right?' he asked, taking a step towards me.

'Yes . . . no,' I replied, feeling the equivalent of a panic attack swamp my spirit-body. My heart, back on the sofa in Fionnula's cottage, would be racing hard, I knew. I took a breath, forced myself to calm down. A cardiac arrest wasn't going to help anybody.

'I'm OK, Gabriel,' I said. 'That was just a bit . . . intense. Thank you . . . for letting me. But I won't be doing that again in a hurry.'

'Why not?' he said. 'What did you see?'

'You don't know?'

'No – I was trying too hard not to scream like a girl. I had no control over what I was thinking, and can only hope it wasn't anything too embarrassing. Or anything that . . . scared you.'

He looked deeply concerned, and I wasn't naive enough

to think he didn't have yet more secrets hidden in that brain of his. The peace we shared, this man and I, was always fragile, and allowing me into his mind had probably taken more bravery than flying into battle with the Blade of Lugh. He'd taken a risk, made a sacrifice, and now he was starting to think he'd made a mistake. That I'd seen something so upsetting, I'd fled, trembling, across the room.

In reality, though, it wasn't some deep dark revelation that had scared me. Not just scared me but petrified me, leaving me stunned and shaken and fluttering with the overload of it all. The shocking revelation had been that he loved me – a love so fierce that most women would kill to experience it even once in their lives.

But then, I'm not most women, am I?

I'm a woman who has lived her whole life in a bubble of quiet solitude and isolation – a life of adaptation and contented acceptance. What I'd seen – what I'd felt – in Gabriel had been the opposite of that. It wasn't contented. It wasn't quiet. It was loud and passionate and it blazed so bright and so hot that I was scared to go near it for fear of being consumed in the flames.

Try explaining that in words of one syllable. With time, I might be able to think my way through it – but right then, I still felt singed.

'I need to go,' I said quietly. 'I'm starting to feel a bit weird. For all I know, Carmel's shaved my eyebrows off by now. Thank you again, and I'm sorry – sorry that I did that. I shouldn't have intruded. I don't even have the excuse that you do, of not being able to control it. Hope I didn't kill off any vital brain cells, or anything, by trampling round in there.'

'I'm sure I'll cope, Lily,' he said, his expression telling me he wasn't buying my light-hearted spirit-girl act. 'Take care, and learn well – I'll see you soon, *a ghra.*'

Chapter Nineteen

When I came to, Carmel and Fionnula were sitting on either side of me on the sofa, like a pair of demented bookends.

'Oh, thank the Gods!' said Fionnula, grabbing my hands and shaking them, hard. 'We thought we'd lost you!'

'I'm fine!' I shrieked. 'Now back off. If you breathe on me much more, I might pass out from the fumes! What's the problem? What happened?'

'The problem is, you kind of went unconscious,' said Carmel, staring daggers at me. 'For ages. Eyes rolled back in your head – not a good look, for future reference. Lady Barfly here was going nuts – said it wasn't right. She thought something had gone terribly wrong; portents of doom and all that. And there was nothing we could do but watch, and wait. And in *her* case, belch a lot.'

'Well, I'm fine,' I said. 'As you can see. Nothing wrong with me at all. Fit as a fiddle. Feeling groovy, in fact.'

I jumped up from the sofa and danced a little jig to prove I still had full use of my limbs, but it didn't seem to do much to reassure them. Fionnula stood up as well, and managed all of three seconds upright before she tumbled back on to the sofa.

'Oh dear,' she said. 'That wine must have been corked.'

'The first bottle, or the third?' asked Carmel, bristling

at Fionnula, and glaring at me. I'd scared her, and she was bitingly angry because of it. I'd need another Champion to protect me from the first if she carried on like this.

'I really am all right,' I said. 'And I'm sorry if I worried you. It wasn't intentional. Nothing I ever do these days is intentional. So just bloody forgive me, OK?'

She thought about it for a beat or two, eyes still sparking, then held up her hands in surrender.

'OK. As you asked so nicely, and you did that Lord of the Dance thing so well. Now tell us what *happened*.'

'I went to him. Gabriel. I was there, in his basement, with him. He could see me, and I could see him, but I couldn't touch him – I mean, anything, not just him. I was like a ghost, there in spirit only. And, you know, we chatted.'

I left out the parts about the mind invasion, unwilling declarations of love, and my retardo-girl response to it all. For the time being, that would remain firmly beneath my ever-expanding secrets hat.

'You were actually there?' said Fionnula, hiccuping at the end of the word. 'Not just in a visualisation of it?'

'Yes, I was actually there. In the non-flesh. Walking and talking.'

Her bleary eyes narrowed, and I noticed that the liquid eyeliner she took such a pride in applying was now most definitely smudged.

'That's very . . . interesting,' she murmured.

'That's exactly what he said. What is it with you people and "interesting"?'

'Well, sweetie, when you've lived as long as we have, there's not much new under the sun, is there? Been there, done that, bought the pashmina. But for you to have had the power to do that, to go to him in your other form, is important. Especially when you're so new to it all. Your powers are there, but still developing – and I'm only just starting to think you might be capable of a lot more than I suspected. The connection between the two of you must be impossibly strong . . .'

She tailed off into silence, and for a minute I thought she'd passed out cold. I started to do a visual drool check to see if she needed putting to bed, but she suddenly looked up at me, blue eyes shining with what looked suspiciously like tears.

'Lily, you are so very, very lucky,' she said.

'Right,' I replied, feeling a wave of exhaustion flood over me. I needed to rest, be alone, and recharge my now very frazzled nerves. 'Lucky Lily. That's me. Remind me to buy a frigging lottery ticket tomorrow, why don't you? Now if it's all right with you, I'm going to bed.'

The next morning, I had to fight two hungover hags just for the chance to go out on my own. I'd had a terrible night, tossing and turning so much the sheets were bound around my legs like twists of ivy.

I'd been tortured with dreams – of him, of Gabriel. And me. Of a different me, one that was ready for all of this. One that was ready to love and be loved, to share and open up and be . . . well, normal. Because in the midst of all this craziness, the one thing that had terrified me was that: the idea that all of this came down to love, to an equivalent of Julia Roberts' dopey 'just a girl, just a boy' speech in *Notting Hill*. The thought sent me into spasms of dread. Go figure.

I showered, looked on as Fionnula prised her eyelids apart with a crowbar, and announced I was going out for a walk.

'I'll come with you,' said Carmel, recovering faster than her partner in wine.

'No, you won't,' I said.

'Yes, I will,' she replied.

And thus it went on for several minutes, the two of us setting the room alight with sparkling repartee. Eventually Fionnula rediscovered the power of speech and butted in.

'It should be safe for her, Champion,' she said.

'My lands are held sacred. I have my privacy here, and that is extended to my guests.'

Carmel looked like she was going to argue, but swallowed it down. Probably thinking of all the Alka-Seltzer she could glug while I was gone.

'But,' said Fionnula, turning to me, 'you must promise not to leave the grounds. The barriers are all clearly marked; you can't miss them. Not a foot outside, do you understand? Outside, I can't protect you.'

'From the Hooded Claw?'' I asked sarcastically. I knew she wouldn't have a clue who Frankie Goes to Hollywood are, but she was annoying me. She was laying it on as thick as her foundation, and I was getting sick of being mollycoddled.

'I don't know what that means, but yes, if there is a Hooded Claw out there, it won't trespass on my land.'

I nodded, and turned to leave.

'One more thing!' she shouted, just as I reached out to open the front door.

'What?'

'Take your coat. It's pissing down out there.'

'Yes, Mother,' I replied, grabbing the parka and slamming the door behind me. Not very gracious, I know, considering they were worried about me. What can I say? It was that time of the month. The time of the month when I had to decide the fate of humanity and all.

She had been right about one thing – it really was pissing it down. The sky was a cracked steel grey, black clouds hovering over the distant sea like vultures spreading their wings. The temperature had plummeted overnight, and I wrapped the coat around me like one of those foil blankets they give to marathon runners.

I trudged off behind the cottage, past a neat vegetable patch and a washing line. There was a pond, the surface bombarded by raindrops, and a small family of frogs perched on the rim, looking up at me and croaking as I passed. I say frogs. They could have been people, for all I knew, suffering the wrath of Fionnula the Not-Always Fair. Just in case, I waved and smiled as I headed further down the field.

I walked for about an hour without seeing any visible boundary between this patch of land and the next. There were no other buildings in sight, and the trees were bent and withered in the wind, stripped nude by autumn. It was bleak and barren and fitted my mood perfectly.

I needed this space, out on my own getting my hair blown into tumbleweed, to think, to ponder. To give myself a damned good talking to. How would I handle it, the next time I saw Gabriel in person? How would I react? Would he realise that I'd been poking around in his brain a bit more than I'd intended? Would I be able to even speak to him without blushing? Nah, I decided. I'd never been able to do that. He was a one-man blush machine.

I was stamping a bit harder than necessary on the muddy footpath, my Docs splattered with sludge like the side of a four-by-four, streaks of rusty-brown dirt striping the backs of my jeans. I was angry. With the world, with fate; even – unfairly – with my parents, for not being around to help me with all this. Most of all, I was angry with myself. For being such a total wuss. Boo hoo, poor little Lily – a completely gorgeous man-god was in love with me, and I was crying about it.

I realised as the thought crossed my mind that I *was* crying. A lot. The tears were whipped away from the corners of my eyes as soon as they spilled, the wind was so ferocious. But, yes, I was bleating. Not a good look. I needed to get a grip. That was going to be my new catchphrase: get a grip. As soon as I was back in civilisation, I was going to get it printed up on a T-shirt, or possibly tattooed on my knuckles. I could say it to myself in my best Scouse accent: gerra grip, girl.

It wasn't, I told myself, so bloody bad. OK, there'd

been several attempts on my life during the last week. I'd been kidnapped by a bloodthirsty fairy, transported to the Otherworld, met my deceased parents, faced the news that I wasn't even totally human, and possibly filed my last ever pop page, which saddened me more than it should under the circumstances.

And now, I had another sledgehammer to deal with – Gabriel. Not just the protector, or the Great, or the man-with-the-amazing-blow-up-body, but Gabriel, the man who had kept an eye on me for all these years. Who'd been proud of me when I thought nobody was. Who'd cursed himself for the pain he'd had to cause me. Who loved me, with every ounce of his not-inconsiderable being.

Could I live with that? I'd be a fool to not even try. And the by-product could be, you know, saving the world as I knew it. Shopping malls and all.

I turned it around and around in my head, trying to calm my hysteria, and started to feel a tiny chink of light creeping in: I could do this. I could accept Gabriel. He wasn't perfect, but his heart was good. And his body wasn't bad, either . . . Whichever way I looked at it, there could be worse fates. I would try, I decided. Try harder; be better. Live up to my alleged goddess status. I mean, how could I be a fertility goddess and not even have it in me to love a man and be loved in return? Surely that was a big part of it? How could I bless the land if I couldn't even bless my own life?

OK, I decided as I stomped the life out of innocent ridges of muddy soil. Fresh start. Try not to run for the hills; give Gabriel a chance. Get Fionnula to show me how to stop my touch-type visions. Accept him as my mate; maybe even get laid at last, har-de-har. Put some effort into being less cynical about the world, about love. About life. And yeah, try not to get killed in the process. It wasn't much of a plan, but it was the only one I had.

The tears started to slow, and my breathing faded back to something like normal as I slackened my pace from

Olympic-standard walking speed. I was exhausted, but it had worked. I'd walked myself calm again.

I was busy wiping loose strands of hair out of my eyes when I first heard it. A tiny whimpering sound. So tiny I had to strain my ears against the wind to catch it. A mewing, faint and stricken. I glanced around, but couldn't see anything except the wild, sodden landscape and a fence running horizontally for miles in front of me. The border of Fionnula's land. I'd finally made it.

I walked towards the downtrodden shrubs along the base of the fence, kicking aside withered briars way past their bloom, using the toes of my boot to mooch around. Nothing there except some fat ugly woodlice. Yet still I could hear it, that pathetic, strangled mewing. It was a cat, I was sure. In distress, by the sound of it. Maybe another of Fionnula's experiments.

I pulled back some of the off-greenery, and saw a stile in the fence, complete with a little hop-up step to help you over. On the other side was a kitten. Black and white and so small it could fit into the palm of my hand. It was tangled in the trailing fingers of the briar, sharp thorns stabbing into its soft fur. Its coat was drenched with the rain, laid so flat to its puny body that I could see the shape of its skull clearly outlined.

'Oh, poo . . .' I muttered, peering over the stile, just as an ominous roll of thunder started to lumber in from somewhere to the west. Lightning followed seconds after, for one eye-searing moment drenching the sky in vivid platinum stripes.

I blinked away rain, looked over the stile again. There was nobody there. No thunder gods had appeared wielding hammers. No men in black. No soul-sucking Tuatha. No Hooded Claw. Nobody for miles and miles. Just me and this teeny tiny creature, writhing against the briar and getting itself more and more tangled each time it tried to roll free.

Nobody there but little old me, soaking wet, in an

ear-splitting thunderstorm, weighing up whether or not to save the life of a defenceless kitten who just happened to be trapped on the other side of Fionnula's boundary. Double poo.

I did another quick danger-check, then hoisted up the flapping wings of my coat and climbed – not very elegantly and with a few swear words involved – over the stile. I jumped down with a squelch and stepped towards the kitten, kneeling down in the muddy grass and making what I hoped were soothing cooing noises as I took it into my hands. The cooing was all but drowned out by the drum roll of thunder and the subsequent shock of bright light. I don't know who was more spooked, me or the kitten.

The poor thing squeaked and squealed as I tried to pry it free of the thorny tendrils, pricking my fingers so much drops of blood started to spot its fur. Eventually, I managed to pull the last cord away, taking a clump of downy-soft white hair with it. As soon as I did, the kitten wriggled out of my hands, did an amazingly acrobatic backflip, and ran away, without so much as a thank-you meow. Typical.

I stood up, wiped my mud- and blood-smeared hands on the thighs of my jeans, and pulled my hood tighter around my head. It was so windy I felt like my head could come clear off, like a scarecrow, and go tumbling off across the field, still talking to itself.

'Hello again, Lily,' said the voice in my head. *'I know you haven't heard from me for a while, but I thought you might need my help.'*

I physically jumped at the sound, only just keeping my boots steady in the mud pool around the stile, holding on to the wooden rail to calm myself. No, I hadn't heard from Fintan for a while, and I'd seen and learned a lot since then. I'd been in Gabriel's mind. I'd seen the Otherworld in a whole new light. And I'd found out that Fintan had definitely been behind the deaths of my sisters.

I didn't want his voice in my head. Or anyone else's. It had to be first on my hit list when I got back to Fionnula's. If I got back.

'What do you want, Fintan?' I asked.

'Ah. I see we've been informally introduced. I'm sure you've heard terrible things about me, Lily.'

I stayed silent. I had. And I believed them. But still, Fintan had never actually lied to me, made a move against me, or broken his word. That was enough for me to keep his occasional presence in my mind a secret. Everyone needs their secrets, and as my mind seems to get treated like a rummage sale by all and sundry these days, me especially.

'Where have you been?' I said. 'Out marauding and plotting the downfall of humanity?'

I sounded braver than I felt, but this was the New Me. The Gerra Grip, Girl me. The me that Coleen would be proud of . . . Maybe some good had rubbed off from her after all.

'Oh no, I don't maraud,' he said, disdain dripping from every word. *'I'm more of a strategist. And I think you already know that I've been unable to contact you while you were on Fionnula's land. Hardly fair, do you think?'*

I pondered. I'd been right. It was Fionnula's power keeping him out. And all it had taken was stupid me to climb over a stile to let him back in. She'd warned me not to cross the boundaries, and I'd ignored her at the first sign of feline fluff. I'd be in for a proper bollocking when I got back.

'Did you get that poor kitten wrapped up in thorns just to get me over here?' I asked.

For some reason, that bothered me as much as anything right now.

'Would you believe me if I said it was serendipity?' he replied.

'No,' I said.

'Then you'd be right. No harm done: it's scampered away now, back to a cosy hearth, or chewing a mouse or whatever it wants to do. It was a pawn, Lily. A sacrifice to get you here, so I could talk

to you. Set a few facts straight, as I can imagine what Fionnula is filling your mind with.'

'She's been very helpful with make-up tips,' I said, spoiling the bravado slightly when the latest crash of thunder made me leap into the air. I screwed up my eyes and waited for the lightning to follow.

'Has she been explaining about your visions?'

'No . . . no, we haven't got to that part yet,' I replied reluctantly. It felt wrong to be telling him anything, but there was no point lying. I'm really crap at it.

'I see. It's important, though, isn't it? For you to be able to control them? You've spent your whole life tortured by them. Spent your whole life scarred by your loneliness, never able to reach out and touch someone, never able to be held or comforted. Never able to share physical intimacy with anyone. No hand holding, no kissing, not even a casual hug from a friend. Not without anxiety. Never able to relax unless you're on your own, scared of even brushing by someone on the street for fear of what you might see. How has that affected you, Lily?'

I stayed schtum. That, frankly, was my business, but I felt my spine stiffen as he made his list. He was right, about it all. If I survived all of this nonsense, I'd need to be in therapy for the rest of my bloody life. My inner child was well and truly pissed off.

'Well, don't worry,' he said. 'Fionnula will be able to show you. She's a good teacher, despite her many faults, and it's actually quite simple to do. Very simple, in fact. So simple, Lily, that really, you should have been able to do it by the age of ten. Your sisters were older than you. They'd already started their training before their . . . untimely deaths. Fionnula did it for them. The visions had started by then, but because of Fionnula, they were able to control them, live normally. Can you imagine how different your life would have been if you'd had that training, Lily? If you didn't have your visions?'

I really couldn't. I would have been a different person. I would have had a different life. I'd only need a few years of therapy instead of decades. I'd have been able to reach out in ways I've only ever fantasised about, and even the fantasies stopped once I got through my teens.

At six, all I'd wanted was a cuddle, for someone to tuck me in at night, stroke my face like my mummy used to, hold me tight and tell me everything was going to be OK. I was used to being loved, to being hugged, to having my small hand held as we skipped to the shops for an ice cream. I lost that overnight, and badly wanted it back. Wanted to feel that safe again, to lie in someone's arms giggling and listening to stories and knowing that I was the most precious thing in the world. But even at that age, I'd realised I shouldn't touch Coleen, or anyone else. Because if I did, scary things happened. Bad things.

By fifteen, like most girls, all I'd wanted was a boyfriend – one I could kiss without seeing him halfway through a colonoscopy in a few decades' time. And by eighteen, I'd realised there was no use torturing myself with it any more. I was never going to have a boyfriend. There was no white knight. I was Lily McCain, and I saw dying people. It wasn't ever going to lend itself to romance, or even to friendship. I was only safe when I was alone. Not a barrel load of laughs, but that's just the way it was. No point crying over milk that's been spilled, stood in, and gone sour.

So what if my sisters had been trained, and I hadn't? For some reason, maybe to do with Fintan's slaughtering of them, I'd had to go through it alone. Yes, it had been hell, but on the plus side, I wasn't dead.

'Fintan,' I said. 'Do you have a point? Because I'm really, really wet now.'

'Very brave, Lily. Yes, I do have a point. The reason you weren't trained, the reason you were taken away and placed in Coleen's hands, the reason you were left to the fate of your visions when you needn't have suffered them at all is this: the man you call Gabriel chose it for you. He decided it, Lily. He not only chose Coleen, he chose to leave you with the visions, and with no way

of controlling them. He chose to let you grow up like that. He's also a strategist – and that was one of his gems. To let you drag yourself up, damaged and alone and broken. So, whatever sweet lies he tells you, remember that: it's all his fault.'

I felt a blur in my eyes, and realised I'd been staring so long without blinking that rain had gathered inside my lower lids. I shook it away, and stood as tall as I could, my knuckles white as I grabbed the fence. I felt all soft and slippy inside, and didn't want to fall. Not during a brain invasion.

'What do you mean?' I said. 'I already know he took me to Coleen. He said it was to keep me safe. From you.'

'Really? Well, he would, wouldn't he? Yes, he took you to Coleen for that reason, trying to hide you away. But what do you think was the reason he left you with your visions, Lily? What advantage did that give him? He could have sent Fionnula, as he had to your sisters, within a year or so. He could have done that and still kept you safe. But he forbade it. He ruled that you should not receive the same training, that she shouldn't show you how to protect yourself. He barred Fionnula from contacting you, even though she wanted to, even though it was the only way of giving you any peace. It was him – he decided to leave you, alone, with Coleen, unable to touch or be touched, rigid with fear every time someone stood next to you in the playground. So I ask again, Lily: how has that affected you?'

The rain had turned my hair into thick auburn ropes the colour of rusty nails, whirling in the wind and lashing me across my icy cheeks. I saw it happening, but could barely feel the contact. I couldn't feel my hands, or my feet. I couldn't feel anything. I'd known Gabriel had secrets, but this? This was . . . too much.

I pondered Fintan's question, the one he'd repeated. How had it affected me? And why had Gabriel – the man who loved me, and the man who was also ruthless beyond imagining – decided to deliberately force me to live like that, if it could have been so easily avoided?

'It made me . . . alone,' I said at last. I could have elaborated: it made me lonely, isolated, sad, practical, independent, frightened, strong, weak. All of those things were true. But mainly, it had made me very alone. Surrounded by people, by life, but afraid to touch. Scared of everything but my own company.

'Yes. Alone. And pure, Lily. Free from ties, free from relationships, free from any kind of emotional or physical entanglement. It kept you alone – like you were spending your life in quarantine, waiting. Waiting for him to come along and kiss it all better. He distanced you from everyone else; he put your life on hold until he was ready. He left you completely and utterly alone, until it suited him. Until he needed you.'

Could that be true? Was that what Gabriel had planned? Had he done it to keep me apart from other people, so I'd be ready and waiting when he arrived for me? So I'd feel like I had nothing to lose by giving myself to him? Had he wanted my real life to be so miserable that I wouldn't think twice about giving it up to run off and play house with him?

Was he really that cruel, that devious? I knew the answer already. Yes, he was. He could be, no matter how much love I'd seen in him. He could be that ruthless, because his love for me, and the love he wanted in return, was nothing compared to his duty. His calling. His bloody destiny – and, so he'd have me believe, mine as well.

The thunder had started to fade, rolling away to another hill, another place. Another girl standing in the rain, wondering why she'd been stupid enough to think she could even try to love.

'Lily? What are you thinking?' Fintan said.

I ignored him. Turned around and climbed back over that stile. I felt a strange silence when I landed back on Fionnula's land, like someone had turned off the static in my brain.

I set off back to the cottage. Things were about to change.

Chapter Twenty

I stamped all the way back. I was aiming for angry yet dignified, but was hindered by the fact that every footstep was accompanied by an obscene squelching sound.

I didn't even get to do a dramatic door-slamming entrance, as Fionnula and Carmel were already outside to meet me. Carmel was drenched to the bone, her black blouse a second skin, raindrops gathering and dropping from the end of her slightly prominent nose.

Fionnula had wrapped herself in a flouncy lilac poncho affair that made a small tent around her shoulders, her hair starting to frizz in the storm.

Both of them ran over towards me as I approached the cottage, Carmel grabbing my shoulders and shaking me, hard. I pulled away, ready to lash out at somebody and not wanting it to be her.

'Where the fuck have you been? Are you all right?' she demanded, big whisky eyes rolling wildly, like a spooked horse at the starting line.

'No! I'm not! But what do you know about it? Was it her?' I said, gesturing towards Fionnula with a nod of my head. It'd be just like her to have some kind of privacy-invading magical CCTV set up around her home.

'It wasn't me,' said Fionnula quietly, her tone calmer

but her eyes just as wide. Whatever I'd done, I'd triggered DEFCON 1 back here. She reached out, stroked a sopping rope of hair back from my eyes.

'It was Carmel,' she said gently. 'She sensed something. I know it hasn't happened to her before, but things are different now. She's your Champion, and she sensed danger.'

'I sensed more than that,' said Carmel, shoulders shaking in the cold. 'I felt . . . like you were going to explode. What the fuck happened?'

I stared at them both, and bit my lip so hard I lost a chunk. Bugger.

'Let's go inside. We're all freezing,' I said, walking towards the cottage, leaving them trailing behind me.

Once inside, Fionnula walked into the kitchen and straight to the door I now recognised as the Cupboard of Booze, and grabbed a bottle of whisky with a very old-looking label. Looked like she was pulling out the big guns.

Carmel wrapped her arms around herself, still shuddering, looking at me uncertainly.

'OK,' I said, hanging the drenched coat on the back of the kitchen door. 'I suppose I have to explain.'

'Too fucking right,' she said, which made three 'fucks' in the last three sentences. That was a lot, even for her.

'And I will,' I replied. 'But after that, Fionnula is going to answer a few questions of her own, and then we're going back to Dublin. Straight away.'

I heard Fionnula gulp, and didn't know if it was anxiety of just half a bottle of whisky going down.

'For a little while now, I've been hearing voices. Well, one voice to be precise: Fintan's.'

'How long has this been going on?' asked Fionnula, peering at me from under her finely plucked blonde eyebrows. I knew she'd suspected I was hiding something, so she didn't look as shocked as she could have. Don't suppose you live to be 420 years old and still shock easily.

'Since I went to the Otherworld. And not all the time,

just occasionally. He . . . tells me things. He told me he'd call off the men who were chasing me, and he did. He told me he'd allow me free will, and he has. I know he's the big bad guy – I feel it myself – but he's done nothing to hurt me.'

'Have these conversations continued while you were in my home, in my sanctuary?' she said, eyes blazing. I wouldn't want to be on the wrong end of that temper, immortal or not.

'No. Not at all. Your territory wasn't breached. I had to . . . cross the boundary. I climbed over the stile and into the next field.'

I didn't want to elaborate on that because, well, it was frankly embarrassing. Big tough goddess-girl falls at the first hurdle. Maybe Gabriel was right to have surrounded me with secret squirrel bodyguards for the whole of my life. I was clumsy in every possible way: saying the wrong thing, tripping over my own feet, climbing over stiles and laying myself bare to shady Otherworld henchmen. I was rubbish at this.

'And why would you be doing that, now? Climbing over the stile when I distinctly remember telling you not to leave my land?' asked Fionnula, her voice deceptively soft and Irish. I ignored her. It wasn't relevant. And I didn't want to tell.

'Ha!' said Carmel, her shakes finally subsiding, pointing one long, dark-skinned finger at my already blushing face. 'How did he get you? Free Easter Egg? Labrador puppies wrapped in ribbon? New Stone Roses album?'

'Kitten,' I muttered, keeping my voice low in the hope she wouldn't hear me and would forget all about it. Fat chance.

'That's pathetic,' she said, shaking her head. 'Truly pathetic. You need to buck your ideas up, or you're going to get yourself killed. And I won't be able to do a thing to stop it. You understand?'

I looked into her eyes, at her furrowed brow, her clenched fists. Jesus. She was serious. I was getting a proper telling-off from my best and only friend, my best and only Champion. And even worse, she was right, and I knew it.

'All right,' I said, nodding. 'I understand. I'll be more careful. And maybe you and Connor can teach me to fight, or something. I'm sorry.'

She nodded abruptly, and a splatter of rain fell from her hair on to the floor. She was letting me off lightly. For now.

'What did he say, anyway?' she asked.

'Well, that's the interesting part. And that's where Fionnula comes in.'

I turned to face her. She met my gaze with a lot of attitude, which was fair enough: I was in her home, under her protection, and I was about to give her a bloody hard time. She knew it was coming – I could tell from the set of her shoulders and the way her chin was pointing out and up at a strange angle, trying to compensate for the fact that she was four inches shorter than me. Fionnnula's battle stance.

'I want the truth. I don't want any excuses, or any sugar-coating. You're supposed to be Switzerland, and I don't want any more lies or evasions. You will answer me honestly, Fionnula the Fair, or I will walk right out of this cottage, off your land and back to Fintan. One more lie, and I'll be his. All of this will be over. Do you believe me?'

'I believe you, Goddess. I hear the truth in your words,' she said, her tone still defiant. 'And I will do as you ask – but be aware that the truth is never simple. Never absolute. There is always more than one version of any truth.'

'That's bollocks,' I replied. 'And you're preparing me for something you know I don't want to hear, aren't you?'

'Maybe I am, Lily. And maybe I'm right – maybe you don't want to hear it. Maybe it would do you no good to hear it.'

'I'm sick and tired of other people deciding what is good

for me, and what isn't. I've spent my whole life under the shadow of strangers conspiring to decide my fate, and now it stops. Today, it stops. Now answer me this: did you train my sisters, and help them control their visions? I only need a one-word answer to that, by the way.'

Carmel had gone silent and still, weighing up the heavy-weight tension in the room. This was between Fionnula and me, and she sensed it.

Fionnula stared at me, her eyes glinting like ice-cold crystal. Her coral-painted lips were clamped shut, as though she was trying to stop the words from escaping.

'Answer me. Or I will leave. I mean it. I am the Goddess, and there is nothing you could do to stop me. One word. Yes or no.'

'Yes!' she finally said, in a whisper that still seemed to fill the room.

'And they were about seven or eight?'

She nodded, one swift plunge of her head, as though even that affirmation caused her pain.

'And that was normal – that's what you would usually do? I remember you telling me that you were teaching me later than you'd like, that in normal circumstances you'd have preferred a younger mind to mould. So, why not me – why wasn't I sent for training? Why was I the only one left with the bastard visions?'

'You were the only one left alive!' she hissed. 'Gabriel had to keep you hidden. He couldn't risk sending you here to me; it would have exposed you.'

I rolled the thought around in my mind, analysing what she'd said, and – more importantly – what she'd carefully left out. Witchy bitch indeed. I was up against centuries of cleverness.

'I accept that,' I replied, trying to sound calm despite the mounting hysteria inside me. 'But why didn't you come to me? I'm sure Gabriel in all his Greatness could have arranged that. You, with your vast experience of sneaking around, could have managed that. Why didn't you come to me, and teach me? Didn't you want to, Fionnula?'

'It wasn't that,' she said. I could swear I saw tears in her eyes, and wondered why. Maybe she was like me and cried when she was angry.

'What was it, then? Was it him? Did Gabriel order you to stay away? Did he want to keep me the way I was, leave me crippled by my visions? Is that what happened?'

'I told you there is nothing absolute about truth! It's complicated, and I won't be forced into guessing his motives!' she screeched, throwing her whisky glass across the room so hard it smashed dramatically against the white wall, splashing amber fingers over the paintwork.

I recognised it for what it was: both an expression of frustration, and an attempt to distract me. It wouldn't work.

'Fionnula. Answer my question. Did Gabriel tell you to leave me alone, to leave me with my visions? Did he forbid you from helping me? One word only. That's all I need.'

She sagged back against the kitchen counter like a popped balloon, suddenly devoid of all fight. She stared at the floor, and the tears finally spilled over, a steady stream falling to the kitchen floor. A pause. A deep, shuddering breath.

'Yes,' she said quietly.

One word. One small word that changed everything.

Chapter Twenty-One

Fionnula went quiet after that. I'd expected her to try to talk me out of it, to explain, to plead Gabriel's case. Instead, she agreed to drive us back to Dublin and watched silently as we packed up our belongings. I guess she really was Switzerland.

In the car, she stayed sullen, driving with abandon around hairpin bends with nothing but a rickety fence separating us from the cliffs below. Clearly I was going to have to get used to the way these supernatural types treated a car.

'Nothing to say?' I asked, finally, clinging on to my seat belt for dear life. 'No impassioned speeches about my duty to save the frigging world?'

'No,' she replied quietly. 'This is between you and Cormac Mor now. I've already said too much.'

'I don't think so,' I replied, hearing the bitterness seep from my own voice like acid burning through my soul. 'I don't think you've said anywhere near enough. For starters, I need you to tell me how to stop getting these visions when people touch me. I don't want to see anyone else's future, ever again. Fix it.'

She braked so suddenly I jerked forward, the breath knocked out of me as the seat belt tightened around my stomach. In the back I heard a quiet 'oof' as Carmel's head banged against my seat. I peered out into the darkness through the windscreen, and saw a solitary fox wander out in front of us, its eyes shining opal in the headlights. A quizzical twist of its tail and it was gone.

'I can't just fix it,' she said, immediately hitting the accelerator again and going from a dead stop to sixty in what felt like zero seconds. I needed to get some of that G-force training astronauts have.

'Maybe not fix it – but explain to me how it works. If my sisters learned when they were only children, I can learn now – and you can teach me. I need this, and I deserve this. You owe this to me.'

'It wasn't my fault, you know,' she said, turning to look at me when I much preferred she looked at the road. 'And it wasn't really his. He had his reasons.'

'Yes, I know. He always does. No matter what I hear about him, he always has his precious bloody reasons. Like you said, that's between him and me. Now tell me what I can do to stop the visions.'

She sighed, and thankfully turned her attention back to driving.

'When you contacted Gabriel last night, you used the power of your mind. You went far beyond anything I've seen a novice ever do, Lily. You have great natural talent – that's probably why your visions have been so strong, so frequent. Does it sometimes happen with places as well as people?'

I recalled the long-ago incident with the mystic monks on the Mersey Ferry. And another time, when I was a bit older, on a school trip to Croxteth Hall, a vast Edwardian manor house on the outskirts of town. As we'd all piled off the coach, flicking elastic bands at each other and guzzling bottles of Sunny D, I'd seen it as it had been back in its heyday: buzzing with uniformed staff, coachmen, gardeners, maids in black dresses and frilly white caps, gamekeepers with pheasants slung over their shoulders, trailing blood as they made their way to the kitchens. The vision had vanished as quickly as it had appeared, but made the trip round the Hall a lot more vivid.

'Yes,' I said simply. She didn't need the details.

'I thought so. How did you contact Gabriel, would you say? There were no magic words, no special herbs, but you did it. How?'

I thought about it. At heart, it had been about will. About focus, and using my own energy to achieve something I really wanted to do.

'I did it by funnelling everything I had into that one aim. And by listening to what you were telling me to do.'

'Yes. And you did it quickly, and with relative ease. I never expected you to be able to do that, Lily. That's because of who you are, your nature. It's the same with the visions. You can control them; you can switch them on and off, choose when to accept them. You have the power. It's up to you to do it.'

'What you seem to be telling me, Fionnula, is that it all comes down to trying really, really hard. Is that it? Is that your whole magical training spiel in a sentence? Because, believe me, I've tried really hard over the years, and it's still happened.'

I was getting angry, and frustrated, and fidgety. The seat belt was way too tight, and the heating was on full blast, and Fionnula was talking a crock of shite. It all added up to one irritable chick.

'No, you haven't tried, Lily. Not really. You've panicked, been scared, and retreated. Chosen the path of least resistance because you didn't know any better. Avoided touching people instead of learning to control it. Hidden from the visions instead of confronting them. But again it comes down to will – to focus. It won't be easy to start with, but it will get better with practice. When someone touches you, you need to summon up all your resolve, all your determination, and switch it off. Put up a barrier, a wall of willpower to hold them off. Visualise it, any way you please. Like you did to reach Gabriel. I won't be there to guide you, but I am sure you can still do it. Try now, with Carmel.'

Carmel silently stretched a hand forward between the two front seats, offering her fingers. I looked down at them, felt the familiar fear rise in my throat.

'Don't be afraid,' said Fionnula. 'That's what clouds your judgement, makes the visions worse. You need to stay calm, and channel everything into it.'

I stared at Carmel's fingers again. She was wriggling them up and down now. Hilarious.

'No,' I said. 'Not with her. Not with Carmel. I believe what you say, but I won't try it with her.'

The fingers gave a sad wave, then fell back, as though disappointed. I felt Fionnula's disapproval swell and fill the car; saw it in the tight line of her lips. Tough titty. I refused, absolutely refused, to be put in a position where I could see anything bad happen to Carmel. And in our current circumstances, the something-bad could be happening quite soon, and possibly related to me. No way, José.

'You should also know that you can use your power to see the past, Lily, like you did with me. If you choose. You can see everything that has gone in a person's life, if you pay attention to what you're doing.'

'How far back?' said Carmel, the first words she'd uttered since we'd set off. Other than 'oof', and that didn't count.

'To birth. Sometimes to before, to time in the womb.'

Yuck. That sounded pretty gross, and in most people's cases, would probably be boring as well. But Carmel . . . that would be different. She's spent years trying to find out who she is, where she comes from, what happened to her parents. Why her birth mother abandoned her. Could I really answer her questions with the touch of her hand?

I knew she'd be thinking exactly that right now, and I also knew that I couldn't risk it. Not yet.

'I'll do it for you when I can, Carmel. I promise. But not right now.'

'That's all right,' she said. 'I know you will. And I trust you to do it right, rather than some other people I could mention.'

Fionnula stiffened at the implied insult. Carmel was right. Fionnula could probably do it as well, but I didn't blame Carmel for not wanting her involved. I wasn't sure who I trusted right now either, apart from the foul-mouthed Scouse-Irish-Egyptian in the back seat.

'You should know something else,' said Fionnula. 'You can change things. The things you see in the visions. Nobody's fate is cast in stone, Lily. You can use them to help people, for good. For your own advantage. The visions give you information; it's up to you how you act on them.'

That one was too much of a mind fuck. Should I have spent the last two decades following people round warning them about their fate? Telling them to double-bag the condoms? Not to take that first hit from the cute girl with the dime bags in her pocket? Not to miss that smear test? I couldn't handle the thought of that. I'd be swamped by guilt, even though I knew it wasn't my fault. I locked it up in the 'things to consider later' box, and moved on.

I cast my mind back to last night – God, was it only last night? – and the way I'd found Gabriel. The images I'd used, the white walls and the empty mental spaces. It had been hard, but clearly not impossible. If what Fionnula said was true, I would be able to do that again. Summon up that level of concentration, and use it on command. The thought of being able to touch people made me feel light-headed. I didn't think I'd ever become one of life's huggers – too much water under the bridge for that – but to consider a life where I didn't have to fear it either was intoxicating. I'd be able to go shopping in summer without wearing seven layers of clothing; and dance at a gig without worrying about bumping into someone. And touch a man, other than a dead one. I'd be able to touch Gabriel . . . which would be helpful when I tried to throttle him.

I spent the rest of the journey practising concentrating and trying not to have a heart attack at Fionnula's driving. Both were very difficult.

By the time we arrived in Merrion Square, it was late afternoon. The autumn light was fading, and the greenery had toned down to a dull grey as the sun slid behind dark clouds. Street lights had flickered on, casting hazy golden circles of light, pooling on the tops of cars that all looked dark and shiny. The wind was up, and fliers that had been popped behind windscreen wipers by some entrepreneurial publicist were whirling around in small paper twisters.

I banged on Gabriel's front door, feeling my stomach clench with a mix of nerves and anger as I waited for someone to let me in. Goddess or not, nobody had thought to give me a key. That's men for you.

A few seconds passed until the door opened, and Connor stood there in front of us, buffed up and wearing a Converse T-shirt that made him look like a displaced surfer, with his blond hair and blue eyes.

'Goddess,' he said, bowing slightly. What a gent. 'We weren't expecting you.'

'Good,' I replied, using my backpack to shove past him in a way that could only be described as rude. Carmel came behind me, and I sensed her pause when she saw Connor, maybe giving him one of her full-on hundred-watt smiles. Glad to know she could still flirt. I presumed Fionnula followed, carrying her dinky Versace overnight bag, but I'd given up caring about that.

'Where's Gabriel?' I asked.

'Training, with Finn and Caemgen. We were awaiting the rise of the vampires, as they are handy to have in a battle.'

I just bet they were. Big, strong, immortal, with handy retractable fangs for all that throat ripping.

I could hear the sharp clash of swords, and the occasional muffled boom coming from downstairs in the basement. I traipsed down the stairs, and was faced with two doors. One, I knew, would lead to the gym. The other must be the training room. I shoved the door open, and the smell of sweat, testosterone and gunpowder told me I was right.

The room was vast – more of a hall – with one end partitioned off as some kind of firing range. Kevin, my floppy-haired fake barman, had been busy riddling human-shaped paper cut-outs with small black holes. Gabriel and Finn were sparring, using huge broad-bladed swords that, at least in Finn's vertically challenged case, were as long as a man. He seemed to have no problem holding his own, though, massively muscled arms hoisting the blade over his head.

He took advantage of my arrival and Gabriel's momentary distraction to stick the pointy end at Gabriel's throat. Now why didn't I think of that?

Chapter Twenty-Two

They all stopped, then turned to look at me. It probably wasn't a pretty sight. My hair was dry now, but had done the curly thing, a big red halo around my head. Make-up hadn't seemed relevant under the circumstances, and I was still wearing mud-splashed jeans, and a dark-green parka with fur round the hood. Very glamorous.

Apparently, I also looked a bit pissed off, as the smile fell from Gabriel's lips as soon as he saw the look on my face. I don't think he needed to mind-read, though, to work out what I was feeling.

'Tell them to leave,' I said. Again, so rude. Being the Goddess was turning out to be very bad for my manners. And I couldn't give a damn. I've spent my whole life trying to be polite, to fit in, to play by a complicated set of both society's rules and my own. I was sick of it. If they didn't leave, I'd scream at Gabriel in front of them, and see how Mor that made him look.

Gabriel gestured towards the door, and Finn and Kevin both left, giving me respectful nods as they passed. Maybe I looked a bit scary as well. Not a bad thing.

The door closed quietly behind them. I wondered briefly if they'd stay outside and listen, but decided they were too old school and obedient for that. Carmel, however, was probably rooting round for a glass to stick to her ear right now. I didn't care. What I had to say to this man was sincere, from the heart, and likely to damage the hearing of anyone within a ten-mile radius.

Gabriel was wearing sweat pants, dark grey, and his feet were bare. His chest was bare as well, but I blanked that out. If I was going to start using the incredible power of my mind (ha!), I'd start with that. I would no longer allow myself to be swayed by the sight of bare man-flesh, even if it was perfectly formed, rippled with muscle, and covered in freshly earned sweat.

'Put some clothes on,' I snapped. Best be on the safe side. He complied, pulling a black sweatshirt over his head, tousling the waves of his dark, damp hair. He wiped his face with a towel, and stood before me. Fully dressed. Calm. Collected. Giving every appearance of normality, or what passed for normality for him. I knew better. His eyes were a deep shade of violet, and the sensual curve of his lips was grim. I stared at him, staying quiet, focused. Forced my mind to calm, filled it with white space. Pushed my thoughts outwards, like a wire, threading its way towards him . . . and felt it. Just a tremor at first: anxiety, worry, fear that I'd found something out. Dread of what was coming. Resolve that he'd handle it – handle me – the arrogant bastard. The random thought that he loved my hair, and wanted to bury his face in it.

I pulled back. I didn't want to be in Gabriel's mind. Last time I'd done it, it had ended up giving me a bad case of the warm and fuzzies, and that really wasn't appropriate here.

'Lily,' he said. 'What's wrong?'

'You are,' I replied, my voice so quiet it surprised me. I'd intended to yell, but it didn't come out that way. 'You're wrong, Gabriel. About everything. I know now what you did. It wasn't just giving me to Coleen, was it? We've been through that. I understood it. I didn't like it, but I accepted it. But now I know there was more.'

'Like what?' he asked, his eyes staring into mine so intently, I thought he was trying to work some kind of mind control on me; trying to find out exactly what I knew so he wouldn't give too much away by accident.

'Stop playing games, Gabriel. We're way beyond that. I know what you did. You deliberately chose to leave me with these visions. You chose to leave me half-alive. You chose to let me grow up in isolation, scared of my own shadow. You didn't have to do it. It wasn't just to keep me safe. It was to keep me alone. To keep me away from everyone else around me, ready for you. Don't deny it, you manipulative bastard.'

He flinched slightly at the last sentence. My behaviour was obviously unbecoming in a goddess. Couldn't say that I cared.

He reached out as though to take my hand, saw the look on my face and backed off. He closed his eyes for a beat and when he opened them again they were a lighter shade of purple, hypnotic and intense – and sad.

'All right. I won't deny it. I did what you say I did. Fionnula had trained your sisters. And yes, I could have found a safe way for her to see you as well. But I didn't. You're right. I chose a different path for you.'

'Why?' I said, and this time it was a yell. I was full of pain, full of anger. Full of a sense of betrayal I couldn't quite understand. Apart from my father, this was the only man who had ever loved me, and he was forcing me to hate him. If this was love, I'd be better off without it.

'I sent you to Coleen to keep you safe. I sent the others with you to keep you safe. I watched you myself, to make sure. But you were the last one . . . the last chance to defeat Fintan. And the fate of the world is more important even than you, Lily.'

Huh. When he put it like that, it sounded sane. Reasonable. And yet, I still felt that hurt, deep inside me, like an axe to my abdomen.

He took my silence as an encouragement, and continued.

'Your sisters had parents. They had training. They had protection. And still Fintan found them and killed them. I was lucky to get you out alive, and I couldn't risk anything happening to you. Not just Fintan, but the other things that can happen in a human life. I couldn't risk you falling in love, or backpacking round Thailand, or getting married and having children. Taking up rally driving and getting killed in a crash. I couldn't risk you doing anything that would put you in danger, or allow you to become so entwined with your human life that you wouldn't leave it. You were the only one left, and I had to keep you the way you were. Believe me, I know what that cost you. And I'm sorry.'

This time he did take my hand: it was strong, solid, warm, and my fingers felt small inside his grip. I wanted to twine them into his, fall into his arms, allow myself to forgive him and feel safe.

Instead, I gathered my will around me, focused on putting up a barrier between us. I needed to prove to myself that I could hold someone's hand and not see their future. Especially his. I really didn't want to know his future, as it probably had a lot to do with mine. It seemed to work. All I felt was his hand, nothing more, nothing less. It was harder than I'd expected, but Fionnula had assured me it would get easier with practice.

I took some deep breaths, held the focus in place while returning to the conversation. If he had any indication of what I was doing he didn't show it, just looked mildly surprised that I was allowing him to touch me.

'You're sorry,' I said, finally.

'Yes. I am. Truly sorry,' he replied, holding my fingers tighter, pulling me towards him. I let him, and found myself leaning into his body, my head resting against a solid wall of chest, inhaling his scent. His thighs pressed against mine, and I felt his face in my hair, like he'd imagined it earlier.

He pulled it back, exposing my neck, kissed me softly on skin that had never been touched. It fizzed and tingled in response. My arms slipped around his waist, tentatively resting on the curve of his back. It felt wonderful. It would be so, so easy to give in to this. To relax, to allow myself to feel safe, desired. To stay in his arms for ever.

'And would you do it again?' I murmured, as his breath nuzzled my ear, sending a whisper of lust through my whole body.

He paused. I felt the muscles of his back stiffen beneath my touch.

'Yes, Lily. I would.'

His heartbeat thudded, and I felt it through the thin layer of his sweatshirt. Tears welled in my eyes, and I screwed up my lids until they disappeared.

I pulled away from him. Away from his warmth, and his strength, and his security. Because it was not enough. It was never going to be enough. He loved me, but he loved his duty more.

I didn't have time to analyse my feelings. Didn't have time to consider whether I was being a monumental arse to expect anything different. But I knew one thing: he would always choose his duty over me. I wasn't exactly experienced in the arena of loving relationships, but I did know that wasn't enough. Maybe I'd never fall in love. Maybe I'd never have a man truly love me. Maybe I wouldn't even survive the day. But neither would I settle for this.

His body sagged as I moved away, as though I was still there. There was a vague shifting around in the sweatpants that told me he'd been enjoying the moment as much as I had, and he had the grace to look marginally embarrassed about it. Good. If I could leave him in any discomfort, I was happy with that. The aftermath of an unwanted hard-on was hardly comparable to the life he'd thrown at me, but it was all I had right then.

'Again, Gabriel, I come back to one thing – you

were wrong. You might have thought you were keeping me safe with Coleen. You might have thought leaving me with my visions would keep me safe for you. But you were wrong. Because what they actually did was keep me safe from everyone, and everything. I don't love anybody. I've never loved anybody, not since my parents died. I haven't lived life. I haven't been involved in this precious world of yours. It's passed me by, all of it. All of the wonderful things you say you want me to save. And if you want me to love you? If that's part of your master plan? Then it was an even bigger mistake. You're fighting for love, for humanity, for free will. For people to be able to carry on living, loving, making their own mistakes. Don't you see that's exactly what you took away from me? I've never had any of it. And you know what? I'm not sure I even care about it.'

It was a good speech. I meant every word. So I left before I messed it up.

Chapter Twenty-Three

I trudged back up the stairs. Every step I took was an effort. I felt weary, defeated, battle-scarred. I felt as old as the Earth.

There was a familiar thrum in my pocket, and I scooped out my phone. All the texts and messages that had been sent over the past few days were landing. One from the Dormice, thanking me for the review and inviting me to their Halloween gig. Ha. That seemed unlikely. One from Big Bill, asking if I was interested in interviewing the city's most successful male Cher impersonator. 'Most successful' implying there was more than one, which was weird. And one from an unknown caller, asking me to phone the Liverpool General Hospital 'at my earliest convenience'.

I may have led a limited life, but even I know missed calls from hospitals are never a good thing. I fumbled a couple of times, got through, gave my name, and suffered through a minute and a half of muzak while I was transferred. A nurse answered, sending a shiver down my spine as she said the words 'Intensive Care Unit'.

I explained who I was, heard the tapping of buttons and the rustling of paper.

'Yes. Right. Miss McCain, we have a Coleen McCain in here. Your grandmother, I believe? You were listed as next of kin.'

'That's me. Is she all right?' I asked, feeling adrenaline zip through me. Of course she wasn't all right. Nobody goes to Intensive Care if they're all right. It's not a fun place.

'I'm afraid she's not, no. She had a slight fall, at the bingo, I believe, and was brought in with two broken ribs. Ordinarily that wouldn't be serious, but at her age, and in her poor health, it's caused some severe complications. In fact, it would probably be best if you came in as soon as you can . . . I'm sorry, but we're not sure there's anything more we can do for her.'

'What do you mean, her ill health?' I asked, confused. OK, so Coleen was skinny as a whippet and smoked forty a day, but she'd always seemed fit. Strong. Scarily so, in fact. The kind of woman that could take on a Cortina-full of hoodie-wearing ASBOs and send them running for their mamas.

'She hasn't told you? Mrs McCain has advanced-stage lung cancer. She was diagnosed six months ago, but has refused all treatment. We assumed you knew.'

I held on tight to the phone, scared I was going to drop it. Coleen had cancer. She was dying. And she'd never even told me. Jesus. How much more fucked up could my life get?

'OK. Thanks for letting me know. I'm away at the moment but I'll hopefully be there later tonight,' I said, closing down the call and leaning against the wall. I needed to catch my breath. I needed to think. To stay calm. To get the hell out of Dodge, and back to Coleen. She might be a nasty old bitch, but she was the only family I had, and she didn't deserve to die alone. Nobody did.

I made it up the rest of the stairs without stumbling or sliding back down on my arse, which counted as a major victory, and tried to make my face as normal as possible before I went into the living room.

Carmel was standing with Connor, feigning interest in the Celtic tattoos that were traced around his arms, and blatantly using them as an excuse to feel up his biceps. Fionnula was, predictably, eyebrow-deep in a glass of something red. The vampires were awake, and Luca was lounging across a sofa, taking up the whole length of it, his bare feet propped over one armrest, silky dark-blond hair trailing over the other.

He gave me a smile as bright as the North Star, and patted his lap. Leather-clad, obviously.

'Hello, beautiful lady!' he said, gesturing to his knees. 'Come sit with me – I promise not to bite!'

Any other time I might have been tempted. But not now. Right now, nothing would be tempting, apart from a real-life body swap with someone dull. Someone boring. Someone who wasn't me, or anybody I knew.

'Sorry, Luca. I'm all flirted out.'

'You break my heart, Lily. Some other time, perhaps?' he said, pretending he was crestfallen.

Maybe he was, but I doubted it, somehow. I nodded, tried to smile. He didn't buy it, I could see. He raised one eyebrow at me, a question all on its own, but I turned away. Didn't have time for that, or for anything, really.

'Carmel,' I said, interrupting her muscle patrol. 'I need to go to the loo.'

'Erm . . . fine. You know where it is,' she said, looking confused.

'But I'm a girl. And there are rules. I need another girl to go with me.'

Fionnula belched, and held up her hand. 'Count me out – Switzerland is busy getting drunk.'

Carmel got the message, reluctantly let go of Connor and accompanied me to the bathroom.

As soon as we were alone and the door shut, I started running both taps and flushed the toilet.

'What gives?' she said, watching as I created waterfalls all around the room.

'Gabriel. He has ears like Dumbo, and I don't want him listening in. Carmel, look, I've got to leave. And I need you to help me.'

169

'Of course,' she replied. 'Whatever you need. Mind if I ask why? And I take it your chat with lover boy didn't go well?'

I felt my face slide into misery, and couldn't stop it. I must be a heck of a shallow person. Coleen was lying almost dead in a hospital bed, and I was still playing wounded damsel about Gabriel. All together now: Gerra Grip, Girl.

'It went as well as it could, considering he's a lying, conniving piece of shit.'

'Oh,' she said, which was fair enough. Not much she could add, really.

'Anyway, I've just had a call from the hospital. It's Coleen. She's been in an accident. And she has cancer. And she's . . . well, she's dying, Carmel. I need to get back to her. Back to Liverpool.'

'Without the aforementioned lying, conniving piece of shit, you mean?'

I nodded.

'Will you be safe?' she asked, Champion instinct kicking in.

'Yes. Fintan promised he wouldn't send anyone after me, and so far he's been true to his word. Just stop Gabriel from following me. Stop all of them.'

'O-kay . . . but how do you propose I do that? They're all, like, superheroes and witches and mind-readers. I don't know how long I can hold them off.'

'Just try, enough to give me a head start. Buy me the time to get to the airport and get out of this place. Please. I need not to have to deal with too many barrels of shite at the same time. I need to get to Coleen, and not be distracted. I owe it to her to be there.'

Carmel frowned, and I could tell she was battling her inner demons, and trying to keep her trap shut. She hated Coleen with a passion. She wouldn't think I owed her anything. In fact, she'd probably go and do the Macarena on her grave.

'All right. I'll do my best. But be careful, and call me. If you don't, I'll dob you in.'

'Thank you,' I said. 'I mean it.' I did. It felt good to have someone on my side. Someone without a bigger agenda. Someone who put me first. Gratitude spread through me like warm coffee on a cold day, and I didn't know what else to say.

There was a pause, and she looked embarrassed, awkward. As though she'd caught me in the loo with a pregnancy test in my hands.

'Can I give you a hug?' she asked. 'You look like you need one. I know Coleen's all you've got. If that were my mum lying in there, I'd be in pieces.'

There was no comparison to be made between Coleen and Carmel's adoptive mum, Mrs O'Grady. Mrs O'Grady was fat and smiley and made soda bread and called all her kids 'feckin' idiots' as she whacked them round the head with a rolled-up copy of the *Gazette*. She was wonderful. Coleen was none of those things, but as Carmel said, she was all I had.

I drew myself up, deep breaths, white space, willpower on max . . . and hugged her. Briefly, and without a great deal of enthusiasm. But I did it. And nothing bad happened. A day for small triumphs to be savoured.

Carmel beamed at me.

'Now go,' she said. 'Crawl out the window, whatever. I'm going to tell them all you're so pissed off at Gabriel that you've gone to that male strip club in Temple Bar.'

'They won't believe that!' I said.

'OK, I'll tell them you've gone to the park to sit on the swings in the rain and sulk.'

Tragically, I had to admit they were far more likely to swallow that one. God, I really needed to get a life.

'Now scoot,' she said, turning off the taps.

I scooted.

Chapter Twenty-Four

Hospitals have a smell all of their own. A smell nowhere else would ever want.

I'd pushed my way through the cloud of smokers at the front of the building, some of them sitting in wheel-chairs or hoisting around drip stands or puffing away with oxygen tanks on their laps. It was enough to put you off cigarettes for life, and I say that as an occasional indulger. They should take pictures of people like that and stick them on the back of fag packets.

Inside, and on the ward, it hit me: that mix of bulk-produced cleaning products, overcooked vegetables and human misery. People wandered the corridors, phones glued to their ears, hollow-eyed and tired. It was all so fragile, so depressing. But I suppose you're never going to see the best of life on the ICU.

The nurse was über-glam, über-Scouse, all pointy black eyebrows and midnight hair and spray tan. She probably needed something to cheer her up, doing her job. She smiled and chatted as she showed me to Coleen's side room, her tone becoming hushed and respectful as we walked through the door.

I stopped, dead still. Coleen lay in her bed wearing a hospital gown that had been washed so many times the floral pattern had faded to a dull grey. It matched her hair, which was plastered to the sides of her thin face, trailing cobwebs over the pillowcase.

She had blankets tucked in at the top of her chest, and she lay perfectly still. There was a tube up her nose, and an oxygen supply hissed in the background. A drip flowed into one arm, the sticky tape puckering her skin, and the machines next to her beeped loud and red as they monitored her heartbeat. A swing table was pushed to one side, an untouched jug of water sitting on top of it with a dented plastic cup.

I knew all of this without even looking. I knew because I'd seen it all before. As a child at my parents' funeral, in my vision – the one I'd never forgotten.

There was a loud crash from outside, and both the nurse and I turned to see what was going on. Staff ran round in a commotion, a male nurse waving a broom handle and running backwards and forwards. He clattered into tables and chairs, swinging the brush like a staff, and I caught a glimpse of what looked like black wings beating and swooping in the air around his head.

'Don't worry,' said the nurse. 'It's just the crow.'

She said it like it was normal, instead of freakily surreal.

'It's been hanging round all day. Must have got in through an open window. We can't seem to catch it, and the poor thing keeps flying into this door and crash-landing.'

She patted me on the arm, left, and closed the door quietly behind her. It was weird, but then again, I was getting used to that.

A doctor had met me on the way in, corralling me into his tiny, cluttered office before I was allowed to see Coleen. He'd looked young, harassed and empty, his mousey-brown hair straggling across his head, which was going prematurely bald. Maybe he should consider getting a job stacking supermarket shelves. Maybe I should, too.

'I'm afraid the outlook isn't good,' he'd said, rifling through Coleen's file as he talked, as though reminding himself which patient he was talking about. 'Mrs McCain's cancer is at terminal stage, and one of the broken ribs nicked her left lung as well. She's having extreme difficulty breathing, and unless we take drastic measures, she won't be able to breathe at all.'

'What does that mean – drastic?' I'd asked.

'It means putting her on a ventilator, which can breathe for her. I realise you are next of kin, and that Mrs McCain has no living will. But she has been very insistent, throughout her illness, that she is to receive no treatment. In all honesty, the prognosis was gloomy even if she had accepted it, but she has always refused. I suppose the question we have to ask ourselves is whether she would want us to put her on a ventilator at all, or to let nature take its course.'

I almost smiled at the way he said 'we'. As though it were anything at all to do with him. As though he wouldn't end his shift, go home, and have a beer in front of the women's beach volleyball on Sky Sports. I'm not stupid – not all of the time, at least. I knew the decision was mine. That the decision I had to make was whether to keep Coleen alive, or let her die.

'Will she ever recover?' I'd said, already knowing the answer. I felt like he expected me to go through the motions.

'There's always a chance, but it's ninety-nine per cent certain she won't ever regain consciousness. Then it's just a matter of waiting. We can keep her on the machines, certainly, for as long as it takes. We can keep her out of pain. But no, she won't be able to communicate. She won't be the grandmother you knew.'

The grandmother I knew. Funny, that. He'd said it as though I'd miss her . . . and against the odds, I probably would.

'Anyway,' he'd said, tidying up his papers and straightening his specs. 'Maybe you should go and see her first. But before you leave, we should talk again. See what you decide.'

I'd nodded, played the good little girl, and been led here. To this small room, besieged by a crow, looking down at the only parent I've ever really known.

She looked tiny, shrivelled. Like one of those shrunken heads I've seen at a museum in Oxford. Her hands had been placed on top of the blankets, in a mockery of peaceful sleep. The skin was wrinkled, furrowed, so very, very old. Her fingers were yellowed with nicotine, and her nails cut short, stubby, clean.

I sat down on the hard plastic chair next to her. I'd had my whole life to prepare for this moment, and now it was here, I had no idea what to say, or what to do.

The only sound was the beeping of the machines, and the gentle ooze of oxygen. That, and Coleen's laboured breath, coming in slow, ragged bursts, like each one could be her last. There was a slight rattle in her chest each time, as though it was forcing its way through blocked drainpipes.

I should say something. Hold her hand. Be of some bloody use. If this was the last time I'd ever see her, it should mean something. But how do you condense a lifetime of shared history into a few moments? Especially when the shared history isn't exactly the stuff of Enid Blyton stories.

I focused, screwed up my eyes to help me blank out the background noises, and took hold of her hand. It was cold, freezing, despite the warmth of the room and the blankets she was wrapped in. Her skin felt like crinkled paper, wrapped loosely around the fragile bones of her fingers.

There was no jolt of energy, no fizzing behind my eyes. No vision of her future. Although I could guess what her future was already – it was only a matter of how quickly it came.

I gripped her tiny hand, and felt tears spill on to my cheeks. I'd never even felt them coming, and was almost shocked at how emotional I felt.

'Hi, Coleen,' I said. 'It's me, Lily. We're here in the hospital.'

I paused, trying to think of what else to say. In movies, they always show these moments as so perfect: the death-bed confessions of love and regret; the apologies and reunions and emotional highs. In reality, it felt odd – slightly embarrassing, even – having a one-way conversation with someone I knew probably couldn't hear me. If this really was my last chance to tell her how I felt, I was blowing it.

'I'm so sorry about all this, Coleen. And I can't believe you didn't tell me you were so ill. Why didn't you? I would have been there for you. I would have helped; you know I would. We've had our ups and downs, but you've been my only family for . . . well, most of my life. And you did your best, I'm sure.'

That sounded lame, even to my ears. But a heart-rending monologue seemed beyond my imagination, and it was all I could come up with. I stopped again, wondering how to phrase my next words, how to say goodbye, how to express how much I'd miss her.

Just as I was about to launch into my next line of plati-tudes, she grabbed my hand back, the tight, firm grip I knew so well. I was so shocked that I almost fell off my chair. Where did that come from? She was supposed to be unconscious. Was it some kind of muscle reflex, or could she actually hear me?

The grip tightened, and her blue-veined eyelids sud-denly snapped open. I may have made a sound like 'eek', because scarily it looked like something from a horror film. She stared up at me, the shine of her eyes glazed over with lack of oxygen.

'S'all right, girl,' she murmured, her voice low, gravelly, fighting to escape her chapped lips. 'I know you would. Didn't want to be here any more. Had enough of this bleed-ing world.'

She was talking in abbreviated sentences, rationing her energy. She paused, and I stared, wondering if she was going to black out again. She was taking so long between gasps of breath I started to think she was actually dead.

'Coleen?' I said. 'Nan?'

'Still here, love. Just about. Not long now. Wanted to see you first. Wanted to tell you something.'

'What was that, Nan?' I replied, stroking the parchment skin of her hand, trying to warm it up. Again that long pause as she rallied.

'Love you,' she said, dragging her other hand across the bedspread and placing it on top of mine.

I closed my eyes. The tears were pouring now, pooling in the hollow at the base of my neck. A sob started to work its way through me, so strong it jerked my whole body.

She loved me. The words I'd been desperate to hear my whole life. The words nobody had spoken to me since I was six years old. The words that had now reduced me to a mound of jelly on a plastic chair.

Why now? Why not earlier? Why not when I needed it? How different would our lives have been if she'd been able to express that when we'd first met? When I was lying alone and scared in the dark, telling myself fairy tales and imagining my daddy coming to the rescue? I'd cast Coleen as the evil witch in those, and she's always seemed happy to play the part.

Fuck. I didn't know what to say. I was so stunned, so moved.

In the end I went with the basics.

'I love you too, Nan,' I said, my words now as shuddery as hers. I had so many questions, so much I wanted to know from her, and there wouldn't be time. I knew there wouldn't.

'You'll be all right, girl,' she said. 'You were all right when you were Maura. You coped when you were Lily. You'll be all right now. Strong. You're strong. Better than me.'

I shook away tears and leaned forward to get closer.

Her words were quiet now, barely scraping out loud enough for me to hear.

'But I need you, Coleen – I don't know what's going to happen! I don't know what to do . . . what to choose.'

'You'll . . . do right. Always do. Sorry, Lily. Sorry. I was scared. Of them. The others. You. Didn't give you a chance.' Her grip tightened so much it actually hurt my fingers, and her eyes rolled wildly. I didn't know where she was getting the strength, but I suspected it was her last. 'Forgive me?' she wheezed.

'Yes!' I said quickly, in case she popped off before she heard it. 'I do. And everything's going to be OK.'

I don't know why I said that. It probably wasn't, and certainly not for her. But what did I really know? She could be headed for choirs of celestial angels, or an eternity sipping nectar from tulip cups. It might be OK. It could be.

She nodded, a barely there gesture from an exhausted body.

'Don't let them put me on those bloody machines,' she rasped. 'Let me go. Time to go now.'

I nodded back, unable to speak for the sobs and tears and snot. I was a mess, and absolutely no help to the dying woman in front of me. I felt desperate, and useless, like I wanted to climb into that bed with her and keep her warm and safe and alive. To share what life I had, and keep her with me.

There was a bang on the door, and a sliding noise as though something had scraped across it. I looked up, through the glass panel. Saw the crow, beating its wings against the pane.

'Let it in,' said Coleen. 'It's for me.'

I frowned at that one. Why would she want to let some crazed bird inside the room with us? Oxygen deprivation?

'Do it, Lily,' she urged in that ragged whisper. I did it. Deathbed détente or not, I was still conditioned to do what Coleen said, and when. As I pulled open the door, the crow swooped in, spread its iridescent black wings, and perched on top of the drip stand. Once there it seemed perfectly content, and started preening itself with its beak. It looked at me once, seemed to nod, and then ignored us both.

'I'm off now, girl,' said Coleen. 'Have a cuppa for me. Don't remember me bad, love. I'm sorry.'

She tried to smile, but the expression had never come easily to her. Her facial muscles had mainly been used for shouting and smoking, and it looked strained to see her try to form a proper grin. Especially under the circumstances.

'I won't,' I said. 'I love you, Nan. I wish you weren't leaving me.'

'Well, life's crap sometimes, Lil. You just need to gerra grip.'

And with that, she closed her eyes, and loosened her hold on my hand. She took one deep, rattling breath, sent it juddering through her body. The crow cawed over her, the sound magnified in the small, hushed room. The heart machine bleeped and blinked. The oxygen hissed, unneeded.

She was gone.

Chapter Twenty-Five

Afterwards, I walked. For miles. I had paperwork shoved in my backpack, and a million things to do. Next of kin meant responsibility. It meant organising a funeral, and registering the death, and speaking to utility companies. It meant clearing a house and taking clothes to the charity shop and throwing the junk that made up a human life into a skip. It meant too much.

So I walked. I stuck my iPod earphones in and walked, listening to the sad, soulful wailing of Jeff Buckley as I made my way through Liverpool town centre. It was late, or early, depending on your point of view, and the clubs were spilling their contents on to the damp city streets. It was the Saturday before Halloween, a massive party night in Scouseland: men were in Zorro masks with vampire teeth, girls were wearing flashing devil horns and not a lot else, despite the plunging temperatures. They all seemed drunk, happy, angry, spoiling for a fight or searching for sex. Alive, and hopeful, and full of energy beneath their fake blood and witch hats.

It was me who looked like the freak in this crowd, in my ordinary clothes and my boots, shoulders down, automatically trying to avoid contact as I passed through the jostling throngs.

Without even realising it, I'd made my way to the waterfront at the back of a south city dock. I knew it would be
quiet there. Apart from some new-build flats, a handful of
offices and a kids' play centre, there wasn't much around.
Not at night, at least. Nobody in their right mind came
down here at night, which made it just about perfect for
me.

I perched on the stone wall along the edge of the river,
legs dangling through the wrought-iron railing. The water
was flat and vast and black, swallowing up the tepid pools
of light cast by the lamps along the prom. There was a slow
drizzle seeping into my hair – and presumably the rest of
me – but I was too cold and too numb to feel it.

Across the water I could see the lights from houses built
close to the riverbank; imagined the people inside, living
their normal lives. Tried to imagine what it would be like
to worry about work and the next gas bill and what I'd be
wearing to town on a Saturday night. I couldn't. My life
had been so far removed from that for so long, I couldn't
even connect with it any more.

I knew I should phone Carmel, let her know I was all
right. But that was one more thing I couldn't do right now.
She'd be upset, sad, for me. She'd sympathise, but she
wouldn't understand. Coleen was gone, and she for one
would probably think the world a better place for it. But
for me, it was everything. A glimmer of love, of how things
could have been, then nothing. Just emptiness, and one old
lady left to bury. I'd never felt so alone in my entire life.

Very few people would miss Coleen, and that saddened me as much as anything. Her whole life had passed
by without any meaningful relationships other than the
messed-up one we'd shared. And suddenly, now that she
was gone, my head was filled with questions: what had
her life been like before I arrived and took it over? Why
had she never married? How did she get mixed up in all
this in the first place? So many questions – and no way to

ask her. I wasn't clear on the whole Otherworld thing, and how it related to the heaven and hell I'd grown up being told about, but somehow I couldn't imagine Coleen lounging in a cherry orchard sipping nectar. Not unless it came in nicotine flavour. She was gone, and I felt the finality of it like an anchor weighing me down.

Fionnula had told me I could change what I saw in my visions, that I could intercede, but this was one instance where I felt sure I couldn't have done anything differently. Even if I'd spilled, told her everything, she'd have just shrugged those bony shoulders of hers, lit up another Silk Cut, and said something like, 'We've all gorra go sometime, girl,' in her thick Liverpudlian twang.

No, I couldn't have changed a thing. Couldn't have saved her. Some goddess I was turning out to be.

The tune on my iPod came to an end, and I switched it off. Next up was some crazy-ass Irish rock that one of Carmel's brothers had put on there for me, and I wasn't really in a getting-jiggy-with-it kind of mood.

As I pulled the buds from my ears and started to wind up the wires, I sensed, rather than heard, somebody approaching me. I tensed up, realising how vulnerable I was. Sitting on the edge of a river, alone, in the dark, when a host of villains was out to get me. No weapons, no black belt in karate, no Champion. None of the cast members of *Finian's Rainbow*. Way to go, Lily.

I rooted round in my parka pocket and discovered my house keys. Hardly a thousand-watt taser, but all I had. I clenched them between my fisted fingers, like Coleen had always taught me to do when I was walking out after dark. I could always try to poke an eye out with them, and if that failed, throw the whole bunch at their head.

I stayed still, trying not to show that I'd heard them. Sensed them, whatever. Maybe, if they tried to sneak up, I'd at least have the element of surprise with my cunning eye-stab-key-throwing plan.

'It's only me, Lily, no need to worry.'

I knew the voice, but I'd never heard it out loud before. Usually, it was tugging away in the inner recesses of my mind, making me look like a mental patient as I tried not to respond in public. It was Fintan.

I looked up, couldn't make him out in the shadows and the rain. He scrambled down to my level and adopted the same pose, legs poking through the fence. Very short legs, I noticed.

He was dressed in an old-fashioned great coat, with dark-coloured velvet trim on the collar. The kind spivs used to wear in movies about World War II. His hair was slicked back, a glint of Brylcreem glistening in the moonlight, and he wore small, round, wire-framed specs. I'd seen him before. I knew I had.

I stayed silent as the computer in my brain whirred away, trying to match up this face with another one I'd come across. It was recent, I knew . . . but where had I seen him?

'Want a clue?' he asked, smiling across at me like we were chatting at a party, instead of hanging over the edge of a river that would kill us both if we slipped. Me, at least. He probably had wings, or a button he could press that turned his shoes into a speedboat. I'd just go splat and spend eternity with the fishes and an assortment of shopping trolleys.

I nodded. Yes, I wanted a clue. Maybe he could act it out like a game of charades; after all, we were having such jolly fun.

'Ireland's finest,' he said, making a sipping gesture with a pretend cup he 'held' in small, delicate hands. As he mimed drinking, it finally clicked into place: Bewley's. The morning after the night before.

'You're the man who said hello to me in the coffee shop,' I said. 'The one that Gabriel shunted me away from. The one that made him go all big.'

'Yes! How clever of you to remember, Lily. I'm – hush! – in disguise! Your Gabriel didn't quite recognise me – he's not as all-powerful as he likes to think he is – but he sensed something, didn't he? Created quite the scene, I seem to remember. He never did have much control, that one. Too lazy to learn; all instinct and no work ethic.'

Interesting. After everything I'd been expected to take in over the last few days, everything I'd been supposed to accept, Gabriel was apparently the one with the learning difficulties. I'd enjoy throwing that one back in his face. If we ever spoke again. I screwed up my eyes, anticipating a wash of pain at the thought, but there was nothing. Maybe there'd just been too much. Seeing Coleen die had finally filled me up past the maximum-level line. I felt numb, like those veteran soldiers who've seen all the horrors of the world and can't react to more. Lily McCain was officially closed to new pain business, it seemed. Which was good. I needed some time off.

'So . . . is this what you actually look like?' I asked. 'I was expecting something . . . more.'

'Well, when it comes to disguises, Lily, less *is* more. But no, I don't actually look like this. I hope to meet you in my proper form one day, and you can see for yourself. This is Larry. Larry Hoey. I'm playing it safe, and leaving my real body back in the Otherworld, where it will be kept nice and warm and happy. Not like poor Larry here. I borrowed him for the occasion.'

'What do you mean, borrowed him? Will you give him back?'

'Just that, borrowed. Until I'm sure of my status here, until I'm sure of *you*, Lily, I'll be keeping my distance . . . Can't be too careful in these tempestuous times, can you? Last thing I need is some rampaging High King in the grip of the green-eyed monster blundering in to spoil our chat. Anyway, Larry's a bit of a sad case, to be honest. Not married. No friends. Parents dead. Not even a dog to welcome him home at night. He'd just been made redundant from his job at an accounts firm when I found him. He was trying to kill himself. In fact, he was right on the edge of the Liffey, much like we are now, trying to pluck up the courage to jump in. I didn't let him.'

I felt a wave of sympathy for Larry rush over me, and could clearly picture him, in his dapper coat with his overly polished shoes, feeling so useless in this world he wanted to end it all. Life really sucks, a lot of the time.

'What did you do?' I asked, dragging myself away from the image. Now was not the time to get vacuumed into the suicidal mindset of a man I'd never even met.

'I took him over. Slipped into his body while he was distracted, worrying about whether it would hurt or not when he finally took the plunge. He wasn't fully committed, you see. Then I got him up and away, home for a nice bath and an early night. Called for a Chinese on the way.'

Fintan the Fearless, chowing down on some dim sum and a chicken chop suey. Strange but true.

'So . . . if you're in his body, where's he?'

'Oh, still in here, I suppose. I feel the odd fidget sometimes – a bit like I've got a fly up my nose, you know?'

He was so offhand, so casual, but the very thought of it made me squirm. The idea of being squashed inside your own body, unable to make yourself heard, make your will known, while someone else entirely walked round and used it. Yuck. Poor Larry. His life sucked more than most.

'Will you let him have it back when you've finished?' I said, realising I couldn't see his eyes behind the glasses. It was dark, and they were hidden in shadows and reflections. It unsettled me in some strange way, as though not seeing his eyes meant I couldn't see anything at all. Maybe it was for the best. I wouldn't want to see a glimpse of poor Larry in there and imagine him squealing like Jeff Goldblum at the end of *The Fly*.

'If it's still usable. Wear and tear, and all that. These human bodies don't last for ever, you know.'

He looked at my expression and gave me that creepy fake-jolly smile again.

'Well, he didn't want it anyway, did he? Don't think me heartless, Lily. I was doing him a favour. He wanted to die, but he didn't have the courage to do it. I was helping him out.'

I wasn't convinced. Many people probably have moments in their lives when they feel there's no point in carrying on. In fact, I was having one right now. But until they made that choice, until they decided, until they took that plunge from the side of the bridge, nobody should have the right to just swoop in and take it from them. That was wrong – wasn't it? Or had I been spending too much time around Gabriel, the man who talked a lot about the glory of choice but had taken all of mine away from me? I'd definitely been spending too much time with someone – because I was sitting here, next to a man I knew for a fact had wanted me dead, and the fear factor hadn't even kicked in. That was either very brave, or very stupid. The latter seemed most likely. I decided to make the most of my stupidity and ask a question that had been hovering round in my head like a bluebottle.

'What about my parents? How can you pretend to be a friend when you killed them, and my sisters, and that girl Lucy?'

'Ah. Well, friendship is a complicated thing, wouldn't you say, Lily? And that "girl" Lucy . . . well, she was no girl. She was a grown woman infected with Gabriel's ridiculously blinkered sense of duty. She changed her form, and off they drove for a jolly car ride. To start with, the car wreck felt like a victory, to be honest – they almost had me fooled. And all the time, poor little Lily was enjoying her second childhood in the loving arms of Coleen. And now she's gone too. Oops.'

'Life seems very cheap to you, Fintan,' I said after a pause. My voice sounded neutral to my own ears, like I was discussing my plans for tea, not a human life. Maybe that's exactly what Fintan was aiming for. He was testing me, pushing me, trying to find out how much I still cared. If I still cared at all.

Did I? It was an interesting question. And no, I didn't, right at that moment. I was finding it hard to care about my own fate, never mind the rest of kingdom come. Yet . . . poor Larry, a quiet voice inside me still murmured, unable to quite shake the thought of this sad, middle-aged man who thought his death would be worth more than his life.

'No. Not at all, Lily. I love life. But this . . . this isn't living. These *people*' – he said it with as much affection as I'd say 'slugs' – 'have taken this world, this life they were given, and destroyed it. Turned it into a constant battleground of greed. This isn't life. It's existence – a wounded animal still crawling through the dust, too stupid to realise it's already dead.'

I felt my eyes widen. Well, that told me. And at least he was honest, which is more than I could say for some.

I stayed quiet. There was too much to ponder. Too much to turn over in an already overstuffed head. I wanted him to go away and leave me alone, let me stare at the river for a little longer while I thought. I wanted to cling on to the last few words that Coleen had said to me, to try and erase years of bad memories with a few minutes of good. I'd promised her I would.

'Are you sad about Coleen, Lily?' he said, breaking the silence. I didn't even ask how he knew. Expect the unex-pected was my new mantra.

'Yes,' I replied. 'Yes, I am.'

I was sad. Sadder than I'd ever thought I was capable of being. Not only sad that she was gone, but sad about all the missed chances, the missed opportunities. The missed life that we could have shared. The other Lily I could have been; the other Coleen she never got to be.

'If you choose me, Lily, you won't feel like that any more. Nobody will ever need to feel like that any more. You've been to the Otherworld. You know what it's like, what it offers. Is it really worth the battle to save the Larrys of this realm? To save all those poor idiots out there, wriggling around like worms, looking for love? Fighting and cursing and deluding themselves that happiness is just around the corner? I know you're not like that, Lily. You're different. You see this world, this pathetic life, for what it really is. You know you'll never find joy or contentment here, in this realm, as it exists. But you can have everything you want if you choose me. And it's time to choose. I've been patient; I've respected your wishes; I've upheld your safety. But I can't wait for ever.'

As he said the words 'time to choose', I heard a resonant beat in my head, like the heavy tick-tock of a grandfather clock. I shook my face, cleared it away. It was a trick, and I recognised it now.

Fintan's tiny legs had stopped their playful swinging, the shiny shoes now resting back against the algae-covered dock wall. His voice had lost all pretence of jollity, and his face – Larry's face – had fallen into a blank expression. It looked like he was working hard to keep it that way, his nose occasionally twitching. Small fists were clenched so hard I could tell Larry's nails would be cutting crescents into his own palms. The moon was perfectly reflected in his glasses – two huge yellow orbs, still hiding his eyes. In the distance I heard a foghorn blaring its warning, and saw the far-off fuzzy glow of ships' lights further up the river.

'Choose, Lily. Choose me. Take what you want.'

It was with those last few words that I started to smell it: the soured-apple aroma that I associated with Eithne. Over-ripe fruit. Decadence. Indulgence. Something once sweet, now rotting. My nostrils flared, and I glanced around. No sign of her – it must be generic. The signature scent of the Fintna Faidh.

I don't know if it was the smell, the thought of poor Larry trapped inside his own body, scarring his own skin, or the rush of emotion I'd felt when Coleen died, but my stomach tightened with revulsion. How could I choose him, when the essence of his being made me feel nauseous? My tummy was clenching and cramping, and my throat was compulsively swallowing down my own saliva. I was awash with that awful feeling you get just before you vomit, when you fight to control it.

For all his attempts at camaraderie, for all his flattery, persuasion and honesty, this was how Fintan affected my body. How he affected me. And as I didn't have anyone else to trust right then, maybe I should listen to myself.

I might not want to choose Gabriel, but I could never choose Fintan either. Yes, he'd been fair. He'd been patient. He'd treated me a damned sight better than everyone else had, bar the occasional assassination attempt. But he was also . . . wrong. I felt it, deep in my bones, deep in my heart. Deeper than anything else I'd ever felt. It was like an old soul was living inside me and decided to speak: no.

I remembered so clearly the way that woman had felt, the woman trapped in the Otherworld, miserable when all around her were joyous. Wanting to go back to a home that was no more. And I remembered the way I felt when I sensed Gabriel's love, and when Coleen told me of hers. I was just starting out in this world, an infant in everything but body. I was still learning, still finding my way. Still discovering the depths of feeling I never knew I had, or was even capable of. Much of it had been bad. Painful, agonising. The last few hours had been torture.

And yet . . . I'd never felt more alive. I'd learned more about myself in the last few days than I had the previous twenty-six years. Life hadn't been safe; it hadn't been quiet.

It hadn't been any of the things I'd tried to make it before. But it was mine.

I wasn't Larry. I wasn't ready to take the plunge and leave this world. It still had so much to offer, so much I wanted to experience. And I knew, with a certainty that came straight from that old soul inside me, that nobody else should be forced to leave it either. I was going to say 'no' to Fintan. That didn't mean I was going to say 'yes' to Gabriel, but there was no way I could play a part in making this creature's ideal world a reality. Not at the loss of this one.

I swallowed, taking deep, damp breaths to calm my body. I looked around me: breath steaming in curls on the cold air; the lights twinkling upriver; car headlights beetling their way around the Wirral waterfront. Fog and wind and the remnants of someone's Big Mac meal rolling along the pathway. No, not at the loss of this one.

Once I'd made the decision, I knew it was right. I felt relieved, like a pressure cooker had switched off inside me. I felt certain, and sure, and suddenly scared. Very, very scared. As the cooker switched off, the reality kicked in: no matter how harmless he looked tucked away in Larry's ventriloquist's dummy body, Fintan was dangerous. And he wasn't going to be at all happy with me. I clenched my bundle of keys again, knowing even as I did that it was futile. If he wanted to hurt me, he could, no matter how pointy Mr Yale was. I'd fought for free will, and I had it – but this could well be the last decision I ever made.

'No, Fintan,' I said, bracing myself, fingers trembling around the keys. The spirit was strong, but the flesh was pathetically weak. 'No.'

'Why? You owe me an explanation!' he said, his tone so whiny, so petulant, I half expected him to stamp his feet against the dock wall, or cry with frustration, like a little kid getting told off for something he hadn't done.

'I owe you nothing, Fintan, but I will tell you this much – I cannot choose you, or play any part in your ambitions. I am Lily McCain. I am Maura Delaney. I know little of your world. But the spirit of Mabe is in me, and while it is, I cannot help you. For Mabe and for this world, I refuse your request, and will offer no succour to the Fintna Faidh as long as I live in this mortal realm.'

I didn't know where that little speech came from, or the formulaic language. But it flowed from somewhere deep inside, and it felt right. To me, at least. Even as I spoke the words, I felt my body almost shimmering with energy, like I'd just treated it to the world's most vitamin-packed fruit smoothie. I'd done the right thing, and something inside me was celebrating.

Fintan, however, was not. The smell of rotten apples intensified, gathered so strongly I could almost see it hovering around him like an aura, like colourless smoke. I heard a sharp, distinct pop and looked down. He'd snapped one of Larry's fingers in two, and it was slanted at a tragic angle. Another pop. The next finger went, bent out of all human recognition. Fintan felt nothing. I wondered if, somewhere inside him, Larry was screaming.

His teeth started grinding together, so loud it made me feel sick, harsh and relentless, building up in its intensity until it was all I could hear. The seconds ticked by like hours, passing to the sound of decaying dentistry and rain pelting into the river. I should make a run for it, I knew. Try to scarper while I still could. But that sudden shimmer of energy had burst through me and fled, and now, somehow, my legs were immobile. I felt paralysed, and couldn't so much as move my big toe.

Fintan was staring at me, hard, and I knew he was the reason I couldn't move. That somehow, without so much as lifting a broken finger, he had paralysed me. I tried again: nothing. I felt panic rising in my throat, a choking combination of fear and nausea. He was going to hurt me, and I couldn't even run, couldn't even try to protect myself. I told myself to calm down, that the anticipation of the pain was probably worse than the pain itself – but I knew it wasn't true.

He gazed at me, through those moon-orbed glasses, and smiled. Then his mouth puckered, and he started to whistle – 'Sitting on the Dock of the Bay'. He watched as I struggled against his control, thrashing around inside, cold sweat beading my forehead at the pointless effort. No matter what I told my body to do, it remained still and frozen in the dank night air; the only sign of me existing at all was the steamy puffs of panicked breath panting from my mouth.

Fintan watched, and he whistled. This, I was sure, was not what Otis had in mind.

'So be it, Lily McCain. The choice is made, and Mabe has spoken. Who am I to defy the Goddess?' he said quietly.

And with that, he put both hands behind my lower back, and shoved, as hard as he could. I felt my bottom sliding away from the ledge, away from the safety of the wall, my boots banging against the slimy brickwork. I slid down through the railing, banging my back on jagged shards of stone. Fintan laughed, a small, neat laugh, and suddenly I was free of the paralysis that had been holding me still.

As I felt life flow back into my arms, I reached up desperately, trying to grab hold of the wrought-iron railing even as I slid down, off the edge of the river wall. I managed to get a tenuous grip, fingers wrapped round the slick iron up to my knuckles and no further. I clung on, clutching the rain-slicked metal, my body dangling over the black water.

I panted, wriggled, tried to gain some purchase on the slippery river wall with my boots, trying to support my bodyweight with anything but just my fingers. My tired, battered fingers, ice-cold, nails broken, circulation gone, almost out of strength.

'I let you go, Lily,' he said, standing above me and looking down. The moon was behind him, casting him in dark shadow. 'As you're so keen on free will, I thought I'd let you enjoy one last choice. Now: will you join me?'

I looked down at the water, bleak and glassy and waiting. Then up at Fintan, with his fake face and borrowed body and mouth twisted into fury. I'd been wrong before. *This* was the last decision I'd ever make. It had better be a good one.

'No,' I murmured, exhaling the word on a desperate out-breath, too exhausted to say anything more. The effort of even that was too much. As I spoke, my left hand slipped from the railing. I flailed around, trying to find the energy to throw it back up, but I was empty. I was now clinging on with one hand only, and the strength was sapping from my fingers.

He leaned down, the hem of the great coat sloshing into a puddle. He stared at me, nose wrinkled slightly, as though both fascinated and repelled by what he saw. Then he edged forward and started to prise my fingers off the railing, one by one. He did it deliberately, slowly, and I saw at least one of them pop backwards so far it had to be broken. I didn't even feel the pain; I was concentrating so hard on clinging on with my last four fingers. Three fingers. Two. One.

I tried to heave myself upwards one last time, trying to get a grip on the railing, his legs, his hands, anything, but he moved too quickly, watching and smiling as gravity finally took me.

I screamed as I tumbled down, down into the darkness, arms and legs windmilling as I grasped thin air, looking for something to break my fall. My yells were drowned out by the foghorn, and swallowed into the night. I cartwheeled, then plummeted, choking for breath as I fell. I threw out a prayer – a prayer to God, the God I'd been raised to pray to. Please, please, don't let me die. Not here. Not like this.

I spiralled down, in a flapping turmoil of hair and coat, to the water. Cold air whooshed past my face, dragging the breath out of me. I slammed into the icy glass of the Mersey with a slap that cut through skin.

Black. Cold. Blood.

It was over.

Chapter Twenty-Six

'Extra cold or normal?' he said.

'What?' I replied.

'Your Guinness – how do you want it?'

'Um . . . extra cold, I suppose.'

The man nodded, and walked away. To the bar. The bar in heaven, I had to presume, working on the theory that I was dead. My last memory had been of that harsh slap of still river meeting flesh, crippling pain, and of seeing my own blood swirl above me as I sank, curlicues of rust in dark water. I remember looking up, seeing the moon shimmering and shaking above me through the ripples of the Mersey closing over my face. Then nothing. Until now. Until heaven.

I glanced around. Heaven looked strangely familiar. It looked a heck of a lot like the Cavern Club, in fact. A place where I had indeed consumed rather a lot of extra-cold Guinness over the years. This must be my happy place.

I was dry, warm, and sitting on a deckchair. A proper old-fashioned, wooden-framed deckchair with red-and-white striped canvas. The kind I was always scared of getting trapped in. A quick look at my hands told me the nails were still broken, blood encrusted in the cuticles, and that the finger that Fintan had popped out hadn't magically popped back in. It looked a lot worse than it felt, because it felt absolutely fine.

I craned my neck to look around, not wanting to risk trying to stand up out of the deckchair, which was a recipe for a falling-over disaster. There were a few wooden chairs, no tables. No DJ-pumped music, no stags and hens, no students, no musos with guitars over their backs . . . No tourists, either. It was the Cavern that I knew – but at the same time it wasn't. The brickwork was there, the arches and nooks and crannies, as well as a great big sign that said 'CAVERN' in capital letters, which was quite a strong clue. But it was darker, and dingier, and grimier. The floors shone with moisture, and the floor really needed a good clean. There was a pungent smell: sweat, disinfectant, and something that belonged in a toilet.

The place was packed, completely rammed full of hipsters, like a Sixties convention come to life. They were scenes I'd only ever seen before in black-and-white photos, but in reality it was even more vivid: the faint smell of sweat and cigarettes, the women with their bouffant hairdos and A-line skirts and little cardigans, men with sharp cuts and sharp suits. A sense of overwhelming excitement, the kind I'd felt before: hundreds of people crammed into a small space to see a great band. The common bond of loving something; of being a part of something. Of a 'scene' unfolding around you.

The man walked back over, the sardine-tin crowd parting to let him through. He placed the Guinness in my hand, and gracefully lowered himself into the deckchair next to mine. Nobody looked in our direction, or pushed or shoved to get past, or even seemed to notice us at all. It was like we simply didn't exist, which was odd as we were sitting smack bang in the middle of a very small room. In stripy wooden deckchairs.

He was average in every way: height, build – all normal.

Brown hair, blue eyes, a pleasant face. An appreciative smile at the first sip of Guinness.

'They don't really have Guinness here, especially not the extra-cold,' he said. 'That's a long way off. But I prefer it, so that's what we've got. How are you feeling? Ready for the show?'

'I'm feeling . . . a bit confused. Who are you? And where am I? And what show?'

He rolled his eyes, as though he was dealing with an awkward teenager, and made a suitable 'tsk tsk' sound between swigs.

'I think you know exactly where you are, Lily. Assuming you can read, anyway. As for the show – who do you think? I wouldn't bring you right here, right now, to see just any-body, would I?'

'I don't know. I have no idea what you'd do, as we've never met before. The last thing I remember is—'

'Unpleasant, I know. But you called me, and I came. Fintan, as ever, wasn't playing by the rules. I sent him off with a flea in his ear . . . well, a crow in his ear, actually, but that's another story. Now, settle back; the crowd's about to go nuts.'

I stared at him, with his neat hair and neat clothes and neat lines, talking gobbledegook. I called him? What on earth was he raving on about? I hadn't called anybody all day, which I really should have done – Carmel would be going insane by now. But it's difficult to work your mobile when you're clinging on to a railing, hanging over the Mersey, and facing certain death. Even the most dextrous of texters would struggle with that.

It was all very confusing, so I took the sensible option – drank some Guinness, and sat back to watch the show. I had no idea what was going on, but on the plus side, I wasn't in the river inhaling glugs of filthy water; I was dry, nobody was trying to kill me – yet – and I wasn't in any pain. In comparison to the last few days, that was a majorly good result. Heaven indeed.

The crowd started to thrum with energy so raw you could almost see it. In fact, I realised, I *could* see it – floating above their heads in little puffs of red and orange, like speech bubbles made of fire. It was as though someone had thrown a rainbow of paint down from the ceiling, and it stayed, hovering, inches from all that hairspray and Brylcreem, swirling with cigarette smoke.

The lights dimmed, and on they came. Four young men, all dressed in impossibly cool suits. White shirts, black ties, black waistcoats. Hair not quite moptop, so earlier days. The fans went wild, shoving themselves even closer to the tiny stage, which was overshadowed by the brickwork arch of the cellar. Some of the girls sat down at the front; others were perched in the side arches, looking on with wonder.

The Beatles. At a guess, '62 or '63. John and Paul at the front, John laughing and joshing with the audience. George behind them. Ringo on drums – so definitely after August '62, when he replaced Pete Best as the drummer. God, where does all this crap come from? Did I really need to know all this? No wonder I was easily befuddled: my brain is full of rubble.

The band started playing. A cover of 'Some Other Guy'. The fans going berserk. Then . . . 'Love Me Do'. They recorded it in '62, and like most people, I've heard it a million times. But nothing compared to this – to seeing them, young and raw and full of arrogant potential, strutting as much as the crowded stage would allow them to, buzzing from the adrenaline rush. I felt a small 'wow' slip from my lips as I watched. This was history, folks – live from the celestial deckchair. Who knew that heaven came in stereo? It certainly beat the Otherworld for the fun factor.

A few more songs, screaming from the crowd, energy poofing and floating and circling right up to the flaking brickwork of the cellar ceiling. The trademark group bow at the end. All of them leaning down, greeting the front row, Cheshire cat grins topping off the suits before they slinked off to the dressing rooms, leaving the room abuzz. Wow again. I sat back, took another drink. Said wow a couple of dozen more times.

'See that girl over there? The one with the red lipstick?' the man said, interrupting my quiet rapture. He was gesturing to a pretty young thing who was still holding the sides of her face with her hands, tears running in rivulets of mascara over her cheeks. I nodded.

'Go and say hello to her. Touch her hand. Or maybe lend her a tissue – she really needs to sort out that eye make-up . . .'

'No!' I replied, starting so suddenly I spilled my Guinness. I felt a cold blob land on my chest, spreading through the fabric of my long-sleeved T-shirt. 'I . . . I don't do things like that.'

'I know you don't, Lily. And I know why. But now is the time to trust me – don't block her out, just go and see what she's feeling right now. You don't need to see her future if you don't want to. You can control that; you know you can. Anyway, don't argue – do as you're told.'

I looked at him, ready to tell him where to stick his instructions. One pint of Guinness and I am most definitely not anybody's. Who was this mystery man to be bossing me around anyway? First Coleen, then Gabriel. I must come with an invisible sticker on my forehead that says: 'No will of own – all donations gratefully received.'

He smiled, and raised his eyebrows. A shimmer seemed to radiate from his body, like a sudden heat haze over a desert road, waves of distorted light surrounding his shoulders. His eyes shone, vivid and brilliant and glaring, chipped diamonds swirling together. He suddenly looked anything but average, and I realised that whoever I was sitting next to in that deckchair didn't usually look like a common or garden mid-twenties male. Nobody I ever met was actually what they seemed – you'd think I'd be used to it by now. I sniffed; there was no rotten apple smell, no cloying sense of death. Not Fintan again, in some other body, looking to kill me a second time. Just this bright, gleaming form, and eyes I found it impossible to look away from.

'You called me,' he said again, simply, the movement of his lips making the iridescent air around him whirl. I shook my head in confusion, and he paused, as though waiting for the penny to drop. Suddenly, it did. It dropped with the weight of a cartoon anvil right on top of my head.

Fintan had broken my fingers. I'd lost my grip. I was falling. Plunging downwards to the ice-cold surface of the water. And . . . I called him. Asked him to save me. Please, please, don't let me die, I'd thought. Not here. Not like this. I'd called him.

'God . . .' I muttered, not sure if it was a way of naming him, or simply an exclamation of wonder.

'Yep. Although your High King friend would call me the Overlord. I have many names, in many languages. You may have called me one thing; they may call me another. Names don't matter – and they're mainly cried out in times of desperation. This isn't one of those times, Lily. Look around you. Feel that energy. See it. This is a time of celebration and excitement, the joy of being human. Now close your mouth – I can see your tonsils – and go and talk to that girl.'

Still reeling, I stood up, without getting trapped in the canvas, which in itself was proof that God was indeed there, and working his miracles. I took one last glance at him, still shimmering, still shining, and walked away. For once I really was going to do as I was told. I could ask questions later.

I headed towards the girl he'd pointed out, and tapped her on the shoulder, tentatively. She whirled round, the sweet chemical smell of her perfume and hair lacquer floating in a cloud as she did. She smiled at me, so happy she was sobbing.

'Weren't they brilliant? I can't believe it! Everyone's say-ing it's their last time here . . .'

I nodded. They were, indeed, brilliant. Couldn't argue with that, especially when you knew what their future back catalogue would sound like.

I smiled back, and wondered what she was seeing as she grinned up at me – surely not a bedraggled girl from the future, wearing mud-spattered jeans and battered Doc Martens, red hair lying in thick chunks around her shoul-ders. I was so not rocking the Sixties look, but it didn't seem to bother her at all. She was high on life, and I was just another part of it.

I took a deep breath, inhaled more of her perfume, and reached out, taking hold of her hand. I tried to do what Fionnula had taught me, and control what I was seeing. I wanted to feel her emotions as they were right now, because they looked like fun. Not thirty years in the future, when her only son was killed in the Gulf War, or whatever. That might, I admitted to myself, have reflected a slightly negative attitude.

She gripped my fingers, and pulled me against her in a tight hug. Yes, she was that happy. The hugging com-plete strangers kind of happy that I'd witnessed before, but strangely enough had never been tempted by.

I was nestled into her bouff, and swamped with second-hand joy. Her name was Theresa Brady. She was nineteen years old, and worked in ladies accessories at George Henry Lee, the local department store. She was a little bit in love with Paul McCartney, who she'd snogged one time when she was fifteen, but she was even more in love with her fiancé, Brian. In fact . . . she was pregnant by him. And terrified of telling her mum. Even though Brian had said they could bring the wedding forward, do it before she was showing. Even though he'd said he'd stand by her.

Theresa's emotions cut through me: anxiety, fatigue, love, hope, and the sheer unadulterated thrill of being in the thick of all this – here, tonight. Of seeing this band, on this stage; of having this last wild memory to share with her unborn child. Of being part of something so special.

I could feel the baby too, heartbeat throbbing away in her tummy, high on amniotic fluid and the motion of its mother's body as she jigged around, holding on to me. That was too freaky for words, so I pulled back, concentrated on Theresa, and the present.

The present was awe-inspiring. The present was all joy and hope and just a nag of uncertainty. Theresa Brady, on this one night she'd never forget, was experiencing emotions I'd never even felt, and they were wonderful – even if I was only borrowing them for a few minutes. But what about her future? What happened next for Theresa and Brian and their baby? There's a reason I never usually do this kind of thing, and I was probably about to be reminded of that – but I had to try.

I lifted some of the white cloud I'd been using to guard myself, let it fade slightly, and nudged forward, dropping control. With a near-physical whoosh, it happened: Theresa's future life, running through my mind like a movie montage on fast forward. The wedding – her not showing, as promised – and Brian, suited and booted and beaming. Mrs Brady senior looking on, a slight twist to her lips, thinking that her daughter had blotted her copy book but not to mind, worse things had happened at sea.

The baby – a boy. Colin. Followed by another boy, and finally a girl. The mundane happiness of an ordinary life: school gates and Nativity plays and Holy Communions and teenage sulks. The dark cloud of a stillbirth, and a brief unsatisfactory affair with a man from work who reminded her of the bloke from *The Sweeney*. The death of Brian, after a lifetime of smoking and drinking, and the long trek to adjusting to life without him. Grandchildren – lots of them – and aching joints and a lump removed and nights filled with telly and bingo and TV dinners.

No lottery wins, and no huge tragedies, just normality. It was . . . nice. It was full. And even more pleasantly, there was no nasty ending – which meant that Theresa Brady, nineteen years old and high on life, was still out there somewhere. Still living, still loving. Still remembering this one very special night.

I dragged myself away, still feeling woozy with her excitement. Like I'd been inhaling someone else's spliff. Adrenaline rushed through me, the sheer force of Theresa's happiness becoming my own. I turned around, looking for the Man – that definitely needed capitalising now – ready to give him a super-thrilled thumbs up, in honour of McCartney's traditional gesture.

As I turned, I started to tingle all over; the sounds around me became blurred and fuzzy through my ears, and my vision clouded. Uh-oh. Fally-down time again. I felt my body crumple, and hoped I wouldn't get trampled to death beneath a crowd of stampeding Beatlemaniacs. Better than my last two deaths – fake car crash and death plunge – but not ideal.

I woke up back in my deckchair. The Man – no longer shimmering, just back to being normal old God, Overlord, whatever – was next to me. I rubbed my eyes, feeling like I always did after a see-'n'-swoon session: like I'd woken up from an unpleasantly long sleep.

'It's all right,' he said. 'I caught you. I'll always catch you, Lily. And I got you an extra pint in as well.'

Sure enough, a fresh glass was waiting at my feet, the glass sweating in the heat. Right next to my backpack, which I'd assumed was gone for ever.

'How was that?' he asked. 'Did you like Theresa? I always had a soft spot for her . . .'

I reached down for the glass. Gulped down half a pint in one go.

'Are you telling me you know all about her?' I said, wiping my Guinness tash off my lip to distract myself from the craziness of the whole conversation. 'About everyone? I mean . . . how can you? There are so many of us!'

'The very hairs on your head are all numbered, Lily. Don't you remember that? Yes, everything. About every-one. Especially you. You're extra special.'

I stayed silent and drank. There was nothing I could pos-sibly say that would sound remotely close to 'intelligent'. I took in what he'd just said, and couldn't quite shake the ridiculous image of God sitting at a computer station, fill-ing in the world's largest-known spreadsheet. Excel to the max.

There was a ripple through the crowd, and an extra-loud hum of excited chatter. The little puffs of energy in the air started to swirl, creating mini tornadoes just beneath the ceiling. Something was happening. I craned my neck to see what the fuss was about, as people thronged around a spot off to the left.

'Ah,' said the Man. 'I wouldn't advise you go and touch his hand, to be honest . . .'

I looked again. John Lennon had emerged from the dress-ing rooms, and was talking to his fans. More handsome in real life, with his equine face and waistcoat swinging open. Laughing – he laughed like the world was at his feet – which it was, right then. No. Indeed. I was in no rush to go and meet the living legend – I didn't need psychic powers to know what his future held, and it wasn't head-ing anywhere nice.

'Right,' said the Man, bringing my attention back to the here and now. Or the then and there, I wasn't quite sure. I still thought there was a strong possibility I was dead, or at the very least in a mind-altering, coma-based alternate reality. 'We have some more bands to see,' he continued, 'and you have some more people to meet.'

Over the next hour, the Cavern swirled and changed around me, flying through the decades and surviv-ing closures, bankruptcies, demolitions and rebuilding.

But, ultimately, not changing at all. We remained in a small, cosy hole beneath the ground, brick arches winging over our heads, and musical history appearing before our eyes. They were all stars who had actually appeared at the club during its history, which was a pretty impressive list.

Soul singer Wilson Pickett. Queen. Elton John. The Who. The Rolling Stones. A brilliantly sneering Liam Gallagher in Oasis. And even some I'd been to see first time round, and had very different memories of: Bo Diddley, Paul McCartney as a solo artist, the Arctic Monkeys.

I set aside the mysteries of life to just enjoy the experience. After all, it was the best gig ever in the history of the universe. My life has been pretty crappy in a lot of respects – but really, how many people can say they've seen Mick Jagger, Freddie Mercury, Chuck Berry, Rod Stewart and Stevie Wonder all on the same night? Not many, I reckon.

All the time, the fashions were changing around us: from beehives and Brylcreem to bad afros and hippy hair; from sharp suits to bell-bottom jeans and Afghan coats, right up to the current indie chic of skinny pants and Converse trainers and zipped-up puffa jackets. The smells changed too: less ciggie smoke, less eau de drainage, and a lot more booze.

After each show, I was asked to follow the same routine – find someone in the crowd, and connect with them. I saw so much. I felt so much. Some of it sad, some of it tragic, but most of it wonderful. Joyous. Long lives, well lived. Bright lights shining the most vividly on that one night, in that one place. Sex and love and hope and sheer excitement all blending in with the sounds and the smells and the sights. Gigs and hen nights and stag dos and birthday parties and good old-fashioned Saturday nights out on the town.

By the end of it, I was dazed. Filled to the brim with other people's emotions. High as a kite, in fact.

I'd touched so many people – seen so much about them. And survived it all, bar a few swoons. I'd crammed in more human contact in one evening than I've had the rest of my life, and I was giddy. So giddy that when the final band came on stage, I was ready to rock.

'This,' said the Man, 'is a special treat for you. They never actually played here, but I thought it would end the night well. But before we start – and before you go off and snog some random student, you're buzzing so much – what have you learned? Sit down, and tell me.'

I didn't want to sit down. I didn't want to discuss what I'd learned. I was flying, and I wanted to spread my wings. I wanted to dance, and jump up and down, and sing out loud, and laugh with strangers, and yes, snog random students. This was all stuff I'd never done before, and I was starting to see why it was so popular.

But I looked at the Man. Remembered he could shimmer, and that he had eyes like diamonds. Remembered that he'd caught me – said he'd always catch me – and that he had counted all the hairs on my head.

I sat down.

'I've learned . . . that it's not all about pain. That I've never given pleasure a chance. That most of these people will live happy lives, even if they don't appreciate how lucky they are to be ordinary. I've learned that being alive is . . . wonderful. Joyous. Exciting.'

'And what else?' he prompted.

'That Freddie Mercury used to wear really tight trousers?'

'Yes. That. But what else?'

I sighed, drew my arms around myself. I was hot, sweating from the crowds and the music and the dancing.

'I've learned that I could . . . I suppose . . . feel all of those things myself, one day. If I let myself try. And if I work hard. And if I eat all my greens. Happy now?'

The Man smiled, and I was swamped with a feeling of pure love. I closed my eyes and savoured it, tucked it away to bring back out on bad days. And there would, I was sure, be plenty of those on the road ahead – but at least now I *saw* a road ahead. I saw a future. I saw potential, for me and for everyone else. A future that didn't only include hurt and pain and death. It's amazing what a good night out can do for a girl.

The lights dimmed, and a moody-looking indie crowd started to sway and chatter. Hooded jackets, baggy jeans, T-shirts with smiley faces on them.

The Man stood up, and gestured for me to do the same. The band came on. The bloody Stone Roses. The best gig ever had just become perfect. I really wished Carmel was there.

A distinctive opening drum beat. Guitars kicking in. Ian Brown's offhand vocals.

'I Am the Resurrection'.

Chapter Twenty-Seven

Nobody warns you about your sense of smell. When you lose someone – when you become part of that happy little club, 'the bereaved' – you are swamped with a mass of information: how to register a death; how to organise a funeral; how to contact a counselling service.

What they should really be doing is telling you stuff that saves your sanity. Things like: 'Erase all your voicemail messages, as hearing them again will make you sob up a lung'; and: 'Empty their bin right away, or you'll see their discarded fag packets and tea bags and imagine they're still there.' That kind of thing. In fact, I might do it myself, get it printed up into booklets: self-help for the apprentice griever. It could be a hit in hospices around the world.

In my case, it was the smells that got me. I'd let myself into Coleen's little terraced house late at night. My newfound friend had dropped me off in a cab, while the street was silent and empty and still. I'd looked around – rows and rows of terraces, all the same. Close-packed cars and wonky lights shining from wonky street lamps. Litter in the gutters, cats on the prowl. Just another night in Anfield.

Except this night, I was letting myself into a house that would be for ever different. For ever changed. Just like me.

As soon as I stepped foot into the hallway, my nostrils flared. I'm sure for some people, returning to their childhood home brings a rush of happiness, or at least a sense of security. Memories of good times shared, and love doled out with the cornflakes. Not so for me – there was no happiness here, despite Coleen's deathbed proclamations. Every single time I'd opened this door, during my entire life, I'd done so with a sense of dread, not anticipation – and being told you were loved seconds before someone took their last breath couldn't change that. At least not this fast.

But there were still memories; way too many of them, in fact. You can't live with someone for most of your life without storing them up, hoarding them in your mind like unwanted shoes shoved to the back of the wardrobe.

Cigarette smoke, that's what came first. The place always reeked of it, which wasn't surprising as Coleen had chugged her way through forty a day, every day, since I'd met her. She'd always tried to chase away the smell of the ciggies with air fresheners, and that was there too: the fake floral smell of a plug-in. There was one in every spare socket, and she kept the refills in little stacks in the cupboard under the sink. Tiny cardboard boxes promising Essence of the Rose and Garden of Eden. As though collecting them was her hobby.

I walked through into the living room, with its old-fashioned video player and an antique telly – the kind with the fat back. She'd never moved into the realm of the flat screen, or even the DVD. As long as she could record *Casualty* to watch after the bingo, she was happy. Ish.

The kitchen was tiny, built as an added extension to the original two-up, two-down design. It was in there that the smells really kicked in. Even more cigarette smoke, as this was her lair of choice, the place she would while away her hours. A scorched scent, which I realised came from a kettle left to boil without enough water. She only ever put in enough for one cup – stingy, even with the stuff that flowed freely from a tap. A big mug with 'Best Nan Ever' on it was next to the kettle.

I'd bought it for her on a school trip to Chester Zoo. It was patently untrue, but lots of the other kids had been buying them for their parents, so I'd felt obliged. I was only little – part of me was probably hoping that if I said it, it might come true.

She never said thank you – that wasn't in her vocabulary – but she hadn't thrown it away either, which I'd half expected. In fact, it had been given something of a starring role in the kitchen – as her tea bag mug. Each time she made a cup, she'd lob the old bag in there, wait till it was full, then put them all in the bin. There were about five in there now, the once-white insides of the mug stained deep brown from years of abuse.

The ashtray was still on the table, full as usual. One of her crossword magazines had been left folded open nearby, a pen lying on top of it. I sat down and picked up the magazine. She'd been struggling on seven across. So was I, so I put it back down. Looked around. At the pen, the mug, the kettle, the ashtray. All signs of a life very much interrupted. I've heard people say this before, so I know it's not a startlingly original thought, but it really did feel like she'd just popped out to the shops. Maybe to buy a plug-in, or something.

She could be walking back in at any minute, bustling and scowling and moaning. Emptying her carrier bag, then shoving it into the tiny drawer next to the sink that was already full to bursting with other carrier bags. Making a cuppa, lighting a fag. Giving me a dirty look for being in the way, or possibly for existing at all.

I simply couldn't imagine this house without her in it. For all her faults, she'd been a permanent feature in my life. Like malaria – deeply unpleasant, but always there. For years, we'd sat in this kitchen together, me passive smoking, Coleen doing her puzzles. The kettle boiling and filling the room with steam. The clunks and clicks and glugs of fridge door opening, milk being poured, spoon hitting china. Beans on toast for dinner. Crumpets for breakfast. Heinz soup in cans. A Swiss roll for high days and holidays. Tea, fags, and stodge. If they did an autopsy, that's what they'd find flowing through her veins.

I flicked on the radio – a late-night chat show – and looked in the fridge. It smelled sour, which wasn't a surprise. She'd not been at her best for the last couple of days, what with being in Intensive Care and all. Contents: milk, butter, and two slices of ham curling pink and fetid in its already-opened plastic wrapper. One jar of piccalilli, the metal screw-top lid twisted down tight.

The sight of it made me feel unbelievably sad – not for myself, for once, but for her. This had been her life. This tiny room, with a sandwich for one, using a solitary tea bag at a time. Measuring out her life in fags and brews, constantly scared. Constantly looking over her shoulder, closing herself off from emotion, in case it jumped up and bit her on the arse.

God, we were two of a kind, really. I've always blamed Coleen for the way I am, but, I now realised, it was my fault – in part, at least – that she'd ended up like that. She'd told me in hospital that she was scared of 'them' – but also that she was scared of me. Me, a little girl. Wee orphan Annie, dumped on her doorstep. Of all the big bad things I'd learned over the last few days, this felt the biggest and the baddest – not that I was a goddess in human form, or that I was destined to have a baby with a man I'd just met, but the truth about Coleen. And me. And the 'us' that never was.

I started cleaning the fridge, just for the sake of something to do with my hands. Spray, scrub, rinse, over and over. Then the surfaces – spray, scrub, rinse. Then the tabletop. Then the window ledge. Spray, scrub, rinse. A fine old ditty.

I realised my fingers were hurting, but carried on anyway. I welcomed a bit of physical pain. It distracted me
from the confusion of missing someone I'd been halfway
to hating.

When the kitchen was spic and span, I went and flicked
on the heating, adjusting the thermostat to high. As ever,
it was freezing in here, so cold I could see breath clouds
every time I exhaled.

'Sorry, Coleen,' I mumbled, knowing that if she was
watching me from on high (something I should really have
asked while I was in the Cavern, instead of getting my
party on), she'd be bloody seething. I didn't even have a
hat and scarf on, for Christ's sake, and I was going all out
on the gas bill.

I wandered through the house to the stairs, drew a deep
breath, and went up. My own room held nothing but horror for me: those long-ago memories of the night I arrived,
left to shiver and shake and sob in a tiny bed in a cold, dark
room. Crying for my mummy and daddy, and scared of the
wicked witch downstairs. Nothing much changed over the
years – apart from the crying. I gave up on that pretty soon,
when I realised it did no good. Nobody was coming to help
me, and the wicked witch downstairs didn't care if I cried
so hard my eyes fell out. 'Cry more, pee less,' as she'd once
said in a particularly charitable moment.

I'd never been able to figure out why, if she was my
mummy or daddy's mummy – like grandparents were supposed to be – she was so horrible to me. Why she seemed
to hate me so much. Why she was nothing like them at all.
That bedroom – and all the lonely nights I'd spent in it –
had never provided me with anything like an answer.

So I left the door closed, and moved on. I paused at the
bathroom, and my nose betrayed me again at the lingering smell of Radox bath salts. It was as close as she got
to a luxury: a soak in the bath at the end of a long hard
day smoking and complaining. Obviously being that

mean – and, I now knew, that frightened – took it out of a woman. She'd go in, lock the door even though there was only me in the house, and stay there for an hour, topping up the hot water every few minutes. I wondered now what she thought of, while she lay there in an avocado-coloured bath suite, surrounded by steam that billowed in the always-frigid air.

I'd assumed at the time she was indulging in fantasies about torturing kittens, or hunting down endangered species on the Galapagos Islands with a blunderbuss. Now, I suspected, she'd indulged in other fantasies. Perhaps one where she'd been allowed her own life; where she'd married and had kids and held down a little job at Iceland. Coleen, unlike most, probably appreciated the value of a normal, mundane life. Because despite appearances – the fags, the radio, the little terraced house – her life had been anything but mundane.

Yes, she had been a miserable old hag. And most likely she always would have been, no matter what had happened. But she'd also been a miserable old hag who was terrified. And, of course, who'd said she'd always loved me.

Hmmm. Much as I tried that coat on for size, it never seemed to quite fit.

I went into her bedroom – the only room where she didn't smoke, and a place I'd not been allowed on pain of a sovereign ring to the side of the head. Obviously – being a child – I'd snuck in there on a few occasions, knowing she'd batter me if I was caught. Kids will do these things. I was always very disappointed at what I found. No torture chamber. No clothes racks full of ball gowns. Not even a naughty book on the bedside cabinet.

It was just a room. A room with hideous floral wallpaper that hadn't been touched since the Seventies, and a big, bulky, dark-wood wardrobe that might now be classed as vintage but was actually just plain ugly. A view from the narrow window into the small backyard. A double bed which, as far as I knew, only ever had one occupant. And, bizarrely, a huge stuffed lion in the corner: big enough to sit on, it looked ancient and well used, missing one eye and part of its nose. She'd never let me play with it, and I'd only ever seen it during illicit smash-and-grab visits, but I'd always wondered if it had been hers as a child, impossible as it was to imagine her as a child.

I sat on the bed, suddenly exhausted – must be watching my nan die, nearly following suit myself, and my mammoth night out with the ultimate deity. The five pints of Guinness probably hadn't helped, either. It felt like years since I'd had normal food in normal company followed by a normal night's sleep in my own bed – but, in reality, it had only been a few days. Just . . . very busy ones.

The bed squeaked and sagged down on one side, and I saw the indentation on the pillow where Coleen had laid her head for all those years. Had she read before she fell asleep? Done her crossword? Said her prayers? I had no idea at all.

There was a dusty glass of half-drunk water on her cabinet, along with a box of tissues and a packet of Rennies. Standard-issue night-time fare for women of her age, I suspected. I could see a solitary silver-grey hair shining on the pillow, and found myself leaning over to pick it off. It looked almost magical – a last remnant of the sadly departed.

As I leaned down, I smelled her on the pillow. Her shampoo, her bath salts, her cigarettes. Her. All of her. Years' worth of her.

I lay down on the bed, picked up the pillow and hugged it to me, clinging to it while I cried. This is going to sound weird – in fact, this *is* weird – but for a few minutes there, that pillow actually became Coleen. Like some freaky transubstantiation shit had occurred, and that pouffy, squishy collection of fake duck down and cotton really did turn into her. The actual physical woman. Except, you know, rectangular and made of fabric.

It's hard to explain how or why we react like we do in these situations, but that's what happened. Maybe it was the smell and that single, shining hair, or the sight of the neglected old stuffed lion, but something made me think that Coleen was there with me once more. In the form of a pillow.

So I did what Coleen would never have let me do in actual real life, not while she had strength left to fight me off: I hugged her and squeezed her and cuddled her and cried all over her. I told her I loved her, and I kissed her, and I rested my head on her and I blubbered and I howled.

And you know what? She didn't mind. She was a lot more compliant – not to mention comfortable – in pillow form.

Seeing everything I'd seen tonight – touching all those lives, experiencing all those joys – had made me even more appreciative of what I'd never had. And what Coleen – poor, sad, lonely, frightened, indigestion-riddled Coleen – had never had, either. Her whole life had been wasted, unless you counted keeping me alive for the last two decades. Gabriel would see that as all that mattered – as a victory – but I couldn't feel that way. She'd missed out. I'd missed out. And maybe, if I'd done to her what I was doing to this pillow, I might have found a way to break through her fear to the woman who lurked inside. It was when I was busily shedding snot and tears all over my fake, far-more-affectionate nan that I heard a noise on the stairs. A creak, which meant someone had trodden on the fourth step up.

There was someone in the house.

Chapter Twenty-Eight

I jumped up from the bed. The Overlord had warned me during the cab ride that I needed to be careful, that Fintan, cheated of his prize and chased away, would now have declared all-out war. The place could be crawling with men in black, all looking to kill me – and here I was, stuck on my own in an empty house in Anfield. No High King. No warrior slaves ready to use their sword arms. Not even Carmel and a plant pot. He'd also told me that he'd be sending a protector – but there was no sign of this mythical being right now, when I needed it most.

There was nothing pointy or lethal-looking in the room, and my own fighting skills were about as much use as the stuffed lion. The very, very large stuffed lion . . . I ran over, grabbed it, and climbed into the cavernous wardrobe, pulling Leo over me. The thing was huge. If I huddled in a corner, on top of the shoes, it would just about cover me.

OK, I admit it. Not the most brilliant of battle plans – but it was all I had right then. At some point, assuming I survived the night, I needed to learn how to look after myself. To fight, to run faster, even to use the power of my mind to protect myself better. Fionnula used spells to enclose her land, and I'd seen Gabriel use magic to cause rockfalls. Maybe I had that in me too. It had to be better than hiding and quaking and waiting for something to happen. It was going to be hard to protect the fate of the whole world if I couldn't even protect my own.

But that was for the future – and tomorrow, as everyone knows, is another day. Right then, I had nothing. Apart from the ability to stay very quiet, and hide beneath a giant cuddly toy, pondering how rubbish I was.

I held my breath and waited, hearing the door to my old bedroom open. A pause, then it was quietly closed again. The bathroom was next, and the sound of the airing cupboard door being swung to and fro, the slight swoosh of the shower curtain being pushed aside. Whoever was out there was searching for something. Probably me.

I realised I was still holding my breath, and let out a long, slow, hopefully quiet stream of air. I was sweating, through a combination of the fear and the heating and being crushed by the lion. My heart was building up to a full-on cardiac, pounding so hard I was convinced it could be heard outside in the street. The sharp end of one of Coleen's shoes was poking into my backside, and all I could see was one tiny chink of light gleaming through the keyhole. This, I decided, was most definitely not a dignified way to spend your last minutes of mortality.

The slight creak of Coleen's bedroom door opening. Quiet footsteps, getting closer. A small silence, as presumably they stopped, and looked around. I remembered I'd left my phone and keys on top of the bedside cabinet, and tried not to swear out loud. A rustle on the bed, the metallic clinking of my key chain being moved around. I'd been rumbled.

Footsteps again, now so close I expected my heart to explode with fear. I felt my chest rising and falling in a panicky pant as I sucked in tiny gulps of musty mothballed air. Not enough oxygen; my lungs were screeching, as though I was about to have my first ever asthma attack.

My forehead beaded with sweat, my fists were clenched

into balls, and my throat was so parched I couldn't even have swallowed my own non-existent spit. Please, please, just walk on, I thought. Decide I'm not here. Please. If I'd been more experienced, more gifted, more everything, I could have tried doing an Obi Wan Kenobi, a variation on the 'these are not the droids you're looking for' theme – but I was too panicked, too spooked. Too dehydrated and hot and scared to concentrate on anything other than trying to breathe – and what was on the other side of that door.

The tiny pinprick of light disappeared. The keyhole was blocked by the body of an unknown assailant. I sucked in one last, desperate breath and held it as the doors were gripped and flung open so hard I felt the base of the wardrobe rock. Oh well, I thought. At least I got to see the Stone Roses . . .

I screwed up my eyes, and felt the lion yanked away from me. A rush of light, almost as blinding as the panic. I wanted to jump up and attack, to yell and punch and bite, and do everything that I knew Carmel would do if she were in my boots. But my legs were cramped and twisted, one ankle tucked beneath me at an impossible angle, and my broken finger was scorching with pain from being wrung and clenched so hard.

I looked up. Still couldn't see properly. Too terrified even to scream, to do anything other than blink.

'That was the lion,' he said, pulling Leo out and throwing him clear across the room. 'And here's the wardrobe. You must be the witch.'

Gabriel.

Relief came quick and hard and choking. I found I could breathe properly again – but my heartbeat was going to take some time to rediscover its natural rhythm.

He leaned in and took hold of my hands to help me out, noticing when I grimaced in pain at his grip.

I stood up, and he stroked the hair back from my face; he ran his hands down my cheeks, my shoulders, my arms, my hips and waist, all the time staring intently at me. I realised there was nothing sexual in his touch – he was checking me for injuries, like a concerned vet examining a spooked horse.

'I'm fine,' I said, batting his hands away and frowning, anger flowing hot and fast now I felt safe from Sudden Death. 'Apart from the fact that you almost gave me a heart attack there! Would it have killed you to shout out so I knew who you were, you stupid bastard?'

He frowned back, and I could see responding anger in his eyes. They shaded down darker when he was roused, I'd noticed – when he was furious, or aggressive . . . or turned on. All of which seemed to happen a lot when I was around. This must all be such fun for him. Right now, he probably had a lot in storage: me firing him up then rejecting him back in Dublin; doing my amazing escape act with Carmel's help; risking my own life; and, ultimately, unleashing Fintan's wrath. I had been a naughty little goddess. I could understand why he was angry, truly I could. I just didn't give a fuck.

'Yes,' he said coldly, 'it might have killed me, actually – I had no idea if you were here, if you were alone, or if the Faidh would be waiting for me. It's war out there, Lily, and hiding in a bloody wardrobe isn't going to save you.'

'What is, then?' I snapped, taking my weary body over to the bed and sinking down on to it. The pillow was next to me. It was just a pillow now, and I carved out a moment to feel sad about that.

I let my head droop down, hiding my face behind my hair to create the illusion of some privacy while I regrouped ready for the oncoming screaming match. Gabriel and I seemed incapable of talking for more than three minutes without one of us going nutso. Maybe we would make the perfect married couple after all.

I knew that if I just leaned back and closed my eyes, I could go to sleep, right here on Coleen's bed, snuggled up to that pillow, and let the war rage on around me. The adrenaline of the hunt had drained from my body, leaving me weak and limp and exhausted. I really needed to sleep. To breathe. To grieve. To be back where I felt most comfortable: alone.

Gabriel, obviously, was having none of that. He wasn't about to kill me, which is always a plus point in a potential boyfriend – but he wasn't about to leave me be, either. I already knew him too well to expect that.

'How did you find me?' I asked, looking up again. He was staring at my broken finger, and the encrusted blood on my nails. His body was inching bigger, and his eyes were flaming. He'd allowed me to be hurt, and that wouldn't be sitting well with his High Kingly sense of duty. He had one mission in life – to protect me – and he'd failed.

'Carmel,' he replied simply, spitting out the word like he couldn't spare the breath.

Huh. Carmel. Maybe she'd started invading my brain as well – I mean, what difference would one more make? There was a whole street party going on in there. Might as well invite the entire family, bring a picnic and some cherryade. Spread out a blanket and watch the frigging show.

Gabriel proved my point with a timely psychic eavesdrop. (Repeat after me: must try harder to keep the nosy bugger out of my head.) 'No, she hasn't been invading your brain – she just knows you too well. Eventually we phoned the hospital and found out what had happened to Coleen, and she knew this was where you'd come next.'

He sat down next to me on the bed. I could feel the tense muscles of his thigh pressing against mine, thrumming with strength and restraint, and knew he was trying very, very hard to calm down. Not something that ever came easily to him. I appreciated the effort, because I couldn't deal with a Celtic warrior going apeshit on me right now. I really couldn't. If he started to tear a strip off me, I was going to walk to the nearest police station, punch the desk sergeant on the nose, and get myself locked up for the night. Three squares and a bed was sounding like a luxury mini-break right about now.

'What happened to your hand?' he asked gently, reaching out to touch the injured fingers. I saw the contact coming, and didn't have the energy or the will either to fight him off or scoot to the other side of the room. Instead, I reached inside my mind and hastily pulled together a flimsy white cloud, trying to put up a mental barrier between us – hopefully keeping him out of my mind, and out of my visions. Steel bars would probably have worked better – maybe a nice brick wall – but white seemed to be the thing that worked for me. I closed my eyes, and tried to let the image solidify.

He was holding my hand. I concentrated, alert to an untimely tingling or a sudden rush of blood to the head. I felt nothing but his touch. Fionnula was right – it did get easier with practice. Like pilates. I just needed to make myself do it in the first place. Also like pilates.

'Fintan happened,' I replied, wondering if Gabriel had any idea what I was doing. If he did, he wasn't telling.

'I arrived at the hospital in time to watch Coleen die – just me, her and a passing crow. Then I went to walk by the river. Fintan found me there – and yes, I know, I am an idiot. We had a nice chat, then he broke my fingers and pushed me into the Mersey. To my – as it turns out – not-so-certain death. Then I got rescued by God, and we went for a night out in the Cavern. It's been quite a day. What have you been up to?'

He paused and rubbed my fingers gently between his until they started to tingle. Not in a freaky about-to-fall-down way, but in a way that felt warm, and comforting, and healing. I swear the pain seemed to be rolling away, disappearing in tiny waves like the tide going out. Which was both unexpected and lovely. I only realised how much the throbbing had been bothering me when it started to fade. I didn't know if it was something magical, or if it was just the pleasure of human contact – or whether, for me, there was really any difference between the two.

I felt a huge temptation to give in. To stop fighting; to stop arguing. He'd tried telling me what I should be doing, and that hadn't worked. I'd stomped my feet and said no. He'd tried charming me and bossing me and persuading me, and none of that had worked, either. Yet staying still and quiet and massaging my poorly fingers was making me go all gooey-eyed; making me want to fall into his arms and lay my head on his chest. To let him hold me, and kiss me, and take care of me. To give up on this whole free-will lark, and simply go with the flow. Be his mate. Save the world. Have babies. Make curtains and cook his dinner. Eek. I've been starved of affection for the whole of my life – and now I was on a sugar rush.

'I've been killing,' he said, spoiling the romantic mood somewhat. 'I almost started with Carmel when I found out she'd helped you leave.'

'Ha!' I said, resting my head a tiny bit against his shoulder. Because he was big, and solid, and there. And because it had been a very hard day, and I kind of wanted to feel a bit like a girl for a moment. 'I'd like to see you try!'

'No, you wouldn't like to see me try. She'd die, and you'd never forgive me – and that's probably the only thing that saved her. You need to tell me everything that happened, but we can't stay here for too long – if I found you, they'll find you. We are both in danger. Fionnula told me about the deal you'd had with Fintan.'

'Oh, good,' I replied jauntily. 'I bet you wanted to kill me as well, then, didn't you, for not telling you?'

'Never that, Lily. But maybe a good spanking wouldn't go amiss . . . at some point.'

I lifted my head, looked up to check. Yes, he was smirking. Only a joke. Amazing how we were finding it within ourselves to flirt, under the circumstances. Maybe the best flirting always goes on under these kinds of circumstances.

'Anyway,' he added, running a hand through his hair so it fell back down in thick, dark waves to his shoulders. 'Whatever deal you had seems to be off. The house in Dublin was attacked this evening. Luckily the vampires were awake, so we escaped without serious injury. Kevin lost an eye, but he'll be fine.'

I gulped and held on to his fingers just a tiny bit harder. Jesus. Kevin – the floppy-haired barman from the Coconut Shy – had lost an eye. Gabriel mentioned it so casually, as though it were a paper cut, as though it meant nothing. But it was, I knew, all down to me that he'd never get to be a fireman when he grew up. Fucking hell. I was responsible for someone I'd viewed as a friend, and certainly as a protector, losing a bloody eye. If only I'd said yes to Fintan, then Kevin would have been safe . . . but, I reminded myself, the rest of the world wouldn't.

The Larry Hoeys of the world would disappear. Fintan would take them, and use them, and force them to live a life he deemed more suitable. I had done the right thing – I knew I had – but the consequences of my actions were going to send me on a very long guilt trip.

I tried to talk myself down from it. Kevin's eye – and let's face it, he had two – versus the rest of humanity. No competition. And Kevin was a soldier. He'd offered to lay down his soul for me, in fact, as well as to use his sword arm. What was one eye between friends, when vows like that had been made? He'd known this kind of thing might happen. For all I knew, he'd plucked out a few eyes himself in his time. Saving the world was his full-time job, when he wasn't pulling pints in a Liverpool nightclub. Plus . . . well, he generally had hair over one of his eyes all the time anyway.

It was a valiant effort, but it wasn't really working. I still felt awful, and no amount of self-justification was going to help. I reminded myself that Kevin, as Gabriel had said, would be fine, and tried to move on.

'Then what happened?' I asked, not even bothering to try talk to Gabriel about feeling guilty. He just wouldn't get it, and might even see it as an insult to Kevin's monumental macho. These guys were weird like that.

'Then we came back here, to Liverpool. Carmel is with the others, training. The apartment is safe – for now. Fionnula went back home, where she will be safe too. You were the loose end, Lily.'

Ha. Story of my life. Hanging from the back of the tapestry, waiting to be tugged.

'Now I've found you, we need to get back to them,' he said. 'Fintan will be searching for you. Eithne will be out. Their soldiers will be coming. What happened, Lily? Why did he hurt you?'

He wrapped an arm around my shoulder, and I felt the twitch of his flesh expanding. Clearly the thought of Fintan hurting me was not making him a happy bunny. Can't say that the memory did much for me, either.

'He asked me to be his new BFF,' I replied, allowing myself the brief luxury of being held by him. 'And I said no. It was . . . awful. He'd taken over someone else's body, and he smelled, and . . . I said no. He tried to kill me then – like you say, all bets are off. And then . . . well, I met the Overlord. We watched a few bands. He showed me a few things.'

'What do you mean, the Overlord? Nobody ever meets the Overlord, not even the minor gods themselves. Do you even understand what the term means?'

I felt a minor huff coming at his tone, and told myself to chill – it was a fairly unbelievable story, after all.

'Yes, as I'm not quite as stupid as you seem to think I am, Prince Snot. The Overlord. You know, God. Sorry I've upset your sense of snobbery, but he was the real deal. He saved my life, and he was . . . beautiful. And the people there were beautiful, and he did his very best to persuade me that my life could be too.'

'And did he?' he replied, nuzzling my hair. It probably stank of fags and booze and sweat, but it didn't seem to bother him. 'Persuade you?'

'Maybe he did. But don't get cocky about it – he also told me that the choice is mine, Gabriel. It's not my destiny. It's not preordained. I don't have to do what you say.' I thought back to my conversation with God in the taxi to Coleen's house, everything he had told me, and focused on the sense of resolution it had given me. 'The decision is mine, and you need to accept that. Saying no to Fintan doesn't mean I'm saying yes to you. And he also said he's sending someone to me. No names – he was mysterious like that – just that I needed some protection, from you as well as from Fintan, and that I'd know her when I saw her. So don't get any ideas about locking me back in that wardrobe until Samhain, then expecting me to meekly say yes to your every command, OK? God will know. And he'll be pissed off.'

He was silent. Which was unusual. That was the kind of speech that normally sent him into a huge rant about honour and duty and fate and all those pesky things. I presumed he was weighing up whether he felt tough enough to argue the toss with God or not.

He didn't. At least for now.

Instead, he just nodded. 'It's been quite an ordeal, hasn't it? Coleen's death alone would have been enough . . . I understand that, Lily. You don't live as long as I have without loss. So much loss, I sometimes wonder why I bother carrying on . . .'

'Who?' I asked quietly. 'Who have you lost?'

'Both my parents for a start. Friends, family. Human companions I've met through the years. Even the bloody dogs – it's not easy, knowing that everyone you meet, everyone you allow yourself to love, will die before you.'

I'd never thought of it like that. I had – understandably – been too wrapped up in my own concerns, evading death, et cetera. I didn't know what to say – this was a whole different side to him, and one that confused me. I should reach out. I should hold him. I should offer him comfort . . .

'All right,' he said abruptly, standing up so fast I fell over sideways, landing on my face on the bed. Elegance and charm, as ever. 'We need to leave. Now. Is there anything you need from here?'

I looked around, at the terrible wallpaper and the ugly furniture and the half-drunk glass of water. Coleen was gone, and there was nothing left here but ghosts, memories and a really hard crossword book.

I walked over to the wardrobe, feeling the need to tidy it up and close the doors. If this was the last time I'd be here, I wanted to leave the house as she would have wanted. Which meant I'd better remember to switch the heating off before we scarpered.

'I want that lion,' I said, kneeling down to collect scattered shoes and rearrange them in the bottom of the wardrobe.

'Really? The whole of the Tuatha are pursuing us, and you want a stuffed lion?'

I glared up at him.

'Yes, I want the bloody lion – now make yourself useful and go get it!'

He rolled his eyes – dealing with prima donna goddesses was clearly testing his patience – and walked away.

As I leaned into the wardrobe, blindly feeling around to find the other half of an especially grim pair of slippers, my hand touched the edge of what felt like an envelope or package. I poked at it; it was about A4 size, and bulging with documents. I pulled it out. Maybe Coleen had left a will, and I'd inherit the gas bill. That'd show me.

I sat back on my heels, and looked at it. Plain Manila. Dusty and powdery, the way paper gets when it's really,

really old. Nothing was written on the front, and the flap wasn't sealed. I quickly overcame a momentary qualm about invading her privacy – which went along the lines of 'she's dead, get over it' – and lifted it open.

I poured the contents out on to the carpet, aware that Gabriel was walking up behind me and looking over my shoulder.

Photographs. School photographs – the type that get taken once a year, with tidy uniforms and neat plaits and gappy teeth and forced grins. The type that come in cheap cardboard frames, and are usually displayed on the mantelpiece of parental homes across the land. Mrs O'Grady's house was full of them – portraits of her seven offspring over the years. Coleen's, unsurprisingly, never had been. In fact, I vividly remembered that every year, she refused to fill in the little order form or send in the money, claiming it was a waste of cash – what did she need photos of me for, when the real bloody thing was forever getting under her feet anyway?

And yet here they were. Every single one. I laid them out in order – a parade of little Lilies: rarely smiling, always serious, getting older and bigger and even more serious in every picture. She'd bought them, she'd hoarded them, she'd hidden them. Tucked away in a plain brown envelope at the bottom of a wardrobe, in a room where I wasn't allowed, like a dirty secret she wanted to avoid facing up to.

Maybe she didn't want to let me know she cared. Maybe she was under instructions from Gabriel not to give me any warm and fuzzies, and spoil his dastardly plans. Maybe she just didn't like them – my grim little face would be enough to scare anyone off.

But she'd kept them, all of them. Like her deathbed confession, it almost broke my heart. I saw a small blob of liquid splat on to the forehead of an eight-year-old me, and I realised I was crying.

'I'm sorry, Lily,' said Gabriel. I twisted round to look at

him. He was standing behind me, tall and strong and eerily beautiful, with the stuffed lion tucked under one arm.

'For what?' I asked, wiping my eyes with my sleeve.

'For many things, but right now, for Coleen's death. She never told us she was ill. We could have helped her. We have . . . ways of helping. But it was her choice.'

'You're right,' I said, squeezing my eyelids shut to get rid of any more wussy-girl moisture, 'it was her choice. And nobody could ever change Coleen's mind about any-thing. This one, at least, isn't on you.'

I started gathering the photos together – they would definitely be coming with me, Gabriel and the lion – and put them back into the envelope. As I did, I noticed one more, tucked deep inside at the bottom. An old print, in that particular tiny square shape they favoured in the Sixties, before the age of digital cameras or Polaroids.

It had been caught in one corner, and I tugged it free. Black and white. Late Sixties, from the look of the clothes on the guests . . . the wedding guests. A predictable enough group shot, with some kind of garden in the background. Maybe Stanley Park, which was nearby. Happy, smiling faces – with the happiest of them all belonging to Coleen. Coleen many years ago; a different Coleen to the one I'd always known. She couldn't have been more than eighteen – but it was definitely her.

I'd never seen pictures of my nan in her youth. In fact, I'd half assumed she never had one, and had sprung fully formed and miserable from the bowels of the Earth. But here she was, blonde and coiffed and wearing a very fancy frock with white lace sleeves. She was looking up at the man next to her, gripping on to his arm and grinning, a posy in her hand. The man – small, dark, just as happy – looked directly into the lens.

Coleen. On her wedding day. The wedding day I never knew she'd had, marrying a man who was most certainly not on the scene any more.

I looked up at Gabriel, and raised an eyebrow. Really, was there anything about my own life I actually knew and understood? One tiny little thing? One small scrap of information I could actually rely on?

He hefted the lion closer under his arm, and smiled sadly.

'You have questions. And I have some of the answers. But not now, and not here. Gather those up and we'll—' I suspected he was about to say 'leave', or maybe 'flee for our lives', but it was drowned out by a loud boom from downstairs. The sound of splintering wood, and heavy footsteps pounding down the hall. He cocked his head to one side, and I knew he was doing something spooky and psychic.

He grabbed me and pulled me to my feet, me still busily shoving the photos back into the envelope as he dragged me towards the window. He glanced around, then picked up the bedside cabinet. The water glass, the tissues, the Rennies and my keys and phone went hurtling through the air as he lifted up the cabinet and smashed it through the glass of the bedroom window.

He used it to butt out all the remaining shards, the sound of the breaking glass competing with the hammering of feet running up the stairs. I grabbed my keys and phone, stashing them in my bag, before looking at Gabriel.

'Do we really need the lion?' he asked plaintively, arms swelling beneath his jacket.

'Yes, I'm afraid we do,' I replied.

He nodded, not at all surprised, and pulled me towards him, wrapping one arm around my waist and keeping the lion in the other. He used the broken cabinet as a footstool, and leaped out of the window. I gripped as tightly as I could around his neck, his hair and mine whipping together around our faces as we fell through the chill night air.

I felt the bone-grinding judder as we hit the ground, even though he'd broken my fall by lifting me up slightly at the last minute. The rough landing didn't seem to bother him, and he bounded away towards the back gate. Lifting one black-booted foot, he kicked in the wood, clearing the way for us to run into the back alleyway. God. What was it with these men and doors? Would it have killed him to just open it?

Holding on to my hand, he sprinted down the alley, both of us leaping over black bin bags of rubbish and discarded milk bottles as we ran, my feet skidding on damp cobbles. A lone cat wisely scattered out of our way, and I could see the glimmer of the street lamps out on the road. He held me back with one hand as we reached the end of the passage, and I took a moment to catch a breath. It was all right for him. He was a super-fit, nigh-on immortal. I was a bloody journalist, for Christ's sake – and on the whole we're not made for sprinting.

He pushed me back into the alley, and I fell arse-over-tit backwards when my feet hit one of the bin bags. The bag split and puffed open as I landed, and I found myself covered in used tea bags and old banana peels as I dragged myself to my feet.

Gabriel was ahead, fighting with two black-clad men, and seeming to be on the winning end of it. Their limbs were a whirl of darkness, too fast to see properly, and I could hear sickening dull thuds as boots and fists made contact with flesh.

I looked around me and saw a child's broken scooter abandoned in the alleyway. I picked it up, ran screaming towards the flurry of arms and legs and karate chops and punches, and cracked it as hard as I could on the head of one of the bad guys. At least I hoped it was one of them – I realised at the last moment that I couldn't see well enough to be entirely sure.

He went down like the traditional sack of spuds, and I felt utterly delighted with myself, considered doing a little Rocky dance and punching the air.

The elation didn't last long, as the next thing I knew Gabriel was taking hold of the other man's head in his hands. He clamped down on either side of his face, and twisted so hard and so abruptly that I actually heard the bone snap, and saw the head partly come off at the neck. He dropped the body to the floor, and the head lolled to one side, sinew and bone and glistening flesh exposed under the street light. I felt my stomach lurch as I stared, and put a hand to my throat as the vomit rose, burning into my mouth.

I looked at Gabriel in the shadows, knowing that I couldn't possibly keep the horror from my face. He was huge now, over seven feet and built to go with it. There was blood dripping from his mouth – I had to presume he'd bitten something off at some point – and had a vicious curl to his lips. His hands were the size of shovels, and his nails had lengthened into talons, gleaming with gore. Even in the darkness I could see the battle lust in his eyes, as he kicked the body out of the way and took a menacing step towards me.

'This is me, Lily,' he growled, 'in all my glory. Now get in the bloody car.'

Chapter Twenty-Nine

I got in the bloody car. The car that now was, quite literally, bloody. Gabriel took a few moments to calm down – he had to, so he could fit in the Audi – then climbed into the driver's seat. His hands immediately slid from the steering wheel, they were so slick with blood and tiny gobs of flesh.

The sight, and the coppery smell, made me want to puke again, so I turned away and stared out of the open window. Looked at the busted-down door of my former home, and saw the outlines of the invaders rampaging from room to room upstairs. I could hear the banging and smashing even from outside. They were destroying the place, but I couldn't have cared less.

I had my lion. I had my photographs. I had the scariest protector in the universe. He was on my side, and even I was now a bit scared of him. That was a new one for me. Gabriel had aroused many feelings in me since that first night in the Coconut Shy: anger, frustration, affection, lust, a slight hint of hatred. But never fear. I'd always known, from the moment we first met, that he wouldn't hurt me. Not in the physical sense, at least.

Now, having seen him in 'all his glory', as he put it, I wasn't sure I could feel one hundred per cent that way ever again. Watching a man tear a head off will do that to you – and the fact that he was doing it all to keep me safe didn't make me feel much better.

Don't get me wrong – I had no sympathy for any of Fintan's men. That would be stupid – they were trying to kill me, after all. But there's a vast difference between preferring your own survival to theirs, or clonking the odd one on the head with a toy scooter, and seeing their torn throats shining in the moonlight.

That probably qualifies me as a hypocrite, but I couldn't argue with the way I felt. I shuddered and huddled as far away from him as I could, arms wrapped around my own torso, staying silent and looking out of the window. There was nothing that could come out of my mouth right then that could do either of us any good. I caught him sneaking the occasional glance in my direction, and I knew he must have been feeling awful. I even felt sorry for him – but not enough to close that distance.

Fionnula had told me he was ruthless – and now I'd seen it first-hand. In the flesh, as it were. It made me wonder how well I really knew him – and made me remember Donn's insistence that I be forced to accept Gabriel as my mate, willing or not. I'd been so utterly convinced that he would never walk that road, but now I couldn't be sure. The monster I'd just seen in action would be capable of anything.

There was a lot to think about, and not enough time between traumas to do it. One minute he seemed like a man I could love, the next he seemed like the bogeyman who'd do anything necessary to get his own way. I felt like asking the real Slim Gaby to please stand up – but I suspected they were all versions of the same man. Heck, he was a complicated person.

We drove in silence through the darkness of the city, pulling into the underground parking garage beneath his apartment and getting out without a word. I managed a small smile as he pressed the buttons in the lift, but that was that. I'd taken the lion and the photos from him – I didn't want him to get any blood on them – and followed him into the building.

It was probably my fault that he was so distracted. That he didn't sense that something was wrong. That he didn't feel that the warding spells were blown, and that violence had come to visit. It's definitely my fault that I pushed my way past him and went through the door first.

Inside, we were met with what I can only describe as carnage. The furniture was wrecked, smashed, and toppled. The TV screen and the games console were shattered, glass and wiring strewn over the floor. At first glance I saw five bodies – all of them dressed in the trademark *Men In Black* uniform. One more was still alive, twitching and bleeding and crawling along the polished wooden floorboards.

Finn screamed, and drove his sword through the back of the man's head so hard it impaled itself in the planks beneath. The sound of cold metal slicing through skull and brain is not something I'll ever forget – that or the look on Finn's face as he did it. The sheer, wild joy of killing.

Gabriel pushed me out of the way, and I dropped the lion. He ran yelling into the room, battle rage well and truly back, looking for something to destroy.

'It's all right,' said Carmel, standing in front of him and laying one hand on his chest. God knows how she found the guts to do that, I remember thinking – before I truly looked at her. Saw her properly, in the moody lighting of the flat. Most of the lamps seemed to have been smashed, and only one remained, over the bar, casting the whole room in a sinister glow.

'They're all dead. She's safe,' she said, gesturing around her. Her hand was covered in blood. Hers or someone else's, I had no idea. There was a gash along the left side of her face that would leave a scar, and her hair was streaked and clumped with deep-red liquid. Her blouse was torn, and her bare feet were leaving bloody prints as she moved.

Carmel. Carmel O'Grady – night-news editor and friend – was walking around in a pool of blood as though she was indulging in some new kind of spa treatment.

Despite all of that, it was her eyes that worried me most: wide, amber, sparkling with excitement. Whatever had gone on here – and obviously it wasn't good – she'd enjoyed it. Revelled in it. Relished every blow she'd taken, and every one she'd dealt out. It was almost as scary as Gabriel. I guessed this wasn't my night for feeling entirely comfy around my loved ones.

Gabriel nodded, once, a hard dash of chin to chest, as Connor stepped forward to explain what had happened. The attack had come shortly after Gabriel had left, and the working theory was that they snuck in when he snuck out. The warding spells had worked, and all of them – this apparently included Carmel – were immediately alerted to the threat.

Great, I thought, looking at her. She was definitely one of the boys now. How many had she killed, I wondered, gazing around at the disaster zone that was once Gabriel's neat and tidy bachelor pad.

Connor continued to recount the battle – with unmistakable delight – as Carmel finally caught my eye. She ran over, feet slipping in gunk, and threw her arms around me. I stiffened as she did it – partly just my usual reaction, partly repulsion. I mean, she was covered in blood and the gloop of other people's body parts. It just wasn't nice.

'Don't be such a tit,' she said, pulling quickly away. 'I'm still me. Just . . . you know, scarier. More Champion-like. How are you? Why didn't you ring me, you silly cow? I had no choice but to tell him. And I honestly thought he was going to kill me.'

She was staring at me, hard, and I stuttered an apology. After what I'd witnessed tonight, I could better imagine what that particular scene had looked like. Was I the only one who didn't get off on all this bloodshed? No wonder they needed a fertility chick to lighten the load – left to them, the whole human race would probably be walking round with swords and scabbards and missing limbs.

And eyes, I thought, turning round to look for Kevin. I saw him behind the bar – ever the professional – trying to salvage what he could from the broken glass scattered on the floor. I walked over, wondering what I'd say. 'Hi, Kevin, sorry about almost getting you blinded. Could you do me a quick rum and Coke, please?'

The eye in question – or, I had to presume now, empty socket – was covered by a bandage, but the other one looked pretty pleased to see me. Generous, in the circumstances.

'Kevin, I'm so sorry – I don't know what to say . . .' I muttered, reaching out to touch his arm. Yuck. That was a mistake, as it wasn't the cleanest arm I'd ever come across. Clearly being visually impaired hadn't prevented him from getting stuck in.

'What about?' he asked, looking genuinely confused.

'Um . . . your eye?' I replied, adding a silent 'duh' at the end.

'Oh! That! It's nothing,' he said, grinning. 'Except all the others are starting to call me Caemgen Caech now!'

'Are they?' I said, wondering why this was such an amusing thing, as to me it sounded like he'd just said 'klunk klik klak'.

'Yes, it means half-blind!' he added, as though this was the best gag the world had ever heard. Maybe it was, but I was obviously having a sense of humour failure that night. Kevin passed me a mug of Peroni – looked like the glasses were all done for – and I took it gratefully. At some point I needed to do myself a favour and eat, but right now I'd take anything I could get.

Around the room, Connor, Finn and Carmel were start-ing to clear up, shoving the dead bodies into one corner like leftover rubbish at a party. I could hear glass crunch-ing beneath their feet, but if it was hurting them, nobody seemed to notice. Morgan, one of the vampires, managed to find an unsmashed iPod dock, and called up some tunes. I wondered idly if he had a special playlist, titled 'Music to Kill Men By'. It turned out to be Frank Sinatra doing 'Moon River', which was just plain weird.

'Is everyone all right?' I asked Kevin, assuming that they wouldn't be getting all jiggy in a Rat Pack fashion if they weren't.

'I think so . . .' he replied, looking around with his one functioning eye, as though he was doing a head count. 'Isabella?' he shouted. 'Your guys all good?'

Isabella's beautiful black head appeared from behind the upturned sofa. Her mouth was still attached to the neck of one of our attackers, and she took the time to finish her meal before she answered. I heard the last glug of blood leaving the body, like the sound a gas nozzle makes when the car tank is full, and she dropped it with a dull thud back to the floor. She stood up, wiped her face so the blood smeared across her cheeks, and smiled. Her pupils were dilated, and she looked like she'd just had the best shag in the world.

Yes. I was definitely the odd one out here.

She glanced around, spotted Morgan crooning away in the corner, and Marcus wielding a sword in one hand and a dust-buster in the other. She frowned, her head swivelling from side to side as she surveyed the wreckage.

'Luca!' she bellowed, leaping over the sofa like a superhero. I looked around too. He was nowhere in sight, and I felt panic rise through me. He could be in another room. He could be behind the bar, eating a human being. He could be taking a nap. He could be anywhere at all – but, in the tried and tested tradition of every movie I'd ever seen, I had a Bad Feeling About This. Luca was the only one of the vampires I'd bonded with – which is a polite way of saying I'd gyrated on his genitals – and he was missing. Kevin's eye was bad enough. Losing Luca would be . . . worse.

Morgan and Marcus, alerted to their leader's distress, stopped what they were doing and grouped together with her in the centre of the room. They started to sniff the air, like bloodhounds on the trail of an escaped convict.

As if at some silent signal, they all moved – half running, half leaping, scooting on their arms and their legs like animals – towards the open-plan kitchen area. They disappeared behind the countertops, and as I ran over, all three of them started howling. Like a pack of wolves. It was loud, and eerie, and terrifying, watching their blood-streaked faces lift to the ceiling as they bayed.

Scary as that was to see, it was nothing compared to the sight at their feet. Luca lay collapsed in a bloody heap, the bodies of three attackers dead around him, throats torn and oozing. He'd gone down biting. He was terribly, dreadfully still, and his torso was ripped open, the ragged edges of his blood-soaked T-shirt clinging to the jagged tears of flesh. I could see his insides on the outside, looped and curled and glistening pink. The wound sheared up to his chest, and his rib cavity gleamed red and white and wrong.

It was revolting. And it seemed to mean he was dead. I knew they weren't immortal, that they could be killed – it was just pretty damned hard to do.

Gabriel loomed over us, face set and grim and rigid.

'They caught his heart,' he said. 'It's over.'

'No!' shrieked Isabella, leaping to her feet. 'It still beats – I can hear it! He lives, and while he lives, we do not give up on him! He needs human blood!'

Carmel pushed her way forward. 'I'll do it,' she said calmly, as though she was offering to take him out for a latte instead of open up a vein.

'No . . . it's *hers* he needs,' hissed Isabella, desperate eyes focusing in on me. 'She can save him. The *Goddess*.'

Gabriel stood between the two of us, sheltering me with his swelling body. 'No,' he said, voice made of iron. 'I forbid it. Her blood is sacred, and it shall not be spilled.'

I peeked around him to look at Luca, the physical wreck-age of his once fine body. The body he'd sacrificed because of me. The body I'd danced against to The Doors. The body that, according to Isabella, I could save.

I dashed out from behind Gabriel, my feet slipping in the blood, and skidded to a stop on my knees in the stuff. I felt it soak into my jeans, and knew it would dry crisp and coppery. Gabriel stepped towards me, hands outstretched as though to physically drag me away, and I glared at him.

'Back off!' I yelled. 'I am Mabe – Mother of the Mortals! And I will not be treated like a child! Touch me, and I will kill you!'

I had no idea why I said that, or what deluded portion of my brain thought I was capable of killing a warrior High King, but it stopped him in his tracks.

'Feed him!' screeched Isabella, grabbing my wrist and slashing at it with a red-painted talon. The attack was so quick, so sharp, that I didn't even feel the pain – it was only when the blood oozed to the surface and started to flow that I realised what she had done.

Gabriel roared and went for her, grabbing her by the head and tossing her into the sky like a rag doll. She flew up and up, somersaulted through the air, all flapping black hair and flapping black dress. She landed with a sickening thump against the wall on the other side of the room, slid-ing down it until her body reached the floor. She twitched and roused and stood up, and I could hear bones and joints popping back into place as she growled at him. It was like watching a Halloween puppet reassemble itself, with the soundtrack from hell.

Without a word, Marcus and Morgan attacked, flying at Gabriel with teeth bared and nails flaring, snarling and snapping like starved lions. Finn, Connor, Carmel and Kevin waded in, and I knew – just knew – that they could all end up dead. Me too, the way the blood was pooling from my wrist to my lap. Luca, bless his sweet soul and his lovely leather pants, looked like he was already gone.

I stood up, planning to make some kind of goddessy scene, or at the very least to throw myself into the middle of the ruckus – that would make them pause if nothing else.

I took a deep breath, held up my hand to try and staunch the blood, and took a step towards them. Party time.

Just then, the floor-to-ceiling windows shattered in an almighty explosion, sprinkling us all with shards. I covered my head with my hands, screaming like a baby, and saw a body fly through the broken panes. A body that landed, sure-footed, in a pair of enormous shit-kicking black boots in the centre of the room.

The boots belonged to long, long legs; and the legs belonged to a woman who stood six feet tall, with the body of a blacksmith. A black leather coat flew around her ankles, and her hair – a startlingly vivid red, streaked with white – streamed behind her, a flaming curtain.

'Enough!' she yelled, her deep voice ricocheting around the room as she grabbed hold of the nearest body – which happened to be Connor – and wrenched him away. He fell to the floor, glanced up, saw who had attacked him, and stayed there. Kneeling and sniffing the ground like a grovelling dog.

I have to be honest. I almost peed myself just looking at her, so I could totally understand why he reacted like that. But I couldn't quite believe my eyes when the others followed suit. All of them. The vampires. Gabriel. Even Carmel, who had so gone native.

The ones who were standing fell to their knees in worship, and the ones who were sprawled raised themselves up to the same position, their foreheads scraping the floor as they spread themselves before her. This was one scary dudette.

'You will fight among yourselves while the Goddess

bleeds?' she said, so loud it made my head vibrate. 'You will brawl while she sheds her sacred blood upon the floor of this hovel? You are not worthy! Cormac macConaire, stand before me and explain yourself – why you, as her protector, her mate-in-waiting, allow this to happen?'

Gabriel stood, and I swear to God he looked scared. It was the one and only time I have ever seen that look on his face, and in turn it made me breathe that little bit faster. If the scariest man in the room looks worried, it's time to run and hide.

He kept his head bowed, not making eye contact, not wanting to challenge the top dog, and spoke: 'One of the vampires received a near-mortal blow, My Lady. His brethren want her to save him. They . . . they cut her.'

The woman looked over at me and raised an eyebrow. I was the only one still standing – more because I was frozen like a petrified block of stone then because of any intended disrespect. I walked towards her. Without being told, I knew it was what she wanted, and knew that I should obey her.

She took my hand, held it up to the light so she could see the still-flowing blood. My entire sleeve was soaked in it now, and as soon as I saw it I started to feel a bit light-headed. Gabriel's face fell as he realised how hurt I was. Yep. Another epic fail, protector-boy.

'Do you wish to feed the fallen vampire, Goddess?' she said.

I nodded, feeling woozy but determined.

'Then you shall.'

She turned to Gabriel, who despite his best efforts to remain acquiescent, was glaring at her and starting to grow some extra muscle. He opened his mouth to protest, and she held up one hand to silence him.

'Do not try your puny tricks with me, High King – I am the Morrigan, and I will be obeyed. Who are you to tell me what to do? To tell the Goddess what to do? You are but a child in a man's body. She will do as she pleases, and you will leave her be.'

Wow. That told him, in a way I'd never seen before. In fact, the only person I'd ever known to answer him back was me. I was liking the Morrigan already. Carmel lifted her head slightly and caught my eye, mouthing two words at me: girl power. I stifled a laugh. The Morrigan seemed to be big on being taken seriously.

'She,' said the woman, 'is the cradle and the apple in one. She will save whom she will save. It is within her gift.'

'But the consequences!' shouted Gabriel, still not quite cowed enough to get the message and shut up.

'What consequences?' I asked, suddenly even more interested. Apart from, you know, potentially dying of exsanguination.

The Morrigan turned to me, emerald-green eyes shining in her face. Eyes that shone like jewels and reminded me of the Man in the Cavern. Eyes that promised passion and strength and death.

'If you do this,' she said, 'then the vampire will be yours. You will own him.'

'I don't want to own him. Donn can have him. I just want to keep him alive. Or dead. Or whatever.'

'There is no room for "whatever" in this, girl – and there is no room for negotiation. If you do this, you sever his ties with Donn, and his existence is yours. What do you say?'

I looked at Isabella, her exquisite face staring up at mine, desperate. Back at Luca, still and dying. At Gabriel, silently beseeching me to refuse.

'I say yes,' I replied.

Gabriel looked down at his feet. Nodded once. Said: 'I cannot watch this,' and left the room.

Chapter Thirty

Isabella jumped up and ran at me, grabbing my wrist and tugging me towards Luca. I planted my feet as firmly as I could, and shoved her away.

'I will do this myself – don't try to force me!' I said, hissing at her. She hissed back, and her fangs gleamed white and terrifying. It was potentially a bad move, but I was *sooo* sick of being bossed and dragged and bullied. It's happened to me my whole life, and I needed to make a stand. Choosing a feral vampire to test it out on might not have been the wisest of decisions, but the time had come – the time for people to just back the fuck off and leave me alone.

I could see her body trembling with the need to rip my throat out, but one glance at the ginger Amazon hovering behind us told her that would be a bad thing. They were way more scared of her than of Gabriel, so I was going Team Morrigan all the way. Miraculously, she backed the fuck off.

I kneeled down beside Luca, the blood and gore sloshing beneath my knees, and stroked his pale face with my good hand. He was so beautiful. Why wouldn't I want to save him? And as for owning him . . . well, I'd find a way to give him back later. Assuming Donn had the same returns policy as M&S, that is.

I leaned forward, cradled his blond head in my arms, and pressed my bleeding wrist to his lips.

At first, there was nothing. Not a twitch, not a lick, and I thought it was too late. That all the arguing, all the fighting, had been wasted.

'You're not doing it properly!' whispered Isabella, still hovering at my shoulder, her tone a mixture of plea and threat. 'You need to bleed better!' I ignored her, and pressed my flesh deeper on to his mouth, willing him to wake up and drink. To feed. To live.

'Come on, Luca . . .' I muttered, stroking his hair back from his face. 'Be a good little vampire, and drink up.'

It was tentative to start with: the tiniest flicker of his tongue. Like a kitten lapping at milk. It felt soft and gentle and pleasant, and I was just starting to think that this wasn't so bad when his mouth crunched down on to my flesh.

I wanted to scream – in fact, I suspect I may have – as his lips clamped down on my wrist, sealing off the wound. The suction was so powerful I thought a few internal organs might slip out with the blood, and I found myself straining backwards, trying to pull away from him.

After the first couple of mouthfuls, he regained enough strength to move, and grabbed my arm to hold it forcefully in place. I could feel his fingertips hitting bone, and knew I'd be bruised. His eyes flickered open, deep and dark and shining, going a fraction wider when he saw it was me.

He yanked his mouth away, letting his head fall back into my arms, and licked his lips.

'No!' shouted Isabella, dashing forward. 'He needs more – you need more, Luca!'

I heard rather than saw the Morrigan intervene, and the sound of Isabella screeching as she was thrown yet again across the room. I guessed it just wasn't her night.

'Do you?' I asked, really hoping that the answer was no. It hurt. God, it hurt. I felt dizzy and sore and ached all over.

I liked Luca, and I wanted to save him, but I was praying that was enough. I glanced down at his body, at the tattered rags of his T-shirt. The flesh had started to knit back together, and his insides were back where they belonged. But the cuts were still open and gleaming, blood seeping from the edges as his body tried to heal itself. Shit. He was better, but still not right.

He shook his head, too weak to speak, and I knew I had to make the decision for him.

'You need more,' I said, offering my wrist to him again, clenching my eyes shut and hoping for the best.

'Relax, *bella* – this can be fun, you know?' he murmured, pausing to lick a few stray droplets from my skin. Yeah, right, I thought. Fun in the same way getting electric shock therapy was fun. And as for 'relax' – well, that sounded about as convincing as when the nurse doing a smear test says it.

I took a breath, deep and long, realising that he had stopped. That he was waiting for me to give him some sign.

'Do it, Luca,' I said, 'but please – be quick.'

'That's not what the girls usually say,' he replied, and I realised that if he was joking again, this must be working. I was doing it. I was saving him. Yeah, it hurt – but so what? This was bigger than that. This was what I was meant to do. It made me feel good. It made me feel powerful. It made me feel like when I'd finished with Luca, I could go and grow Kevin a new eye, and then make my way to the nearest hospice and carry right on. Yeah. Go Goddess.

It was also making Luca feel good, I couldn't help noticing. Despite the fact that his torso was still covered in half-healed wounds, his leathers were shifting and filling in an obscenely male way. I wondered if this was normal – if that happened every time he fed – or if I was, you know, special.

I decided I didn't care, and pushed my wrist back to his mouth. He clamped back down and started to suck again, but this time he was slower, gentler. More controlled. He reached up, placed long fingers on the side of my face, softly stroking. I leaned into his touch, rubbing my skin against his in the way I always felt free to do with him. God, he was right. It was starting to feel . . . nice.

His sucking was slow, rhythmic and sensual. He started to time it with my heartbeat, and that sent a great big shuddering throb all through my body. His hand was twined into my hair, and I rubbed against it, murmuring quietly, feeling his fingers stroking my scalp.

I glanced down at his body. The cuts had closed. There were still faint pink lines where the wounds had been, but he was whole again. And gorgeous again. And so damned sexy again.

He stopped just drinking, and replaced it with feathery touches of his tongue, licking and probing and quite frankly making me go all wriggly in the knickers department. He never broke eye contact with me as I hitched a leg over his lap, straddling him until I could feel his body pressing into mine through the fabric of my jeans.

He sucked. And I squirmed. And he got even bigger. And I got even hornier. I leaned down, started to nip and nuzzle at his neck, licking the tanned skin and strong muscle at the top of his shoulder. His hand in my hair twined deeper, pulling me closer, and his whole body bucked up to meet mine. I shook and trembled and ground down even harder against him. I had no control over it at all, and the fact that I had an audience hadn't even entered my mind – I was going on pure, delicious physical instinct, for the first time in my life.

I honestly had no idea what was happening to me. Bear in mind my sexual history is completely and utterly blank. Nothing had ever prepared me for this. Sex was something that other people did. That other people felt. And yet here I was – writhing around on top of this drop-dead gorgeous hunk of newly healed beefcake, feeling my face flush red with desire, thrusting away at him with every beat of my heart, every suck of my blood.

I pulled my wrist away, looked down at him. Blond hair falling to the sides of his cheekbones; pupils huge in chocolate-brown eyes. My own blood smeared on his lips. And I kissed him – long, and hard, and desperate, as he snaked one hand up beneath my top, stroking erect nipples through the lace of my bra. I gasped, and kissed, and wriggled, and sighed as an intense feeling of need built up through my whole body. Something very good was coming. I just knew it was . . .

The next sound out of my mouth was a scream – but not the kind I'd been hoping for. The Morrigan had grabbed me by my hair, and dragged me away, boots kicking against the slippery floor as she pulled me back to her.

'Ow!' I yelled, rubbing my sore scalp. 'Why did you do that? You could have just told me to stop!'

'I did,' she said, 'several times. You were distracted by the vampire, and he would have drained you dry in your need.'

'I would *not*,' said Luca, sitting up and grinning over at us. 'I would never harm her – unless she wanted me to. She is my mistress, and I live to serve her – in any way she chooses . . .'

I looked at him. All healed up now. Cheeky again, brown eyes glinting with humour and the remnants of desire. I still wanted him. I wanted to sit on him, and bite him, and have him bite me, and see him completely naked while we did it . . .

'Pay attention!' said the Morrigan, taking me by the shoulders and whirling me round to face her. 'This is not real – this is not right. We will leave now, whether you want to or not.'

I didn't want to leave. And if I did, I wanted to take Luca with me. I opened my mouth to argue, just as Gabriel walked back into the room.

He'd been in the shower, and was wearing only a battered pair of faded Levis. Feet bare. Chest bare. Hair damp and curling on his shoulders, trickles of water running over ridged muscle and smooth skin. His eyes met mine and they were bright, brilliant violet. He'd known. Of course he had. He looked at Luca, looked at me, and dragged a hand back through his hair. More water. On even more muscle.

He looked angry. And edible. And like the most gorgeous creature I'd ever laid eyes on. My body was still thrumming with need, and all of my desire detoured from Luca, and headed in Gabriel's direction – channelled by the clamouring want I could feel beating through me. I shook the Morrigan's hands from my shoulders, and ran towards him.

I didn't slow as I approached, and slammed him physically back against the wall, pinning him up against it and leaning into his body. My hands flew to his bare chest, stroking the outlines of his pecs, his nipples, leaning down and licking the droplets of water from his flesh with my tongue. I wanted to lick him clean, then make him dirty, then lick him all over again.

'No . . .' he muttered, trying to push me away. 'This is not right . . .'

I crooked my neck to look up at him, and knew that whatever he was saying, he didn't mean it. He wanted me. I wanted him. I'd never given in to anything like these urges before – hell, I'd never known these urges even existed. All I knew was that I was going to bloody well have him.

I twined my hands behind his neck, and tugged his face down to mine, meeting his lips like an invading army. His arms went around my waist, and I was crushed against him, left in no doubt that I was right. He wanted me – a lot.

Gabriel. My mate. Just then, it didn't sound wrong. It sounded . . . perfect. I started to fiddle with the buttons on his fly, and he groaned in response, swept away by the lust that I was throwing out like a garden sprinkler. For a moment my mind collided with his, and I caught a snippet of what he was feeling: regret, and anger, and pride that he had at last proved himself irresistible. But all of that was overshadowed by need: hard, driving, ignore-everything-else-in-the-universe need.

I'd just about managed the first few buttons when, once again, I was torn away – and, again, by my hair. I was going to fucking kill that woman.

The Morrigan grabbed hold of me and threw me against the wall, face first. She twisted one arm behind my back and tugged it upwards, all the time crushing my head into the wallpaper. It hurt, and it showed no signs of stopping. Maybe I wasn't going to kill her after all.

'Stop pulling my hair!' I hissed. 'I'm not a naughty puppy!'

'But you are behaving like a bitch in heat,' she said, leaning so close to my face that I could feel her warm breath on my cheeks. 'Time to go to sleep now, Goddess.'

As she murmured the words, I slid down. Down to the floor, and out. Sleep. At last.

Chapter Thirty-One

I twisted my head upwards.

I was looking at birds. Thousands of them, streaking through a sky that was tinted with the grey haze of dawn. They flocked and swirled like starlings, but I could see all kinds in their twirling nimbus: gulls and pigeons and sparrows and many I had no name for, all swooping and screeching and wheeling around us in a dark cloud of fluttering wings.

If that wasn't strange enough, I could also, when I looked to the side, see Carmel's legs. Or Carmel's jeans, at least – those slinky Karen Millen numbers, now customised with dried blood and goop. I was upside down, looking up at crazed birds and my friend's thighs, my head bobbing around like a nodding dog in the back of a car.

I was not only upside down; I was being carried. I twisted myself up as far as my abs would allow me, and saw the Morrigan's red-and-white hair streaking down her back. I was over her wide shoulders, dangling in a fireman's lift, and I could feel a tingling sensation as the blood started to move more freely around my body.

Carmel leaned down to my eye level and gave me a quick smile. Her scar was vivid, red and angry, stitched together with black thread. She looked like something from a Tim Burton film.

'She's awake!' she piped, as she straightened up again. The Morrigan immediately dumped me to the ground, which happened to be a patch of scrappy grass, surrounded by wind-blown old crisp bags snagged in clumps of long-dead flowers.

I closed my eyes for a moment, clenching my eyelids shut and trying to regain my balance. When I snapped them back open, the birds were still there, blocking out most of the sky. Carmel was still grinning. And the Morrigan was staring down at me, now looking seven feet tall and built like the proverbial brick shithouse. She nudged me in the side with her massive biker boots, gently enough to break a couple of ribs, I should think.

'Get up,' she said. 'It does not befit the Goddess to lie in discarded trash.'

Cow, I said. Silently.

'It probably doesn't befit the Goddess to be dumped there in the first place . . .' I muttered, staggering to my feet. Minor defiance, but better than nothing at all, I supposed.

The Morrigan ignored me, and instead looked up at the riot of birds above us. She grinned – the first time I'd seen her crack a smile – and it transformed the sharp plains of her face from 'scary but handsome' into the realms of 'knock-out beautiful'. No wonder she didn't do it often – men would fall at her feet, and she'd get gunk on the soles of her boots as she crushed their puny skulls.

The smile, needless to say, wasn't at the sight of me, hopping on one leg while I wiped mud and a half-eaten Snickers bar off my arse. The smile was for the birds.

She lifted up her hands and made a swirling gesture, like a conductor in front of an orchestra. The birds clouded and leaped in response, coming together to create a downward flurry of thrumming wind: like a tornado pointing to the ground, larger beasties at the top, cawing and honking and endlessly circling, and the tiny ones fluttering together at the bottom to form the spout.

The Morrigan flicked her fingers, like she was sprinkling water from them, and the flock immediately flew away, a single black mass scudding off into the distance, presumably to go back to eating worms, or building nests, or shitting on cars, or whatever it was birds did all day. I was glad to see them go. It had all been getting a bit Hitchcock. She chuckled and watched as they flew, like Mother Duck saying goodbye to her kids on the first day of school. I guess we all have our weaknesses.

I looked around me, trying to figure out where we were. I had no idea how long I'd been out, and I didn't trust these Otherworldy types one bit when it came to transport. For all I knew, we could have jumped through a fairy portal and be in a back street of Mozambique, or about to take a front row at the Colosseum to watch some heavy-duty gladiator action.

Instead, I saw a dim, abandoned car park, cracked concrete, and a vast tower block looming above us in the grey half-light. Across the road were neat terraces, with well-kept front yards and brightly painted front doors. I could almost smell the Mersey whipping up towards us on the same wind that had been playing havoc with those crisp bags, and heard the hungry wail of gulls over the water.

'Are we in Dingle?' I asked Carmel.

'Yup,' she said, nodding. 'And you got a lift the whole way.'

Great. Another dignified exit from . . . well, a highly embarrassing scene. As I recalled the way I'd behaved back in the apartment, I felt a fiery flush claim my cheeks. God. How awful. Bitch in heat indeed. I didn't know what had come over me – maybe my lager had been spiked – but I was hoping it never happened again. At least not with an audience.

The Morrigan stamped away ahead of us, and used her

mighty boots to kick open the door to the tower block. Once, it must have had some kind of intercom system, but that now hung in shredded wires from a small metal box. I didn't know if that was her handiwork, or just the natural fate of a block of flats mid-regeneration.

The air was dank and chill inside, and the walls were decorated with graffiti of varying quality. The lighting was strip neon, flickering on and off over our heads, and the smell was akin to a male urinal. Old newspapers – the weekly free sheets that sometimes got dumped instead of delivered by enterprising youths – were rotting in a damp, mouldering pile, and the quiet rustling inside them led me to believe that a few four-legged residents had moved into a new des res.

Looking around at the silent, dim lobby, edged in grime and months of neglect, I immediately knew three things: that nobody human lived here any more; that the lifts wouldn't be working; and that the Morrigan would most definitely be holed up on the top floor.

Some time later, I'd been proved right on all three counts. I was also, finally, catching up with the others. I'm pretty fit – for a mortal – but those two sprinted up the stairs (all twenty-two storeys of them) like superheroes heading for a cape sale. I needed to up my game, maybe invest in a Zumba video or something.

I arrived on the top floor huffing, puffing and even redder in the face, also itching to wash my hands from holding the scum-coated railing for the last few flights. I felt marginally peeved that I hadn't been magically transformed into a superior physical being by all this supernatural crap, in the way Carmel seemed to have been. I got to save the world, and Carmel got to run up stairs really, really fast. Them's the breaks, I suppose.

They'd thoughtfully left the door open, and I took a moment to catch my breath before I followed them in.

I found both in the living room, which was dingily lit

and decorated in unsurpassed Eighties chic. A Florence and the Machine poster was tacked to the wall, and I wondered if it was a remnant from a previous inhabitant, or if the Morrigan had brought it with her. Maybe it was her daughter; they looked enough alike.

I wandered over to the window, and saw a row of pigeons outside on the ledge. Dozens of them were crammed together in a line, their feathery chests puffed out against the cold. Lookouts, Morrigan-style, I guessed. One whiff of the men in black, and they'd dive-bomb them all, in that special way that only city-tough street pigeons can. Avian ninjas to the rescue.

Further off, I could see the panorama of the city, and sunlight finally starting to spread its fingers over the steely surface of the river. I could see buses crawling over the streets, and the shapes of the two cathedrals and St John's Tower piercing the sky. The flat was a tip, but the views were spectacular. I felt a surge of affection for the place well up inside me. My life would never be the same, but Liverpool, I hoped, always would be. I wanted to come back here when this was all over, ideally without a trail of assassins on my back. Maybe I'd get to interview that male Cher impersonator after all.

'I have prepared you a place to sleep,' said the Morrigan. She gestured at what looked like two army-issue sleeping bags on the floor, still rolled up and toggled. Ooh. Luxury. 'For you too, Child of Menhit,' she added, looking through narrow eyes at Carmel.

I had no idea what that meant, and I saw Carmel open her mouth to ask. She was silenced by one slight shake of the Morrigan's head, and her lips clamped shut. I'd never seen her so subservient to anyone before, not even the editor at the *Gazette*. Especially not the editor, in fact. It wasn't a criticism – I wouldn't argue with the Morrigan, either. She put me to sleep and hefted me to the Dingle last time I tried it.

I stared at the vicious slash across Carmel's cheek, and felt a wave of shame sweep over me. I'd dragged her into all of this, and she'd been marked for life as a result. Kevin's eye. Carmel's face. Luca's almost everything. After last night's performance, my own self-respect. Where would the list of casualties end?

She saw me looking, and her fingers flew up to touch the ragged edges of the wound, a trail of loose thread still hanging from one corner like a drooping comma.

'It's all right,' she said, 'it doesn't hurt. Connor sewed it up for me. He used TCP and everything, so chill out, OK? It'll only make things worse if I have to worry about you worrying about me on top of everything else. I made my choices, and I don't regret them.'

'Of course she doesn't – she has the heart of a warrior,' said the Morrigan, bustling away in a crinkling carrier bag in the corner of the room. 'And there will be more injuries and more death to come, Goddess, possibly your own – you need to get used to that. You are being – what's the word you people use . . . a wuss. Your Champion isn't. Learn from her, and find the courage I know you must have hidden within you.'

Now, as pep talks went, I'd had better – but I suspected she had a point. The issue, at least for me, was that everyone around me was getting hacked and thwacked all over the shop, whereas I was fine, bar the odd broken finger and a few nervous breakdowns. I felt as though the world around me, and everyone I ever cared about – admittedly an exclusive list – was being torn apart, all because of me.

Me, me, me . . . OK, she *definitely* had a point.

The Morrigan emerged from the carrier bag bearing plastic-wrapped sandwiches and bottles of water. She'd obviously managed a quick trip to the Tesco Metro on the way home, for which I was eternally grateful. I almost knocked her over in my eagerness to grab the food, and to abandon a thought process I wasn't enjoying very much at all. There was time for self-analysis later – now was the time for stuffing my face. That was much less stressful.

We sat on the ground – bare, apart from a few tufts of purple carpet left behind when the last owner tore it from the floor – and ate. It was the best BLT I'd ever tasted, and we all remained silent, happily munching away, for a few blissful minutes. Nothing like being plunged into life or death situations every other hour to make you appreciate the simpler things.

'Now,' said the Morrigan, finishing her sandwich and throwing the plastic package back into the bag, 'we will rest, and we will learn. You know who sent me?'

I nodded. Didn't want to say it out loud, though – it sounded a bit up myself to say, 'Yeah, God asked you to look after me, cos I'm so super-special and all.'

She nodded, as if pleased to see that I wasn't a complete imbecile. Maybe just 95.5 per cent.

'There are two nights until Samhain, when you must present yourself at Tara and make your choice,' she said. 'Do you understand me?'

She spoke slowly and clearly, enunciating every word, and I started to wonder if she really did think I was mentally impaired. And whether she might just be right.

'Yes, against the odds, I've somehow managed to keep up with you so far . . . but, well, what if I just don't go?' I asked. 'I don't really want to.'

Carmel looked at me in exasperation, as though she just couldn't believe what I was saying. I made an apologetic face in her direction – she thought I should go, I knew. Accept Gabriel. Bless the world. The whole nine yards. She'd bought into it all, and even had the scars to prove it.

'That is not an option,' replied the Morrigan, icily. 'If you refuse to go, I will take you forcibly. Do you doubt my capacity to do such a thing?'

I looked at her, taller than most women even though she was sitting cross-legged on the floor. Her red-and-white hair was scattered like snakes over her powerful shoulders, and she was fixing me with a green glare that was brighter than the sunshine leaking through the grimy windows. Umm. No. I didn't doubt that for a minute.

So much for Plan A: avoidance.

'No,' I said, 'I know you could make me to go, and I was foolish even to ask. You've made yourself clear, and I'm not as stupid as you might think I am. I'll go to Tara, OK? But once I get there, it's up to me, right? Nobody can force me to do anything once we're there? I may be a wuss, but I'm really unhappy about all this . . . forcing. And with Fionnula, and with Donn, there was mention of someone else taking me forcibly. Of taking away my choice.

'I don't know Gabriel well enough to understand where his boundaries lie, and I don't want to leave it until it's too late to find out. I'm told I have power – and I need to know how to use it if things seem to be heading in that direction. Or if I react like I did tonight, when I, uh, really wasn't myself.'

That, of course, was an understatement. The way I'd felt just a few hours ago, I'd probably have accepted my school lollipop man as my eternal mate if it got me laid. I couldn't let that happen at Tara, when of all times I would need a clear head.

The Morrigan nodded, thinking about what I'd said – and what I hadn't said, for fear of being too crude. Old habits die hard.

'That was the vampire's fault – that and your lusty nature. It will not happen like that again if you guard against it,' she said. 'I can show you how.'

I swallowed back a laugh, and heard Carmel sniggering in the background. Lusty nature? Me? Abso-bloody-lutely hilarious. If only she knew.

'What about the . . . other thing?' I prompted, blushing. Must be my lusty nature getting the better of me again.

'Men are feeble creatures,' she finally replied, 'dominated

by petty needs and selfish drives. It has always been so, and in many ways your High King is no different. You must understand that he has been raised in a world where to take – women, wealth, territory – is seen as a sign of strength. And that this pairing, this mating, is what he has been destined to do for the whole of his existence. If he fails, then his life will be without meaning and without aim. He will most likely fall upon his own sword, rather than continue to live with such failure.'

There was a pause, as I tried to digest what she'd just told me. It was taking longer than the BLT.

'What do you mean, fall upon his own sword? Like, commit hara-kiri? He'll kill himself if I don't say yes?'

Even to my own ears, my voice resembled that of a lab rat being tortured: I was squeaking several octaves higher than usual, and felt like all the air had been punched out of my lungs. Jesus. So, I had to agree to be Gabriel's mate, or the world as I knew it ended, and he topped himself? Wow. No pressure there, then.

'I do not understand, girl, why you squeak so?' said the Morrigan, frowning in confusion. 'If you do not care for him enough to take him as mate, why would it cause you concern to see him dead?'

That, I decided, was the kind of question only a centuries-old otherworldly being could ask. And there wasn't enough time left to try and explain it all to her now.

'Anyway,' she continued, seeing that I was too busy hyperventilating to reply, 'I still do not understand why you would choose not to mate him, when so much rests upon your answer. I have been wanting to ask this of you since we met in my other form.'

I dragged myself out of puffabilly land long enough to stare at her again. We'd never met before, in this form or any other. She wasn't the kind of woman you easily forgot.

'Look closer,' she said quietly, reading my reaction, and smiling spookily with one side of her mouth.

I did as I was told and looked harder at her, trying to recall if she was one of those faces from the past that Gabriel had mentioned. Someone who'd been lurking on the edge of my life without me even knowing it.

When that failed, I tried half squinting my eyes, as though distorting the angle to get a different picture would help. But no – she was still a ginger-haired behemoth, squatting in the corner, looking amused.

I drew in a breath, suspecting this was one of those occasions when looking with my eyes wouldn't be enough. I closed them, as they were useless, and instead called up the power that Fionnula had told me I had. I started with the white – I do like my routines – and blanked out everything else, scooping it all to one side as though there was a moving wall that bulldozed the present away. It was, as she'd predicted, getting easier. Maybe I'd even be able to experiment with different colour schemes soon.

When my mind was clear, I opened my eyes again – and that's when I saw it. A flickering around the edges of her body; a dark juddering atop her shoulders. The fluttering got stronger, and the colours coalesced into an iridescent black. Shining, oil-dark wings unfurled and haloed around her, swooping up and down, fanning tendrils of red-and-white hair up around her face. Her human shape was still there – but the wings surrounded her, like a moving curtain of black satin.

It was lucky I was already on the floor, or I'd have been crash landing on my backside any minute now.

She was the crow. The crow from the hospital. The crow Coleen said had come for her.

My fists clenched so hard a spike of pain shot up from my damaged finger, and my concentration shattered. The wings disappeared, leaving nothing but a smirk on the Morrigan's face, and confusion on mine.

'You?' I spluttered. 'You took Coleen?'

'I didn't take her, you fool – it was her time. She knew

that, and so do you – surely you had foreseen it? Her miserable existence had come to an end, and that was nothing to do with me. I was there only to share the moment with you, Goddess. But other times . . . yes, other times I take people, and I *relish* it,' she said, her lips twisting into a joyous grin.

'That's why they're all so scared of me – why they grovel so. They fear that, one day, I may land on their shoulder during battle. Is it not so, Champion?'

Carmel had gone pale – which is quite an achievement for someone with her colouring. The black cotton stitches stood out even more starkly as she gulped in air, and struggled even to nod. I was a bit freaked out, but Carmel seemed to be in the grip of a genuine, voice-stealing terror. I had no idea if she'd seen what I'd seen, but she was quaking like a very shocked blancmange.

I felt magic crackling in the air, and the Morrigan seemed to shimmer with energy – her body floated a few inches up from the ground as she smiled, apparently reliving glorious moments from battles gone by. Her hair was lifting with her, streaks of red and silver reaching out to the corners of the room as she laughed quietly away to herself. Death, disaster, mayhem. Such jolly times. Meet Mentor Number Two – a sociopathic crow to follow Fionnula the alcoholic dolly bird. No wonder I wasn't exactly rocking out in goddess school.

The shimmer faded, and she hovered back on to her substantial haunches, muscular thighs swelling through leather that crackled and groaned as she resettled herself.

'I still cannot grasp it, though, child,' she continued, as though nothing at all out of the ordinary had happened, ignoring or simply not noticing the fact that Carmel and I were cowering out of reach.

'Erm . . . what?' I asked, hoping it wouldn't be anything that was likely to get her all happy and excited again. She was hard enough to deal with when she wasn't levitating and laughing like an evil genius.

'I cannot grasp why you cling to your objections. Is Cormac Mor repellent to you? Do you find his physique not sufficient for your demands?'

'No! There's nothing wrong with his . . . physique!' I gasped out, so not liking the way this conversation was going. I wanted to put my hands over my ears and sing out loud to avoid what I suspected was coming next.

'Indeed there is not,' she said emphatically. 'Many women have lusted after him over the decades – he is much younger than I, but still I find he incites desire within me. Is it that you doubt his sexual prowess, then? You need not fear on that front – he was been well trained, and shared his bed with thousands of willing partners during his short life.'

Eek, yuck, and poo. His *short* life? And *thousands* of partners? Was this really supposed to be convincing me? I saw from the Morrigan's serious expression that the answer to that was a resounding 'yes', and realised we were experiencing what you might call a mild culture clash. I'd grown up in the era of safe sex and condoms, and in my particular case, latent Catholic indoctrination – never mind my own problems with skin-to-skin contact. I was feeling a slight roiling sensation in my stomach, and had no words to express what I wanted to say. They simply didn't exist.

Carmel looked at me, at my mouth flapping and skin flaming, and managed to find her voice again. Ever the Champion.

'It's like this, Morrigan,' she said. 'Lily doesn't do men. Not so far, at least.'

'You mean she prefers women?' the Morrigan replied. 'Because that is not the impression I formed when she tried to couple with both the vampire and the High King this evening . . .'

'No!' replied Carmel, nipping that train of thought in the bud. 'I mean she doesn't do *sex*, full stop. Her visions have left her . . . a little behind on that front. She's playing a big game of catch-up, and, well, being forced to choose a mate when she's only just started snogging is a bit of a head fuck for her.'

Eloquently put, I thought. Couldn't have said it better myself – mainly because I was still guppy-gulping.

The Morrigan stared over at me, and narrowed her glittering eyes.

'You mean you have lived without touch for all these years?'

I nodded, and met her gaze as brazenly as I could, considering that I was about to poo my pants. It's not my fault that I've lived the way I have, and I wasn't going to start apologising for it. That was someone else's job.

'Then I better understand your worries,' she said. 'You are but a child in the ways of man and woman, and deserve more kindness than I have shown you thus far.'

She went silent, screwing the top off her bottle and casually crushing the plastic cap with her fist, and I wondered if she'd finished. She downed the water in one, then crushed the bottle too. Maybe all the crushing helped her concentrate.

'You should know, Goddess, right now,' she continued, just when I was starting to think it was safe to breathe again, 'that nobody will be forcing you to do anything. If you choose Cormac as your mate, it can be ceremonial to begin with – a ritual that needs not be followed with the carnal act until you are ready. Until you have more . . . experience? And accepting him as your mate also does not mean that you must take him and him alone to your bed – that is not our way. You will always be free to take more – even the vampire, if that is what pleases you.'

I couldn't see Gabriel being less than pissed off about that one, but hey, it was good to know. Maybe subconsciously my whole reluctance was based on wanting to get out there and slut around a bit – and from what the Morrigan was saying, I could still do that. I could have my beefcake and eat it. Yay.

She crawled across to me, and I instinctively shied away. Because, you know, she was huge and terrifying and could turn into a crow that ate people.

When my back reached the wall, and there was nowhere else to run to, she reached out and took my hand. Hers was half as big again, and her skin was cold and calloused and ridged with scar tissue.

'Look at me, girl,' she said, in her best *or-else* voice.

I looked at her.

'Now, we will sleep. Tomorrow, we will learn. And when night falls, we go to Tara, where you will choose your fate. But hear me, and remember this: I am your protector, and your servant. If any man – mortal, High King or god – lays a hand upon you that you did not invite, I will slay him where he stands, crush his bones beneath my feet, and feed his entrails to the dogs.'

Huge. Terrifying. And on my side.

Chapter Thirty-Two

You see a lot of interesting things on a late-night bus in Liverpool. I've spent years riding them, people-watching, huddled on my own by the window, dreading the inevitably huge woman with seventeen shopping bags who usually wants to sit next to me and share her life story over a packet of custard creams.

There was the man who smelled of wee and read *The Economist* upside down; the woman from Haiti who muttered sinister-sounding curses under her breath every time the bus stopped to let someone on. And – my personal favourite – the old lady who had to be, like, a hundred and counting, with a carrier bag full of brochures for 18-30-style holidays, flicking through them, gnashing her bare gums and cackling, all the way to Aigburth.

This time, I suspected we were the weirdest people on there, and we were getting the surreptitious glances to prove it. The Morrigan loomed large behind us, her sheer bulk – and the battle-ready glint in her eyes – deterring even the most hard-faced scallies from daring to sit next to her. Carmel looked almost like a normal girl, until you noticed the jagged, fresh scar across her face with its stylish shabby-chic stitches.

And me?

I had my new hairdo. I'd woken up that morning channelling Morticia Addams, with a huge dazzlingly white streak in my hair. It ran from root to tip on the left side of my face, and no matter how much I tried to mix it in with the rest of the red, I kept catching sight of it from the corner of my eye. I looked like the Morrigan's wannabe little sister.

It wasn't that it was unattractive – it had a certain Goth pizazz, to be honest. But the fact that my life was now so weird that my hair had spontaneously started to change colour overnight was right up there on the freakity-doo-dah scale. I'd yelped when I'd first seen it draped over my face as I emerged from the shockingly warm cocoon of my army-issue sleeping bag.

Both the Morrigan and Carmel had leaped into action to do some heavy-duty laying-down-of-souls on my behalf – which was very sweet of them – but there was nothing they could do to help, unless they happened to have a bottle of Casting Creme Gloss about their person, and knew how to use it.

'It is nothing – merely the sign that you have given life, as you are meant to do,' pronounced the Morrigan, inspecting the snow-white streak with complete indifference.

'What do you mean, "given life"?' I shrieked, wondering if I'd accidentally gone through labour in my sleep. Immaculate conception and then some.

'The vampire,' she sneered, obviously laughing it up inside big time at the way I was reacting. And I got that – I mean, in the ultimate scheme of things, my hair really didn't matter. Except, you know, I *am* still a girl – and hair always matters.

'You gave him your blood, and with that you gave him life. This is what happens,' she said, back to her you-are-a-mental-patient voice, and then added, 'Look at my hair, child – see how it glows!'

She shook her mane around in an unintentional parody

of a shampoo advert, sunlight filtering through the white-and-red tresses.

'You . . . you've given a lot of life,' I muttered as I looked. It was hard to tell whether it was red striped with white, or the other way round.

She laughed so hard I felt the floor vibrate through the sleeping bag; she held her stomach as if to stop her sides from literally splitting. It was the kind of laugh that could cause tsunamis and earthquakes, and wild horses to stampede across the prairie. I must be *so* funny.

'No, child,' she said, once she'd got herself under control, wiping tears from beneath her eyes. 'Death! I have given a lot of death! And every one is marked here, on my head . . . I carry them all as marks of honour.'

Carmel was looking at her in sheer admiration while absently running her fingers through her own hair. I hadn't asked, but I was guessing she had dispatched a few the night before. Guess we're not all lucky enough to get the Supernatural Barbie makeover.

We'd spent some time in the flat talking – well, mainly listening, in my case. It's fair to say the Morrigan had been around the block a few times, before possibly going on to demolish it. She knew a lot of stuff – about Gabriel, about Fintan, about Tara and what would happen there – that I was glad to know.

She also taught me some useful things about my own powers, puny as they seemed to her, and how to better harness them. As if that wasn't enough, I now had logged in my brain several quick ways to gouge out an eye with my thumb, and stop a man in his tracks by crushing his windpipe.

'Ignore the genitals,' she'd said, snarling. 'They are always the first to be guarded. The fools leave far more important flesh exposed to attack every time. Oh, I could tell you so many tales of men I have killed, ripping out their throats as they stand there cupping their hairy balls!'

Again, good to know. And ignoring men's genitals was something I'd always been especially good at, so I didn't think that would be a problem. It did, however, provoke some very interesting dream sequences during the couple of hours' sleep she allowed us.

Later, as we consumed yet more sandwiches, and Carmel once again phoned in sick to the newsroom, she explained what would happen next. Having kept me safe for the last day – apart from the hair thing – we would rejoin the others, and travel to Tara. I still wasn't clear on how that would happen – Mr Ben-style or a trip to the airport – and she seemed unconcerned with the trivialities.

Travelling, she said, was a base concern for menial fools, and anyone with enough power about them could simply move themselves from A to B through sheer force of will.

I had no doubt at all that the Morrigan could do that – but I was a different matter. I was about a minus two on the goddess scale, with some definite room for improvement. Hence, just after midnight, I found myself sitting on the number 82 Arriva as it drew into the bus station at Paradise Street.

The journey had passed largely without incident – bar the Morrigan seeming tempted to decapitate a couple of security guards who got on wearing their all-black uniforms, and the fact that enormous flocks of birds had followed the bus for the whole journey. It was, without doubt, weird – seeing giant black clouds of them swirling outside the windows as we drove, but nobody else seemed to give it a second thought. What can I say? Liverpool crowds are hard to shock.

We disembarked with the usual ragtag of late-night souls and headed towards the apartment, marching through ice-cold drizzle and a fierce wind that plastered my hair to my face, hiding a ferocious blush that even I was embarrassed about having. Blushing about blushing. My lunacy knew no end.

I was feeling a bit nervous, if truth be told, about how I'd react when I saw Gabriel and Luca again. Other than with mind-searing awkwardness, obviously. The Morrigan had given me some Top Goddess Tips on how to control certain aspects of my nature, and I was going through them as we walked across town.

I was of the Earth, she'd said, and I was born with a default setting to be fertile and fecund and all that good stuff. Obviously something I'd missed out on in the intervening years, but I had a sense it was starting to kick in just a little bit now – if me trying to shag two blokes in public was anything to go by. Part of that had been the inevitable result of my feeding Luca, she thought, but part was also my natural instincts coming out after decades of suppression. Maybe if I'd spent my teenage years bonking my head off like Carmel had, it wouldn't feel so overwhelming – but I hadn't, and there wasn't much I could do about it now. As far as I knew, retrospective slutdom wasn't yet possible.

I needed to concentrate, to maintain my self-control. She'd explained all kinds of ways to do it – many of them revolving around reminding myself that all men were fundamentally flawed dickheads – but I suspected I had a better way, at least for the time being. I'd just go back to being regular old Lily: She Who Shall Not Be Touched. If I didn't touch, I wouldn't be tempted.

I was even walking with my hands shoved deep in my pockets, just in case I accidentally bumped into some passing person with a penis and was consumed by a sudden earth-shattering lust. If that happened, I might be tempted to mount them on the massive concrete steps of the shopping centre, and that just wouldn't do – it was really cold, for starters. I'd get frostbite on my girl bits and they might drop off. I wouldn't be much use as a fertility goddess then, would I?

I knew I was probably over-obsessing. I hadn't seen a man who tickled my fancy at all, never mind one I wanted to straddle. But it was, I think, my own way of distracting me from the bigger issues. Like what was going to happen at Tara; whether Fintan was going to try to kill me; and, at the heart of it all, what I was going to do about Gabriel.

My feelings towards him had been as erratic as a blind-folded tightrope walker, drawing together a huge list of emotions that included hatred, fear, affection, gratitude, anger and a huge dollop of lust. I didn't know what to make of it all – but I knew it was big. Too big to handle right then, if ever. It might be pathetic, but I was kind of hoping that if I ignored it for a bit, it might just go away.

We were walking along The Strand by the waterfront when they first noticed something was wrong. Carmel had been busily quizzing the Morrigan about her various bat-tle techniques – as girls will do – and both of them had been happily and quite correctly ignoring me as I bumbled along at their side, chewing my lip and muttering like I was their autistic stepdaughter.

We were within the moon-cast shadows of the Liver Birds when they both suddenly stopped, their whole bodies on the high-alert mode that I could at least now recognise, if not share. They stood statue-still, nostrils flaring, before their eyes met in a way that clearly held some warrior-shit significance.

Carmel took a small, glinting knife from her coat pocket, choosing it over the larger sword that I knew she had hidden in her jacket. She flicked it open in a way that sug-gested she'd been practising, and the Morrigan flung aside the swoop of her leather to heft out a huge sword half as long as her leg. I'd had no idea she'd been carrying it with her, and her easy stride had showed no signs – that would be centuries of experience for you, I expect.

My eyes flickered between the two of them, and I took a deep breath – I knew what was coming next, and I wasn't going to like it.

'Run!' yelled Carmel.

Chapter Thirty-Three

She was immediately away, sprinting after the Morrigan, who was already disappearing off into the darkness of Water Street.

I legged it as fast as I could, following the two of them down by the side of the Liver Buildings, weaving through parked cars and around ornate cast-iron lamp posts, pounding in their footsteps until we reached the wide stretch of paving in front of the river.

There's a long boulevard behind the Liver Buildings, leading from the artily stylish concrete box of the Museum of Liverpool down to the cruise terminal and a long line of office blocks. At that time of night, there should be nothing there. Workers have gone home to watch the telly and make their packed lunches for the next day; tourists are watching Beatles tribute acts in Mathew Street, and the ferries have long since stopped running.

It should be empty. It should be deserted. The river should be roiling and churning alone in the moonlight, watched only by the beady eyes of the Liver Birds and the occasional passing drunk.

Instead, the whole promenade was pulsating with bodies, what looked like hundreds of them, writhing and screaming and fighting. The din was brutal: shrieks of pain and cries of rage and the constant underlying clanging of metal on metal, and the dull, wet thud of steel on flesh. All of it overridden by the gale-force winds howling up towards us from the might of an angry river.

I scrambled up on to the railing along the riverside, bracing myself against the tug of the wind, giving myself the extra height to see what was going on. The lighting was dim, scattered street lamps and cloud-covered moondust shining down on the scene, striping everything a sickly shade of gold.

I dragged my hair back from my eyes, and gazed ahead. As far as I could see, all along the waterfront, there was nothing but battle. Fintan's men in black were camouflaged in the night air, but as cloud scudded away across the yellow of the moon, I saw them – so bloody many of them. Like an army of vicious ants, hacking and yelling and stomping and moving together, so many it looked like the road had turned black and started to roll like fresh tar.

I spotted Finn, sword raised above his head, whirling around like a mini tornado, making up for his lack of height with his huge strength. As he spun, the sword sliced and diced, and I saw skin and blood flying, his face splattered with it as his enemies fell screaming to their knees at his feet.

Connor and Kevin were back to back, like some deranged parody of a school three-legged race, swords flying through the night air as they manoeuvred. There was dark liquid flowing over Connor's face, and although it wasn't light enough to see, I knew it was blood. His blood or someone else's, I couldn't tell.

The vampires were slithering low to the ground, a lithe, undulating pack of teeth and muscle. They were taking men down by their knees and setting on them like hounds, ripping and tearing at their flesh with their fangs. A flurry of scuffling black scurried towards the glow of a lamp, like the rugby scrum from hell. I saw Isabella's beautiful black head rear up. Her face was distorted with rage and hunger, and what looked like a torn-off ear was flapping from her mouth, still dripping and oozing. She shook it from side to side, like a cat worrying a bird, then spat it out, diving back down to go for more.

I almost gagged at the sight, and that's when the smell hit me: the rotten stink of death and blood and pain and shit. I clenched my eyes tightly shut, trying to stop myself from puking, fainting, or just plain losing my balance and tumbling head first into the Mersey. I'd been in there once this week, and that was quite enough for anyone.

Carmel was at my side, knife in hand, her whole body thrumming with the need to throw herself into the carnage. Her eyes were huge, whisky-coloured pools of longing. What I saw physically sickened me – but I could see it called to her in a way I'd never understand.

The Morrigan grabbed hold of Carmel, shaking her by the shoulders to drag her gaze away from the battle and back to her face.

'Your job is to guard her! Keep her safe until I return, or your life will be forfeit! Do you understand?'

She shook her even harder with every word, until Carmel's curly black hair was jiggling, and the lust in her expression faded. Lust. Seemed a strange word to use, but it was the right one – because what I'd seen in her eyes was more lustful than any look I'd ever seen her give to a man. God, what had I done to her?

Carmel nodded vigorously, and pulled away from the Morrigan's bone-crunching grip.

'Yes, I understand! I am her Champion and I will remain at her side until the Dark Day comes!' she replied.

'We pray that is not yet upon us,' murmured the Morrigan, turning to look up at me. 'And you, child – you stay out of it!' she commanded, pointing a long finger at my face.

With that, she glanced once more at the devastation

unfolding before us. As far as we could see, there were black-clothed men, all of them advancing steadily on the group that stood at the heart of the seething mass. The group that could never stand against them, no matter how brave, how skilled, how vicious they were.

The Morrigan frowned, then ran, hair and black leather streaming behind her as she pounded off in the opposite direction. I felt disappointment scythe through me: she was the baddest of the bad, the ass-kicker to end them all, the only one who could help – and she'd abandoned us. The Morrigan, the Harbinger of Death, had run away into the night.

I forced myself to look back at the fight. To hear the terrible sounds, and smell the terrible smells, and see the way that oil-black swell of the Faidh was pressing ever nearer to people I knew. People I cared about. People who were willing to die to save me.

I didn't want to look back – but I had to. Because I needed to know where he was, if he was safe . . . if he was even still alive.

'Gabriel!' I shrieked, standing as high as I could on the railing, feeling the wind steal my words and the cold spray of the river water leap up to slap my face, icy fingers telling me to wake up, grow up, man up. Gerra grip, girl, I heard, in the quiet, rasping tones of Coleen as she lay dying in her hospital bed. Get a grip and stop all of this death. You were born to give life – and all you've done so far is look on and weep as people die.

There was an almighty howl in the dead centre of the war raging in front of me, and an explosion of bodies flew into the sky. Six, seven, maybe eight of them – black-clad and limp, thrown up and over the heads of the crowd in a sudden arc, windmilling limbs, flying for yards before thudding down, landing on hard ground or on the heads of their fellow soldiers, crushing down whole screaming crowds.

He emerged from the pack, roaring my name.

So much taller. So much bigger. So much scarier.

Gabriel.

He'd created a temporary vacuum around him, but it took seconds for more men in black to fill it. They surged forwards, surrounding him, swords glinting, pressing closer and closer until all I could see of him was his head and shoulders, staring out and looking for me.

His mighty arms worked as he searched, his clawed hands tearing and searing and ripping flesh from bone. Some of the blades that lunged in his direction hit home, and I could see the gashes open up on his skin – across his chest, his forearm, his neck. Still he searched, yelling 'Lily!' over and over again in a voice that boomed over the sonic drone of the wind and the battle and the death.

I could see him weakening, and more of his precious blood flowing. Kevin and Connor were working their way towards him, trying to protect their king, but they were too far away. They wouldn't reach him in time. There were too many of them – swarming over Gabriel like cockroaches now, trying to drag him back down. Two were hanging off his neck, climbing around his shoulders, attempting to hold his arms still so the others could attack.

He flung them off like toys, only to be faced with more. He was huge, vast. Twisted and vicious and ugly and magnificent, all at the same time. But there were too many of them. He was going down, inch by bloody inch he was going down. One of the Faidh used the pommel of his sword to hit him repeatedly in the face, and blood spattered from his nose as he staggered backwards, dazed and blinded.

Sensing his weakness they flew, a tide of oncoming death, towards him, screaming curses and stabbing blades and kicking him over and over again until he started to stumble, to topple back in giant, shuddering steps. If he fell, they'd have him, I knew. Even he couldn't fight off this many – not with his magic, not with his claws, not even with the Sword of Lugh, which he was trying to wield as the black wave drowned him.

I heard my name called once more, a searing growl so inhuman it belonged in a fairy-tale forest, not in front of a row of abandoned office blocks in Liverpool. I called back to him, and our eyes met briefly – for one sweet second.

He might look like a monster. He might occasionally act like one. But the eyes were still his – distant discs of dark in the moonlight, though I knew they'd be shining, dark and violet as he struggled to reach me. He was still the man who loved me, in the only – flawed – way he knew how.

There was another rush of incoming Faidh, a swathe of black that pushed and shoved and chopped its way towards him. Dozens of them, racing over him, until finally . . . finally, he fell. His body disappeared beneath them, engulfed by darkness, and he was gone.

As I watched, I felt a stab of anguish and desperation sear through me, sharper than any broken fingers or vampire bites or any pain I'd ever experienced in my whole fruitless existence. He was going to die – and here I was, watching. Again. A helpless onlooker as his life seeped away.

I couldn't do it. I wouldn't do it. Even if it meant the end of me, the end of the world, the end of everything, I couldn't do it. I heard the shrieks of horror go up from Connor and Kevin as they reached him too late, followed by the pack-hound howls of the vampires. By my side, I saw tears falling from Carmel's eyes, her face washed pale in the moonlight as she quietly sobbed. With the High King gone, it would take only minutes for the rest to be slaughtered: without their centre, they'd be doomed.

I shook my head, clearing my eyes of limp strands of hair. No. I wouldn't let this happen. The time for losing people was over. Gabriel was mine – whether I wanted him or not – in the same way that Carmel was mine, Luca was mine. All of them. They were mine, and I was not going to let Fintan take any of them.

The Morrigan had told me to stay out of it – but how could I? And where had doing what I was told ever got me? I've been a good little girl my whole life, and now people were dying for me.

I reached out while she wept, and grabbed the pocket-knife from Carmel's hand. I flicked it open, and stood as tall as I could on the railing, battered by the storm and drenched by the rain that had started to sleet down on us like ice.

'I am the Goddess Mabe, Mother of the Mortals!' I screamed as loud as I could. 'And I offer myself to the world in sacrifice – my life for these!'

I don't know where the words came from, and I certainly don't know where the sound came from – my voice was amplified, like I was hooked up to a PA, booming and echoing over the din, over the battle screams, over the wind.

A brilliant white light suddenly shone over everything, spilling across bloody faces and shining swords and crawling, damaged bodies – like a floodlight switched on at a late-night football match, making them shield their eyes against its dazzling ferocity.

I looked down, and realised it was coming from me, that my whole body was wavering and flaring and shimmering with brightness.

I took a gulp, almost floored as a shocking flood of awareness flowed through me: I could feel it all. I could feel everything. The pain and the agony and the determined fury of the Faidh. The sadness and desperation of Gabriel's men. The communal grief of the vampires, the ferrous tang of the blood still in their throats. I could even feel the confusion of the fish in the water, the tiny fluttering heartbeats of the woken gulls, the frantic scurrying of thousands of insects being crushed underfoot. The aloof fascination of a lone feral cat, watching from a safe distance on one of the office-block rooftops.

It was all there, inside me, so pure and clear I wanted to scream. I wanted it over with. I wanted my own head back.

The light shining from my body intensified, and I cried out: 'This must cease! By the command of the Goddess, this must *cease*!'

My words thundered through the air, and I felt my power swoop down over the heads of them all – the Faidh, the vampires, all of them. They were mine to command, whether they liked it or not, I knew that now. I didn't have to stand and watch. I didn't have to be the onlooker. I was the cause of all of this destruction – and I could be the end of it.

I held my arms aloft, and the light swam and flurried around me, leaving my shadow cast huge over their confused faces. Suddenly, everything stopped. It was as though some almighty remote control in the sky had pressed the pause button. Everything – everyone – became still, as they felt the strength of my words and my power binding them. I'd found it accidentally, through fear and desperation, but I'd found it at last.

I saw swords paused mid-air, fists stopping mid-punch, and the vampires standing upright and huddled together. The undulating movement of the massed Faidh came to a halt, and they all turned as one to look at me.

Me. Lily McCain. Standing incandescent on a railing in the rain, at the edge of an ancient river, with a knife held to her breast.

Carmel was screaming at me to get down, to stop, to give her the fucking knife. She tried to pull me back down without pushing me over, scrambling around my legs and cursing at me. I kicked at her with my right Doc Marten, feeling the boot connect with the flesh of her shoulder, and pushed her away. She landed on her back, still yelling, still raging. I ignored her, and looked ahead.

The sounds of the battle had finally quieted, replaced with the gusting wind and a quiet hum of communal expectation as they all waited to see what I would do next. What the Goddess would command of them.

That, of course, was a mystery to me as well. But instinct had got me this far, and instinct was all I had.

That, and a very sharp knife.

The secret was in my blood. The damned blood of the Goddess that flew through my veins. The blood had saved Luca, and now, if I played it right, could save Gabriel too. And Kevin. And Carmel. And all of them, even the foot soldiers of the damned Faidh. All of them, in exchange for my blood.

I wasn't thinking straight. I was operating purely on adrenaline, and what I felt to be right. I was scared of losing Gabriel. I was scared of what I'd turned Carmel into. And I was so tired – so very, very sick and tired – of all the death and violence and waste that was going on around me. And it was all because of me. Enough people had died in my name, and I would always carry that burden – but no more. Never again.

I took the knife, and dragged it, hard, across my chest. From the top of my right breast to above my heart, which was thudding so hard the whole world must have been able to hear it.

The blade cut easily through the thin cotton of my blouse, and almost as easily through my skin. I was so cold, so pumped up, so completely sure that this was the right thing to do that, at first, I felt no pain. I just looked down, and saw the blood. A fine line of brilliant red instantly appeared along the cut. At first it oozed and dripped, then it flowed and seeped, turning the white fabric of my top into a Rorschach test of scarlet.

Maybe it was seeing it, maybe it was real – but suddenly it started to hurt. Like a complete bastard. There was a lot of blood, more every moment I stared at it, spreading across my whole torso and creeping in a warm, viscous furrow towards the waistband of my jeans.

I was dimly aware of Carmel, still screaming; of Gabriel, roaring at me, calling me a stupid fool; of the sound of my own pulse banging louder than all of it, thundering through my brain like Satan's steam train; of distant car alarms wailing, and the glass in the windows of the offices shattering and shedding and sprinkling to the floor.

Above it all, there was a whooping and beating and wrenching sound, hurting my ears, getting closer by the second.

I felt fuzzy, strange, cold and hot all at the same time. I was wobbling and wavering and felt the knife slip from my wet fingers, splashing down into the river.

I looked up and saw the Morrigan's face inches from mine, drenched in rain and sweat and fury. She was sitting astride an enormous bird, its wings spanning two dozen feet or more, its cold, unblinking eye staring at me like a worm it was about to eat.

I smelled copper, and heard a mechanical clank as the beast swooped its wings around me, flapping my hair up into a red-and-white cloud in its backdraft.

The Morrigan reached out, grabbed hold of my hands and tugged me up, throwing me across the bird's almighty back. It was hard and cold and completely devoid of feathers, fur or anything other than rough, jarring metal, slick with rain.

'Hold on!' she shouted, and I felt a stomach-churning jolt as we were up and away. Swooping and clinking and banging and screeching as we climbed higher and higher. I gazed down and saw the faces of my friends staring up at me. I saw Gabriel reach out, one clawed hand grasping uselessly at empty air. I saw Luca howling, and Carmel screaming and waving as I disappeared off into the night sky, all of them getting smaller and smaller as we flew. I saw the river, flowing steel-grey, churning in the wind, carrying swords and shields and bloody, broken bodies away with it.

And I saw the Liver Buildings. Minus one bird.

We were so high, I thought I could reach the moon. I stretched up one hand to touch its yellow surface, wondering if it was made of cheese.

The effort was too much. My hand drooped back down by my side, and I drooped back out of consciousness.

Chapter Thirty-Four

I was naked, and lying on something soft, furry, and very, very warm. I squished around a bit, luxuriating in the way it felt against my bare skin, then rolled over on to my side.

I risked opening one eye, and came face to face with the extended jaw of a bear, face for ever frozen in its death howl. Yikes.

I sat up, a bit quicker than my body wanted me to, and had a brief dizzy-making head-rush. I glanced back down at the bear. It looked as startled as I was, poor thing.

The bearskins were thrown over some kind of wooden pallet, in the corner of a room that appeared as much cave as boudoir. The walls were hewn from rock, and traces of silica and crystal glinted in the light thrown from the huge open fire.

Broad tapestries were hanging from the stone walls, bearing scenes of torture: witch-burning and giants biting people's heads off, along with dozens of other gruesome scenarios. Must be what people did for kicks before they got cable, I supposed. I shuddered, and tore my gaze away – they made Hieronymus Bosch look like a pastoral idyll. Burning braziers were suspended from the ceiling in black iron bowls, flickering shadows across the pictures and making them all look a bit too lively for my mental health.

Even though my flesh was bare, I felt warm – partly due to the fact that the room was a fire marshal's worst nightmare, and partly due to the fact that I was sitting ass-naked on Winnie the Pooh and his pals. The room was vast, and smelled of smoke and coal and rich damp earth and the kinds of herbs you get bombarded with at Christmas markets.

I could see piles of books, the tops of them used as shelves for ornate rocks, intricate gadgets and miniature oil paintings, all propped upright and leaning against the walls. I was in his room. Its name was Teach Chormaic, my brain told me.

I opened my mouth to ask where I was, then realised two things: (a) I was alone, so it would be pointless, and (b) I already knew.

I was in Tara. I'd never even been to Ireland before, other than my jaunts to Dublin's fair city and Fionnula's cottage, but I somehow knew it. It felt familiar. Safe. Comforting – despite the bloodthirsty artwork. It was a place of refuge. A place of protection. A place of choice.

There was a bottle of Evian on the floor next to me, which looked completely out of place in the midst of the whole medieval-cellar-chic look, but I leaned down to grab it. I was so, so thirsty . . . which, I thought as I swigged greedily, might be down to the blood loss.

The blood loss incurred shortly after stabbing myself with a pocketknife, and shortly before being spirited away on the back of a Liver Bird by an ancient Celtic warrior goddess. Just another day at the office for Lily McCain.

Apart from the dehydration, my body felt fine – but I still couldn't quite face looking down and inspecting the damage. It was like a hangover – purely self-inflicted – but not as much fun. With that thought in mind, I took another look at the side of the pallet. Sure enough, there was an unopened blister pack of paracetamol sitting there, along with an open can of still-fizzing Diet Coke. I smiled.

Water, paracetamol, Diet Coke. Carmel had definitely been here. Which meant, you know, that she was alive and all.

I left the painkillers where they were. Admittedly, I hadn't moved much yet, and hadn't dared look at my chest for fear of swooning like a baby girl, but nothing was hurting enough to justify taking the tabs. The fact that my friend was not only in the land of the living, but well enough to resume usual post-booze-up business, was all the high I needed. And if Carmel was all right, the chances were that everyone else was as well.

I knew the Morrigan had been fine. Fine enough to pilot an eighteen-foot metal bird from Liverpool to County Meath, anyway. And I'd seen Gabriel as we'd flown overhead . . . He'd seemed a bit angry, now I cast my mind back. He may even have called me a few names. He was probably, in fact, storming around the building banging his head on the cave roofs and swelling like a big fat lip at this exact moment in time.

Huh. Interesting. I hadn't wanted him to die – but now, I was in no rush to see him, either. I was kind of fed up of being shouted at by Mr Tall and Mighty. I really needed to find a way of stopping him from doing it. Maybe I should take some tips from the tapestries in the room, and cut out his tongue with a red-hot poker? That'd cramp his scolding style.

I stood up, stretched tall, lifting my arms in the air and testing my body. Nope. No searing pain. No tearing flesh. No sudden urge to squeal for the paramedics. I glanced downwards towards my boobs, but kept my eyes squinted half-shut, like I did when I was little and there was something scary on the telly. I could make out the hazy outline of a dark mark, just above my breasts. I prayed to God – my close personal friend – that whoever had stitched me up had done a better job of it than they had Carmel's face.

It was too dark to see properly, so I walked over to one of the braziers, as yet unlit, to see if I could perform some magic trick and make it poof into life. Surely handy stuff like that should be included in my new skill set? I mean, did it all have to be doom and gloom and sticking knives in my tits? Couldn't I at least get one break, and have fag-lighter fingers or something?

As it turned out, I didn't need them, so I never got to find out. There was one of those old-fashioned long metal gas lighters resting on the edge of the bowl, the kind Nan used to use to light the oven before the days of automatic ignition. I clicked the button, and a blue flame shot out. The minute it touched the coals they blazed into magnificent orange life, and I jumped back to avoid getting my eye-brows singed. Possibly I said 'eek' as well.

As I stared at the fire, hypnotised by its flickering dance, I realised I wasn't entirely alone after all. A huge dog appeared from the shadows and ambled towards me, all legs and muscle and haunches. Like a five-foot-tall lurcher. His coat – her coat, I corrected myself, after a surreptitious glance at the relevant body parts – was a smooth, sleek black, giving her inquisitive head the look of a curious seal. Her fur was shining and glinting in the firelight, the sparks dappling over the elegant lines of her long body, as though a thousand tiny jewels were trapped beneath her skin. Maybe it was a trick of the light. Maybe it was a magic dog.

She came closer, sniffing and snuffling and fixing me with huge, freakishly intelligent eyes, arctic blue ringed with gold. I held out my hand, and she took a gentle push at it with her wet nose. I had the strangest feeling that she was giving me time to get used to her, letting me become accustomed to her look and her scent, in the same way we all teach kids to safely approach new dogs. That she was the sentient being, and I was the easily spooked animal . . . well, that was fine by me, as long as she didn't expect me to start sniffing her arse as well.

I leaned down, ran my fingers over her sparkling, smooth seal's head, scratching behind her ears in a way that seemed to meet with her approval.

'Hello, girl,' I murmured, 'aren't you the beautiful one? What's your name, then?'

'What would you do if she answered?' came a new voice from the corner of the room. A familiar voice. One that was, as usual, laughing at me. I shrieked, and ran for the cover of the bed, skidding my fine naked self so far across the shiny bearskins that I thudded against the eroded stone wall on the other side.

I ignored the sharp scrape of rock on my flesh, grabbed one of the coats, and threw it over me.

'Jesus!' I said, so loudly that the dog cocked her ears and looked at me in question. She closed the distance between us in two athletic strides, jumped straight up on to the pallet, and circled exactly three times before curling herself up in a tight ball, nose tucked into tail. Dogs on beds. Probably not in the Barbara Woodhouse training manual, but I kind of liked having her there. I'd learned to take my allies where I could find them.

'Where are you, Luca?' I shouted. 'And how long have you been there?'

He emerged from the same dark corner of the room as the dog had, and strolled close enough that the light from the braziers flickered across his body. His completely, totally, day-he-was-born naked body.

'Long enough,' he replied, grinning so broadly I could see the tips of his fangs. Ugh. He'd been there long enough to see me tarting around starkers, obviously. And while that state of affairs didn't seem to bother Mr Free and Easy over there, I was feeling decidedly squeamish about it. As well as decidedly . . . well, curious would probably be the right word.

I realise this may seem a strange confession for a grown woman, but I had, up until that point, never seen a real-life penis up close and personal in my entire life. Unless you counted that time I caught Jason McGee wanking over a poster of Mariah Carey on the backseat of the school bus – and I had looked away pretty damned fast on that occasion, as any sane person would.

Now, here was Luca, strutting his pretty magnificent stuff right in front of me, stretching and twisting and doing all kinds of things to make his muscles pop and his skin ripple in all the right places. Probably, knowing him, one hundred per cent on purpose. He was a damned fine specimen of manhood, and boy did he know it.

I found my eyes drifting from his dark-blond head to his golden-brown shoulders. To the powerful chest, scattered with silky hair, and the super-flat stomach, ridged with gracious lines of muscle. And after that . . . yes, there it was. In all its dangly glory. I tried not to, but I really couldn't help but stare. I knew he wouldn't mind. In fact, I deduced from the fascinating amount of twitching and swelling going on down there, he actually quite liked it. Pervert.

I snapped my eyes shut, and physically slapped myself across the face, hard enough to leave finger-shaped tingles across my skin. The dog quirked one eyebrow at me, obviously wondering what all the fuss was about.

'Put some fucking clothes on!' I hissed. 'I won't open my eyes until you do!'

I heard him laughing, and gave some serious thought to asking Fionnula how I could turn him into a toad. Or a hyena, so he could chuckle away to himself all day long, the twat. But I also heard him rummaging around on the floor, and the welcome sound of a zipper being tugged up.

I risked a quick peek, and saw that he was dressed – on the bottom half, at least. The half I'd been most concerned about. There was pretty much a fifty-fifty mix of relief and disappointment in me at that one, so I concentrated on playing with the dog's ears instead – trickier than it sounds when you're also trying to use a bearskin to protect your fast-disappearing modesty in front of a sex-charged vampire Adonis.

He sat down next to me on the pallet, and reached out to

give the dog a scratch under her chin. She rolled over, lifting her legs in the air to show him her belly, and gave his hand a quick lick. The floozy.

He made a clapping noise on his thighs, and gave a quick whistle. Another three dogs appeared from the darkness, and trotted towards us. They all had the same build as my dog – because, well, in my newly acquisitive frame of mind, I had decided she was mine – long, lean, with racing legs and powerfully muscled haunches.

They also all had the same shimmer to their coats, even though they were all different colours, as though there was something glowing beneath their skin. They all sank to Luca's feet, and he started to tickle their tummies with his bare toes.

'We're old friends,' he said. 'I snuck in here last night and slept with them. Donn has forbidden me from staying with the others for my slumber, and I found I missed the warmth of a body next to mine. I didn't think you'd be overly thrilled if I climbed in there with you, so I stayed with the curs. I needed their companionship, and I needed to be near you. Was that all right?'

All right? Was it all right that he chose to sleep with the dogs instead of me? That Donn had forbidden him from staying with the others? That he *needed* to be near me? That he was even asking my opinion about all of this anyway? No. Precisely none of it was all right. Apart from the bit where I got to see a nice big willy for the first time, anyway – that had been bearable.

'Depends,' I said, refusing to look into his eyes, and making sure our hands didn't touch over the now-snoozing form of the dog. No touchy, no tempty. 'On what you mean by "slept with" the dogs . . .'

He laughed, and I felt the bed shake. He was edging a bit closer as he guffawed, obviously hoping I wouldn't notice. That I'd be so distracted by the sight of his perfectly formed pecs bouncing up and down that it would pass me by.

'Stay right where you are,' I said, holding out a hand to ward him off, 'and tell me what I've missed. And tell me why Donn's pissed off with you.'

He took his attention away from the dogs, and turned to look at me. His chocolate-drop eyes suddenly swam with tears, and it was all I could do to stop myself from reaching out to console him. I bit down on my lip, using the pain as a reminder of all that could go hideously wrong in my life if I let this man get too close to me. I could, with one touch of his fingers, turn entirely into the World's Biggest Ho. Seriously, the world's biggest – people would queue up to see me as a freak-show attraction.

'My former lord is pissed off, as you say, because I let you feed me. I drank of the Goddess's blood, and now I belong to you. After centuries of living with them, of sleeping with them and eating with them and travelling with them, I am now cast out. I am cast out, and he is punishing Isabella for allowing it to happen. She is forbidden to drink human blood for a month, and instead must sustain herself on the fruit of rats and other vermin.'

Nice image, I thought, all too vividly picturing her chomping down on a wiggly tailed rodent. *Bon appetit*, Isabella.

'You mean he would've preferred it if you'd died?' I replied, after glorying in that concept for a moment. OK, so she'd saved my life on the odd occasion – but we weren't exactly BFFs. She tended to rip holes in my flesh a bit too often for that level of bonding.

I didn't much care about her new pest-food diet, but I was worried about the situation. For a start, the band was going to have to find a new drummer – always tough. And more importantly, what was I going to do about Luca?

I hadn't expected Donn to be delighted with this turn of events, but, well, there were extenuating circumstances, m'lord. I'd hoped to be giving Luca back sometime soon, and certainly wasn't keen on the idea of him following me around and sleeping with my dogs. Somewhere, in the back of my mind, I also registered the fact that having the Lord of the Dead as your frenemy probably wasn't the coolest thing in the world.

'Yes, of course he would have preferred me to die,' he said, as though it was obvious. 'Isabella should by rights have let me pass . . . It was a weakness on her part that we must now all pay the price for. I have certainly lived long enough, by anybody's standards, *bellisima*. But what is done is done. Donn has no further use for me, and I am yours to do with as you will.'

He raised an eyebrow at me with that final line, and I saw some of the usual flirty spark return to his eyes. Enough of it that I just shook my head, and moved on. Vampires, eh? Can't live with 'em; can't shag 'em in case they eat you.

'What about everyone else? I assume they all made it here OK? I'm sure Carmel did, but what about—'

I was about to say 'Gabriel', or possibly fudge it a bit and try to appear unconcerned by saying 'everyone else', but I didn't get the chance. The dog on the bed leaped off, flying through the air in a graceful, glimmering arc, and ran to the door. The rest of the pack all followed her, whining and barking and scratching at the ground with their claws, as though they were trying to dig an escape tunnel to the other side.

They'd obviously heard something out there that I couldn't, and before I got pissed off at still having no new superpowers, I reminded myself that even normal dogs could do that. Carmel's family pooch was always waiting in the window way before the car pulled up, smiling its daft Staffy grin, its stubby tail wagging its whole fat body in a frenzy of happiness.

The door swung open, heaving wood on inches-thick hinges, and the Boss walked in. At least, he was obviously that as far as the dogs were concerned. They all jumped up around Gabriel, which was an impressive sight as they were as tall as him on their back legs. They rested their paws on his chest, his shoulders, anywhere they could find a spare bit of flesh, and set about licking him and nipping him and generally adoring him, cord-thin tails whipping like windscreen wipers in a storm.

For a moment he completely disappeared inside an excitedly wobbling canine curtain, and I had an unwelcome flashback to the night before: to Gabriel staggering and falling and finally succumbing to the pressing crowds of Faidh around him. I drove back the anguish, but held on to the thought: I might feel decidedly ambiguous about the man right now, but when he was under threat, I'd cared enough to sacrifice myself to save him.

That wasn't an easy thought to maintain, as he pushed the dogs aside and strode angrily into the room. His poor face was battered and bruised, his beautiful nose slightly less straight than it used to be, purple flowers blossoming over the high arcs of his cheekbones. I could see scars and scrapes and jagged, half-healed cuts running over his neck where they'd hacked at him, and I should, by rights, have felt nothing but sympathy and regret.

But the look on his face did a pretty good job of chasing all of that away, and replacing it with a stone-cold anger of my own. He stared at us sitting together on the bed, Luca half-naked and me clasping the bearskin to my exposed flesh, clutching it over my chest like a starlet caught out by the paparazzi, and growled. Actually growled, in a way that made the dogs cower and whimper at his feet, and didn't do much for my state of mind, either.

His eyes were blazing, and he stood tall and arrogant before us, taking in the scene. No 'How are you today, Lily?' or 'Good morning, Lily,' or 'Hey, thanks for saving my life by sticking a knife in your own heart, Lily.' Nothing but that violet glare and a sense of rapidly building fury swelling through his trembling body.

'Get out, leech!' he hissed, and I guessed he was talking

to Luca. I'm clever like that. The vampire responded with a hiss of his own, which was far more impressive – sibilant and bloodthirsty all at the same time. He was definitely winning on the hissing contest front.

Luca leaped up from the bed, seeming to fly through the air kung-fu legend stylee, and landed in a crouch in front of Gabriel. I recognised the pose now – the battle-ready stance of the vampire, half-human, half-animal, ready to attack at the knees and bring down their prey. I could see tiny sparks physically jumping from Gabriel's fingers as they faced off, and felt the crackle of magic pervading the air.

Luca was snarling and circling. Gabriel was channelling Carrie. This, I decided, was a situation where one of them could very easily die. If I was lucky, both of them . . .

I sighed, realising that I was getting a bit fed up of playing the human buffer zone between the various psychopaths that now inhabited my life. Give me a bar-room brawl in Liverpool any day – at least there were always bouncers to break things up. Here, I was the bouncer, and I hadn't even shaved my head that week.

I stood up, trying to keep the bearskin wrapped around me, and quickly realised that unless I wanted to hobble towards them and fall in an undignified heap at their feet, it wasn't going to work. So I dropped it down, and strode tall and naked in their direction. Naked, I thought, would probably score higher on the distraction scale anyway. And I'd definitely look better than the average bouncer.

I will confess to feeling a very ungracious rush of empowerment as I placed myself between them, and looked on as their collective jaw dropped to the floor. The flickers faded from Gabriel's fingers, and Luca stood up straight, eyeing me appreciatively as I flaunted myself. Yep. That had definitely worked.

I placed my hands on my hips, and stuck out my boobies. If you're going to do something, might as well do it right.

'Luca,' I said, when I'd got their extremely undivided attention, 'leave us. Go take Isabella a ferret, or something.'

'I do not wish to leave you,' he said, his voice dripping with a strange blend of anguished need and good old-fashioned lust.

'You have no choice, right? If I tell you to do it, you do it? So jog on, kitty – leave us alone.'

Gabriel was sneering, grinning at Luca in a way that clearly said 'my dick's bigger than yours'. He obviously thought he'd won some kind of big battle, the dumbskull. Honestly, hundreds of years on the planet, and at heart he was still a teenage boy fighting behind the bike sheds.

'Yes,' said Gabriel, 'leave us. And be cautious, Luca, of how you behave around the Goddess – her blood is sacred, and her body is mine. She has no use for you or your kind, with your parasitical ways and your concept of love and death – I will not let you use her, or drain her for your sex. She is not your plaything.'

Ooh. There was so much wrong with that little speech I didn't know quite where to start. My body was very much my own, thank you very much – apart from those brief interludes where I seemed to be possessed by the spirit of a Playboy Bunny. And as for Luca killing during sex? I could *so* see how that would happen, and it sent a little chill all the way down my spine. I'd have to remind myself of that next time I was leching over his boy bits.

Luca looked at me again, and I made a 'take a hike' gesture with my head, nodding towards the door.

'If it is what you wish, Lily, then I will leave you,' he said, 'but only because you ask it of me – not because Cormac Mor tells me to. And remember this – yes, there are aspects of my nature that might be repellent to you as a mortal woman, but at least I never speak untrue to you, Goddess. I don't expect you to live your life as a child, forever doing my bidding, wrapped in a web of lies that I have spun all around you.'

With a final glower at Gabriel, he stalked towards the door, making us, and the dogs, all jump with the ferocity of his exiting slam. I waited for a moment, half expecting a rockfall.

Right. One down, one to go. I glared at the one in question, then started to patrol around the room, looking for clothes. I finally found a T-shirt and some leggings neatly folded on top of a chair, and climbed into them as elegantly as I could, given the fact that he was staring at me so hard I could almost feel boreholes singeing into my skin. I felt so much better once I was covered – that whole 'knock 'em dead naked' power trip had a very limited shelf life, before I just started feeling mortified and wanting to join a nunnery.

'Is everyone safe?' I asked, sitting down on the bed and popping out a couple of those paracetamol. Strangely enough, I could now feel a headache coming on.

'Are you well?' he asked, ignoring my question and frowning as he pulled a chair up to sit opposite me, looking on as I fumbled with the tabs.

'Yes,' I shot back, gulping in a couple of mouthfuls of Diet Coke to swill them down. 'I think I'm just suffering from testosterone poisoning after that little scene. Now, answer me – did everyone make it back OK?'

'We did,' he replied, staring at my chest. I suspected his gaze was less about being a perv than recalling the events of the night before. I waited for the thank yous, although I knew they'd never come.

'You're welcome,' I said, fixing him with a pretty angry stare. 'No need to thank me.'

'Thank you?' he snapped. 'You are expecting gratitude, for jeopardising everything I have ever worked for? For not trusting me to triumph in a battle that has been centuries in the making? For leaving me there, not knowing if you were alive or dead? I will not thank you for that, Lily. Your last actions were foolish, ill-conceived and stupid beyond even my usual expectations of you.'

As he ranted, he grabbed hold of my wrist, and held it so tightly it hurt. I looked down at his fingers, and tried to breathe through the usual rush of panic at someone – anyone – touching me.

I pulled together that mental barrier I'd been working so hard on, trying to block him out, and found it was easy. Maybe it had been last night's events; maybe I was just getting better at this shit – but I knew that unless I deliberately lowered my guard, he wouldn't be able to get into my mind, and I wouldn't get an inappropriate fit of visions. I didn't have time to celebrate that fact right now, but I knew at some point it would feel pretty good – finally being liberated from a burden I'd carried my whole life.

As I was having so much fun, I decided to step up my game and try something new – conjuring up an image, and throwing it at him, as fast and as hard as I could. The image I chose was of a gun firing out a stream of liquid manure, and I aimed it right at his face.

He dropped my hand suddenly, rubbing his own fingers like they'd been burned, and looked at me with a tinge of his own panic clouding the deep-shaded navy of his eyes. I'd obviously hurt him somehow, and I have to confess it felt good.

'Don't call me names,' I said, sharply. 'I'm getting pretty fed up of it. Now, why are you here, and what do you want?'

I saw a rush of emotions play over his face – he wasn't a man used to being challenged, especially not by little old me. In the end, he just sighed, and smiled, and stroked the white streak of hair back from my face in a way that made my tummy do a little flip. Damn. I might be able to control the supernatural mind patrol, but I was still a sucker for the gentle touch of his fingers against my skin. I suspected that was a far more difficult condition to control. It was called being female.

'I shouldn't be here at all,' he finally said, letting his

hand drop and rest tentatively on my shoulder. Probably scared I was going to start slinging cow shit at him again. 'But I needed to see you, to see for myself that you were as well as the Morrigan insisted – her standards of "well" are not the same as most people's. Technically, I am forbidden to see you until the ceremony. Until the . . . choosing.'

I noted the careful way he used the word, savouring it on his tongue as though it was a new delicacy he was sampling, and he wasn't at all sure if he liked the taste or not. The choosing. Yes. That would be a whole new concept to him, and I acknowledged the effort he was making in using it.

'Why forbidden?' I asked, shrugging his hand from my shoulder. I didn't mean to be rude; I just didn't want to start feeling all naughty down below.

'I suppose,' he said, moving his hand safely back to his lap, 'that they fear I'll make some kind of final pitch. That I'll try to charm you into submission, or win you over through sex.'

I laughed – very long and very loud. Charm. Yeah, right. Storming into my room, having a slanging match with Luca, calling me his property, then ranting on about how stupid I was. He had a way to go till he could pass his Swiss Finishing School exams. The sex, though, I thought – that was a risk. Because despite his battered face and his scarred skin, he was still quite the work of art to look at.

He was a super-hot hunk in a super-tight T-shirt, and I knew – despite the fact he'd not covered himself in glory so far today – that he loved me. He really did, as much as he was capable of. He just did a damned fine job of hiding it beneath multiple layers of knobdom. Knowing that was one thing; figuring out what I felt was a different matter entirely. Could I love Gabriel? I'd have to revisit that one when life was a little calmer. Like in a decade or so.

'Sorry,' I said when I'd finally stopped laughing and he'd started to look amazingly peed off, 'but if we have a few illicit minutes together, there are more important things on my mind than getting laid. Yeah, really, there are – don't look at me like that! I have questions, and until they're answered, I won't feel ready for this . . . choosing.'

His body tensed, and even without a brain plunge I could tell he was nervous about what was coming next. Quite rightly, too. He nodded, once, sudden and sharp, and gestured for me to go on. I felt tense myself: this man had me on an emotional carousel. One minute he could do a pretty good impression of the man of every girl's dreams (presuming she'd been eating a lot of cheese the night before), and the next I was slapped around the face with a revelatory wet kipper. It would be easy to stay quiet, to give in to the urge to hide from truths I knew would hurt me – from truths that would make the tricky issue of Gabriel and me even more tricky. But I couldn't. I had to know. I had to poke, to prod, to ruffle the undergrowth and see what came out. No wonder I'm single.

'Coleen,' I said simply. 'The wedding photo. Her. Tell me.'

He ran his hands through his hair in a way I recognised as something he did when he was anxious. When he was playing for time. When he was entirely possibly thinking up a big fat lie to tell the kids.

'The truth,' I said, 'or I'll know.'

'The truth is a complicated—'

'Oh, spare me the bullshit. I've heard that speech before from Fionnula. What it usually means is I'm about to hear something I won't like. Well, I'm a big girl now, Gabriel, and I need to know. So tell me, or I can pretty much guar-ántee I'll be running straight into Fintan's arms and doing a conga with the Faidh come nightfall.'

He closed his eyes, and started to crack his knuckles, and stared first at the dogs and then at the fire and then, finally, at me.

'Coleen's husband, Philip, was one of ours,' he said, his

voice low and quiet and reluctant. 'He was human – but he'd been raised here in Meath, and his family was tied to ours. He was, I suppose, a servant. He helped us on the mortal side, one of many allies we had here.'

Hmm. Like Miss McDonough and Roisin, I supposed – not one of them, but working for them. OK. I got it so far. I raised my eyebrows, asking what was next.

'Then he developed cancer. He was young – in his thirties. Leukaemia, just at the time when he and Coleen were starting to talk about having children of their own. She was . . . well, she was different then. She was happy. They were happy. When Philip found out he was dying, he told her about us, and she made contact. She asked us for help. She asked us to save him.'

Jeez. I could only imagine what a head fuck that had been. One minute you're a happily married Scousewife planning the rest of your life, the next you have a dying husband and a whole new world to come to terms with.

'I'm guessing,' I said when he paused, 'that you didn't – because I certainly never met a Philip, and Coleen wasn't exactly what you'd call a blushing young bride, was she? What did you do?'

'We . . . I . . . did help her. In a way. There was nothing we could do for Philip on that side – he was too far gone down the path of the disease. So she begged us to . . . take him. To the Otherworld. To keep him there, keep him safe. Make him forget all about her and their life together, give him a fresh start, unencumbered by memories or sadness or regret. In exchange, she took on his duties for us. For me.'

'So . . . Philip is in the Otherworld, living a carefree life. And Coleen was left . . . alone. With a new job,' I said, frowning as I struggled to wrap my meagre brain around the whole idea.

The woman I'd known – the cold, hard-faced battle-axe who'd raised me – had seemed completely devoid of warmth, or love, or any human emotions other than anger and bitterness. Yet at that time, at that crossroads, she'd made the most amazing choice. She'd sacrificed the rest of her own life to save his. It was beautiful, and brave, and so completely fucked up. No wonder she'd been scared of them. No wonder she'd seemed so resentful of me: I was a symbol of everything that had gone wrong in her world. A constant reminder of everything she'd lost.

'Why couldn't you take her as well?' I asked. 'Let them both go to the Otherworld, and stay together? Is that . . . not allowed?'

He met my eyes, and I knew there was a nasty coming.

'It is. And I could have. I chose not to. I needed her on the outside. I needed her for you, as my backup plan. So I refused her when she asked, and told her she must live her life the way I wanted her to, or—'

'Or what?' I said, leaning forward so our knees were touching. 'Or you'd . . . hurt him?'

'Or we'd make him leave the Otherworld, and the safety he knew there. Return him to the mortal plane, where he would most certainly die.'

He was silent after that. We both were, listening to the hiss of the fire and the gentle snoring of the dogs and the quiet clunk of a whole new reality sinking into place. They – he – had taken advantage of the love a young woman had for her husband, and then threatened to torment him if she didn't do as she was told. I'd known he was ruthless, but this . . . this really was taking the whole packet of Hobnobs.

'I think you'd better leave,' I said, finally. I felt suddenly cold and alone and overwhelmingly sad. Coleen was gone, my parents and sisters were on the other side, Carmel was a blood-crazed lunatic, and the Morrigan had a hairdo made up of slaughter. The man who sat beside me, the man who loved me above all others, was so single-minded in his ambitions that he was borderline evil. That left me with only Luca – my vampire slave – and possibly a shiny dog. In the whole wide world.

I stood up and pointed at the door. I really needed to be alone with my aloneness.

'Leave,' I said. 'Now.'

He ignored me, and reached out, tilting my chin up so I was looking into his eyes. Eyes that were filled with a sadness almost as big as my own.

'I did as you asked,' he said. 'I was honest. And now you'll punish me for it?'

'Yeah,' I replied, slapping his hand away. 'Sometimes life sucks, doesn't it? Just ask Philip and Coleen about that one . . . Now, please, get away from me. I can't bear to be near you right now. As final pitches went, that was the world's worst.'

'I know,' he said, 'and I didn't come here intending to make you suffer. Or fight with Luca. Or scream at you. I came here to tell you how brave you were last night. To thank you for saving me, even if it wasn't the sensible thing to do. To tell you I'm sorry, for everything. To tell you that . . . I . . . that I . . .'

He hesitated, and I could sense it coming. I could hear the 'L' bomb hovering in the air between us, burning fiercer than the fire and stronger than the stone and brighter than the jewels beneath the dogs' coats.

'I know,' I said, turning away before he could say it. 'I know you do. I just don't know if it's enough.'

Chapter Thirty-Five

Carmel threw herself back on the bed, and rolled around laughing. Literally rolled around, disappearing beneath a cloud of black hair and bearskin as she drooled into the pillow.

'I'm glad one of us finds this amusing,' I said, sharing my glares between her quaking body and the view I could see in the full-length mirror. The view of me, goddess-style. The one that had so affected my friend, the laughing policeman over there.

Shortly after Gabriel had left, I'd been attacked – and that is the only word I can use for it – by Tara's version of Tracy and Cheryl from the salon. Not that I know a Tracy and Cheryl from the salon, but you get my drift. They might not have had the Scousebrows and Botox needles, but they had exactly the same appraising glint in their eyes as they looked me up and down. The one that said, 'Shit – we've got our work cut out for us tonight, girls.'

So now, after several hours of torture, here I was. Wearing a long white gown straight out of the Druid Girls' Guide to Fashion, coated in oils and potions, and with my hair knotted up in dozens of tiny plaits. The plaits were pinned around my head, apart from the one white streak, which had been decorated with miniscule red berries and left down to flow over my left shoulder and fade into the fabric of the dress. I looked . . . faintly ridiculous, by modern standards. Certainly by Carmel's, looking at the state of her. But, well, I kind of liked it. As long as I didn't trip up, wee myself in public, or swear, I'd at least appear dignified – even if I didn't feel it.

I'd drawn the line at the stupid sandals, though, and insisted they let me wear my Docs instead – I definitely needed a bit of grounding on a night like this. Never mind the fact that it was the end of October, and bloody cold out there. I wasn't sure they really went with the rest of the outfit – but then, neither did I.

They'd left us, then, with plates of food, a bowl of fruit and carafes of wine, so we could get on with the important business of eating, drinking and bickering.

'You know,' I said, sitting down next to her, 'this is a pretty important night. The Feast of Samhain. The moment when I have to do all my goddess stuff. You could be a bit more . . . supportive?'

She sat up, leaned back against the wall, and wiped tears from beneath her eyes. The dog was curled up at my feet, and leaned over to lick my ankles. At least one of the bitches in the room understood.

'I'm sorry,' said Carmel. 'It's just . . . well, look at you! And it's not just that – it's everything. Everything that's happened over the last few days. The madness of it all. How I'm feeling. How we've both changed. I mean, it's wild, isn't it? If I didn't laugh, I might lose my mind.'

I nodded. Wild. That was one word for it. I'd add insane, horrifying and fucktarded beyond all recognition to the list.

'It's all been kicking off at home as well,' she said. 'I checked the paper's website at the airport, and did you know they'd put all that crap last night down to some kind of performance-art piece? Some super-expensive performance-art piece that has the boffins at the museum salivating over all the genuine historic artefacts that ended up in the river? Don't know what happened to the dead people, but some of the swords floated up in the Albert Dock! I kind of wish I was in the newsroom right now . . .'

I knew exactly what she meant. Newspapers are crazy places, and the buzz is never buzzier than when a big piece of news is floating around. Big events – tragedies to anyone else, like Princess Diana dying, or 9/11 – are torn about by the hungry newshounds, a bunch of borderline alcoholics and overgrown students working as one well-oiled machine to produce the stories that everyone wants to read.

I felt a stab of nostalgia for it: the way they'd all be scurrying around now, getting photos and expert comments and witness accounts using the inevitable phrase, 'I heard a big bang . . .' Except that wasn't my life right now. Maybe it never would be again. And depending on what happened tonight, maybe it wouldn't be anyone's life ever again.

That whole idea felt ridiculous. How could I – Lily McCain – have ended up with this kind of responsibility? How could I, who'd only ever dipped her little toe into the great pool of life, now be asked to decide what happened to it next? And how could I separate my feelings about Gabriel, and the things he'd done, from the fate of all humanity?

Rejecting him meant accepting Fintan – and his version of the way the world should be. Accepting him meant . . . well, I didn't know what it meant. Not happy ever after, that's for bloody sure. Not for me, or him, or the world, I suspected. It's not like I'd say yes, and suddenly planet Earth would be wrapped in a big blanket of rainbows and unicorns, with the whole of humanity acting like they'd taken an E. It all felt impossible to judge.

Life would, as Gabriel had always known, be a lot easier if I'd just been a good little girl and done what I was told. Never questioned his version of events, swooned into his manly arms, and thought myself lucky to be there. Oops.

'So,' said Carmel, serious again, 'what are you going to do, then?'

The dog jumped up, and laid her long face on my lap so I could scratch her ears. I did exactly that as I pondered Carmel's question.

'I . . . don't know,' I replied. 'In all honesty, I don't know. Fintan is, well, a sicko. No doubt about it. But I've been to the Otherworld, and it's kind of beautiful, in a *Logan's Run* sort of way. It definitely beats walking through Bootle on a Saturday night, anyway.'

She opened her mouth to speak, then thought better of it. I smiled – I knew exactly what she'd been about to say. That she'd had some cracking nights out in Bootle on a Saturday night. I, though, hadn't. I hadn't had those many cracking nights out anywhere, which is exactly why this decision would have been much easier for her: her life wasn't perfect, but she loved it. It loved her. It was full of friends and fun and her unspeakably fantastic family. This would've been a no-brainer for Carmel. Me? Very much a brainer.

What I'd seen of this world was ninety per cent pain. What I'd seen of the Otherworld wasn't, because that's where my parents lived. I knew I wasn't seeing the full picture – Fionnula had shown me how the Otherworld would be for some, and I'd had enough glimpses of normal human life to realise that it, too, could be totally awesome. And stuck right in the middle of the two was Gabriel. My High King and mate. My saviour and my tormentor. My wannabe lover and potential jailor.

'I'm hoping,' I said, thinking out loud, 'that when I get out there, I'll just know. Some pretty weird shit happened last night—'

'You mean like you turning into a glow-stick and speaking in stereo?' she interrupted.

'Like that, yeah. I didn't plan any of that. It just . . . happened. And maybe it'll happen again. That I'll just know what to do, as if by magic.'

'OK . . .' she replied, pulling a face that told me exactly what she thought of my devious master plan. 'But what about the really important stuff? Forget all this saving the world crap – what about him? What about Gabriel? I've seen the way you look at him, and it even confuses me. I never know if you're planning to eat him or stab him.'

She was right. That was exactly the way I looked at him – because that's exactly the way I felt.

Before I could answer, she plunged back in: 'I get that there've been a few untruths, Lily. I get that you're angry with him, with fate, with everything. And it's not like I'm a fully paid-up member of the High King Fan Club or any-thing . . . but, well. You know, don't you, that he loves you? That if it wasn't for his sacred duty, blah blah blah, he'd still love you? That you two could have a chance at . . . God, this sounds like puke, but a chance at being really happy together?'

At that point I'd have quite liked to take an apple from the fruit bowl and stick it in her mouth. I didn't want to hear all this stuff – not now, not ever. Because again, damn her, she was right. If life had been different, I could so eas-ily have fallen for Gabriel. The head over heels, happy ever after, love of my life kind of fallen. Maybe I still could – but there had been too much, too fast, for me to have any sense of balance about it.

'Um . . . yeah,' I said, eloquently.

She nodded, realising she wasn't going to get anything more from me, jumped up from the bed and went to look at herself in the mirror. She'd fared a lot better than I had on the ancient mystical ceremony wardrobe – tight black pants, long-sleeved black top, and kind of funky knee-length boots made of soft brown leather, with black leather laces criss-crossed all the way around them.

'These,' she said, lifting up one foot and pointing a toe at me, 'are a bit on the kinky side, I think. Which may be why I like them. So . . . what you seem to be saying, Lily, is that your master plan consists of: (a) wait and see, and (b) hope for the best?'

I nodded. When she put it like that, it did sound kind of lame.

'Why? What do you think I should do?' I asked.

'I can't answer that,' she replied quickly. 'You know what I'd do. But I'm not the Goddess for a reason. That's your job, and I wouldn't want it. But I know this – whatever you do, it'll be from the heart, and it'll be right. I think so, and I'm pretty sure the Diamond Dogs agree.'

The Diamond Dogs . . . I looked down at the mammoth head on my lap, and the way her coat seemed to sparkle with jewels you could only see from the corner of your eye. She was right. They were Diamond Dogs. I couldn't believe the thought hadn't occurred to me earlier. Only I could fall through the rabbit hole and land in the middle of a David Bowie song.

'Just in case you need it, though,' she said, 'I want you to keep this.'

She handed me something, and I took it. It was a pocketknife like the one she'd been carrying the night before, the twin sister of the one I'd dropped in the river. I had a small looped purse hanging from the belt of my dress, which for some reason was full of keys to doors I'd never tried to open. I tucked the knife in there, and looked up at her, wondering how she'd managed to fish the knife out of the Mersey.

'It was buy one get one free at Assassins R Us,' she said, grinning.

I was halfway to a giggle about that one when a bell started to chime, deep, loud, and rattling with vibrato. The kind of bell that told the puny villagers the Kraken was on its way to eat them all, and to run for their lives. It echoed through the room, rattling the mirror on its uneven ground, and making the dogs restless.

Carmel walked over, and gave my hand a quick squeeze.

'Ooh,' she said, pulling a face, 'it's all a bit Hammer House of Horror now, isn't it? I suspect that's our call – are you ready, chickie?'

'No,' I replied. 'But we'd better go anyway.'

Chapter Thirty-Six

We opened the heavy wooden door to be met by two men brandishing burning torches – the kind that don't need batteries. They led us through a maze of low-roofed tunnels cut from rock, and eventually to a long, dark corridor, lit by chunks of built-in stone that glowed eerily in the dark. Without a word, the men stopped, and gestured us forward.

I looked at Carmel, my friend and my Champion, and she gave me a jaunty little salute as we walked on.

'Now,' she said, as we neared the end of the corridor, 'when we get out there, stand up tall, stick your boobs out, and in your head, sing the opening chords of "Foxy Lady". It never fails.'

Against the odds she made me laugh, and after a couple of very deep breaths, we stepped out. Out on to the Hill of Tara, and the rest of my life. I felt like lion-bait entering the arena.

The night sky was glittering with what looked like millions of stars, and the full moon was bright enough to make me blink. As we emerged, we walked into a central clearing, damp grass squishing beneath my boots, dark flutterings overhead as birds circled around us. Or bats. Or possibly pterodactyls. The air was cold and frosty against my cheeks, and smelled of damp earth and freshly burned leaves. The scent gave me a sudden yearning for a cigarette, the first in weeks. Stress reaction, I suppose. Nothing like facing those lions to make you want a Marlborough Gold.

There was a circle of enormous upright stones standing in front of us, jagged and crooked and each casting their own twisting moon-shadow. Some of them looked firm, solid, earthbound. Others shimmered and wavered in and out of vision, like they couldn't make their mind up which world they belonged in. That, I suspected, was pretty close to the truth – this was Tara, on the night of Samhain, when the veils between the worlds grew thin.

Standing in front of each stone – both the present and the not-so-present – was a person. Male, female, different ages. All dressed in grey, and staring at me intently. The Witnesses, I thought. Chosen from both worlds to watch the ceremony unfold. To watch the Goddess choose.

At the centre of the circle was one giant stone, standing alone. It was very, very real – firmly rooted in this earth, as though it had stone roots that spread underground like the stretching subterranean tendrils of an oak tree. Despite its solidity, it shone white in the darkness, casting silver light on the faces that surrounded it. The Lia Fail. The Stone of Destiny.

On one side of it stood Gabriel, wearing the same kind of clothes as Carmel, but looking ever so slightly more magnificent in them. On his head was a simple gold ring, and in his hand was the Sword of Lugh, its cold steel reflecting back the dancing light of the Stone. I met his eyes, and immediately wished I hadn't. I'd never seem him look so serious, or so beautiful.

Next to him was a stranger, almost as tall, blond, and blandly handsome. The kind of boy who's good at tennis and has girls collapsing at his feet, and dates the prettiest girl in school. He gave me a dazzling grin, and I frowned in return, wondering who he was. He continued to smile, then mimed drinking a cup of coffee . . . Ireland's finest. It was Fintan, presumably in his own form for the occasion, instead of poor Larry Hoey's.

On the other side of the Stone stood the Morrigan, sword drawn and clasped in front of her. She looked at me and nodded, sternly, in acknowledgement. Next to her was Fionnula, teetering on high heels that I knew must be sinking into the soft ground. She gave me a small thumbs-up gesture, and I wondered if she was already drunk. I wouldn't blame her if she was.

I gulped, suddenly swamped with nerves as they all stared at me as though they were waiting for me to do something extraordinary. I saw Finn, and Connor, and Kevin, all ranked behind Gabriel. I saw Donn, glaring at me with his angular, slitted eyes, the vampires huddled together behind him. I saw Luca, distant and alone, his tall form silhouetted against the moonlight.

The gang's all here, I thought. And I haven't got a clue what to do with them. If they left it much longer I was going to start a round of the hokey-cokey just to break the tension. It was spookily quiet, as though even the night owls and foxes and shrews and pterodactyls had all stopped what they were doing to watch.

Just as the silence was starting to feel oppressive, it was shattered by a sonorous, booming voice.

'The Goddess is in our presence!' it declared, and I jumped in surprise, looking around to find out where it was coming from. I blinked up at the moon, wondering if there really was a man up there after all, until a figure stepped out from the other side of the Stone. He was small, dressed in deep-autumn-coloured robes, with long white hair flowing around a bearded face. Gandalf the Green.

'The Goddess is in our presence, and we shall worship her!' he said, voice carrying and lifting and flowing through the stones, the hills, the earth, the outstretched fingers of naked October trees, and off into the distant sky.

As one, everybody present fell to their knees. Including, to my utter horror, Carmel. I fought the urge to drag her back up, and instead did as she'd advised. Stood tall. Stuck 'em out. And sang a bit of Jimi.

I walked towards the man – he was obviously some kind of priest or shaman, or Celtic bingo caller – and he bowed, deep and low, towards me.

'Now the true High King must present himself to the Stone of Destiny!' announced the priest, as everyone swished back up to their feet. Looked like I only got a few seconds of worship, which was fine by me.

Gabriel stepped forward, and without looking at me, reached out and placed both his hands on the Stone.

'I am Cormac macConaire, the true High King!' he said, leaning forward to touch the rock with his forehead. I heard a collective intake of breath as everyone watched and waited, then felt my eyes widen as the Stone screamed at him. Literally screamed – a huge, banshee wail that floated over the heads of the crowds like a cloud of sonic smoke.

Gabriel took a step back, and the screech died down to a whimper. Fintan looked decidedly put out, and I was just glad I hadn't fallen over from shock. Being told in advance that a stone was going to scream was one thing – standing next to it when it did was a completely different matter. And that's from someone who's stood next to the speakers at a Slipknot gig.

'The High King is recognised!' shouted the priest. 'Tara acknowledges Cormac macConaire!'

There was a murmur of approval from most of the crowd, then the priest turned to face me. As he did, I saw a shimmer and a shake behind him, a flickering of shadow and light that grew and spread all around us, a wind-blown curtain of gloaming surrounding the circle and everything it contained.

I saw figures twisting and roiling in its mist, like half-formed shapes in a cloudy sky, almost but never quite solid. Horses made of swirling grey air, stamping at the ground and snorting, steam blowing from their wavering nostrils. Their riders clasped hard on to invisible reins, and faces started to take form: Eithne at the head of the pack, hair that I knew was black in my world streaming white in this one, surrounded by dozens, hundreds of others, all jostling against each other. The visions circled us, trapping the entire hill in a kaleidoscope of not-quite-there images.

I twirled around in a dizzy circle, casting my eyes over every half-drawn face I could see, searching for the two I knew would be there. The two I wanted to see. At last, I found them – my parents. My mother, with two small children at her side. My sisters. And sitting tucked in front of my father, hanging on to the horse's broad neck, a small girl with long red hair. Lucy. The girl-woman who'd died in my place. I still knew nothing about her, and vowed that one day I would – when she wasn't galloping around on a spirit stallion, perhaps.

The horses and the figures and the smoke that wasn't smoke whirled and circled around us, like a fog-shrouded fairground carousel. I span with it, round and round as fast as I could, trying to keep my eyes fixed on my mother and father, until I felt dizziness and nausea swamp me, and the trailing tail of white hair slap me in the face.

Firm hands clasped my shoulders, and held me straight. I blinked my eyes a couple of times, and let the head-rush die down. Carmel was right there, in my face, her eyes huge and worried. I nodded once to let her know I was all right, then shook off her grasp.

'The Otherworld is here with us,' boomed the priest, ignoring my petty drama and sticking to his script. 'They are in our midst, as we celebrate the Feast of Samhain. The harvest of the earth is done, and now we look to the Goddess to plant the harvest of souls, and give her rich blessing to the mortal plane!'

I looked at him. Looked at Gabriel, and Fintan, and the Morrigan, and searched for the faces of my parents in the twirling, flickering Otherworld that surrounded us. I found them all, but none of them had answers. None of them told me what to do. I was helpless and stupid, a little girl playing grown-up in the land of the giants. Panic rose up like bile in my throat, and I wanted to scream: *Just tell me what I'm supposed to do!*

I felt a sharp nudge in my back, and turned to see Carmel pushing me.

'Go to the fucking Stone!' she hissed, shoving me forward again.

The Stone. Yes. She was right. Of course she was. I'd just been too freaked and dizzy to realise.

I walked up to it, and laid my hands on the glimmering rock, feeling it strangely smooth and glassy beneath my fingers. I placed my forehead against it, as I'd seen Gabriel do, and waited for something to happen. I had no idea what, but . . . something. Anything.

Within seconds, I felt its power course through me with an almighty whoosh. It was like being physically blasted by a supercharged hosepipe, energy rushing through my blood and my nerves and my skin, pulsating and throbbing and pounding its way into my body.

My hands flew back, and my arms lifted towards the night sky, and I shone – brilliant white light exploding over the hill and across the faces of everyone before me.

I was of the Earth, and in the Earth, and for the Earth. I felt all of its tiny cries, from the creaking of the nude willow branches to the echoing heartbeats around me. The wind caressed my face as a friend, and the damp soil beneath my feet welcomed me home.

I was of the Earth, but I was also of the Otherworld, and could feel the warmth of the horses' breath streaming across my skin, sense the heavy thud of their hooves against ground that didn't exist. I could feel the taste of the grass they'd grazed and the stream water they'd drunk and the sun dappling against their coats.

I was the Goddess. And all of this was mine.

I walked towards Gabriel and Fintan, and they screwed up their eyes against the light that was shining from inside me. I ignored their discomfort and went closer, placing my hands on either side of Fintan's face.

He kneleled, submitted, and my vision filled with his needs: his anger at what mortals had done to a world that was once his; his pure belief that what he was doing was right. His image of a new, stronger Otherworld – no longer the Other, but the Only. His desperation and fury and humiliation that he was kneeling there before me, a mere human female.

I pulled my hands away, and he wavered as though he might fall to the ground, before finding the backbone to stand again. I smiled at him, and knew it was a twisted thing – for so long this man had threatened me, tormented me, tried to kill me. I'd been plagued with fears that tonight, at Tara, he would do the same – but now I realised that he was nothing. He was an insect I could crush beneath my feet. At least he was right there, right then.

I paused in front of Gabriel, and saw uncertainty flicker across his face. No . . . fear. Fear of the power that stood before him, of how I would use it, and what I would see when I pillaged his mind. Even through the mist of my own strength, I had a moment of concern, of regret – then I pushed it aside, and clasped his head between my glowing hands.

He didn't fall, but I could see the effort it took not to. To stand there, so tall and yet suddenly so weak, and submit to his Goddess.

The images streamed through me: of beauty and passion and fire and need. Of me, as a child and as an adult. Of the world around us, the hill we stood upon, fast-forwarding scenes of the seasons in Tara, the summer blossoms and snow-covered stones and first snowdrops at the foot of the willows. And beneath it all, his need, his duty, his purpose: to keep it all alive. No matter what he wanted or what he needed, that was his role. That was everything he was.

I removed my hands, and stared at him. I knew my face was harsh, cold in the white light, and I also knew that if I chose to, one tiny touch of my fingertip against his forehead would send him sprawling to the ground.

I saw them both, now. Saw them clearly, for what they were and what they wanted to be; for what they wanted me to see and what I could see. But still, despite it all, I was no closer to making the decision that everyone was here to see me make. No closer to choosing between them.

I turned to walk back to the Stone, aware of the silence pressing in on me like closing walls, crushing me with expectation.

I had to choose. And I had to do it now.

The priest stood beside me, his furry face illuminated by the light from my body.

'Goddess,' he intoned, 'will you take the High King as your mate, as has been tradition for all of time, and cast your fertile blessing on this world all who live within it?'

I saw Fintan tense, and the dark shadows of Connor and Kevin moving behind him. I saw Gabriel look to the ground, almost in defeat. I saw the faces of my parents whirl by, riding their ghostly Otherworld horses, twisting in their seats to try and meet my eyes.

And still the words would not come. I was frozen, and still, and lost, trapped by my own indecision. I wanted – so badly – to choose the Otherworld. To leave this place behind, to abandon all its petty concerns, and run to my mother's arms. To stay there for ever, their Fairy Princess, living for all eternity safe in the warmth of the only love I'd ever truly known. All I had to do was say no . . .

I opened my mouth, not knowing what was going to come out of it, and never getting the chance to find out.

I was grabbed, suddenly and roughly, from behind, my arms pinned behind my back, twisted so hard I felt bone-jarring pain shoot through them. The light I was casting wavered and danced as the agony took root, and I contorted my head over my shoulder to see who held me.

I met the dark, angled eyes of Donn, Lord of the Dead, and felt his hot breath stream across my cheeks as he spoke.

'Cormac Mor!' he shouted, so loud, so close. 'I hold the Goddess here in my grasp! She is yours to take. Now do your duty, High King – the one you were born to do!'

I wriggled and kicked and slammed my boots down against the arches of his feet, sensing a whirl of movement around me, and hearing the sudden shrieking of horses and the panicked cries of the Witnesses. I looked to the priest, and he shook his head sadly – this wasn't his battle to fight. There was nothing he could do.

Donn tightened his grip, and I felt one arm pop from its socket as I struggled against him. The pure, searing pain cleared my mind, and instead I attacked him with power – throwing the force of my mind against his. I was Life. He was Death. An eternal struggle, and one I knew I couldn't win as soon as I met the solid black wall that surrounded him. Walls that I couldn't break, or climb, or destroy. I was the Goddess, and he was a god – but he had centuries of experience over me. He knew what he was doing, and I was grasping at straws. The day would come, I knew, when I could end this thing between us – but I wasn't ready yet.

'Cormac!' he screamed again, spittle flying from his mouth and landing on my skin. 'Take the woman now, and our world will be safe once more!'

He pushed me forward, immune to my desperate attempts to break free, and thrust me so close to Gabriel that only inches separated us, shaking me at him like a prize he'd won at the fair.

I looked into Gabriel's eyes, realising that mine were swimming in tears of pain and frustration and anguish. I'd known it could come to this. I'd always known it, and always dreaded it. Time and again this image had played through my mind, and each time it did I talked myself down from the cliff – no. He wouldn't. Ever.

Now I stood here, one arm dangling limp and useless, dressed like a parody virgin and being presented to the High King like a mare he needed to service.

It had all been a lie. Fintan had lied. The Morrigan had lied. Even God had lied. That there was no choice – and if there was, then Gabriel would take it away from me, the way he'd tried to do in more subtle ways for the whole of my life.

I saw the confusion on his face, the battle raging through his mind: his love for me, his reluctance to hurt me, and above all of that – his damned duty. His need to ensure the mortal plane was blessed, by whatever means he could. The part he'd been born to play, raised to believe – mate to Mabe.

Whether she liked it or not.

The light around me wavered, like a bulb at the end of its life, and finally fizzed and popped and went out. It was gone. My power was gone. I was a mere human woman, held tight by a raging god, facing the man who would have me, whatever it took.

I felt cold tears streaming over my cheeks, and sagged in Donn's grip, looking up at Gabriel's face – hard lines, cold and angry in the moonlight. All this time thinking the choice was mine – when all along, it had belonged to him. I felt a wave of sick rise up to my throat, and wondered if it would put him off if I threw up all over him. Probably not, I decided. I'd been in his mind. I knew what mattered to him – and it wasn't me.

Donn shoved me even closer to him, letting me go and pushing me forward until my body collided with Gabriel's.

He leaned in, wrapped one of his arms around my waist, and clenched me tightly to him, gathering me up in his grip.

I turned my face away from him and tugged my good arm free, casting around for the purse looped around my waist. For the knife that I'd use in any way it took.

I knew one thing, and one thing only: I would not let this happen. I'd seen enough of death, and enough of life, to know that I could cope with ending my own. That I could finish it right now, throw away the burden, and give it up. I'd never liked it that much anyway, and one trip to the Cavern hadn't really done the trick. I'd struggled my whole life to be free – and I still would be.

I could cope with dying. The sad, empty part of me that had always existed even looked forward to it. What I couldn't cope with was a lifetime of subservience, of fear, of regret. Of knowing that this man – this man who loved me – had also trapped me and ruled me and taken me. I was the Goddess, and I was Lily McCain, and I was Maura Delaney. And I would not be used.

I would make my choice, even if it was the last thing I ever did.

My fingers finally curled around the knife, and I flicked it open, as Gabriel crushed me even tighter against him. Donn was cheering and laughing behind me, and I heard the wild yells and screaming of the Faidh in the background.

I held the knife, sharp, to my finger. Felt a prick of ice and then the warm flow of blood. Felt Gabriel's sweet breath against my face, the slick flow of my tears wiping against his skin, and the press of his muscled thighs through my dress. I pulled and tugged until my hand was free, the blade digging deep into the flesh of my palm. I twisted it, and readied myself. I didn't know if I was going to use it on him, or me – but there was going to be blood. I tensed, drew in a sharp breath, manoeuvred the handle until it was tightly clenched in my fist.

Gabriel's lips touched my forehead, once, and then he pushed me away. His eyes were blazing violet, and I could see him fighting his need. Fighting his desire. Fighting his destiny.

I staggered back, arms wheeling to try to stop myself falling, as he stood tall and faced the crowd. He turned, once, slowly, taking in the faces of the Witnesses, his men, the Otherworld, and the poor, befuddled priest.

His eyes fell on Donn, and he shook his head, his violet gaze fixed and determined as he faced up to the god, body swelling.

'No,' he said, simply. 'The choice is hers, and hers alone. I will not take it from her.'

'You would abandon our cause for the sake of one human child?' yelled Donn, long black hair whipping around his face in his fevered frenzy of disbelief. 'You would betray your duty, your calling, your role as the true High King? And leave the fate of the world to this . . . brat?'

'She's not a brat,' said Gabriel, picking up the Sword of Lugh, eyes dark and heavy and filled with pain. 'She's Lily. She's . . . magnificent. And I will not force her to do that which she chooses not to. I know that is your way, Donn. It would have been my father's way, also. But it will not be mine – whatever the cost.'

I wanted to go to him. To hold him. To kiss him. To . . . choose him. Because by giving me up, he'd done the one thing that all his impassioned speeches and anguished tirades and lifetime of scheming hadn't been able to do – proved to me that this was right.

That this was what I was born to do.

I moved off in his direction, boots tangled in the soggy hem of my gown, hand slippery with blood. I needed to be with him. To look into his eyes. To tell him what I felt.

As I took my first step, Donn grabbed me again. He tugged my injured arm back behind me, and yanked my head back by the white streak of my hair. I screamed, and had a moment of sheer white pain that momentarily eclipsed everything else. Fuck, that hurt.

'She is a stealer of souls, and has you bewitched, Cormac Mor,' cried Donn. 'You are not in your right mind! But if you will not take her, as you have been bred to do, then she is *mine*!'

Strong hands took the sides of my head, and I felt him twisting and pulling and forcing until the tendons of my neck stretched and popped, and my windpipe started to close in. I couldn't breathe, or run, or even scream at the mind-searing pain of it. Donn was trying to physically rip my head from my neck – and I was pretty sure he could do it.

I saw Gabriel's face crumple in horror, and saw Fintan smiling with triumph. I was going to die, and one way or another, he'd have his brave new world after all.

With the last drop of energy and will I had left in me, I fumbled with the knife, slippery in my bleeding hand. Panic was flooding my vision, and I saw tiny red spots in front of my eyes and a loud roaring sound thundering through my ears as I found a better grip. I lifted it, and stabbed him as hard as I could in the thigh.

It wasn't much, as far as the Lord of the Dead was concerned. But it was enough to distract him – to make him let go, to stagger slightly off to the side. It was enough to make him close his eyes for a fraction of a second, while Carmel screamed and hurtled at him, throwing her entire weight into his stomach and tumbling him to the ground, landing on top of him in a flurry of hair and curses and gouging fingers.

The Morrigan yelled and ran towards us, but I knew she wouldn't make it in time. She was too far away. With a brutal shriek, she leaped into the air, and transformed into the crow. Vast wings beat overhead, and she cawed and cackled so loudly I could feel my eardrums vibrating. She dive-bombed Donn's head, whipping him with sinewy black feathers and worrying his eyes with her long pointed beak as he tried to bat her away with his hands. I heard the howl of the vampires, and saw Luca standing alone between them and us – prowling low, teeth bared, warning them off as they crouched to attack and protect their lord.

And I saw Gabriel, watching to see that I was free before walking away outside the circle of real and unreal stones. The Sword of Lugh swung loose in his hands as he disappeared off into the shadows. The sword that the Morrigan had said he would fall upon, if he failed in his duty.

I ran back over to the Stone of Destiny, ignoring the tear and screech of damaged muscle and torn skin and chipped bone, and laid my bloody hands upon it. Light and power flooded through me, washing away the pain and filling me with new strength, telling me the words that I needed to say. At last, I knew what to do.

'I am the Goddess, Mabe, the Mother of the Mortals!' I cried. 'And I have made my choice! I accept the High King, Cormac macConaire, as my mate!'

The Otherworld spun and shuddered and whirled so fast all I could see were blurs: Eithne's distorted face, the stomping hooves of frightened horses, and the soft, warm smile on my mother's face as they all spun and shimmered and finally blinked and disappeared. They were gone, and so was Fintan.

The Stone screamed once more, even more piercingly than before, and the priest sat down in a huddled heap on the wet grass. It might not have gone smoothly, but from his perspective the show was over.

'Gabriel!' I screamed, as loud as I could, praying that it wasn't too late. That he wasn't lying alone out there, folded over that sword, dead.

There was chaos going on around me. The vampires growled and stalked each other, the Morrigan dive-bombed Donn again as he tried to stand, and Carmel lay wheezing and puffing on the ground near his feet. I could hear yells and shouting and scuffling as Gabriel's men mobilised, and the confused chatter of the Witnesses and the soft Irish lilt of Fionnula, cursing or casting spells or singing, I couldn't tell. I could hear the echo of the wailing Stone, and the clang of bells and the barks of dogs.

But through it all, I could focus on only one thing – staring off into the darkness beyond the circle, and waiting. Waiting for him to return.

After a minute that stretched into an hour, after single heartbeats that stretched into drum rolls, I saw movement. The shadows swished like long dark grass, and a bright shining light was cutting its way through the dark of the night towards us.

Gabriel. With the Sword of Lugh blazing in his hands.

I ran towards him, standing beneath the flare of golden fire, our fingertips touching.

'You made your choice,' he said quietly, eyes scanning my face for any signs of lasting injury.

'Yeah,' I replied, closing the distance between us, 'and so did you.'

Epilogue

It was raining in Liverpool. Again.

My life-changing decision at Tara didn't seem to have made that much difference to the weather, or the state of the planet. I'd flicked on the TV that morning to watch reports of an earthquake in China, and floods in Bangladesh. The only bright spot had been a semi-serious account of a unicorn being spotted running wild through the Argentinean pampas, so I was holding out for that, at least.

My own life, in the few weeks since Samhain, had also not been magically transformed into a non-stop party of love, peace and understanding. Yes, I'd accepted Gabriel as my mate – but not, as yet, in the down-and-dirty way. I just wasn't ready. It was supposed to be fun, right? And it wouldn't be, until I was one hundred per cent confident of keeping my visions at bay.

Even without all that, I wasn't ready. Mainly because he still irritated the fuck out of me, in ways I didn't know had even been invented. He was still bossy, and still domineering, and still had an annoying habit of swelling to the size of a woolly mammoth every time I dared to disagree with him.

In fact, it was only when I was at risk of losing him that I had this odd rush of . . . yeah, love, I suppose. He'd done the one thing I never thought he'd be capable of doing: chosen me over his duty. That had to count for something, and there were moments when I thought I was the luckiest woman alive to have found him. Moments being what they are, though, they passed very quickly, like flash floods of gooeyness.

The rest of the time, I'd happily chase him round the room with an electrified cattle prod. I'm thinking of investing in one of those anyway, as it might come in handy with Luca as well. Once Gabriel had calmed down enough to let me speak to Donn – who was now minus one eye and copying Kevin, thanks to the impeccable crowmanship of the Morrigan – I'd tried to negotiate Luca's return. I mean, what was I going to do with a vampire drummer? Apart from the obvious, and like I said, I'm just not ready.

But Donn was having none of it, so for the time being I'm lumbered. There are worse fates, I know – and I've seen most of them up close.

Donn was a tad more respectful when I did see him, though. Everyone seems a bit scared of me now. Fionnula keeps trying to test my powers, and nobody seems to have a clue what I'll do next, including me. That makes them wary – which I must confess I kind of like. Next up, I have to go and meet the Council. Obviously that came with a huge and unpronounceable name full of vowels, but the gist of it is a whole boardroom full of supernatural gods. Yay. Such fun.

On a more pleasant note, I acquired a dog. She didn't have a name, so I'm working on that. Carmel calls her Fifi, which is so not right for such a majestic beast. It'll come to me. I know it will.

Fintan is back in the Otherworld, but I know he's not given up. I've been in his mind, and it's not a mind that accepts defeat easily. There's more to come, and there are things that Gabriel is still not telling me. Because, you know, he's a knob like that.

There's a lot to settle. A lot to negotiate. A lot to come to terms with. But for the time being, I'm here. Back in Liverpool, and back at work. I finally interviewed that Cher impersonator – his name was Gary – and Carmel is happily answering phones on the night desk again. We're keeping our heads down, finding our feet, and enjoying our boring old reality in a way that wouldn't have seemed possible a few short weeks ago.

Oh yeah – there is one more thing. My hair. I woke up the morning after, and it was all white. Every last strand of it. I calmed down after about, oh, three days or so of constant screaming, and now I kind of like it. I look a bit weird and scary, and everyone thinks it's a pop-chick affectation. Hah. As if, I feel like saying – I got this saving the world, mate.

So here I am, today. Fighting the wind and the rain with an umbrella that just doesn't want to stay the right way round. White hair blowing around my face. On my own, at the Gothic gates of Anfield Cemetery.

It's not my idea of a fun time, but it's something I have to do. The funeral's over, an affair as small and sad as Coleen's own life, and now I've come to visit. I haven't brought flowers – she'd think that was a terrible waste of money. Instead, I've brought a new Glade air freshener, so she'll always smell of lovely fresh chemicals.

I walk through the rows and rows of gravestones, feet squelching on wet grass and mud, until I come to hers. It's black and simple, and bears only two lines:

Coleen McCain. Loving wife.
Loving nan.

Acknowledgements

First of all, apologies if this goes on a bit. It's my version of an Oscar speech and I've been practising it for decades!

Thank you to my agent, Laura Longrigg of MBA, for tirelessly putting up with my crazy ideas and genre-hopping manuscripts. We got there in the end, Laura. Thanks also to everyone involved in the Harry Bowling Prize, for giving me encouragement, and for putting up with a drunk acceptance speech where I thanked Daniel Craig.

Three cheers also to the Royal Society of Literature, whose Brookleaze Award boosted both my finances and my morale.

Eternal gratitude to Michael Rowley at Del Rey UK for seeing something special in Lily and helping me share her story with the world, and to the whole team there – especially Emily Yau. It's been an exciting journey, and I've received a wonderful welcome from every one there, including the other fabulous authors.

Like Lily I have had many 'Champions' in my life, who have helped me in so many different ways. I couldn't have done this – or indeed pretty much anything – without the support of my friends. They include Sandra Shennan, Helen Shaw, Pamela Hoey, Rachael Tinniswood, Jane Murdoch, Paula Woosey, Vikki Everett, Louise Douglas,

Ann Potterton, and, last but not least, Jane Costello – a successful author now, but a friend first, and an invaluable source of advice and encouragement. Also, the late Brian McNaught, for giving me Liverpool.

Thanks to all my pals at the *Post* and *Echo* in Liverpool (and yes, the night news desk really *is* like that, sometimes!) and everyone I met during my time on the pop page. The *Gazette* is completely fictional, but I have to say a year in journalism gives you enough anecdotes to last a lifetime!

On the home front, eternal love and gratitude to my family – my rock God/librarian husband Dom, and my three beautiful kids Keir, Daniel and Louisa. Thanks for putting up with me, helping with plots, suggesting titles, and generally making life a happy, chaotic place to be. I love the bones of you all. And a big hug to the Crazy O'Malleys in all their glory – Terry, Norm, and the gang – for childcare, pep talks, buffet dinners, and encouragement.

Finally, an apology to any serious scholars of Celtic mythology, or the Irish language. I'm afraid I took it, and brutalised it to suit my fictional needs – some of the names are intentionally wrong, and I've lifted legends and recklessly tinkered with them. Same goes for the wonderful city of Liverpool – I've played fast and loose with its geography, but hopefully retained its spirit. I can't think of any better place to set a story.

Also available from Del Rey:

A Conspiracy of Alchemists

by Liesel Schwarz

In a Golden Age where spark reactors power the airways, and creatures of Light and Shadow walk openly among us, a deadly game of Alchemists and Warlocks has begun.

When an unusual cargo drags airship-pilot Elle Chance into the affairs of the mysterious Mr Marsh, she must confront her destiny and do everything in her power to stop the Alchemists from unleashing a magical apocalypse.

Combining the best elements of nineteenth century gothic fiction with contemporary Steampunk, adventure, romance and the supernatural, Liesel Schwarz has crafted a truly exceptional debut.

The first book in The Chronicles of Light and Shadow trilogy.

DEL REY